"WHAT DO YOU WANT FROM ME?" SKYE ASKED THE PIRATE.

Silver Hawk smiled slowly, assessing her. "I'm not quite sure yet. I've decided that I could tame you. Perhaps I shall not ransom you at all. Perhaps I shall keep you with me forever."

Skye gasped. "Don't tease me!"

His fingers dug more forcefully into her arms. "Indeed, why should you think that I tease you, Skye Kinsdale? We pirates revel in debauchery and conquest. It would be most natural to return the ship . . . but not the maiden."

Also by Heather Graham from Dell

ARABIAN NIGHTS
LIAR'S MOON
SPIRIT OF THE SEASON
SWEET SAVAGE EDEN
LOVE NOT A REBEL
GOLDEN SURRENDER
DEVIL'S MISTRESS
EVERY TIME I LOVE YOU
THE VIKING'S WOMAN
ONE WORE BLUE
AND ONE WORE GREY
AND ONE RODE WEST
LORD OF THE WOLVES
RUNAWAY

A PIRATE'S PLEASURE

HEATHER GRAHAM

A DELL BOOK

To Sherry Woods
always an inspiration and a friend

A PIRATE'S PLEASURE
A Dell Book

PUBLISHING HISTORY
Dell mass market edition published July 1989
Dell mass market reissue / February 2008

Published by Bantam Dell
A Division of Random House, Inc.
New York, New York

ISBN 978-0-440-24472-1

Printed in the United States of America

www.bantamdell.com

OPM 10 9 8 7 6 5 4 3 2 1

A PIRATE'S PLEASURE

Prologue

April 4, 1718
Cameron Hall
Tidewater, Virginia

"Pirates! Damned pirates!"

The explosive words rocked the apparent serenity of the coming night. It was sunset along the James River. Soft hues of orange and tawny yellow were falling against the moss-touched oaks and the gentle sloping grasses leading to the river. Someone hummed somewhere as they worked, and birds sang melodic songs.

"Pirates!" came the resounding thunder once more, and it seemed that a hush fell upon the day.

Lieutenant Governor Alexander Spotswood of Virginia slammed his hand upon the polished pine side table by his chair on the porch to further emphasize his fury and displeasure. Lord Cameron leaned idly against one of the massive pillars and glanced at his friend with a wry smile. Alexander was obsessed. A bright and reasonable man, attractive in his person, dress, and manner, he was quite popular among the colonists, from the lords and ladies to the scullery maids. His eyes were intelligent and grave, and outraged though he was, he still appeared the aristocrat—from his fine white wig, the ends of it neatly curling over his shoulders, to his peach brocade frockcoat to his soft mustard knee breeches and silver buckled shoes. At the moment, though, he was lacking his customary oratorical prowess. He was fixed upon one word.

"Pirates! I say," Spotswood repeated. He did not slam his hand against the table again, but preferred to rescue his glass of sherry before his own vitality sent it crashing to the floor. "Pirates, pirates, pirates! They will be the bane of me yet!" His eyes narrowed sharply upon his host, Petroc Cameron, Lord Cameron of Cameron Hall, and "Roc" to his friends and relations. Cameron was sharp, and like his father before him, he was a tall man, young, striking, with strong, handsome features and some indomitable presence about him that instantly attracted the eye and commanded respect. Like many Camerons, he possessed sharp gray eyes that could sizzle silver by certain light. His hair was dark when he disdained to wear a wig; this late afternoon, with the falling sun upon it, the color seemed like jet.

Even in stillness he was vital.

Now, casually leaning against the pillar and looking out to the James River, he still emitted some energy that belied his nonchalance. Humor touched his eyes, but more. If there were danger, then danger be damned. He was a man to meet a challenge.

"Sir," he reminded his friend, "you cannot single-handedly do away with them. But I swear it, sir, we shall do our best to cast the worst of them into gibbets."

"Bah!" Spotswood protested impatiently. "I would chain them all in gibbets by the docks as warning. A pity that chains and gibbets cost so much money, I cannot afford to display the more petty offenders!" He leaned back and looked down the broad slope of grass to the river. It was a beautiful place, this, the Cameron estate. Strategically planned, it combined the best of an English country manor with the wild beauty of the colony. Because of the depth of the river, ships could come to the Cameron docks as if they came to Lord Cameron's very front door. The house itself was both practical and elegant. Spotswood had been friends with this young Cameron's father in the days when he had planned the governor's mansion in Williamsburg, and he had often thought of Cameron Hall when he spoke with the architects. The house had been begun in late 1620s. There had been just the main hall and upstairs bedrooms then. There was a brick in the cellar in the foundation attesting to the date of the building. "With these bricks we build our house, Jamie and Jassy Cameron, the Year of Our Lord 1627. The foundation will be strong, and God granting, our house and our family will stand the test of time."

The family had, so far, stood strong with the best and the worst of times. The eldest son always grew to be a member of the Governor's Council. To Spotswood, they were proving to be very fine friends, indeed. None so staunch as Roc Cameron.

"Sir," Cameron said now, "you do well against the hordes."

Was he teasing him? Spotswood never knew. He swept out a hand indicating the paper he had just been reading and had tossed down with an incredible flourish just before he had banged the table. "There's another article in there by a so-called wife of that Edward Thatch, Teach, Tech—whatever his bloody name is! The man marries women right and left!"

"And they live to tell of it," Roc Cameron said gravely. Teach was a pirate who was beginning to draw attention to himself. Blackbeard, they called him, because of his ferocious facial hair. It was rumored that he hailed from Bristol, and that he had served in Queen Anne's War, and that he had gone on to be tutored beneath the pirate Hornigold to learn a new trade as a scavenger upon the high seas. But he wasn't the worst of the lot. "Logan is running around out there. And One-Eyed Jack. Those are the two who not only steal cargo, but are heinously careless with human life."

Spotswood looked at him with a slow, curious nod. He sat

back, lacing his fingers together, watching his younger friend. "And then there's the Silver Hawk."

"And then there's the Silver Hawk," Cameron agreed flatly.

"We need new commissions," Spotswood complained. "Queen Anne lies dead, and that German upon the throne—"

Roc's laughter interrupted him and the lieutenant governor flushed. "Well, the man is a German! He's the King of England, and he doesn't even speak the king's good English! What is this world coming to? Pirates ever plaguing the seas, and a king who can't even speak his country's English!"

"Better than a papist, sir, or so, it seems, the country decided." Roc Cameron considered himself a Virginian. The affairs of the mother country were of concern to him only when they concerned Virginia. He was passionately in love with his land. The ultimate gentleman farmer, and a fine merchant, despite his title. That was the way with the New World, or so it seemed. A man could make great riches here, but only if a man were hard and bright and willing to work.

Spotswood loved Virginia himself. But he was an Englishman, appointed by the Crown. He might mutter about the king being a German, but still he bowed to England in all things. Queen Anne, the last of the Stewart monarchs, had died in 1714. That poor lady's many children had all died before her, and rather than accept her half-brother—a papist—on the throne, the English were willing to look to Germany for a Protestant king. The religious issue was a crucial one. In the colonies, men tended to be more tolerant of religious differences. But even here, every man of property or means belonged to the Church of England, and he kept his vows to the church as sacred.

Spotswood sighed. Always a challenge! The Indians had beset men a century ago. Now it was the damned pirates.

"Roc—" the governor began, leaning forward. But he was suddenly cut off by a huge commotion coming from the house.

The porch lay off the grand central hallway. It was situated so that the river breeze swept from the open hallway doors in the back to the open hallway doors at the front, when the weather was hot. Now the governor and Lord Cameron heard a bellowing voice and the clump of heavy footsteps. The governor frowned. Roc Cameron grinned and shrugged. "Lord Kinsdale, I believe," he said dryly.

Peter Lumley, Lord Cameron's butler and valet, appeared first. A man of about forty, he was lean and small, but straight and stiff with indignation.

"Sir, I did tell his lordship that you were engaged, and with the lieutenant governor! But he insisted—"

"That's quite fine, Peter," Roc said, pushing away from his pillar. He thrust back the folds of his fawn-colored frockcoat to plant his hand upon his hips. He waited. A second later a small portly man with blue eyes and wild wisps of gray hair appeared.

"Cameron! Have you heard of it! More and more debauchery upon the open seas!" He held the very newspaper that the governor had allowed to fall to the floor.

"Yes, Theodore, I have heard of it," Roc said. Lord Theodore Kinsdale paused to bow in acknowledgment to the governor. Spotswood nodded and met Cameron's eyes above the little man. They both smiled. Theodore Kinsdale was a good man, a fine man. He supported the governor in all things, and held many a merry ball. He owned vast sugar estates in the islands, but preferred to live in Williamsburg. He did, in fact, despise the three-hour drive out to Cameron Hall, and so, for him to have arrived here unannounced, he must be flustered and upset indeed.

"Alexander, what do you intend to do about all of this!" Theodore demanded.

Spotswood glared at him. "I have ships all over the coast! I am doing things, man!"

"Have a drink, Theo," Roc Cameron suggested.

"Don't mind if I do, don't mind if I do. Scotch!"

He sat in one of the handsome twined chairs upon the porch and mopped his face with a scarf. He stared from Roc to Alexander Spotswood, and then back again. "My daughter sails," he moaned.

"When?" Roc Cameron said.

"Her ship has left this very day."

Spotswood cleared his throat. "There's no reason to believe that your ship will be attacked."

"There is every reason to believe that the *Silver Messenger* will be taken! I am a wealthy man. The ship sails with a tremendous cargo. Why, her jewels alone are worth a fortune." He stared straight at Roc Cameron. Cameron stiffened. The two gentlemen were engaged in a running feud. Roc Cameron's father and Theo had betrothed their children at birth.

Roc now found such an arrangement barbaric. He preferred to choose his own bride, at his own time. And rumor had reached him, even from England. The girl wanted nothing to do with him. He didn't consider himself unduly proud, but admittedly, her rumored refusal annoyed him. Still, it made matters easy for him. He had vowed to his father upon his deathbed to uphold his every promise. To keep his honor.

"I'm sure that she will be safe—" Alexander began, trying to mollify Theo.

But Theo would have none of it. He jumped up, staring at Lord Cameron. "Roc, please! Your father was my dearest friend. You can make sure that she is safe! You have friends among the pirates—"

"Friends!" Roc Cameron exploded.

Theo lowered his voice just a shade, clamping his hands together, trying to hide his agitation. "She is my life!" he whispered. "She is all that I have left! I ordered her to return home to marry you! Now she sets sail. All right. You have not friends among the pirates, you have relations—"

"I do not claim pirates as relations!" Roc said firmly. He knew that the lieutenant governor was staring at him, and he cast the man a warning glare, then returned his attention to Kinsdale. "Sir! You would make it sound as if I fraternize with the likes of pirates."

Governor Spotswood grinned at Roc, sitting back, preparing to enjoy the promised show. Roc Cameron frowned to him darkly but the governor's grin widened.

"They say," Theo said, his fists clenched by his side, "they say that the Silver Hawk is a Cameron—"

"He is no Cameron!"

"That the silver eyes give him away. They say, too, that out of some curious respect for the family name, he is willing to negotiate with you. It is rumored that he is quick to seize your ships, and quick to return them for a reasonable fee. They say that you have some power, that you have even been to that island of his and negotiated with him. By God, Petroc! You must help me!"

Cameron threw up his hands. "So, milord, this pirate comes from some ill-begotten and illegal branch of my family! So he is a bit less willing to cut my throat than yours. What would you have of me?"

Theo was silent for a long moment. Then he drew a scroll from within his pocket. "Marry her. Now."

"What?" Cameron exploded incredulously.

"Marry my daughter now. Fulfill the vow you made to your father."

"The girl isn't even here—"

"I have proxy papers. I acquired them when I was in London."

"But your daughter—"

Theo waved a hand in the air. "She has signed them. Oh, I grant you, she doesn't know what she signed, she was arguing with me—speaking with me, that is—about other matters. But it is all well and legal, I assure you. Marry her now—"

"Why?"

"Because the Silver Hawk is your cousin. Because he might find my ship, and my daughter. And even if he does not, many of the others will respect his relationship with you, they will fear what he may do if they seize that particular ship."

"This is insane!"

"No! Cameron, you do not understand!" The man's voice trembled, his countenance had gone white with emotion. "It's the darkness, you see. She cannot stand the darkness."

Kinsdale was losing his mind.

Roc Cameron wasn't prone to rudeness, but he threw up his hands, turned around, and started walking down the slope of the estate toward the water. Kinsdale! The man was too much. Roc could not agree to the insanity.

Nearing the bottom of the slope, he turned away, not wanting to see the workers on the docks. He stared down at his ship, the gunned sloop the *Lady Elena,* named for his mother. It would be time to sail again soon. Very soon.

Inhaling sharply, he turned away and strode back toward the eastern side of the house. The outbuildings were there. Neat cottages for the servants, the smokehouse, the kitchen, the stables, the blacksmith's shop, the cooper's workhouse, the laundry. Far below them, enveloped by trees, lay the graveyard.

He walked there and paused. His mother and father and an infant child lay closest to the new fence. A hundred years of Camerons lay beyond them.

He walked back to the slate headstones that his father had ordered re-etched just before his death. They belonged to his great-grandparents, Jassy and James. He touched the cool stone and thought of the pair. They had endured. They had come here and created a dynasty, and they had endured. They had braved the Indians and remained despite the annihilating attack of 1622. Their heirs had populated a large part of Virginia. And the Carolinas and New York and the eastern states, he thought with some amusement.

Then his smile faded slightly and he turned around again, leaving the cemetery behind him. He strode back toward the house. Spotswood and Kinsdale were no longer on the porch. He heard their voices coming from the formal dining room. Peter would have seen to it that his guests were fed, he knew.

He hesitated then strode up the wide, sweeping stairway that seemed to climb to lofty heights from the expanse of the hall.

At the top of the stairway was the portrait gallery.

Camerons were always painted. The practice had begun with Jamie and Jassy, and continued to Roc's mother and father. He passed by his parents' pictures briefly. They were wonderful portraits. She was beautiful and dark and shyly smiling; he was proud and dignified, and the strange silver color of his eyes had been well captured by the artist. Still, Roc did not pause long. He walked down past his grandparents and great-grandparents. Then he paused, before Jassy Cameron.

She had been a fighter, so he had heard, and the sizzle of fire was captured in her gaze, while laughter was captured upon her lips. She had been a beautiful woman, stunning, and with fine and delicately chiseled features. Her eyes had been painted so that they seemed to fall upon him. Even as a child, he had often come to the portrait, fascinated by it.

He glanced at Jamie. Lord Cameron. Dignified, proud, young. Roc owed them something. Camerons peopled the New World and the Old, and yet he was the heir to their legacy.

Jassy Cameron's glance seemed to remind him so.

"All right, milady," he said softly to the picture, "I have long been a man, and I do realize that three decades is considered a sufficient age. And perhaps my life is haphazard and reckless. But, you see, I'd had in mind to choose the mother of my children myself. This girl could be cross-eyed or quite insane, you know. She could bring in some horrible disease. . . ."

His words trailed away. His eyes fell over the length of the portrait hall. To every Cameron pictured here, honor had been sacred. He cast his hands upon his hips and walked back to his parents' pictures. "I am against this, sir. Totally. You taught me to be my own man in all things, but you have left me with this vow! For the record, sir, I am totally against the marriage. But"—he paused— "as you wish it, Father. I will do my very best for her." He started to walk away, then he turned back, wagging a finger at the portrait. "Sir, I do hope that she is not cross-eyed or hunchbacked!"

He burst into the dining room. Spotswood and Kinsdale were just picking up tender bits of venison. Startled, they looked at Roc.

"Let's have done with this thing, then," he told Kinsdale.

Kinsdale leaped to his feet. "Peter, Peter! You must run quickly to the rectory and bring back Reverend Martin. And his daughter, Mary. She may stand for Skye."

Roc nodded. "Do it, Peter, please. Sir—" he addressed the governor. "You will stand witness to the legality of this rite?"

"If Lord Kinsdale's papers are in order, and it is your wish."

"It is my wish," he said.

The governor sighed, staring at the table. "And it was such a delectable dish!"

In a matter of minutes, the flustered Reverend Martin arrived with his blushing young daughter.

Words were said, and papers were signed and witnessed, and then the deed was done.

Kinsdale was no longer interested in dinner. Indeed, he no longer had a wish to remain. "I intend that everyone shall know that you have wed her, and the Cameron name will keep her safe."

"Lord Kinsdale—"

Roc tried to stop the man, but Kinsdale was in a hurry, asking Peter to call his coachman and valet so that he might start back, despite the fall of darkness.

"Theo! Listen to me. There are no guarantees upon the open sea! Can't you see, man—"

His new father-in-law clutched his hands. "Thank you. Thank you! Remember, sir, that she fears the darkness above all else. Keep her from it! I left a locket with her picture in it on the table." Kinsdale pumped his hand. Lord Cameron escorted his guest to the doorway. His coach, the lanterns swinging from the driver's canopy, awaited him. "Cameron, I will trust in God Almighty, and in your fine name and honor!"

With that, Kinsdale was gone.

Roc Cameron wandered into the house and into the dining room. Spotswood had sat back down to venison freshly warmed for him.

"Eat up! 'Tis your wedding feast!" Spotswood said, holding the locket in his hands.

Roc Cameron scowled sharply and laughed.

"Don't you care to see your bride?"

"Is she cross-eyed?"

"No. She is quite beautiful."

"What can you tell from a tiny portrait?"

Spotswood closed the locket with a snap and pocketed it. He smiled. "I know the lady. I haven't seen her in years, but the child gave great promise."

"Wonderful," Lord Cameron muttered darkly.

"She has a will of steel, my friend. A fine temper to match, and she is bold and quite intelligent and—"

"She will come here and mind her own affairs and that shall be that," Roc said flatly.

The governor smiled, looking at his plate. "I think not," he said softly.

"Your pardon, sir?"

"I said, 'So, it seems that you will sail sooner than expected.' "

"Yes, so it seems." Lord Cameron stood and poured himself a fair measure of whiskey. "To my cousin, Governor! To the Silver Hawk. May we negotiate the very best of terms."

"To the Silver Hawk." The governor raised his glass.

Roc Cameron slammed his glass down upon the table and left the room in a controlled fury. Lieutenant Governor Alexander Spotswood lowered his glass more slowly. He pulled the locket from his pocket and snapped it open and smiled down at the delicate and beautiful features that looked his way.

"And to you, Lady—Cameron!" he said softly. "Skye, it will be good to see you home. It will be most intriguing to see the sparks and feathers fly when you meet your new lord. Ah, if I wasn't the governor, I would set sail myself, for this promises to be high adventure!"

He snapped the locket shut and nearly set it upon the table. After all, Kinsdale had left it for Roc Cameron.

A slow mischievous grin came to his features. He pocketed the locket again. Let him imagine that his bride was slack-jawed and cross-eyed!

His smile faded slowly. Pirates *would* go after Lord Kinsdale's ship if they heard that she had sailed. She would carry not only his daughter, a valuable hostage, but her personal belongings, and God alone knew what else. Of course, she could cross the ocean unmolested.

She could . . .

But it was doubtful. The world was indeed in sad shape.

"Pirates!" he swore vehemently.

Indeed, it was sometimes a sorry world. Pirates were plaguing the coast, and a German was sitting upon the throne of England.

He patted his pocket where the locket lay within it. "Take care, milady!" he said softly. "I'm afraid that for you the tempest has already begun."

I

July 9, 1718
The Atlantic

"The Jolly Roger! 'Tis the Jolly Roger, the death's-head, the skull and crossbones, bearing down upon us!"

Skye Kinsdale reached the helm in time to hear the lookout's panicked words. She came, teetering and floundering, just as a streak of lightning lit up the heavens, sizzling through the sky and the sea. It illuminated the ship that had been following the *Silver Messenger* like a ghostly echo through the night. Already the crew fought to trim the sails against the storms that plagued the Atlantic; now, new terror was offered as the phantom ship displayed her true colors, those of the bleached white bones against the black of eternal night, rogue's colors, a pirate's colors.

"Captain! She waves the Jolly Roger!" the lookout repeated.

"The skull and crossbones!" Skye said in dismay, now standing by Captain Holmby's side. The beleagered lookout, high atop the crow's nest, stared down upon her. He was Davy O'Day of County Cork, recently hired onto the *Silver Messenger,* her father's ship.

Davey looked down upon Skye, and his fear for himself lessened as his heart took flight with the sight of her fiery gold hair, her fine, delicate, and intelligent features, and her eyes of fierce and compelling aquamarine. Her cape whipped around her feminine form, and the wind that tore upon it seemed to make tendrils of her beautiful hair dance upon the very air. In danger, in fear, in laughter, she seemed to shimmer and sizzle with vibrance and life, perhaps a very part of the storm and tempest.

He had adored her since she had first stepped foot aboard the ship, smiling and laughing, always a lady, and always with her keen interest about everything and everyone around her. He was in love with her, as much in love as a scrap of an Irish boy could be, and he vowed in those moments that he would die gladly to save her. Pirates! Mother of God!

Captain Holmby was impatiently staring up at him. Davey found his tongue again, wondering if the captain had comprehended his words.

"Sir! The Jolly Roger! The flag she waves is the Jolly Roger. 'Tis a pirate vessel! We're under attack!"

"I know that, boy! Mr. Gleason!" The captain called out to his first mate. "My glass, sir!"

Skye watched with a curious mixture of dread and excitement as the captain's first officer came forward and handed the spyglass to the captain. The weather was more than rough that morn, with the ship pitching and swaying upon the whitecaps that rode the Atlantic. The scent of a storm was strong upon the air, for the heavens were darkened by a curious gray and the day was cool, growing cold, and the wind was fierce and salt-laden.

It was a day to fear storms and the wrath of God, but no man sailed the seas these days without some fear of the bloody pirates laying waste to unwary vessels upon the Atlantic Ocean and the Caribbean Sea. Indeed, there were great bounties being offered for the likes of Blackbeard and Anne Bonny, One-Eyed Jack and the Silver Hawk.

It was not the proper weather for a pirate attack. The rogues, Captain Holmby had assured her just last night, did not like to attack when they might receive more harassment from King Neptune than from any guns at sea. Nay, Captain Holmby had said, they would have safe sailing, even though the winds might blow and tempest rage, and their journey across the Atlantic would soon be at an end. She would be delivered to her father in Williamsburg, and soon enough, her lucky beau would be blessed with his glorious bride. The last had been accompanied by a wink, and since the captain had proven to be such a sweet and delightful old man, Skye had smiled sweetly in return.

Whether or not she would be a bride was another matter altogether. Her father had decreed that she would marry a man she had never set eyes upon, and though she knew the arrangement was customary and proper, she was not about to accept it. Perhaps the Camerons had built the finest plantation in all of Tidewater Virginia, and perhaps Lord Cameron was a great gentleman, but Skye was determined that she would not be an object to be bartered and sold and possessed, no matter what. No, she'd never had any intention of arriving in Virginia to be a bride. She'd had every intention of escaping marriage someway.

This, however, had not been the way!

There would be a way, of course, a legitimate way. She was all that her father had, just as her father was all that she had. Since her mother had been killed when she was a child, she had clung to him, and he to her. She had always known his very mind and had been able to wheedle from him anything she wanted.

Until six months ago when he had come to her school in London to tell her that she was coming home. She had been so thrilled. Then he had told her that she was coming home to marry and she had been stunned. She had been careful at first, soft-spoken and respectful. Then she had wheedled, and then she had grown furious. He was being so stubborn. Some silly betrothal had been agreed upon before she could even walk, and since she was supposed to marry Lord Petroc Cameron, her father had no intention of seeing reason. She had talked and cried and stamped her feet, and none of it had done her a bit of good. Lord Theodore Kinsdale had hugged her fiercely and told her he'd be awaiting her at their home in Williamsburg when her term at Mrs. Poindexter's School for Refined Ladies was done, and that was that. She was eager to leave Mrs. Poindexter's, so she determined that she would continue her fight in the New World. She would get out of it!

Yes, because a pirate ship was coming straight at them.

Suddenly, from out of the bleak gray sky and sea came a startling flash of color, of fire, of gold and sizzling red against the day.

The pirate vessel was firing upon them.

"One-Eyed Jack!" the captain stormed. He raised his glass to point across the sea. "He means to ram and grapple us! Mr. Gleason! All hands on deck! Call the men to their battle stations!"

The missile did not strike the ship, but water blew nearby them, as if sent to the surface by a great whale, spewing forth foam.

"Is it One-Eyed Jack?" Skye asked, cold fear lacing her insides despite her best efforts at courage. She had heard tales about the man. He kept hostages only if the fancy struck him. He slew good men as he swatted flies. And women . . .

She did not dare think. Her fear would steal her will to reason, and to fight.

"Aye, 'tis One-Eyed Jack!" the captain said. "See the flag, milady. Even his skull lacks the eyehole." He patted her hand absently. "Bring her about! Call the gunners to their stations, Mr. Gleason." Captain Holmby's blue eyes fell upon Skye. "Lady Kinsdale, I shall have you escorted to your quarters," he told her.

"But, sir—"

"Ah, nay, lady, you must stay in my cabin—less danger in case of fire—" He stopped speaking abruptly and swallowed hard with a certain guilt. "I did not mean—"

"I am not a child, Captain," Skye said. Nor would she sit

meekly and be slain if the heathens came aboard. She knew how to fight well, and she would do so.

"Boy, come down!" the captain called to Davey, atop the crow's nest. "Take Lady Kinsdale to my cabin."

"Aye, aye, sir!" the lad replied, and quickly shimmied down.

"Don't be afraid, my lady! We will prevail."

"I am not afraid of the danger, Captain, but of the cabin—" Skye began, but she had lost his attention. He gave his orders to his first officer, who then boomed them out to the crew over the sound of the coming storm and the waves, and over the sounds of the fire that now began, cannon to vie with the thunder.

"Come, me dear lady!" Davey encouraged her, grasping her hand. He began to run over the hull. They dodged grim-faced sailors and the rigging and they came to the door of the captain's cabin. It was an elegant place, finely set with a huge oak desk, damask draperies, and a deep-set bunk surrounded by bookshelves hewn into the very body of the vessel. The elegant china tea service reserved for the captain's use still sat atop his desk. Presumably he had been at tea when the call had come that the weather worsened and an unidentified ship approached.

"May God be with you, lady!" Davey cried to her. "I will lock you in, milady, and—"

"No!" she protested in a sharp scream. Then she smiled apologetically. She would be all right as long as there was light, as long as the door was not locked. "Please, Davey, I would not be trapped. Do not lock me in."

"No, milady, if that is your wish."

"Thank you. Go on now, and God be with you!" she said quickly, for already he was pulling the door shut behind him. Skye picked up her skirts and ran behind him, placing her hands upon the door and leaning against it. She could hear the footsteps pounding over the deck; she could hear the captain's first officer raging out his orders. She screamed suddenly, thrown back with such vengeance that she fell hard against the desk. She heard the fine china rattle and fall. A ball, she surmised, had struck the ship somewhere.

She heard a man scream, scream with such pain and agony that she could feel his anguish deep inside. Then she felt a deep and terrible shuddering within the ship.

The pirate vessel was upon them. She could hear grappling hooks being tossed and thrown, catching and sinking into the wood of the hull like the giant fangs of some evil monster. Aye, a monster it was.

Rubbing her shoulder where she had struck the deck, she carefully rose. The skirt to her new gold-threaded gown had caught and torn upon the carved foot of the desk and she wrenched at it with all speed. Smoke was seeping into the cabin now. Smoke from the fires caused by the cannonballs, fires that surely blazed now within canvas sails. Men were screaming and shouting, and the clash of steel and the horrible scent of powder and flame were all about.

It was stifling; she could not breathe. She flew to the door and angled behind it, opened it enough that she could see.

Dread filled her heart, and swept through her blood, and congealed as ice in her soul.

The good captain lay dead before her very feet. Though officers and sailors still gave battle about the deck, it was painfully obvious that the pirates were the victors of this particular battle upon the sea.

Skye clutched her heart, then set her hands against her ears as the clash of steel continued. She closed her eyes, sick with anguish for the poor gallant captain, and for his men.

Then her eyes flew open once again. She heard the rise of female screams, and she realized that her young maids, fresh from the Irish countryside, had been discovered down in the hold. Bessie was screaming desperately; Tara was gulping out little squawking sounds.

And even as Skye watched, the two women were dragged to midships, beneath the mainsail. All around them tinder burned and the small fights continued. But there was no gallant knight to come to the girls' defense; all the officers and men were well occupied in their own skirmishes.

"No!" Skye whispered aloud, biting into her lower lip.

But there was no denial.

Despite the gray of the day and the thunder and the lightning and the awful smell of charred wood and charred flesh and the threat of rain, certain of the buccaneers were determined. Tara with her soft blue eyes and snow white skin was being tossed soundly upon the deck. With the pitch and sway and tempest of the ocean, she was thrown hard against the water bucket, and none of the riotous rogues seemed to notice her cry of pain. It was a party of four that attacked the girls, one a youth with a scraggly white-blond beard, one missing a tooth, a graybeard, and a nasty, evil dark-haired fellow with yellow, tobacco-stained teeth.

Skye closed her eyes and leaned back against the door. She could not let this happen.

Yet what could she do? The ship was alive with beasts, and the force of good was surely losing to evil.

And still, eventually, they would find her. Was it not better to go down fighting than to be cornered and caught like a fox?

She was not terrified of fighting for her life. She was only afraid of small dark places from which she could not escape.

She looked above the captain's desk, where a fine pair of Damascus swords were hung, one upon the other. The ship pitched dangerously, as if they would all be swept up by the storm, swallowed, and taken to the bottom of the sea.

She prayed briefly. She asked God to forgive her a multitude of sins, pride not the least of them.

Then she sprang forward, leaped upon the desk itself, and wrested a sword from its scabbard against the paneling.

She felt the steel in her hand. She slashed the sword carefully through the air, testing its weight. Then she swirled about, hurriedly leaving the safety of the cabin before she could lose her nerve and cower in terror in some dark corner.

Skye carried her blade in one hand, sweeping her skirts up behind her with the other. The horrible smells of battle were even worse on deck. So much charred flesh! Broken timber, broken limbs, and canvas that continued to burn. She swallowed hard, fighting an urge to faint at the sight of the still-staring—but sightless—captain. She steeled herself and stepped over the man. So far, she hadn't been noticed in the melee.

They would notice her soon enough.

She flew forward in a burst of courage and strength, flying toward the men who held down Tara and Bess.

"Leave them be!" she commanded, waving her sword toward the graybeard who tore at Tara's skirts.

He paused, staring at her. All of them paused, in surprise. The graybeard slowly smiled, licking his lips. "Well, lookee here, will you now! We've found the crème de la crème, eh, boys?" He started to laugh, rising, tossing down Tara's skirt and adjusting his breeches. "How-de-do, mee-lady. Old Samuel, here, and indeed, mum, I do intend to show you a good time."

"Shut your mouth and step aside, Samuel. And you!" she said sharply to the blond youth who was nearly upon poor Bess. "I suggest you return your protruding anatomy to your breeches, boy, lest I find myself tempted to lop it off!"

Samuel burst into a loud guffaw. The blond boy did not find the threat so amusing. He quickly stumbled to his feet, drawing the cord on his breeches tight.

"A feisty wench, this one!" Samuel called happily. "Toss me a sword; this bird I shall quickly best, and have."

"And share!" the boy said.

"Let's see how the lady does. I think perhaps that the prize might first be mine," a voice called out, and Skye quickly turned about.

She didn't need to be told that she had come face-to-face with the man known as One-Eyed Jack. A black patch covered his one eye. He smiled an evil leer and she saw yellowed, rotting teeth beneath the curve of his lip. He was a small, sinewy man with whiskers.

Her stomach heaved. The idea of fighting to the very death gained new appeal for her.

"Captain!" cried Old Samuel. "I killed the captain of this here ship—she's a prize, and mine! Give me a sword!"

"Take on the fight, Sam, and we will judge the lady," One-Eyed Jack agreed. He tossed a sword the man's way. He smiled at Skye, displaying his rotten teeth again. 'Twould be prettier, she thought, to bed a warthog.

She would die first, she vowed to herself.

Which was a growing possibility!

She quickly bemoaned the warning she had given the man —she should have slain him while he attacked Tara unarmed. He was a pirate, an animal, but she had not been able to slay an unarmed man. Now it seemed that she would pay for her morality—and stupidity.

"Sir!" she snapped out, tossing her skirts behind her, finding her position.

And it seemed that Old Samuel was soon as dismayed as she, for the fight went on. Skye knew that he had assumed her threats were idle; he could not know that before her father had shipped her off to Mrs. Poindexter's School for Refined Ladies, he had sent to France to hire her a world-renowned instructor when she had determined to learn the art of swordplay. Samuel had learned the art upon the sea. He was strong, but he knew no finesse.

She could best Samuel. She knew that she could.

But when that was done, there would still be another twenty to fifty pirates . . . perhaps more . . . to fight off.

"Methinks you are no lady!" Samuel called to her. A mean look crossed his face. He was not fighting for a prize anymore; he was fighting for his life, and he knew it. He tried to shatter her strength, slamming down upon her blade. She was too quick. She parried, and feinted, and eluded his anger. She leaped high upon a charred sail beam, and when he slammed downward, she ducked, and flew into a pirouette, and brought her blade slicing through his midsection.

Samuel died, staring at her in rage and disbelief until the fire left his eyes to be replaced by the cold glaze of death.

She swirled around. She realized suddenly that the ship had grown silent. There were no more small skirmishes being fought upon the deck. The officers who'd survived had swords cast against their throats. And they, like the pirates, stared at her.

One-Eyed Jack slowly clapped his hands together, eyeing her with a new respect. "Madame, in the end, it is me that you will meet."

There was little that she could do; nothing that she could say.

She raised her sword. Her eyes lit upon the lot of them, and she backed against the mast, looking to her left and to her right, awaiting her next opponent.

It was to be the youth. He rose and spat upon the deck. Someone tossed him a sword. He bowed mockingly.

"Milady?"

Then he lunged forward.

He was an easy opponent, too easy. He hadn't the strength or barbaric skill of the older man. Soon Skye saw sweat beading his brow. They moved across the deck, and men gave way.

"Lady Skye!"

For a second, a mere second, Davey's anguished cry distracted her. He warned her that a second man had drawn a sword to come up behind her. A balding pirate with a red kerchief about his head popped Davey hard on the head with the butt of his pistol, and the boy sank silently to the deck.

She started instinctively for his side. The blond youth made a swipe toward her, slicing through her skirt. She swung about just in time to save her flesh from the tip of the blade.

"Go ahead, milady, skewer the young hearty!" the balding pirate encouraged. "The boy's not dead; 'e sleeps!"

"No more interference!" One-Eyed Jack called out. "If she's as feisty beneath the covers, I want her alive!"

This was a game to them, she realized, this fight, this murder, this death. And until they drowned in a pool of their own blood, they would play it.

Until she fell. Until she was at the mercy of the one-eyed creature who watched the savagery with such gusto, and waited.

"On guard, monsieur," she told the youth. "To the death."

"Or . . . other." The boy laughed.

Skye stepped forward. Then she fell forward, stumbling along with the others. Suddenly, out of the grayness of the day, came another monster.

The ship was rammed from portside. Pirates and officers alike teetered and grasped for balance and looked about in dismay.

No one had seen the ship that had come upon them out of the murk and tempest of the day. None had seen her ghostly shape or her haunting form as she came upon them, a wraith from the sea.

None had seen her. . . .

Until she rammed the injured ship.

And now, Skye's duel was interrupted, for new screams filled the air. Skye had hoped in an instant that it might be rescue.

That hope was quickly dashed, like the deck beneath a cannon's fire, for it was not rescue that had come.

It was a second pirate ship.

Muskets flared; screams rose. The screech and thunder of grappling hooks was heard again, and from the rigging of the newcomer, men leaped down upon the decks, and battle was joined once more.

" 'Tis the Silver Hawk!" someone called. "In the rigging! 'Tis the Hawk himself! Lay down your arms, and he'll do no murder!"

"Bah, you coward!" another man called out. "One-Eyed Jack is me captain, and I'll not grovel before the Hawk."

"There, there upon the ropes! See him, he comes!"

Skye forgot her own opponent. Her sword rested upon her torn skirts as she stared upward.

Indeed, he was coming. The Silver Hawk, as they called him.

He was clad in black from head to toe, his shirt seemed to be of black silk; his frockcoat, silver-threaded, was black brocade. His boots, thigh high, were black, as were his skintight breeches. A black hat with silver eagle plumes rested upon his head. A full set of neatly trimmed silver-and-black whiskers covered his chin. A black mustache curled stylishly upon his lip.

And for all of his elegance of dress, he moved upon the ropes with skill and speed and uncanny ease. In seconds, he was upon the deck, and before his boots struck wood, he was engaged in battle.

"Surrender, me hearties, and leave me the prize. Your choice, messieurs, to die!" he called, his deep voice a thunder that challenged the sky, that challenged the very tempest of the day.

Pirates stepped back, and pirates stepped forward. The proud old-timer met and defied him first, and lay down so quickly and silently to die that Skye barely saw the battle.

She saw his blade, the silver blade of the Silver Hawk, and she saw the striking, magical grace with which he leaped and danced and moved then upon the deck. No man challenged him alone. They came against him in groups, a pair first, a trio when they fell. And through it all, Skye watched in amazement, unaware of her danger.

Until more of his men came upon the deck. Until fighting erupted all around her once again.

"Take hostages of the crew!" came a shout, and Skye was aware that the deep, commanding voice belonged to the pirate, the Silver Hawk.

"Hawk, I'll kill you!" One-Eyed Jack roared out.

"Valiant words, Jack! Match the action to them!" the Hawk retorted.

And the men met with a vicious clash of steel. The fighting, all around Skye, was suddenly fast and furious once again.

The blond youth swung around abruptly, his face a mask of fury. Skye, startled, raised her sword to parry his lethal blow without a second to spare. She could watch no one else, for she was suddenly thrust into a violent struggle for her own life. The blond furiously lunged toward her. She leaped aside and parried, and caught his throat with the tip of her sword. With a peculiar whishing sound, he fell before her. She gasped, staggering. She could hear the clang of steel around her.

And then, suddenly, she could not.

The deck had fallen silent once again.

And even the wind had died.

Gray rose around her. The gray of the storm that teased and threatened, the gray from black powder and shot, from battle and burning. It rose like a curious fog, as if she had been cast upon the London stage.

And all those around her were curious players.

Once again, pirates ranged about the ship's deck. The crew, she saw, had been ushered toward the aft cabin and were being held there at sword's point.

The second officer held young Davey, and Davey, coming to, held his own head.

One-Eyed Jack would never leer her way again. He lay dead in a pool of blood by the mizzenmast.

And resting upon the fine teak balustrade leading to the helm was the pirate, Silver Hawk.

Silver Hawk, standing well over six feet tall, with his elegantly plumed hat, his black-gloved hands resting upon the hilt of his sword, the point of that sword scarring the deck. He stared at Skye, and her fallen, blond-haired opponent.

"Bravo, milady. Now be a good girl and cast down your sword."

He had taken the ship, that much was obvious. But she had not surrendered to the first set of pirates; she was not about to surrender to this new rogue.

She shook her head. He cocked his own in curious surprise and pushed away from the balustrade, coming toward her.

"You'll not surrender, milady?"

"Never," she said softly.

A hysterical cry came her way. "Throw it down! Milady, throw it down, he'll let you live!" It was Bess. She'd been thrust into the arms of one of the new pirates, a young fellow with dark eyes and striking features. "Mother of God, milady, he'll let us live, he'll—"

"Shush now, ye hussy!" the dark-haired man interrupted her, squeezing her tight about the middle. "Captain," he complained. "What'll we do with these 'uns here?"

The Silver Hawk shook his head, his eyes never leaving Skye's. "Whatever you so desire, Peter. Whatever you so desire."

A boisterous cry went up among the men.

And then young Davey suddenly broke away from the young ship's officer who held him. He lunged toward the Silver Hawk.

The pirate moved back with the speed and agility of a tiger. Davey would die, and Skye knew it.

"No!" she screamed. She cast herself between the pirate and the lad. Davey flew against her and fell to the deck.

Sprawled in her petticoats and torn skirts, Skye tried to rise. The pirate stood before her, reaching down a hand.

She ignored it.

She managed to roll, and she leaped to her feet, angling back, her blade wagging before her.

The pirate paused, laughing. He bowed to her very deeply. "As you wish it, milady." He cast his left hand behind his back, and raised his sword. "Someone get the lad. He seems to offer his lady a foolish loyalty, and I'd not want to slay him for it!"

A man came forward for Davey. The boy struggled fiercely, but Skye could pay him no more mind. The Silver Hawk stepped toward her, his blade flashed.

The clash was terrible. She could barely keep her hand upon the hilt of her sword.

She had asked for death. She could not fight this man. Yet if she did not fight, didn't she face a fate worse than death at his hands? She did not know, she only knew that the battle was engaged, and that if she turned to run, he would probably cleave her into two pieces. The man reeked of his bloody strength, of his fascinating agility, of a masculinity so strong that it caused her to quake as well as shiver, to falter when she should have found courage.

"Milady!" he acknowledged, dipping back, allowing her to regain her grip upon her sword.

"Sir!" she said, and rallied.

The dark-haired man holding Bess suddenly tossed her to another, stepping forward. "Captain, the lady's at a disadvantage! Her skirts!"

"Shed them!" the Silver Hawk ordered.

Skye nearly screamed. The handsome young pirate raised his sword and it slashed through the air. She was not struck at all, but her cumbersome skirts and petticoats were sheared from her form, and she was left to fight with her hose and sheer shift protruding from the tattered remnants of her gown. Crimson flooded her face, but she raised her chin and did not gaze upon the humiliating exposure of her form. None of it could matter now. She could cling to her pride, for it was all she had left, and if she could find courage, he could not take it from her.

"Milady?"

"Sir, as you have ordered, I am ready."

"I give you leave to attack, Lady . . ."

"Kinsdale."

"Kinsdale!"

She thought that he gave pause then, that she had startled him with her name, that he did, indeed, know it well. Whatever, his pause did seem to give her an advantage, and so she did attack, thrusting forward, seeking his heart.

Deftly, quickly, he parried her thrusts. She feinted again, he parried. He backed to the balustrade and leaped up upon it. Caught up in the fray of battle, Skye followed him. He did not attack at all, she realized too late. He merely watched her with his eyes alive, silver gray like the day, like the color of his blade, like the mist of the tempest about them.

A cry went up. Laughing, applauding, the pirates followed along behind them. There was no escape, Skye realized, but that didn't seem to matter anymore. Her arm felt like lead; it was so tired, she thought that it might drop right off with the sword. Now each clang of steel seemed to echo and reverberate throughout her body. She shuddered with each thrust, and she kept driving faster and faster, seeking some vulnerability.

The man had none.

A dark and sleekly savage beast, he barely breathed hard as he caught and fended off her every thrust and parry. Surely, she seemed the wild one, for her cape was lost, her skirts torn and shredded, and her hair flew about her in disarray.

He was deadly calm, a smile twisted into his features beneath the display of mustache and beard. His accent had been English, she thought, or was it? He was whipcord lean and hard-muscled, and the more she realized that she could not win, the more she became determined that she should do so.

"Watch her now, Hawk, they say she knows how to threaten the right part of a man, or the wrong part, depending on a way of thinking."

"Can't imagine the captain with a high voice!"

"She'll never touch him with steel!"

"Never in a coon's age!"

"She's desperate, Captain!"

She was desperate, very. And so she was trying for desperate measures. She allowed her sword to drop, and when he stepped near, she sliced upward with all her strength, just missing the length of his thigh. He leaped back. Laughter rose. His eyes met hers, burning silver with the challenge, burning silver with stark warning.

"Mam'selle, I begin to think that you are no lady," he said, coming to the same conclusion as her previous opponent.

"You, sir, are most certainly no gentle knight."

"Alas, I am a pirate."

"And I, sir, your victim. And therefore, I will fight you with any means at my disposal."

"Is that so?"

"It is." She had warned him. She swirled with her sword, slicing the air. And she was nearly victorious. With any other man, her thrust would have been lethal. She would have slit him cleanly from his groin to the gullet.

But the Silver Hawk moved too quickly. He sensed her movement and responded to it, fighting with uncanny grace and strength, and it was a combination she feared that she could not match.

"Eh, Captain, we warned you!" someone called out.

"That you did!" he replied pleasantly, his voice loud. Then he dropped his tone and spoke to her softly. "Careful, mam'selle, lest I discover the same wicked rules of swordplay."

"Have you rules, monsieur, of your own? I had not thought that you knew the meaning of rules, or of fair play."

"You receive fair play right now, milady."

"Sir, you are a bastard knave, and give me nothing. What man honors himself to fight a lady?"

She thought that she had found his weakness, for he paused, and it seemed that he mused over the question. She had to best him, she had to! And she had to do so soon, for her strength was waning.

She thrust forward with all of her strength.

He parried with a single, swift blow. The staggering

strength of it caught her unaware. So far, all that he had done was tease her, play with her. He hadn't used a tenth of his power, or skill.

Now he did.

And the force threatened to break her arm. She cried out, falling as her sword was sent flying high, until it blended with the silver and gray of the day, soaring in the sky . . . then splashing softly into the water.

Skye, cast down upon the deck, gasped desperately for breath, her arm aching, her head spinning.

He smiled down at her. "The man who is challenged by a lady must fight her, mam'selle," he said, replying to her at last. "She gives him no choice." He looked up and called out in his deep, ringing voice, " 'Tis all over now, me lads!"

His dark-haired lackey called out. "All over but the cleanup."

The cleanup. And what was that? Skye wondered. She came up upon her elbows, her gaze upon the pirate's glittering, silver-blue eyes. He returned her stare.

"The hostages—" someone called.

The pirate Silver Hawk crossed his arms over his chest. His full, sensual mouth curved into a curious smile.

He stepped forward.

Skye inched away upon her haunches, never turning from him, never losing his silver gaze.

"Take the officers down below. Send One-Eyed Jack's men down to the hold."

"The women—"

"You know what to do with them," he said softly.

The dark-haired man strode forward. "I shall take the Lady Kinsdale—"

"Oh, no," the Silver Hawk said. And he stepped forward. He planted one booted foot on either side of Skye, catching the tattered remnants of her once-beautiful gown and strands of her golden hair beneath his boots. She tried to wriggle away, but cried out as her hair pulled. She stopped, gritting her teeth and looking up past the long, steel-muscled length of his legs to the breadth of his chest and onward to his rock-hard features.

He lowered himself slowly over her, imprisoning her between his powerful thighs.

Their eyes met in a sizzling tempest of fire.

"Get away, me mates," he said very softly. "This one is mine."

And he reached for her, just as a jagged flash of lightning tore across the heavens once again.

His touch was no less powerful than that fire.

II ❧

Before she knew it, Skye was standing again upon her own feet. He had drawn her up against him. Contact with his hard muscular body caused her eyes to widen, and he smiled satanically at her betrayal of alarm. Furiously, she tried to squirm from his hold. The sea even seemed to play to his dictate, for a swell took hold of the ship, careening her ever more tightly against him. He held his stance well, riding the sea as an accomplished horseman might ride a wild mount. He laughed aloud, seeing the combination of fear and anger in her delicate features.

"Why, milady! You met my steel with such admirable courage. Would you meet the man himself with anything less?"

"I would not meet the man at all," she retorted, which only served to amuse him further and bring out a burst of laughter from his rowdy crew. He laughed, too, as he held her. Then another bolt of lightning lit up the heavens as if it threatened to strike the main mast. Thunder burst in a furious roar, and the pirate quieted his laughter to a curious smile. "Alas, milady, but you will have to wait, I fear. The gods of wind and water seek to keep us apart."

"May the gods let you choke—" Skye began, but she never finished, for she cried out as she found herself lifted and cast over his shoulder with determined force. He had played with her, she realized, but he played no more. The day had made him sober. She struggled against him, but he ignored her, holding her firmly with ease, and striding across the deck, shouting commands. "Fenwick, you will captain our prize—"

"Let me down!" Skye screamed, pummeling furiously against his shoulders. "Let me—"

"Milady, shut up!" he commanded, and she discovered herself choking out a humiliated cry, for his hand landed upon her rump with a fearsome power, bringing tears to her eyes. She was momentarily silenced, and he continued speaking to his men, striding for the rigging as he did so. "Take care with our prisoners, for we will demand ransoms. One-Eyed Jack's men to the brig if they choose to surrender. Take the guns and any prizes from his ship, then send her to the bottom of the sea."

"Aye, aye, Captain!" came a dozen replies.

"Get your hands off me!" Skye swore, straining against him. It was a futile effort. With his left hand he caught hold of the mainmast rigging and crawled upon it. The ship pitched and swayed violently again. He was a madman, she decided. The sea was a whirlpool, the wind was vicious, and he ignored them both. Like a wraith he took his ease with the rigging. Rather than fighting him, Skye suddenly discovered herself clinging to him as he crawled high upon the rigging to catch hold of a free-swinging rope. She screamed in sheer terror as she realized his intent.

"Relax—Lady Kinsdale. Relax, and hold tight," he advised her, but otherwise he gave her fear no consideration.

Then a moment later, it seemed that they were flying. They fell against the coolness of the wind and the soft gray of the sky. She didn't know if she was plunging to her death or soaring to the heavens.

She did neither, for in seconds he had made an easy leap to the deck of his own ship. Dizzy, Skye struggled to see around herself, and became aware of more of his crew, most of them barefoot, clad only in cotton shirts and knee breeches and many of them whiskered and bearded. They seemed to be of all ages, and to a man, they smiled and waved at her with good humor. It seemed they were loyal to their captain. A cheer went up as he landed nimbly upon the deck with her. Skye thought that they would both tumble at last upon the wooden decking, for the ship swayed starboard as if it would capsize.

Silver Hawk did not fall or falter. His men, too, held their ground, and raised their voices once again in a loud salute. Their captain lifted a hand to acknowledge them, then swung about with her, his prize, in his arms still.

Skye pressed against his back, seeking to plead with his crew of cutthroats.

"I'm worth a fortune!" she cried suddenly. "See that he leaves me be this instant, and my father will reward you greatly!"

"Will he now?" a graybeard called pleasantly.

"Good night, milady!" said another, and they all bowed to her deeply, ignoring her plight.

She cried out in rage again, once more struggling to free herself from her ignominious position upon the pirate's shoulder.

He spun around again, seeing her eyes as she raised herself upon his shoulders. "What is this!" he said in mock protest. "Why, gents, I swear to you that just seconds ago, she held on to me like an adoring mistress. Women are fickle, are they not?" He did not desire a reply, nor did he get one, and the humor fell from his voice as he spoke again. "I'll be at the helm, me lads. The wind is howling ever louder. Like a woman."

"Which is more deadly, Cap'n, do you think? The lady wind that rages upon the sea, or the Lady Kinsdale, shrieking upon your back?"

More laughter rose. "Why," replied the captain, "the lady upon my back, of course!"

He turned about and strode with her now upon his own ship, past the mainmast and forward. A set of handsome, intricately carved double doors lay before them. He set his hand upon a brass knob and pushed inward. Barely a moment later Skye found herself falling hard upon the large carved bunk in the far starboard corner of the cabin. She gasped for breath, realizing suddenly that the remains of her petticoats and gown were rising precariously to her hips and that she was lying before him nearly naked. She had no doubts as to his intent, but she planned to fight him to the very death if need be. She might lose, but she would fight.

He stood above her, shadowed by the sudden darkness in the cabin, and she rolled as best she could against the wall, pulling the fine-knit bed covering over her exposed limbs as she did so. She tried to meet his eyes in the sudden shadow to dare him to protest, but she could read nothing of his gaze, and fear set into her once again even as she assured herself that she would fight forever.

If she could only see his face now!

But she could not. She could see only the hard, lean length of the man, a silhouette before her. He would pounce upon her, she thought. He was like a hawk indeed, circling his prey, waiting only for the precise right moment to pounce down upon her.

Fear seized her, and in panic she thought to bolt, not knowing where she would run. She tried to leap from the bunk, but landed instead within his arms.

"Bastard!" she hissed, near tears as his arms wound around her.

"Alas, lover, I do apologize!" he said, pressing her back. "That you are so eager to consummate this affair, but I must leave you, milady!"

"Eager! I loathe you, I long to skewer you through—"

His laughter cut her off. She could see his eyes suddenly, or something of their deep blue flame and searing humor. "Take care!" he warned her, and there was a razor's edge to the sound of his voice. "Lest you be the one . . . skewered through!"

She knew not if he meant that he would slay her, or if his words carried a more intimate meaning, but his laughter and the soft touch of his breath against her cheeks made her tremble once again, and she braced hard against the steel power of his arms and chest. She could never fight this man, she realized. He was in the prime of life, muscular, powerful, and skillful. She could not best him with a sword, and she would never best him with her fists. She waged her war with a vengeance, and he merely smiled at her futile efforts. He laughed. He gloated. He was completely assured of his triumph in all things. He held her steady against the continual rock and sway of the ship.

"Let me go!" she cried, and she sought to rake her nails over his bearded cheek, but he caught her hand, and the pressure he grimly set against it caused her to cry out, and give up, sagging against him. She became acutely aware of him then as a man, for the black material of his shirt and breeches was thin, and her own clothing gave her no barrier. He was strikingly warm and alive, vibrant. Energy as hot and powerful as the lightning that lit up the heavens beyond them seemed to surround him. To leap from him.

To touch her.

"Please!" she gasped out.

He pulled her closer, and his words curiously seemed to caress the softness of her face. "Where would you go, milady? Would you race out and join the crew, and entertain them, one and all? Or had you thought of the sea? A watery tomb, cold and eternal? I think not." He released her suddenly. She fell back upon the bed, and his eyes were captured once again by the shadows. She did not think of fighting. She did not think of anything. She did not even think to shrink from his gaze as she lay in dishevelment, her shirts and bodice torn, so very much of her flesh bared to him. She lay back, barely daring to breathe.

She did not even move when he reached out to touch her. His fingers brushed lightly over the rise of her breasts as they spilled from her corset.

She did not even scream, for the touch was brief and gentle, and so quickly gone it might not have been.

"Do not fear, Lady Kinsdale, I will be back."

She came up upon an elbow then, a certain courage returning to her as he whispered out her name.

"You will pay for this treatment of me!" she cried. "My father will see that you pay, my fiancé will see that you pay—"

"Will he, mam'selle?" he inquired. Hands on his hips, he cocked his head to the side.

"Of course!" Her voice only faltered slightly. "I am to marry Lord Cameron. He will see that you hang!"

"How intriguing. Well, I hope that he is a man of selfless honor, lady, for all of Williamsburg knows that you have spurned your betrothed and sworn that you will not marry."

Skye gasped, amazed that such gossip could have reached the colony before she had arrived there herself. Then she was furious with herself because her reaction had given away so very much.

"He—he is a man of honor!" she swore quickly.

"And then again," the pirate captain mused, ignoring her words, "I have heard that Lord Cameron is no more eager for this marriage than you are, but out of respect for your father he has not—as yet—opposed the promises made by his father when he was but a lad of ten and you were within your cradle."

"How dare you—" she began, her voice low and shaking.

"Oh, mam'selle, I am afraid that you will soon discover that I am a man to dare anything. But for the moment, if you will be so kind as to excuse me—"

"Sir, there is no excuse for your vile existence, none at all!"

He merely smiled. "Adieu, milady."

"Wait!" she cried.

He paused, arching a brow. "What, mam'selle?"

"You can't—you can't leave me in here!"

He gazed at her in startled surprise. "Lady Kinsdale, it is the finest cabin on the ship, I assure you. You will be safe."

"Safe!" she screeched.

He grimaced at her with casual humor. "Safe—from the storm, milady. Until later," he said. He bowed with courtly gallantry, and then he was gone. Skye heard his long strides take him to the doors. They closed behind him, and she heard the sure sound of a bolt sliding home. She was locked in, alone and wretched, and surrounded by darkness, and by fear.

She couldn't bear it. The darkness pressed in upon her. The walls seemed to press closer and closer.

She had been trapped within the cabin on her own ship, she reminded herself.

But there had been light then. Not this terrible darkness.

It seemed that endless moments passed in which she just lay there, listening to the wind. It shrieked, it groaned, it screamed. It rose over the sounds of the slashing rain that had begun, and like a woman, it seemed to cry. The ship did not stay still for a second, but rolled and tossed and pitched and spun, and in time Skye realized that she was clinging to the sheets and knit coverlet. She lay there quaking, and when she wasn't fearing the awful darkness, she feared the man. She shouldn't be fearing the man, she told herself, not at that moment. She should be praying that they survive the storm, for she had never seen a night so savage.

Lightning flashed, illuminating the cabin. It was a vast space, she thought, for a ship, set high upon the top deck of his fleet ship. The cabin! She needed to think about the cabin. It was large enough for his bunk and shelves and tables and chairs and a stove, trunks, and a built-in armoire. The high square windows probably looked out on the churning sea by day, Skye thought, but now they were covered by rich velvet maroon drapes.

The glow of lightning no longer illuminated the cabin, but Skye continued to register in her mind the things that she had seen. The shelves were lined with books, the desk was polished mahagony, and the chairs were heavy oak, upholstered in brocade. It was an elegant cabin, a cabin for a captain of prestige and means and manners, not the cabin of a savage pirate.

He'd seized the ship from some poor suffering fool! she reminded herself. Indeed, he was a thief of the vilest sort, a rapist, a murderer, a scourge upon the seas.

And he would come back to this cabin.

Unless she lay trapped forever in the darkness.

Growing more and more agitated, she tried to rise. The sway of the ship sent her flying back down to the bunk. She tried again. She moved carefully this time, holding to the wooden bunk frame, then plunging toward the doors. She slammed against them, and nearly gave way to a flurry of tears. They were bolted tight. There was no way out for her.

She sank against the doors, fearful that the ship would sink, and that she would be caught within the cabin.

Skye brought her fingers pressing against her temples. Fear came against her in great, suffocating waves then. It was worse than facing the pirates, it was worse than facing ruthless steel. She could not stand darkness; she could not bear it. Ever since she had been a child, on the awful day that her mother had died, she had feared being locked away in the darkness.

She leaped back to her feet. She beat against the door, screaming, crying until she was hoarse. Tears streamed down her face, and her voice rose higher and higher, rivaling the cries of the wind. She beat against the wood until her hands were raw. Her voice grew hoarse, and she sank to the floor, nearly delirious.

Then suddenly the door was thrown open. A man, young, dark-haired and clad in nothing but knee breeches, stood there. Rain dripped from his features and sluiced down his chest.

"Lady, what ails thee—" he began, but he was never able to go further for she sprang to her feet and leaped past him, straight into the riveting rain, into the tempest of the wind. She heard the shouts of the men as they fought to stabilize the ship. She heard the waves, lashing hard against the bow. The force of the wind seemed terrible. She didn't realize its strength until it whipped her bodily about, and she was cast to the deck as if by a heavenly hand.

An oath was suddenly roared out above her. She moved her hand over her eyes, shielding them from the onslaught of wind and rain. Hands were reaching for her and she was plucked back up and sheltered by broad, strong arms.

"What is she doing here?" Silver Hawk demanded.

"She raced by me. I'd no idea, Captain—"

"Get to the helm!" His eyes lowered to her. "I'll take you back to the cabin."

"No!" she whispered, but he had already brought her there

with his long, determined strides. He shoved the door open with his foot and cast her down to the floor with a vengeance.

"Fool!" he swore to her.

She ignored him, and sat there in a spill of tattered, damp clothing and wind-tossed hair, cold and wet and shivering.

Lightning scorched the night and created a golden backdrop for the darkness of his form. It shone in upon Skye where she knelt upon the floor in her tatters of velvet and lace, her hair free and tangled and spilling all around her.

He stood before her and she stared upon his black boots. They glistened with the glow of the rain that had drenched him. She looked up slowly. His shirt and breeches were skin-tight against his body, plastered to his form.

Skye drew in a quivering breath that sounded like a sob.

"No! Don't go!"

She was hurt! he thought, and he strode quickly toward her, hunkering down by her side and lifting her chin. She trembled. From head to toe she trembled. But as he looked at her he saw that though her eyes were wide and dilated, she showed no injury.

"What in God's name are you up to?" he demanded.

"Let me out of here!" she told him.

"Nay, lady!" he said harshly. "You've seen the storm!" Her words were a ploy. The fool girl meant to flee him at any cost.

"Please!" she whispered, and despite his better judgment, the curious plea tore at his heart. He had never seen a woman fight as she had earlier. Perhaps she was as good at acting as she was at swordplay.

He shook his head with impatience. "Lady Kinsdale, the storm is lessened, but it has not ended. You must remain here." He stood, and headed toward the doors.

"No!" she cried, leaping to her feet. She caught his hand. "Take me with you! Please, take me with you—"

"You are mad!"

"No, I—"

"The winds nearly swept you over, Lady Kinsdale. And you are worth far too much for such a fate."

"Don't leave me!" she pleaded.

He paused, looking at her hands, small and delicate, upon

his own. They were as pale as cream and as soft as velvet. Her nails were long as were her fingers, and they spoke of a genteel elegance. Amazed, he looked into her eyes.

She wasn't looking at him. She was, but her eyes went through him, and beyond him.

He took her hand, freeing his own. "I cannot take you out there."

"Then give me a light."

"Milady—"

"Please!" He stared at her, trying to fathom this woman, and she took his hesitation as a denial. "Please!" she repeated. Her voice lowered and cracked. "Leave me with a light, sir, and I swear that I shall . . ."

Intrigued, he paused, watching her carefully. "You shall what, mam'selle?"

"I shall—" She paused, but went on then. "I shall repay the kindness."

"You shall repay . . . the kindness?"

"Yes!" she screamed.

He arched a brow, inclining his head, taking his time. "Milady, my apologies, but I would that you be a bit more specific. We pirates are known for being dim-witted."

She wanted to kick him. She might well have done so except that he seemed to sense her intent and carefully caught her by the shoulders, drawing her against him. His eyes bored into hers. She felt his breath once more against her cheeks, against her lips. Curiously, his breath was sweet. It smelled of mint. His teeth were good, his own, and clean and white and straight and handsome, flashing with his every dangerous smile. His beard covered most of his face, but she thought that it was probably a striking face beneath the dark mat, ruthless perhaps, and formidable, but striking nonetheless.

She was thinking this of a pirate. A man who intended to rape her, and barter her back to her father or fiancé.

And worse, she was ready to promise him anything, just so long as he didn't leave her in the darkness again.

"What are you saying, Lady Kinsdale?" he demanded softly.

"I will do anything you want!" she lashed out. "Just so long as you don't leave me again in the darkness." She hesitated again and then whispered desperately, "I promise!"

He stared at her long and hard. Rather than being pleased by her promise, he seemed to be furious. He shoved her away from him. She stumbled, but she did not fall. He strode across the room to the bookcase and she saw that there was a lantern there, protected from falling off the shelf by wooden laths, just as the books were protected from being thrown about the cabin.

Watching her with that same curious fury, he found a striker and flint and went to the stove first, lighting the coals. As the glow rose around him, Skye realized just how cold she had been. He must have been freezing, too, she thought, for he was drenched. Despite herself, she found her eyes wandering over him. Muscle and sinew were delineated clearly.

His eyes fell upon her and she found herself shivering. With great deliberation he found a length of match and lit the lamp from the fire in the Dutch stove. He set the lamp back in its place. "Don't touch it or the stove," he said harshly. "I would not survive the storm to burn to a crisp upon the sea."

"I won't let anything burn. I promise."

"You are quick to hand out promises, Lady Kinsdale," he commented.

She shrugged, staring at the warmth of the fire, ignoring him. He kept watching her. She shivered anew with the warning tone of his next words.

"You will keep any promises you make to me, milady."

She nodded, playing only for the moment. Light and warmth flooded the room, and courage began to seep back into her along with the warmth. Then he took two steps toward her and she knew that he meant to touch her then and there. Despite herself she screamed. He ignored her, catching her shoulders, dragging her close. "No!" she gasped, seeking to stop his hands as they fell upon her bodice. Little was left of her gown; he found the ties of her corset and tugged upon them.

"Wait!"

"Your promise, milady!"

"You said you were going back out! The storm! The wind, it still rages, stop, please, you must—stop!"

"Be damned with the ship, mam'selle!"

"We'll drown!"

"Happily shall I die in your arms!"

Her bodice came free and her breasts spilled forth. Color bathed her face, but he barely glanced at her, swinging her around and plucking her torn wet gown over her head. Desperately she flailed against him, but managed only to entangle herself in her clothing. Then suddenly she was naked, shorn of her gown and corset and even her shift, and left only in her stockings and garters. She stared from the pool of her clothing cast upon the floor to his face, and his eyes so cold upon her, denying his taunting words. He took stock of her in a calculating assessment. His gaze was so icily cold that she did not even think to cover herself, to draw her arms about her. He did not in the least seem to appreciate what he saw; indeed, it was almost with disdain that he swept his eyes over her body. He hated her, she thought. But then he took a step toward her again and she screamed with pure primal dread.

He did not touch her. He wrenched the knit coverlet from the bed and tossed it upon her nakedness. She stumbled to her knees as she caught it, sweeping it around her shoulders and hovering there, her eyes lowered.

"You'll die of pneumonia and be worthless to me, mam'selle, if you do not dry off," he said curtly. She did not answer him. She saw his boots before her lowered eyes. His gleaming black boots. She did not look up.

The boots moved. He turned around and strode toward the door. He paused there and spoke very softly. "Don't deceive yourself, Lady Kinsdale. I have not forgotten your promise. You do give your oath freely, mam'selle. And with little meaning, so it appears. What you promise to me, you will give."

She heard the slam of the doors against the wind, and then he was gone.

Skye pulled the cover more tightly around herself. The cabin slowly became warm, and it was bright and comfortable.

And she slowly ceased to shiver, and when she did, she hated herself. The fear! It was so awful, and so ridiculous. She had humiliated herself before the very dregs of the earth because of it. She had made a promise to a pirate!

Suddenly she was shivering again, remembering the way that he had looked at her, as if he hated her. As if he knew her, or knew something about her, deep inside, and hated her for it. What?

Why should she care?

She should cling desperately to every moment that kept her away from him.

He teased her now. He taunted her. He would come back, and it would be all the worse for her because he hated her, too. . . .

At least he had all of his teeth. And he didn't smell bad. His husky whispers carried the scent of mint. . . .

What was she thinking?

Skye bolted to her feet and raced to his desk. She tore open drawer after drawer. He was a pirate, wasn't he? He had to be carrying about some kind of grog.

But his desk was empty. As she stood there perplexed, the ship took a sudden harsh keel and she landed flat upon her derriere. She swore softly and wished heartily she were back in London. London! Suddenly she loved it. There was so much there! Not the struggling new city of Williamsburg. In London there were balls and there was the theater and the opera and the elegance of court. In London there were rakes and rogues, of course, but they were of the civil kind, and a lady could not fall from virtue unless it was her choice. In London, there were no pirates!

She had loved her home in Williamsburg before she had left it. She had loved the beautiful streets, so carefully laid out when it had been determined to move the capital of the Virginia Colony from Jamestown to the place that they had previously called Middle Plantation. She had loved the College of William and Mary, and the capitol building they had built. The homes were clean and bright with white picket fences, and sometimes it seemed a raw place, and sometimes it seemed incredibly exciting to watch it grow. When she had been a child they had begun the grand mansion for the governor, and now, so father had written, Governor Spotswood was moving in. At one time, it had been so beautiful to her. . . .

But now she was being forced to return home to marry a stranger who lived out in one of the godforsaken plantations.

No. She was a pirate's captive. A plaything. And the pirate didn't think that her fiancé would avenge her honor. Perhaps, the pirate had suggested, Lord Petroc Cameron would not even offer to pay a ransom.

Her eyes fell upon a rosewood caddy, that she hadn't noticed earlier, by the side of his desk. There was a decanter of brandy and four stemmed glasses there, held in place by brass racks. Skye quickly stumbled to her feet and filled a glass with the brandy. It was hot and it burned, and it was the most delicious drink she had ever tasted.

She coughed and sputtered, and filled another glass.

The light, the warmth, and the alcohol quickly restored her courage. She railed at herself for having been such an awful coward, but the moment was past now, and the damage done. She had to look to the future. Setting her glass down once again, she began to search through the desk. There had to be a weapon here, somewhere.

There wasn't. All she could find were ledgers and maps. Frustrated, she slammed the drawers.

She paused for a moment. The ship was not swaying so violently anymore. The storm was breaking.

He could come back at any moment.

Inspired with renewed energy, Skye dove toward one of his handsome traveling trunks. She cast it open and came upon an array of stockings and breeches and vests and shirts and coats. They were in differing styles and fabrics, but they shared one common trait. All were in the color black.

"Damn!" she swore softly, despairing that she could find some help for herself. Then she lifted the last of the shirts and discovered a blade at the bottom of the trunk.

She gasped, for she had come upon a short broadsword, a two-foot weapon honed to a razor's sharpness on both edges. She held it in her hands, dreaming of freedom. Then the blood drained from her face as she wondered how she would manage once she had slain the captain.

His men would slice her to ribbons.

She could capture him. She could hold him hostage and demand that his men bring them into the Chesapeake Bay, and down the James. Perhaps she could capture the entire ship.

She sighed, shuddering. She would not capture the ship. But neither would this pirate, the Silver Hawk, ever touch her again and live to tell of it.

There were footsteps beyond the door, coming very close to it. She froze for a moment, then they moved away. She heard laughter now. Voices rising over the sound of the wind.

They had bested the storm.

Skye hurried toward the bunk. Wrapping herself, she put the evil blade close within the coverlet, then scurried as close to the wall as she could. Her heart raced furiously. What should she do? If she feigned sleep, perhaps she could buy herself more time. He would have to be exhausted when he returned. He had battled the other pirates, he had battled her, and he had battled the storm.

She heard footsteps again. And again, they paused before the double doors. She had just begun to relax, thinking that the footsteps would move away again, when the doors flew open.

And the Silver Hawk stepped into the cabin.

Skye closed her eyes and hoped that she appeared very small.

And very pathetic. Then she wished that she had not curled so completely toward the wall, for her back was exposed to him.

Every fool knew not to expose his or her back to the enemy!

But she dared not turn, lest he suspect that she was awake. And so she strained to listen, hoping desperately that he would leave her be.

She heard him close and bolt the doors, and she heard the sounds of his boots against the wood as he moved into the cabin. He paused before the stove, and she could imagine him warming his hands. Seconds later, she nearly screamed, for the bunk shifted as he sat down upon it. His boots clunked to the floor. Then she could hear little, but she was horribly aware of what he was doing. His sodden shirt struck the floor to be followed by his breeches and hose. She heard the curious smacking sounds as the wet fabric slapped against the floorboards.

She waited for him to touch her, or to stretch out beside her.

He did not.

He rose and silently padded across the cabin. She heard a tinkle of glass and knew that he had gone for the brandy. His soft laughter assured her that he realized that she had been into the liquor already.

He poured himself a drink, and then there was absolute silence for so long that Skye feared she would scream and slit her own throat with the double-edged blade.

She heard nothing else.

She felt his touch. Soft, light, and subtle. It came against her so suddenly that she barely refrained from jerking away.

His fingers ran over her blanketed shoulder, and down the length of her back. He paused, then ran his hand over the protruding curve of her derriere.

She bit into her mouth to keep her silence, and she waited, praying.

His weight came down beside her, and he touched her no more.

She would wait, she thought. She would wait, and he would fall asleep, and she would have him at her mercy.

But it didn't work out that way. Skye tried to listen for his even breathing. It was late, and he had worked hard, surely. No, it was no longer late, but early. The sun was rising. The fire in the stove still warmed the cabin, but light from outside glowed against the draperies. It was day again.

And still, he moved restlessly. He did not sleep.

Skye waited. . . .

At some point she ceased to wait. Exhaustion, perhaps, or betrayal by the brandy. He did not sleep; she did so, in truth.

Moments later—or was it hours?—she awoke. Her eyes flew open and she remembered that she lay in a pirate's bunk with only her hose and garters and a coverlet and a twin-sided blade. She needed to roll and face the pirate and plan her strategy.

She was already staring straight at the pirate, she realized.

She had rolled during the night, or so it seemed. She lay on her side facing him.

He lay upon his back. His eyes were closed, his deep dark hair was tossed about his forehead. His nose, she thought, was long, and very straight, and his whiskers were far more curly than the hair upon his head. He should shave, she found herself thinking. He probably had a handsome face.

He was a deplorable pirate!

But this morning there was definitely no denying that he was a pirate in his prime. Even in sleep his stature was imposing. His shoulders seemed to stretch the width of the bed, and like his arms they were heavily laden with muscle. He was deeply bronzed from the sun, and his flesh glistened and rippled even as he slept. His chest was furred with crisp dark hair that narrowed at his waist. Below his waist it flared and thickened again and formed a neat nest for . . .

Her face flamed and her eyes widened and jerked from the grandly protruding piece of his anatomy back to his eyes.

They were open. He was staring at her.

He smiled at her pleasantly. "Ready to keep your promise, Lady Kinsdale?"

She flushed furiously, wishing there were a way to instantly escape life itself. He rolled swiftly to his side and stroked her cheek, and though she tried not to, she slapped his hand away. She tried not to stare into flashing blue eyes, but to keep her gaze fixed upon the ceiling.

His laughter was quick and easy, as if his earlier anger had dissipated. But his face came nearer hers and he caught her chin between his thumb and forefinger. "You were warned, mam'selle."

"I am exhausted."

"Are you?"

"Utterly. How can one possibly fulfill such a promise in such a state?"

"You're a liar. Why, Lady Kinsdale, I believe that you do not intend to keep your promise at all."

Her eyes sizzled with a fury she could not suppress. "You are a pirate, sir. You are the scum of the earth. No decent man or woman would begin to imagine that such a vow need be upheld."

"The very scum of the earth?" he said. "Mam'selle, how offensive!"

"You are offensive!"

"But I am not, milady. . . ." he whispered softly, his voice trailing away in a haunting whisper. His knuckles brushed over her cheek and his fingers whispered against the length of her throat. She stared at him, unable to move or protest, compelled to silence by the silver-blue command of his eyes. Compelled, perhaps, by more.

"Ah, lady, think! It might have been One-Eyed Jack with his gruesome pitted face, decaying teeth, and lice-ridden body. You've done quite well, I daresay."

"You conceited oaf!" she spat, regaining her composure. He laughed, catching her wrists with one hand, straddling her squirming form. "Conceited, mam'selle? Nay, I offer you cleanliness and sound teeth, and you scoff at the lot of it."

"Bastard!"

"Ummm!" he agreed, and the touch of his free hand and fingers traveled lower, teasing the mound of her breast. She gritted her teeth, preparing to scratch and rail and fight and find some way to reach the blade at her side. His fingers fell lower and lower, rounding her breast, grazing her nipple. She screamed out with protest, but before she could fight him, he laughed, and his touch was gone.

He had released her. His feet swung over the side of the bed and she lay in ardent misery as he moved about, completely naked and completely comfortable with his state. Skye drew her covers close and felt the cold steel of the blade against her arm. She had wanted to put him at a disadvantage. He was awake now. Awake, aware, and rested.

There was a knock upon the door. With a slight oath he reached for one of the linen sheets upon the bunk, ripping it free and wrapping it about his waist. Skye, aware that he meant to open the door, drew her coverlet more securely over her breasts and bit her lip in consternation.

The handsome young pirate who had encouraged her fight the previous afternoon stood there with a tray. "Coffee, Captain. Sorry that there's no cream for the lady, but it's been a bit since we've seen a cow. There's sugar, though, and Cookie's sent some fine dark rolls."

"Thank you, Arrowsmith. Have you heard of the lady's ship?"

"Aye, it's sailing along behind us just fine. We all weathered the storm just fine."

"We'll see that she's repaired in New Providence."

"What?" Sky shrieked from the bed. Startled, they both turned to her.

"Wh—where? We're not headed for the James?"

They smiled to one another. "Why, nay, milady!" the Silver Hawk assured her. "Would you have me hang so quickly? I dare not sail straight up the James! I have no wish to see Virginia."

"But I have!"

"And so you shall—when your ransom is met. And frankly, my dear, I am in no great hurry for that." His eyes roamed over her quite differently. They touched her with a shimmering heat. They seemed to stroke her, as if she were a possession, already known, and cherished.

A cry of rage escaped her and the pirate turned to his man with a shrug. He took the tray of coffee and rolls. "Women. You never can please them, Arrowsmith."

Arrowsmith laughed and cleared his throat. He inclined his head in Skye's direction and saluted his captain. Then he took his leave, closing the doors in his wake.

Silver Hawk set the tray down upon his desk. He munched upon a roll and sipped his coffee, black and steaming. "You've one hell of a temper, milady Kinsdale," he noted.

"You made him think—"

"Precisely."

"You are despicable!"

"Am I? I have merely made you my possession, mam'selle, and that keeps you safe from the others—until, such time, of course, that you do see fit to keep your promise."

"Never!" she vowed to him, her eyes narrowing.

"Another 'promise'? Then I've little to fear."

She didn't reply. She stared at him while he watched her,

and she felt suddenly very warm inside, wondering at his thoughts. Then she swiftly lowered her eyes, wondering at his mercy. He had wanted her that morning, and easily could have raped her. He teased, he taunted, but he did not move against her in violence.

But how long would his behavior remain that way?

"We sail . . . where?" she inquired, gathering her coverlet and the broadsword within it. She came to the edge of the bed, and then she stood, looking at him innocently.

"To the Caribbean, Lady Kinsdale. To New Providence, and beyond."

"And I?" she murmured, stepping forward.

He smiled and shrugged, then turned and deliberately spooned jam upon a roll. His back was to her as he answered.

"I think that you will remain in my company."

"And I think not!" Skye cried, leaping toward him. Her strategy had been planned, and before he could turn she had reached him, dragging her coverlet in one hand, slipping the other about his shoulder to bring the broadsword against his throat.

He did not flinch, nor blink. Despite the sharp blade against his throat, he offered her a slow smile.

"I have the upper edge!" Skye hissed. "Cease your silly grin lest you would die with it upon your face."

"And why not, mam'selle? What better way to die?"

"I do not tease or taunt, sir, as is your way. When I threaten, I carry out the threat."

"Lady, beware, when I threaten, for I, too, carry out the threat."

Skye swore with the vengeance of a fishwife. "Cease! Now you will summon your men and order them to make haste for the James River!"

"I think not."

"What?"

He ducked and swirled with such swift agility that her quick reaction still offered nothing but a scratch to his throat. He caught her coverlet, and as his arm cracked down upon hers, sending the broadsword flying. He jerked upon the cloak she had fashioned for herself, and caught within the folds, she went sprawling down upon the ground facefirst.

She quickly rolled, grasping for the covers again, aware of his bare feet, set firm upon them. He did not release the covers to her fevered grasp.

She did not want to see his eyes, but her own were drawn to them, and she had no choice.

Cobalt and dark, they danced with fury. Beneath the fur of his beard his jaw was twisted and set, his lips were grim.

Slowly, slowly, he crouched down beside her. She gritted her teeth as he caught her chin. She tossed back her hair, defying him.

"That was foolhardly, my love. If you ever bring a weapon against me again, you will pay dearly. That is a threat. Is it clear?"

She hesitated, then she clamped down hard on her teeth and nodded. She didn't want to shiver or show fear today. Not after her performance yesterday. But her teeth were chattering, and when her mouth opened, she softly spoke words that she abhorred. "You will not . . . you will not hurt me?"

He shook his head, watching her. She flushed and lowered her eyes.

She raised them again in alarm, for he was reaching for her, lifting her. She felt his arms around her naked flesh, and panic filled her. "You said that you would not hurt me!"

"I said that I would not hurt you. I didn't say that I wouldn't touch you . . . or . . . er, entertain you!" he whispered.

She cast back her head to scream. She did so and he watched with amusement.

Then he seated her before the tray of coffee and rolls.

"Breakfast, Lady Kinsdale. Do you always scream blue blazes when you are offered a cup of coffee?"

III ❧

When she was settled in the seat behind his desk, he retrieved her coverlet, tossing it over her shoulders. Skye grasped at the garment and sat there stiffly. He moved across the room to his trunk and drew out clothing. He looked her way, arching his brows, and she flushed furiously, turning aside as he dressed. She felt his eyes upon her as he buttoned his shirt and tied his breeches, then sat to pull on his high black boots.

"So, tell me, milady, why is it that you are so afraid of the dark?"

"I am not afraid of the dark," she lied ridiculously.

"You are not?"

"No."

"That's a lie."

She shrugged. "A gentleman would allow a lady the lie."

"But I'm not a gentleman. I'm a pirate, remember."

"Oh, yes. A nasty, brutal beast, and I've nothing to say to you upon any account."

He rose. She still did not look his way, but shivers claimed her despite her best efforts as he moved around behind her. He did not touch her, but his hands fell upon the back of the chair where she sat and his head lowered so that she could hear and feel his whisper. "Nasty and brutal, Lady Kinsdale? Alas! I fear that if I keep my distance, I will dearly disappoint you! You've suffered no beatings as yet, mam'selle. The only violence that has come your way has been that given in retribution for your own intent of murder. Bear this in mind."

Skye stiffened, her fingers curling into the handsomely carved arms of the chair, her gaze remaining straightforward. How she hated this man! she thought. Hated his laughter and his mockery, hated his power. Just as she hated the haunting sound of his whispers and the curve of his smile, and the fine, taut musculature of his body. He was an animal! she thought. A pirate. A vile knave, a beast.

But a striking beast, bold, determined, and blunt. If she were not his prisoner, she might very well find him charismatic, his form alluring, his less-than-subtle innuendo exciting. . . .

Dear God, she was a captive losing her mind! He was young enough, perhaps, despite the silver that tinted his hair and beard. And his speech was cultured, his manner sometimes even inoffensive. But he was a cutthroat, no more, no less, and she would still fight him and hate him until her dying breath.

"Nothing to say, my love?" He plucked up a tendril of her hair. His fingers brushed her shoulder where the coverlet had fallen away and she was startled by the searing sensation that swept through her. She slapped his hand away, still staring forward, trembling. "Nothing but the obvious, sir. Your teeth may be better than One-Eyed Jack's, but you are still the same monster as he was. No better."

He laughed, straightening, and going for the broadsword that lay upon the floor. "I do beg to differ, milady. Had he lived, and had you spent the night in his cabin, I think you would have discovered a vast difference twixt the two of us."

"Really? Perhaps were I tavern slut, I might have managed to say, 'what a wonder! The man has his teeth, and for garbage, his stench is not too severe.' But I am no tavern wench, sir, and from where I sit, refuse is refuse, and all to be abhorred."

His laughter was swift and genuine. "Ah, from your lofty heights, mam'selle! I don't wish to disturb such noble ideals, but I tell you this in all truth, a woman is a woman, and a man must be judged by his measure, and not by his position upon this earth. The finest lady, the most noble duchess, tumbles upon the mattress much the same as the tavern wench. She learns to long and ache and desire in the same fashion, to whisper her lover's name, to curl to his caress and strain to his form." He came back behind her, bending over her. "And she learns so much more quickly when he still has all of his teeth!"

"Your conceit is extraordinary."

He faced her and lifted her chin. "That you can doubt my words, mam'selle, lends credence to the very truth of them. There is a grave difference. Had you spent your night in Jack's cabin, you'd not have awakened thinking there could be no difference in men."

She wanted to wrench from him. He held his grip. "I did not say men, sir. I spoke of refuse—pirates."

"Such harsh words, milady! When I carry still in the boundaries of my heart your sweet promise to please me in any way, to offer any diversion I might desire."

"Diversion!"

His lip began to curl with humor. She did twist her chin from his grip. She raised her hand with a vengeance, halfway rising, determined to strike him. She just barely caught his cheek before his fingers wound around her wrist. He twisted his jaw and she was pleased that she had hurt him, then she was suddenly frightened, for a pulse ticked against his throat and she did not care to be hurt in return, and she had definitely angered him as well. She sank slowly back into the chair, her eyes locked with his. She already knew that when the soft silver darkened to a cobalt blue, his temper was flaring. But he did not strike out at her in return. He swallowed, as if he clamped down on his temper. His smile returned. "Were you aware, milady, that you've splendid breasts?"

"What?" she gasped. Her eyes fell downward where the coverlet had fallen from her and where her flesh now lay bare to him. She must have been cold, for her nipples protruded like hardened rosebuds against the mounds.

"Oh!" she swore, and she sought, clumsily, to strike him again and retrieve her covering at the same time. He was not about to be struck again and caught her wrist quickly and easily. "Madame, I am patient, but I do have my limits. So far you've tried to slice my throat and dislodge my jaw. Do take care!" His husky laughter irritated her to no end, but she lowered her head, seeking desperately to free her hand, to recover herself. She glanced up at him quickly and went still, for the color of his eyes had changed again. They had gone to a warm, smoke color, and they remained upon her person, then slowly met hers. She did not quite understand the message in his eyes, but her breath caught in her throat and her blood surged throughout her limbs with a sizzling force. Something in her abdomen coiled tightly and she desperately moistened her lips. "Please!" she gasped out, unaware of just what it was that she requested.

He freed her wrist. She lowered her eyes, drawing the coverlet about her. She sought desperately for something to say.

"I, er, I did not promise—diversion!"

"Ah, but you did promise me . . . what was it . . . ? Anything! I do believe that is what you said," he reminded her, laughing. He turned from her and picked up his hat and set it upon his head. "I shall be waiting, mam'selle. Thank God that I am a patient man!" He paused just a moment longer, belting his scabbard and cutlass to his side, and taking the broadsword beneath his arm. He took a dirk from the bookcase and cast her a wry glance. "I wonder if it is safe to leave you with the serving tray. Ah, yes, bless Cookie, he is a man of rare good sense. He has sent a spoon and not a knife for the jam. Take care, my dear, until we meet again."

With a sweeping flourish of his hat, he left her. She sat still until she heard the bolts slide into place at the doors. Then she leaped up, led by instinct, slamming against them.

She was locked in once again.

She swore violently and was overcome with a sense of panic and desolation. Shrieking aloud, she stormed about and sent the tray with the coffee and rolls flying. The porcelain cups shattered and the jam jar cracked in two, spilling out blood red strawberry preserves. Skye stood still looking upon the havoc she had wreaked, the coverlet still wrapped about her shoulders. She was startled when the doors burst open again and she discovered that the Silver Hawk had returned.

He stood in the doorway, exceptionally tall in his plumed hat and high boots. His eyes sizzled silver and blue and they fell upon her with a shimmering anger.

"Brat!" he exploded.

And he was striding her way with purpose.

Skye gasped out and turned to run, but there was nowhere to go. She collided with the bookshelves and too hastily turned from them, and tripped. In a tangle of covers she fell facedown on the bunk. Gulping for air, she tried to twist and turn, but he was upon her by then, his weight falling hard upon hers. His arms stretched out and his hands fell upon hers, his fingers lacing with her own.

"Let me go!" she cried out fiercely.

But she had no effect upon him at all at that moment. She kicked, she flailed, she bit at him, catching his arm so savagely with her teeth that he let out a roar. To her vast dismay she realized that he was sitting then and that she was being dragged relentlessly over his lap. Her coverlet was stripped away with every twist and movement and she was both swearing and sobbing in her desperation to elude him. But at that moment, he was ruthless.

"Nearly sliced, broken, and now bitten!" he grated out furiously. "Cups shattered, property destroyed—"

"Property destroyed! Those words from a pirate!" she cried.

The irony of it eluded him. He held her in a vise against him and she could not even twist to see his face, to brush her hair from its tangle over her eyes and mouth.

"Mam'selle, I have had it!" he said. "Act like a child and you'll be treated as one!"

A shriek exploded from her as his hand fell with a searing force upon the exposed and tender curve of her derriere. Tears stung her eyes from both the startling pain of his blow and the humiliation of it. Wretchedly she stretched over the burning muscles of his thighs, her face in the covers as she struggled to be free. She could not bear it. She twisted, crying out again. She hated him! She wanted to take whatever he dished out to her with dignity and silence. She wanted to bear any pain.

And she could not. She could not stand this awful indignity.

His hand was rising again. "Please! Stop!" she sobbed out.

And to her amazement, he did.

His teeth clenched together, his hand slowly fell. He shoved her from his lap and she went to the floor in a disheveled pile of covers and tousled hair. She landed hard on her rump and she nearly screeched again, for he had injured her sorely, and she imagined then that it would be a number of days before she managed to sit comfortably again.

"Damn you!" he muttered darkly.

He stood, stepping over her. She didn't see him look back her way because her head had fallen and her hair hid her eyes. "Pick up this mess!" he ordered her succinctly, each word enunciated slowly.

She tossed back her hair, heedless that her eyes were filled with tears. She opened her mouth to tell him that although he was pirate and she was his prisoner, she would never, never obey him. But he spoke first.

"You will do it, Skye, whether I am a bastard pirate or not! You will do it because I have ordered you to do so, and because I promise you that you will rue the day if you do not, and because that is a threat, and as I have warned you, I carry out all threats. If you find it prudent to defy me over jam, then you are truly a fool, and deserve whatever fate awaits you!"

His hands were on his hips, his long legs were outstretched, and his boots were firmly cast upon the floor. His silver eyes sizzled and burned a startling dark silver, and she knew how he had gotten his name. The line of his mouth was grim against the curl of his mustache and the dark fur of his beard, and in that particular moment, she had no more will to fight him.

"Mam'selle! Do you comprehend me?"

"Yes!"

She saw the expression in his eyes soften and he moved his

hand, as if he would touch her, almost as if he wanted to reach out to her. Then he swore and snorted, and spun around.

Then he was gone. The doors slammed and the bolts slid in his wake. Skye stared after him, not breathing.

Then she gulped in air and cast herself against the floor and gave way to a flood of tears.

An hour later, after a great deal of reflection, she determined that she would clean the mess she had made. She brooded long and hard over the action, but in the end, she had to agree that the pirate had made one good point—a jar of jam was not worth this awful humiliation.

She picked up the tray and the shattered porcelain and glass and cleaned the floorboards with a linen napkin. When she was done, she approached the windows and pulled back the drapes. She was startled to see that the sun was already fallen. They must have slept very late into the day. Night was coming again already.

She tied the draperies by their cords, eager for the light that remained. The lamp had gone out and the stove had issued its last warmth and light. Skye knotted her fingers into her fists.

He would leave her here again, she thought. Locked in as darkness fell. He would see her reduced to a groveling fool once again, and he would laugh all the while. He would assume that she deserved it.

There was a knock upon the door. Startled, she whirled. She did not think that the Silver Hawk would be knocking. She pulled the coverlet tightly around her shoulders. "Yes?" she called softly.

The door opened and the handsome young man the pirate had called Arrowsmith walked in, somewhat burdened by the weight of one of her traveling trunks.

"This is yours, I believe?" he said.

"Yes," Skye said.

"Then you'll excuse me if I put it down. 'Tis heavy! What on earth is it that you women carry?"

"I'm sure you've taken plunder enough to know the answer to that!" she retorted.

He grimaced. "No, milady. We ransom off our plunder, just as we do our hostages."

"You'll swing by the neck for it, just the same."

"Perhaps." He grinned, setting down her trunk next to his master's trunk at the foot of the bed. "I'm afraid we'll have to wait until we reach the Caribbean for me to bring you the rest of your trunks," he said apologetically. "The captain went through this one and thought that it offered all that you might require for the next few days of travel."

"The captain—went through it?"

"Yes, milady."

She thought that she would scream her outrage, but she kept silent. Her clothing and jewels were valuable plunder. She was probably lucky that he had decided to clothe her.

"I shall take this away," Arrowsmith said. He smiled and picked up the tray with the broken cups without blinking. He turned to leave the room.

"Wait, please!" Skye said. He was a pirate, too, she reminded herself. Even if he was young and handsome and even gentle in his way. He stopped, looking to her.

"Could you . . . light a lamp for me, please? It is growing dark."

"I shall take care of it, Robert."

Startled, they both looked to the doorway. The Silver Hawk had returned.

"Aye, Captain, as you wish it." Robert Arrowsmith inclined his head toward Skye and exited the room, brushing by his captain. The Silver Hawk came into the room, turning his back to her and, with slow purpose, closing the doors. He turned around again, leaning against them. He looked over the floor, and over Skye, and to the foot of the bunk where her trunk now lay.

"I came to light the lamp for you, milady," he said softly.

She said nothing, standing still and awaiting his next move. It was a long time in coming. He strode across the room and lit the wick of the lamp. The glow filled the room. Skye lowered her head in a turmoil. She had thought that he would exploit her fear, that he would purposely leave her to her terror of the darkness.

He had not.

And yet it wouldn't be proper to thank the vile pirate for

the kind gesture, would it? Not after all that he had done to her.

He set the lamp into its protected niche. "We head south with a good wind. It will be too warm for the fire, I believe, but the light should be good enough."

Skye swallowed and nodded.

"I had thought to find you dressed by now."

"The trunk just arrived."

"Yes. Find something. I will help you don your clothing, and you can come on deck for an hour or so."

Her eyes widened and she bit into her lip. "I can dress myself, thank you."

"Shall I choose for you?"

There was an edge to his voice. They were engaging in battle again.

Eventually, she thought with a shiver, he would wear her down. Their strange encounters were unnerving her completely.

"Sir, I tell you—"

"I shall choose then." He strode toward her trunk. She found herself running after him, catching his arm, then was dismayed by her action. She gazed at her hand where it rested upon him and recoiled swiftly, startled by the blood that had hardened upon his shirt. She stared at him in horror.

"You're—bleeding."

"I was bleeding, milady. A shrew with sharp teeth caught hold of my flesh."

She swallowed, her eyes locked with his.

"It is no matter, Lady Kinsdale. If you'll excuse me—"

"No! You needn't go into my things again. You had no right to do so before. Sir, I tell you—"

"Milady, I tell you. You had no difficulty riffling through my belongings to find that wretched broadsword. I found no difficulty in disturbing your belongings for a far more gentle mission, that of seeing you clad!"

He was already upon his knees, casting back the unlocked lid of her chest. He found a corset and tossed it back down, then procured a simple shift and a linen gown with short sleeves. It was a soft, cool blue with white lace trim and she had purchased it with thoughts of the long hot Virginia summers in mind.

"This one," he muttered.

She flushed furiously that his hands should be upon her apparel. She tried to shove him aside, taking up the corset he had dropped. "If you will just leave me—"

"I will not. And drop that whalebone torture creation. You don't need stockings, either. Even with the breeze, it is warm this evening."

"Mr. Hawk!" she snapped in exasperation. "Is it Hawk? Or is it Mr. Silver? I mean, really, sir, just how does one address you?" she demanded irritably.

He sat back on his haunches and his slow grin curled into his lip. "I think that I might like the sound of 'milord,' from your lips, Lady Kinsdale. Or perhaps, 'my dear lord.' "

"Never," Skye said flatly.

"Then 'Hawk' will do, milady. Come, let's see you clad in this piece of summer's frivolity."

Skye straightened to her full height. "Sir, this will be done by violence only."

"If that's the way you choose it," he said with a shrug, rising and taking a step toward her. "The manner is of no difference to me."

"Stop!" Skye pleaded, backing away from him. She hadn't the energy for the fight. Her flesh still burned from his earlier, less than tender touch. She promised herself that she hated him still with a vengeance, but for the moment, she needed to lick her wounds and recoup her energy.

He stood still, watching her. She lifted her arms and dropped the coverlet from about her shoulders. She meant to keep her eyes on his but she could not, and her eyes fell in shame.

"Oh, you will quit playing Ophelia!" he said in harsh exasperation. He stepped forward, but took his time easing her plight, raising her chin and meeting her eyes. His gaze passed quickly over the length of her. "Milady, the silk stockings must go. Clad only in them, you are most provocative."

If she had thought to shame him, she had sadly miscalculated, and her own temper flew back to a new high as he lifted her from the floor and tossed her nonchalantly upon the bed to strip away her stockings, all that remained of her clothing from the previous day.

Skye swore, she flailed at him. He avoided her pummeling with amusement and quickly did away with the offending garments. "Calm down!" he charged her. And capturing her shoulders, he straddled her. She wasn't aware at first that he had her shift, and that he was trying to slip it over her shoulders. "Lady Kinsdale, I do swear, it is far more difficult to dress you than it has ever been to charm and unclothe any tender maid in all of my days."

"I daresay you've never known a tender maid!" Skye retorted. She quickly slipped her arms into the silken straps of the garment and faced him again, flushed and furious. He stood by the bed, watching her with a curious expression, his eyes the color of fog and steel, a pallor seeming to touch his face. She noted that his fists were clamped hard at his sides. He did not rise to her retort. It occurred to Skye that her shift defined more than it concealed, that her breasts were pressed strainingly against the bodice of the gossamer undergarment, and that the line of her hip and the soft triangle at the juncture of her thighs were hauntingly evident.

"Why do you humiliate me like this!" she cried suddenly. "Why this slow torture—"

"Milady, I promise," he interrupted her dryly, "the torture I do is to myself."

"Then . . ."

"Then what?"

"Then . . . stop it!" she whispered.

"Alas," he murmured, and the word carried a tender and wistful sound, "I have discovered that I cannot." He turned swiftly away from her, finding the dress. "Come, Skye, let's set this upon your shoulders and ease both our souls."

Skye . . .

He had used her given name. He had used it with the ease of a friend or relation, or of a lover. She should have despised the sound of it upon his tongue, but she did not. She should have ignored his command, but she could not. She crawled from the bed and stepped to him slowly. She reached up as he deftly set the yards of muslin over her head and arms. He twirled her around and set to the twenty-one tiny buttons that closed the dress. He was deft with his movement, as if he was well-acquainted with women's fashion. She began to tap a bare toe as his fingers brushed her back.

"Are you done?" she inquired.

"Umm. You intended to do this alone?"

"The intent of such a gown is to have one's maids along. But since those poor lasses have fallen prey to your men . . ."

He was undaunted. "That is why, mam'selle, you must be grateful for my assistance."

"Grateful!" She pulled away, and whirled about. "May we go?"

"If you wish." But he reached down into her trunk again and plucked from it her silver initialed brush. "Your hair resembles an ill-kept bird's nest."

"That is hardly my fault."

"But if you don't care, lady, then I must. Come to me, and I'll make some semblance of golden curls from that thatch yet."

"I care!" Skye cried quickly. On her bare feet she hurried forward, snatching the brush from his fingers. She tried to work through the length of her thick tendrils quickly, but she was nervous and tugged and tore far more than she cared to admit. He emitted some impatient sound and stepped forward with purpose, snatching the brush away again. "Turn!" he ordered her. Gritting her teeth, she did so.

Again, his fingers were deft. There was no tenderness to his touch, but he was apt and able, and with little pain to her, the dreadful knots caused by the wind and tempest of the storms outside and inside the captain's cabin were quickly untangled. Her hair fell about her back and shoulders in soft, shimmering waves.

"It is an unusual color," he commented almost idly. "It is neither gold nor red."

She turned around, smiling succinctly. "It is the color of thatch, so you said."

"Ah, yes, thatch," he agreed, and smiled. Her eyes narrowed and she swung around again, waiting for the door to open. He came around and opened it for her. He offered her his arm. She chose to ignore it, staring straight ahead.

"Skye, take my arm, else resign yourself to this cabin for the length of the voyage."

He spoke the truth, and she knew it. She took his arm and he politely opened the door.

Sunset was coming. The very sight of the spectacular colors streaking across the heavens gave a curious thrill to her heart. The world had fallen apart. She had fallen prey to the true monsters that roamed the seas. Her own captain lay dead and surely floated in some watery grave. Crew had fought and died, and infamy had ensued. She had spent the night in the company of one of the four most notorious pirates about . . . and still, the sunset spoke of hope.

It was glorious. It was red and gold and all the shades in between. The sun itself was a glorious orb falling slowly into the cobalt and azure of the sea. The colors seemed to stretch into eternity.

"Now I know the color," he murmured suddenly behind her.

"What?" she said, turning to him.

His eyes, smoke now, fell upon hers. "Your hair. It is the color of this sunset." He was silent only a moment. "Come on. I am taking the helm. You may stay at my side for a while."

He gave her no choice but to come, holding her tightly as they walked across the decking from his cabin past huge cleats and piles of rigging and canvas sail until they came to the carved steps that led to the wheel. Men saluted, doffing their caps to her, smiling their knowing smiles. She felt her cheeks grow warm and she did not respond, but she tried to raise her chin.

"Evening, Captain!" came a cry from the crow's nest.

"Evening, Jacko. Is she clear?"

"Clear as the sound o' my sweet mother's voice, captain! It seems we've weathered the storms, and moved into clear weather."

"That's fine to hear, Jacko."

"Milady, you're looking well!" the man called.

Skye did not reply to him. The Hawk laughed and answered

in her stead. "Perhaps, Jacko, the lady, too, has weathered the storm of the previous night and seeks calm seas this eve!"

Jacko laughed. Skye was certain that she heard subtle sneering sounds from all about her, but then maybe she had imagined them. The Hawk's men seemed more cheerful than licentious. They were a well-disciplined lot for scourges of the sea, she thought. And they were clean for pirates. And neatly garbed.

Hawk led her around to a carved wood seat that curved around the wheel, built into the superstructure of the ship. The man at the wheel saluted Hawk, nodded very properly to her, and gave over the helm. "The course is set south, southeasterly, sir!"

"Fine, Thompkins. We'll keep her so. You are at leisure, Mr. Thompkins."

"Thank you, sir," Thompkins responded. He saluted again and left the helm. The Hawk took the huge wheel, legs spread firm and apart as he stood and surveyed the sea from behind it. They might have been alone in the world, Skye thought, for the sea and sky seemed so very vast. The sunset falling portside was still a sight of crystalline beauty and the wind was gentle and balmy.

She drew her bare toes up beneath her and leaned her head back, feeling the wind. She should be thinking of some new way to slay him, she thought. She should not let another night pass by. She desperately needed to find a way to salvage life and dignity and honor from this fiasco.

But she was weary and unarmed and the air was gentle and soft. She needed to regain her strength, to find the will and energy and way to defy him.

She opened her eyes, and discovered that he was no longer watching the sea. He was watching her.

"What!" she cried irritably. "What is it that you want out of me!"

He shrugged and glanced toward the sea once again. "I am curious, Lady Kinsdale, and that is all."

"Curious, why?"

"That a woman raised as you have been—a God-fearing lass, born into the peerage—can take her vows so lightly."

She stiffened. "I do not take promises lightly, sir. Not unless they are given to the rodents and snakes."

"A promise, milady, is a promise."

"Not—"

"Yes, milady, a promise, even given to me, is a promise."

"You are a rake and a rogue and a—"

"Pirate! It is a most noble profession, milady! Why that dear great lady, Queen Elizabeth herself, encouraged the profession. Sir Francis Drake was a pirate, you know. Anytime that England has been at war with the Spanish or French, pirating has been called noble!"

"Drake was a privateer—"

"Pirate!" he claimed, laughing. "Or, to be a thief is fine—as long as we steal from other nations!"

Skye turned away, looking westward toward the sunset. "You would compare One-Eyed Jack with Sir Francis Drake."

"No, I would compare One-Eyed Jack with Attila the Hun, for both were cold-blooded murderers."

"Oh? Are there good pirates and bad?"

"Of course. There are the good and the bad in all peoples."

"You are scum," she said sweetly.

"And you are changing the subject. Consider then that we have established that I am scum. Let's return to you."

"Let's not."

He ignored her words. "To promises."

"I have already told you—"

"That you are not beholden to keep a promise to me. Because I am scum. But what of your fiancé?"

"What?"

"You intend to breech your promise to him."

"I never voiced any such promise!" Skye declared. Then, furious that she had replied to him, she turned again. "It is none of your business, you—"

"Cease. I tire of the barbs in your tongue."

"I tire of your presence."

"That can easily be rectified. Come, I will return you to your prison."

"Can't you please let me be! Have you no mercy within you?"

"I am afraid, milady, that you cannot expect 'scum' to come equipped with mercy."

"Oh!" she cried, frustrated. "What is all this to you anyway?"

"I am curious."

"Why?"

"Pure and simple, milady. I wonder if the dear fellow will or will not be willing to pay for your return."

Skye drew her knees up beneath her, folded her hands upon them, and rested her chin there. "It matters not if he pays or not. My father will ransom me."

"But what if your father has had a bad year? Most of his fortune comes from his holdings on the islands. It's been a bad year for the sugar plantations."

"Lord Cameron will pay!" she snapped.

"He will pay for you, even tarnished as you are?"

"I am not tarnished!" she snapped. Then she lowered her eyes slightly, for it was by a curious mercy on his part that she was not, and she did not wish to test that mercy. Then she remembered his touch and his eyes, and the fact that sitting was still difficult because of a certain placement of his hand upon her bare anatomy. "I am only slightly tarnished," she amended, and he laughed softly.

"I think you are right," he said. "I think that Cameron will pay for you, no matter how tarnished you should become. You see, he is a man who knows how to keep a promise. He was pledged as a child, but from respect for his deceased father's wishes, I am sure that he will pay."

She glanced at him sharply. He was watching the sea once again. She cried softly, "You know him! You know the man to whom I am engaged."

He did not reply for a moment.

"You know him!" Skye cried once again.

"Aye, I know him."

"How!" She hadn't realized that she had stood, or that she had moved, until she saw that her hand rested upon his where it lay against the mighty wheel. She flushed and quickly drew away her touch. "How do you know him?"

He shrugged. "He intercedes sometimes when I return hostages. We meet on Bone Cay. I have—holdings—there."

"Then—then I will not be a prisoner long?" she whispered.

A lazy smile touched his lips and one of his dark brows arched. "Long enough, milady."

She drew away from him and turned about. "What is he like?"

"Petroc Cameron?"

"Yes."

"He is like me."

"What!" she stormed, whirling around with great indignation.

His laughter was deep and husky and seemed to fill the night, and his eyes sparkled a fascinating silver. "At least you are quick to leap to his defense!"

"He is a gentleman. You are—"

"Un-uh. Watch it, lady. I am weary."

"You are a—pirate," she said. She meant "scurvy rodent," and they both knew it. His jaw twisted, but he was still amused. She was, after all, she admitted ruefully, broken down to a certain control.

"He is like me," the Hawk said, "because he is my cousin."

She gasped so awfully that she choked. He patted her firmly upon the back and quickly apologized. "Milady, please do not have apoplexy upon me! You needn't fear the future so intensely upon my account. He is a second cousin of sorts. And I, of course, poor slime, am from the wrong side of the sheets several generations back. The Camerons do not like to speak of it, of course, and they admit nothing. But when you meet your dear betrothed, you will see that there can be no real denial, for the Lord Cameron and I do bear a certain resemblance to one another."

Skye sank back into her seat, staring at him dismally. "And you would tarnish your own cousin's fiancée?" she demanded.

"There is no love lost between us."

"But—"

"And remember, milady, as of this moment, you are only 'slightly' tarnished. And if rumor stands correct, you intend to dishonor your bethrothal anyway."

"That is mere speculation."

"To many. You forget. I know you."

"You do not know me at all!"

"I am learning more about you with each passing hour, Lady Kinsdale."

"Again, you show your conceit."

She crossed her arms over her chest and looked away. "Governor Spotswood hates pirates! He will catch you one day and he will hang you high, and I will make you one promise now that I will keep. The day that they hang you I will be there with bells on. I will watch with the greatest glee."

"Bloodthirsty wench," he said.

"In your case, Sir Rogue!"

He laughed, letting go the wheel, turning to her. She wished to escape his nearness but it was too late. He caught her hands and bowed low so that their faces nearly touched and he all but whispered into her lips. "Milady, one day I promise—a promise that will be kept!—you will call me 'lord' and you will bow to my command!"

"Never!" she promised, but the cry was but a whisper, too, and that against his lips. He so nearly brushed her flesh! So nearly met his mouth to hers. A hammering came to her, and it was the sound of her heart. She heard the rush of the ocean, then realized that it was her blood, cascading and steaming within her. Surely, he saw how she trembled. He would know . . .

Know what? she demanded desperately of herself.

She did not find the answer for someone nearby cleared his throat and the Hawk straightened. Robert Arrowsmith stood with one foot upon the first step to the helm.

"I've laid the lady's supper out in your cabin, Captain."

The Hawk reached for her hand, drawing her to her feet, his eyes deep and hard upon hers. "Mr. Arrowsmith will escort you to the cabin." His voice lowered. "You needn't fear. The lanterns are already lit."

He did not wait for a reply but handed her over to Robert. Robert escorted her past the rigging and to the cabin door. "Good night, milady," he said to her.

And the doors were closed and bolted. But as the Hawk had

promised, two lanterns burned brightly, illuminating the water left for her to wash and the meal left for her upon the Hawk's desk. She would never eat, she thought. But it had been endless hours since she had last eaten and she quickly realized that she was famished and that the stew left for her smelled wonderful.

She sat down. It was a fresh fish stew, she quickly realized, thick with potatoes and carrots. The bread at her side was fresh, too, and vermin free. With less than ladylike manners she set into it, and when she paused at last, she realized that she had consumed it all.

She hadn't even bothered to pour herself some of the burgundy left for her. She did so then, reflecting on the night.

He would not hurt her. He had told her so. If she took care, she would be rescued soon enough.

If her father had the ransom, she thought dully.

Or if Lord Cameron was still willing to come to her aid.

She was only slightly tarnished. . . .

Restlessly, she stood. The food had been wonderful. It had left her with a sense of well-being. The wine was good, too. It went down well, and it eased away the fear and the pain. She was still so very tired.

She looked from the washbowl and French soap and sponge to the door, wondering when he would burst back in upon her. Nervously she dug into her trunk for a substantial nightdress, and even more nervously she set to the endless task of trying to undo her buttons. She let her dress fall to her waist and scrubbed her upper torso.

No one came to the door.

She slipped her nightdress over her shoulders and soaped and sponged her lower half, finishing with her feet. Then she breathed a sigh of relief, for no one had come.

She sat down and finished the wine. Still, no one disturbed her. The lanterns burned brightly, and she was at ease. She leaned back and closed her eyes.

Later, she tried to move, and she struck wood. Panic seized her. She was surrounded by darkness. She was locked into a small wooden space, and darkness surrounded her.

She could hear the screams. . . .

Stay! She had to stay!

But she could not. She could not remain in her prison and listen to the horrible screams!

She tried to scream herself, but the sound would not come. They had warned her not to make a sound, not to make a sound. . . .

It burst from her, the awful sound of her dream. There were hands upon her. They had found her. They had come for her, too. She scratched and fought furiously. They would kill her, without a second thought.

"Skye!"

There was light again, she realized. She blinked furiously, looking about herself. She was in his bed, beside him. She had banged against the paneling at the side of the bunk.

"It went out!" she cried. "The light went out."

"Hush, I'm sorry."

He held her, very tenderly. He was naked beneath the covers, she knew. His shoulders were bare and the hair upon his chest teased her cheek. He was a pirate, and she couldn't care, she couldn't even think about it. She lay against him, trembling and dazed. His hands soothed her, touching her hair, stroking her cheek. "It's all right. I won't let the light go out again. Ever."

She kept trembling. His arms came more tightly against her and she buried her face against the strength of his broad chest.

"Don't fight me, Skye. Lie still, lie easy. I won't leave you and I won't hurt you. Don't fight me. . . ."

She had no thought to fight him that night. None at all. With a soft sob she curled against him. Slowly, her trembling eased. He whispered to her still. In time, her eyes closed. Then she slept, a dreamless, easy sleep.

He waited until that time. Then he uncurled the fingers that still tore into his flesh with terror. He smoothed them out, softly massaging her palms.

He gazed down upon her tearstained face, so fine in the web of her sunset hair.

He admitted that she was beautiful.

And he admitted, too, that he was playing a losing game. He had made her his prisoner.

But now, he was the one in chains. He would never be able to just release her.

Before it all ended, he would have to have her.

And leave her very, very tarnished indeed.

IV ❧

Skye awoke with a start, only to discover that she was alone. She looked quickly about the cabin, assuring herself that the Silver Hawk was nowhere about, then she winced and leaned back again, thoroughly despising herself for her weakness and more perplexed than ever by the pirate. At certain times he was ruthless beyond measure; he didn't bend, break, or give the slightest quarter.

But he could also be gentle, sensitive beyond measure to the terrors of darkness that plagued her heart.

None of that mattered, she told herself flatly. She had lain in bed with a pirate and set her cheek against his chest and her hands against his flesh and she had clung to the very scourge of the seas.

A lamp was lit, but the drapes were still closed against the sunshine. Skye crawled from bed and walked to the starboard windows, pulling back the velvet to look out. It was a beautiful day. All blue and golden. The sea was calm, stretching endlessly beneath the powder blue horizon.

There was a knock upon the door. She wasn't exactly decently clad, Skye decided, but her nightgown did cover her chastely from throat to toe. "Come in," she called out.

The doors opened and Robert Arrowsmith entered with a breakfast tray. "Good morning, milady." She nodded his way as he set the tray upon the table. He seemed pleased with himself that morning as he removed the silver warmer from the plate upon the tray. "I've a surprise for you. Fresh milk and eggs and a ham steak, milady."

She couldn't resist the food, nor her curiosity. "Fresh milk?"

"We met with a sister ship this dawn coming out of Charleston, milady." He hesitated. "The captain had a hip bath brought aboard, too, and he bought a supply of French milled soap. Now I warned him that you might not care to immerse the whole of your body into the water and take a chance with disease, but the captain's regularly into bathing himself, so he thinks as how you might want the opportunity, too."

"I would dearly love a bath," she said. Where was her pride? she wondered. She should scoff at every offer given her by the wretch of a pirate. She wasn't terribly certain if her pride could be salvaged by remaining sticky and dirty and she scoffed at the idea that evil spirits and diseases entered into the body when it was submerged. She had grown up in a hot climate and had learned to love to bathe.

"Fine, then, some of the lads and I will be back with the tub and water. You can heat more yourself, of course, if you wish. I shall light the stove and leave you a kettle."

Skye thanked him and sat behind the desk. He set forth lighting the stove and she watched him as she delicately cut into the ham on the plate before her. She chewed reflectively. "Charleston," she murmured. "And we sail for New Providence?" She knew the general vicinity of the island. And she knew that it was a pirate's haven, a true den of iniquity. The small swift pirate ships were able to manuever the reefs and shoals about her while the warships and merchantmen too often cracked up upon the treacherous coral rock. The English proprietors of the island seemed not to have the energy to deal with the pirate problem, and so, Skye had heard, the only law there came to be that based on the will of the strongest rascal who happened to be present.

Robert hesitated, jabbing at the coals in the stove. "Aye, we sail for New Providence," he said, looking her way. "You know of it?"

"Too well."

"You needn't fear. The Hawk does not intend for you to leave the ship. We won't stay long. Then we'll move on to Bone Cay. The Hawk is the law there. He will see that you are kept safe."

"Safe?" she said sweetly.

"Quite safe," he said. "Until some arrangement is made."

Skye gave him a beautiful smile. "Tell me, Robert, what happens if my father cannot pay the sum of money that the Hawk demands?"

"Surely, Lord Cameron—"

"But what if Lord Cameron does not choose to pay?"

"He will," Robert insisted.

"But if he does not?"

"He will."

"But what if he does not?"

"Milady, you are insistent!" he said, standing.

"Yes, I am."

"Well then . . ." He threw his arms up in the air. "Well, then you will like Bone Cay, I suppose. I don't know. I am quite certain that you will be ransomed quickly."

"How long till we reach New Providence? Two days, three?"

"Yes, depending upon the wind."

She stared at him hard and he shuffled his feet uneasily. He was a striking young man, much like his master. His speech was cultured and his manner refined.

Perhaps, she mused, he was not so horrible a pirate. He treated her like a lady despite the circumstances. He seemed to admire her, and she was not without a certain confidence in her ability to charm. He might be persuaded to help her.

She smiled at him, sadly.

"You must cease this horrible life, you know," she told him. She pushed up from her chair and hurried around to touch his shoulder. She was so intent upon her pursuit that she did not see the doors swing open, or the Hawk enter into the cabin behind them. "Mr. Arrowsmith, if you could, perhaps, help me to escape, I could speak to the governor on your behalf. Oh, he is a man who wretchedly hates pirates, but he is quick to see remorse, and ever ready to give a man a chance! Robert, can't you see? You will hang if you persist in this life! I could help you, truly I could. And oh, sir! I would despair to see you swinging from a rope!"

Her fingers fell upon his sleeve. He flushed, for they were very close, and her gown, though sedate, was made of thin cotton. "Milady—" he began.

"Yes, milady!" came a long drawl from the doorway. Robert jerked and jumped away from her. He stared blankly at the Hawk. The pirate smiled his slow sardonic smile. "That's all, Robert."

"Aye! Aye, aye, sir!" Robert sped on out of the cabin. Skye remained before the desk, her heart sinking as she watched the thunder of a pulse against his throat. He was dressed, as usual, in black corded by silver threads. His shirt was open and much of his bronze chest was displayed. She felt a nervousness leap into the pit of her belly and it was difficult to remain where she was. She wanted to run from him, and from the feeling inside of her. His eyes touched hers with dark and shimmering power, and to her eternal shame, she did not think to be furious or indignant. She thought instead of the night. She thought of her dreadful fear, and of how secure she had felt once his arms had come around her. They were like steel. They were bronze and hard and vibrant. Like the beat of his heart.

The blood began to drain from her face as she remembered their first morning together, and seeing him fully naked. Tremors shook her and she swallowed, trying to keep her eyes wide open and upon his. She did not wish to let them fall. Indeed, she did not wish to recall his anatomy one bit, and yet she did, and the very memory caused her to heat and burn inside. His sexual drive seemed as potent as his fighting force, and yet . . .

He had let her be.

"Alas, love!" he murmured softly, coming in and walking around to take the seat she had vacated. He picked up her coffee cup and sipped the warm brew, sighing with satisfaction as he raised his booted feet to clunk upon his desk. He folded his hands over his chest. "So you were trying to charm poor Robert into mutiny."

"I was telling him rationally what would happen if he persisted in this life of infamy."

"You lie, milady. But then, that is your way."

"I am not lying. I would hate to see him hang."

"And what of me, love?"

"I have told you, I will cheer the loudest when you swing by the neck!"

He watched her for a long moment, his eyes fathomless, his smile implacable. "Yes, I believe that you would. But they will have to catch me first, you know."

"Perhaps Robert will betray you."

"Fallen to your charms!"

"I did not intend to charm him, nor did I do so."

"Be glad then that you did not, mam'selle, for then I should have been forced to slay him."

Skye gasped. *He* was lying now! she thought. But how could she know? The man was an enigma. He leaned toward her then, speaking softly. "Indeed, I warn you, Skye, take care with my men. Any who touches you will die, and I will come to think that I do not give you adequate attention if you must seek out others."

"I seek escape!"

"You will be free soon enough," he said flatly. He started to rise, and she was glad, for she was sure that he meant to leave, and she was trembling terribly. But there was a knock upon the door and it opened and Robert was there again. He looked at the Hawk, who waited expectantly. "We've the hip bath, Captain."

"Bring it in."

Skye looked at him in horror, swirling to the far corner of the cabin quickly. She sought to hide, she realized, but there was nowhere to go. Two sailors walked in with the wooden tub between them and it seemed that a score of others followed with buckets of water.

And they all saw her. Every man saw her there in his quarters like a common . . . harlot.

She locked her jaw but didn't make a move. The men filed out, one after the other, until only Robert remained, explaining that he had set a kettle within the stove and that towels and soap were set upon her trunk. Then he, too, was gone, and she was left alone with the Hawk and her steaming tub.

Still, she remained dead still. Steam wafted above the tub and silence hung heavy upon the air. It dragged on and on. Then the Hawk idly lifted a hand. "Your bath is ready."

"Well, I am not."

"The men worked long and hard to prepare this water for you, milady. I suggest that you use it."

"I see. And I don't suppose that you might consider leaving so that I might do just that?"

"No, I will not consider leaving."

"Sea slime!" she hissed.

"A previously established fact, milady."

"Oh, stop it, will you!"

"Why?" he inquired innocently. "Stop what? I am trying to be a gentleman sea slime and refrain from arguing with a lady."

"This is absurd. I will not get into that tub with you here."

He arched a brow, and she saw that he was not at all in a good humor, no matter how light his words. "How cold, Lady Kinsdale, how very cruel! I bear the burning tortures of the flesh by night to offer comfort and nothing more, and for my pains I return to my cabin—where I strive to keep you in comparative comfort and ease—to find you casting yourself into the arms of my second mate! Then, when I find my own leisure from the travail of captaining the ship, it is only for you to suggest I leave! Have pity, milady."

"You should have sought a career upon the stage, sir," Skye told him curtly. "It would have been a legal profession, and one at which I am quite sure you would have excelled."

"Skye, I will not leave my cabin."

"And I will not crawl into that bath."

"I can make you, you know."

"So you can. But it will be against my will."

"Then is it your will that we clash by flesh again?"

She flushed, grating her teeth. Was she insane? He spoke the truth. It would be easier to move of her own accord. But that would be surrendering to his command, and she could not bring herself to do so.

"I will not crawl into that tub," she repeated.

"By all the saints!" He swore with such vehemence and fury, leaping to his feet, that she cried out and backed further against the wall. She'd been a fool. He would touch her and with violence. He would rip the gown from her and toss her into the steam and . . .

She didn't know what came after the "and."

"Wait!" she pleaded, but he ignored her. With deadly menace he walked around his desk, his hands upon his hips. He stared at her hard, and his voice rang out with a deep tenor that caused a tremor in her heart and made surrender seem a most viable possibility. "Well, milady, if you will not get into that tub—" He paused, and she was halfway certain that he was about to do her severe bodily harm. But he twisted around instead, starting upon his own buttons. "If you will not get in, Lady Kinsdale, then I shall do so myself."

"What?" she gasped, stunned.

He tossed his shirt to the floor and pulled off one of his boots. "I'm not about to waste that water."

"But you can't just—" She broke off. His other boot fell to the floor. He paused.

"I can't just what?" he demanded politely.

"Take a bath in front of me!"

He cast his head back and his husky laughter held a dangerous note. "Milady, I beg to differ. I can. And I intend to."

His hands were at the back tie of his knee breeches. She turned her back to him and stared at the wall. He ignored her. She heard him sink into the hot water with a self-satisfied sigh.

"You have the morals of . . . of . . ."

"Sea slime?" he asked politely.

"Of a gutter rat!"

"We cannot all play the grand hypocrite, milady. Be a love, will you? Yell out to Robert. This soap will not do at all."

"I will not call out to Robert!" Skye protested.

"But then," he said indignantly, "I shall smell like a French whorehouse. Oh, that will not do! It will not do at all. Come now, Lady Kinsdale, lend a hand here."

"You're out of your mind!" she said, staring at the paneling and shelves. Damn him! His sigh had been highly irritating. He was enjoying her bath.

"Will you call the man for me, or not?"

She didn't hear that his tone had changed. "No!"

"Then I shall have to call him myself!"

She heard the water roll and sluice as he stood. Despite herself, she twisted slightly. Whipping up the massive cotton towel that Robert had left for her use, the Hawk strode to the doors and pulled them open. "Mr. Arrowsmith! I need you, please!"

Robert must have been accustomed to running quickly to his master's call, for he appeared momentarily and listened to the Hawk's command for a more gentlemanly soap. Then the Hawk waited at the doors, tapping his foot.

Robert returned and gave him the soap. The Hawk then returned to his bath, humming. He had closed the doors, Skye realized, but he had not bolted them.

"You don't need to peek, Lady Kinsdale. I am here for the asking, you know. Alas, awaiting your gentle promise."

"You will rot in an unmarked grave, you know," she said sweetly.

"Perhaps, but until then . . . oh, this is frustrating. Come here, will you? I need help with my back."

"You will die of a horrible case of insanity," she assured him, "and then rot in an unmarked grave."

"I don't think so. I think that you will come over here and give me the small comfort of your sweet assistance."

"Sir, I would not spit your way if you died of thirst."

"You press Lady Luck, mam'selle."

"Do I?" she murmured uneasily. She did not like having her back to him, but she did not intend to move, and she was not going to rise to any of his taunts or obey a single command.

The doors, she recalled, were open.

Perhaps she just might pretend to obey a command. . . .

"Lady Kinsdale—" he began, but broke off when she spun around. She stared hard at him. He looked absurdly comfortable in the tub, the steam matching the mist of his eyes, his long legs drawn up beneath him, his arms draped comfortably over the sides. A pleased smile curved his mouth as he watched her. "How nice, mam'selle! If you just soap and scrub the upper shoulder?"

She smiled sweetly in return. She strode toward the tub, and then straight by it. She just caught sight of his smile as it faded, then she reached the doors.

But just as she cast them open and started to flee, she felt a tug upon her gown and then heard the awful rending sound as it split down her back. She cried out, swinging around. Naked and dripping, he stood behind her, a large part of her gown in his hands. A strangled sound escaped her as she realized that her lower body was bared to the wind. "Oh!" she railed.

She nearly ran anyway, to jump into the sea if need be. But he was quick. He dropped the fabric in his hands and caught hold of her arm, wrenching her back into the cabin. He slammed the doors shut with a vengeance. And this time he slid the bolt.

He turned around, staring at her. Her gaze fell against his body, then her eyes jerked back to his with growing alarm. He smiled. Like a hawk with a field mouse within its claws. Then his smile faded and he stared at her somberly. His voice was deep, menacing in its very quiet. "End of play time, my love. There is one serious thing here that you have failed to realize. It is imperative that you follow my orders. And from now on, Skye, I promise that you will."

Her lower lip was trembling despite her staunchest efforts to remain calm. She clutched the remnants of her gown to her, gritted her teeth, and backed away, vowing to herself that she would not falter. But her resolve fled from her when he took his first step toward her. She panicked, shrieked, and leaped away. He caught her arm, pulling her back to face him. He wrenched the gown from her, his eyes so dark they were like burning coals upon hers. A breath of air and no more separated their bodies. She could feel him with the length of her. A whisper of space and she would be crushed against him . . . she would know all the hard-muscled coils and planes of his body, she would know the feel of the dark hair that curled over his chest, just as she knew the searing pulse that protruded from him and did touch her body, brushing like a living flame against her belly.

She could not swallow, she could not breathe. His lips were close, so close. He was wet and sleek and all the more menacing for it, the bulge of his shoulders and arm and chest muscles glistening in the sunlight that streamed in from the open window. She wanted to scream, but she could not, for she still couldn't even draw breath. The world would fade. She would fail, she would sink to the floor in a dead faint and he would surely know nothing of mercy. . . .

"Your bath awaits you," he said, his words falling like a touch of mist against her lips. Then he was touching her completely, sweeping her up into his arms.

And he deposited her firmly within the tub.

Instinctively she drew her knees as close to her chest as she could. He rescued her hair, winding it into a knot. The water was steaming hot and delicious. She shivered uncontrollably in spite of it.

"Let's see . . . it's quite all right if *you* smell like a French whorehouse," he muttered. He was behind her. She tried to twist and rise and elude him, but his hands were already upon her. He held a cloth fragrant with the sweet-smelling soap and he moved it over her neck and shoulders and down the length of her arms. Her movement of protest worked well against her, for his hand slipped down, and cloth and soap and man came in startling contact with the full curve of her breast. She gasped, startled and desperate, for the brush of his fingers against the peak of her breast made it swell and harden, and horror filled her, just as the sensation of lightning swept with a vengeance into the whole of her being. Their eyes met. She was caught in some strange hypnotism again, unable to move. She felt the ferocity of her heartbeat and she knew that he saw the pulse that throbbed against her throat. She hardly dared to look at him, and yet she could not help herself, and when her eyes fell upon his body again, panic seized her. He had dropped the cloth. His bare hand lay against her breast. He was as still as she, his eyes burning, the whole of him gone rigid. Her lips were dry despite the steam. She fought to moisten them. To draw breath to speak.

"Please!" she managed to cry out.

She heard the grate of his teeth. He shoved away from the tub with the frightening thunder of an oath upon his lips. Skye sank further into the tub, hugging her knees once again. She heard him jerk on his breeches. He clothed himself no more thoroughly, but barefoot and bare-chested slammed his way out of his cabin.

He did not even pause to bolt her in from the outside. Nor did Skye dare to move at first. She waited, frozen there.

Seconds later, she heard the bolt slide home. Robert Arrowsmith had come, she thought. Always his master's man, tying up whatever loose ends the Silver Hawk might leave.

She came to life then. She scrubbed herself quickly and furiously, then leaped from the tub and dried as quickly as she could manage with the one towel that had been left between them. It carried a hint of his scent, she thought. Of the more masculine soap he demanded that Robert bring him. Of something deeper. Of something that was curiously pleasant and deeply primal, the subtle scent that was uniquely his.

She threw the towel from her and hurriedly searched her trunk for a clean shift. She dressed carefully and completely in hose and shift and corset and petticoats and gown, but it wouldn't have mattered what she had chosen to wear.

He did not come back to the cabin. Not that day. Not that night. Robert came with men to clear away the tub and breakfast tray, and he came again later to bring her supper.

She fell asleep at his desk.

Later, she awoke in his bed, and wondered how she had come there. Had she walked? She was still clad in her gown and petticoats. All that had been stripped from her body were the soft leather slippers she had worn upon her feet.

Had he come back?

He was not within the cabin. Two lanterns burned brightly, and she was not left to the darkness.

Skye lay back down, deeply disturbed. She hugged one of his pillows tightly against her, horrified to realize that she missed the man beside her, and missed the way that he had held her, making her feel secure against each and every terror of the night.

He did not come the next day. Robert Arrowsmith arrived bright and early with her breakfast. He promised that he would return to walk her about the ship. She did not ask about the Hawk, nor did she seek to "rehabilitate" his second mate.

The Hawk had said that he would kill any man who betrayed him, and Skye believed that he did not make idle threats.

By noon Robert took her out on deck. Every man jack was courteous to her, tipping his hat or cap or inclining his bare head her way. They sailed with a good wind.

The Silver Hawk was nowhere to be seen. Skye leaned against the portside hull and felt the wind whip through her hair and caress her face. Robert pointed out the distant shores of Florida, and she nodded, then gazed at him pensively.

"What has happened to Bess and Tara?" she asked him. "The young Irish maids. Do they . . . live?"

She thought that he quickly hid a smile, but he spoke to her gravely. "Aye, lady. They live. They will be returned with you, no doubt, to Virginia."

"Yes, yes! Please see that it is so. My father will pay for them, I promise."

"I will inform the Hawk about your concern," he said.

"Where is the Hawk this morning?" she said, then despised herself for the query. What did she care? She was grateful for his absence, no matter what had caused it, or what it meant.

"He, er, is busy. He will be busy for quite some time. Probably until we reach New Providence."

"How . . . nice," Skye said flatly.

Robert looked at the sky, then cleared his throat. "I'm afraid it's time for you to return to the cabin. Can I bring you anything?"

She shook her head, then she changed her mind. "Er, I'd have another bath if I might." What a lovely opportunity. She would have the sweet-scented soap and the wonderfully steaming water without any fear of his arrival.

"Another bath?" Robert said disbelievingly. "You expose your pores, milady, to heaven knows what maladies!"

She was surprised to discover that she could smile at his very real concern. "So far, Mr. Arrowsmith, I have been quite lucky with my health, despite the bathing. Is this a problem?"

"No, no! Your wish is my command, Lady Kinsdale."

How ironic! she thought bitterly. It was such a pity that her wishes didn't seem to mean a damned thing to his master.

"Thank you," she murmured.

He returned her to the cabin. Restlessly she studied the books in the shelves. They were many and varied. He had texts by Bacon and Shakespeare and Sir Christopher Wren. Greek classics lined one shelf and there were tomes on not only warfare and naval maneuvers but also philosophy and medicine and the astrological sciences.

The Silver Hawk was a well-read man.

Else he had privateered the ship of some well-read gent! That, too, was a possibility. He was a thief. He had probably stolen the books just as he had everything else.

Robert and two sailors brought the tub to her again and the crew filed in and out with their buckets of water. Again, she thought they seemed too decent a lot to be pirates.

She had been locked in the room for four days, going on five, and she was losing her mind.

Nervously she disrobed and hopped in the tub. She expected him to arrive the very second her clothes were shed, but he did not. In a matter of moments, she leaned back. She let the steam enter deep into her and soothe her muscles and her aching spirits. The water began to lose its heat after a while. She had lingered too long.

Had she waited for him? she wondered.

No!

But perhaps she had. Perhaps she had waited to feel the explosive sensation of lightning tearing into the very core of her body, as she'd felt when his fingers had curved over her breast.

"Never!" she whispered aloud, shamed and humiliated. She leaped out of the tub, grabbing her towel, wrapping it around herself.

That was when the doors opened.

Fully clad in his boots and a handsomely trimmed frockcoat, he was holding a ledger in his hands and he seemed preoccupied with it. When he came full upon her, he stopped in surprise. Skye hugged the end of the towel to her chest and stared at him, her eyes wide, and did not say a word.

Nor did he speak. He tossed the ledger upon his desk. For the longest time he watched her, and she felt her blood begin to race within her.

"You like to bathe," he said politely.

"Yes," she managed to reply. He was very grave.

"Did you sleep well, mam'selle?"

"Yes."

He went silent for a moment. "Robert came and took you about the deck?"

"He—he did."

He ran out of small talk then. He took the two steps that brought him before her. She didn't try to run. She didn't even think to do so. His silver-blue eyes held hers in a curious grip, and she scarce had breath in her body. Her flesh burned, and she felt rooted to the floor.

She could not run.

He paused before her and his fingers very slowly threaded through her hair. He tilted her head back, and then he slowly lowered his lips to hers.

His touch brought the lightning to her again, and a sweet fever seemed to rage through her body. His beard and mustache teased her flesh as his lips pressed against hers with a consuming force that swept all thought from her mind. His tongue teased the edge of her mouth, causing her lips to part to the provocative demand. His tongue filled her, and the kiss was planted deeper and deeper.

No longer was he content with the sweetness of her mouth. His hands fell to the small of her back, bringing her flush against him. Then his fingers fell against her cheeks, along the slender column of her throat, to the rise of her breasts.

Not once did she think to fight him.

Not even when his hand closed over the full naked curve of her breast and she dimly realized that her towel had fallen. Not even then did she fight him. She did not think to fight, for thought eluded her completely, and the shattering sensations ruled her heart and soul. The liquid heat of his kiss swept into the length of her, the sensual stroke of his callused fingertips brought a peculiar sob to her throat. . . .

It was the sound of that sob, wanton and hungry, that shocked her from her paralysis. She pressed hard upon his chest, but he held her there tightly. She beat against him desperately, but he did not free her. Her head fell back and she met his eyes. They were dark with a brewing tempest, frightening to behold. "Don't play with me, girl, so help me!"

"Play!"

"Don't tempt, lady, and for the love of God, don't tease!"

"I have not! You are the puppet master here, pulling the strings like an almighty god! You seized me! You imprisoned me, and you give out orders like a tyrant king. You are a master of torture. You taunt until I am insane. I fear rape, I fear death, and you play with me like a cat with a mouse!"

He touched her cheek, his eyes still stormy, his features tense. She strained against him, but his thumb fell over her damp and swollen lips.

"Was that, milady, a threat of rape?"

"Please . . ."

"You made a promise. Perhaps you do mean to fulfill it."

She jerked from him, falling to her knees, reaching for the towel. He came down beside her, resting upon the balls of his feet. "It seems that I am the plaything, lady. You cling to me in the night, and trust in my goodness. In the darkness I could take whatever I desired, couldn't I, Lady Kinsdale?" Her head was down, but he lifted her chin.

"I was kidnapped—"

"Answer my question."

"All right!" she shouted. "It would be easy for you then. So easy. I've oft wondered why you didn't . . ."

"Rape you as you clung to me in terror?" he demanded sharply.

"Yes!" she whispered. Tears came to her eyes, glazing them. He would not let her free.

He shook his head slowly. "I will never have you that way, milady. Coming to me in fear of the darkness. I will have you only when you turn to me because desire, not fear, guides you."

Her eyes widened.

"I will never desire a pirate!"

A slight smile touched his features. His finger rode slowly, sensually over the bare slope of her shoulder.

"If I willed it, you could be coerced into desiring me this very moment," he said softly. Then he rose abruptly, and she felt very small as he spoke down to her. "You are right, milady, on one account. I am a master of torture, and it is myself that I so abuse. I will depart, until you are safely clad."

He turned smartly upon a heel and left her. Slowly she rose, her body on fire, her limbs quaking. She was lethargic at first. She could scarce will herself to move.

She touched her lips with her fingers, and she started shaking all over again. She could feel his lips still, she could feel his hands upon her. . . .

He was coming back. He had said so.

She dove into her trunk. She had one nightgown left within it. Soft blue flowered cotton with satin ribands about the puffed sleeves and waist. The cotton was gossamer, sheer but strong.

She plunged quickly into the gown, and none too soon. There was a sharp rap upon the door, then the Hawk entered once again. For a pirate, he was absurdly regal, striking in his outfit of black, from his elegantly cut coat to the plume that danced upon his hat. Robert entered behind him, and the pirate captain gave his mate the ledger. "Care will be taken, the gravest care," he said.

Robert looked her way and nodded. Then he smiled nervously, finding her eyes meeting his. "Supper comes, my lady," he told her.

She didn't care. She wanted only to escape the presence of the Hawk.

"I am not hungry," she whispered. Robert nodded vaguely, watching her, then his eyes narrowed as he looked at the Hawk again. The pirate captain had taken his chair behind his desk, and seriously studied figures within a second book.

Skye crawled into the bunk, far against the wall. The two men continued to talk about cargo to be bartered, bought, or taken. She closed her eyes. Their voices droned on.

She drifted to sleep, hearing their conversation like some lulling sound. Sleep was sweet, and sleep was good, until the darkness suddenly intruded upon it.

She was trapped. She pushed and shoved and she could not escape. It had come to choke her, the darkness. She could not breathe, she could not swallow, she could not summon the air to scream. . . .

"Skye!"

His voice fell upon her like a gentle ray of sunlight. Her eyes flew open.

His face was above hers. Light filled the room; there had never been any darkness.

"Oh!" she cried, and she tried to cover her face with her hands. The fear had seized her, and would not let go.

He must have come to bed with her that night meaning to sleep, for his chest was bare, and though the coverlet spread over his lower torso, she assumed that his legs would be bare as well. It was the way that he slept.

His arms came around her and the gentle touch of his fingers led her cheek to rest against his chest. He stroked her hair. "What is the terror?" he asked her softly.

She shook her head. He sighed.

At last, her shaking began to ease. She pressed against him, her face rising upon his chest to meet his eyes.

"You—you needn't comfort me."

"It's all right."

"But you say that I crawl to you . . . and taunt you."

"It's all right."

"I do not mean to do so."

He caught her hands, and eased them from his chest. Her

hair spilled over the golden breadth of it. His features seemed tense, for all of the gentle tenor of his words.

"Truly, you do not have to comfort me!" she whispered.

He sighed very deeply. "Milady, it is all right. It is my pleasure, Skye Kinsdale, I swear it. Lie still, and sleep once more."

She closed her eyes, and felt his body shudder.

My pleasure! he thought.

And truly, torture beyond all earthly reason.

V

The Silver Hawk stood high atop the forward deck of his ship, legs firmly planted, his hands upon his hips. The breeze rushed by him as he surveyed the channel they so carefully navigated. They were clear, he knew. Robert was at the helm while certain of his sailors climbed the rigging with the agility of monkeys, leaving them enough sail to catch the breeze, but cutting in deftly for speed and maneuverability. They were coming upon the island of New Providence, to the lusty port town where rogues held sway and thieves and butchers ruled.

He knew the port well. He had come here often enough.

Some curious little tremor seized him suddenly, as if he had stepped from a hot bath into the chill of a winter's day. He shook away the feeling with a shrug of his shoulders. There was danger here still, he thought.

But there was always danger. He had entered into this devil's pact of his knowing that danger abounded.

Still, this was different.

It was the girl, he knew.

He should have gone on to Bone Cay, he thought, even if it

increased his travel time. He couldn't have done that, not plausibly so, but it was from this den of thieves that he would send his messages out and strike his bargains for the return of the ship and the hostages. And he had to come here now, for this was where the captains all came to plot their courses and pick their prizes. It was imperative that he come.

It was just the girl, damn her hide!

She would be safe. He would leave her carefully bolted within her room. They would take the long boats in, and he would leave her in the care of Jacques DuBray. That mammoth Frenchman was a master with a rapier. No harm would come her way.

He took his glass from his pocket and surveyed the scene they came upon. He could see the shanties of the town, the ribald colors and patterns that made up the pirates' haven. Kegs of gunpowder and salt fish lay on a wharf. A dark-haired whore stretched atop the bow of a small cutter, her skirts high against her thigh, her legs bronzed from the sun. She waved a fan in a leisurely fashion, idly listening to the talk of the two men who straightened fishing nets nearby. Further into town, there were more decent structures that resembled houses, but most of the place was beach and shanty . . . and warehouse for ill-gotten gains.

It was not a place for a lady. . . .

He scowled suddenly and leaped down from the bow peak. He waved to Rutger Gunnan at the wheel and nodded out his satisfaction at their course. They would cast anchor soon. "Tell Robert we will set to shore within the hour!" he called.

Rutger nodded his assent. "Aye, Captain!"

The Hawk turned and approached the door to his cabin. To his great annoyance he paused before sliding the bolt and entering his own realm. He'd been a fool to ever bring her here. She'd been such a challenge with her lightning speed with a sword that it had seemed necessary to cast the very fear of demons into her soul.

He had not suspected that they resided there already, nor that it would be he who would suffer the torment of the damned rather than she.

Impatiently he shoved the doors open and entered his cabin.

She was perched upon the window seat. The drapes were back and daylight streamed in. Her legs curled beneath her; she wore a soft white muslin with a brocade bodice, which was fashionably low cut to display the rising curves of her breasts. The skirt spilled out over a volume of petticoats in a soft burst of snow white and soft pastel. She worked on some piece of mending for him, which brought another scowl to his lips. Her hair was free.

The color of a sunset.

Cascading and waving over her shoulders and breast like a web of radiant silk.

He itched to run his fingers through it. Actually, he itched to do much, much more. When she looked up at him, a soft smile on her lips, her aquamarine eyes shimmering like the most glorious Caribbean sea, he wanted to stride right to her and wrench her into his arms. He wanted to play the pirate in the most heinous fashion, rip her beautiful gown to shreds, and leave her with no doubt as to his rapacious desires and determination.

She looked so damned comfortable! And assured. Even domestic.

He clenched down hard upon his jaw and swallowed the force of his emotion, watching her as he walked around to take his seat behind his desk. He cast his booted feet upon the desk and laced his fingers behind his head. She held his shirt, he saw. The full-sleeved shirt he had worn the evening of their first encounter. She mended a tear near the throat. Her fingers, long and elegant, lay still over the material.

Just as they lay by night, long and elegant, over his bare chest.

"You will make a wonderful wife," he found himself snapping out at her with a startling hostility.

She arched a brow. A flicker of amusement curled her lip. "Why, Mr. Silver Hawk," she taunted, "I strive to be the very best of hostages, and still I do not please you! I no longer toss about jam and coffee cups, but spend my endless time pursuing the best interests of your wardrobe!"

He wagged a finger at her. "Beware, lady, you do play with fire."

She lowered her head, smiling. Damn her! She trusted him. Six days and nights with him now and she thought that she had discovered his true measure. Something made a snapping sound. He looked down to see that he had picked up a quill, and crushed it between his fingers.

He dropped the pieces and walked around to her. She barely skipped a beat with her task. She did not look up, nor did her fingers cease to move.

He reached down to her, cupping her chin with his fingers, raising her eyes to meet his. She was, indeed, a startling beauty. No artist could ever capture the blues and greens that mingled within her eyes, nor find the glorious reds and golds of her hair among oils or paints. The greatest sculptors of the Renaissance could not have duplicated the fine and delicate structure of her face, the regal position of her cheekbones, the determined set of her jaw. No man could mold what God had created of her form, an Eve cast upon him from the sins of Eden, slender in the waist, long-limbed, with delicate ankles and lush firm breasts, ripe and provocative beyond measure. To touch her was to stroke silk.

And she smiled . . . in complete comfort in his presence.

She needed to fear him somewhat. It was essential.

He plucked the mending from her hands, casting it aside. A look of startled alarm came into her eyes, and she struggled against him as he drew her inexorably to her feet.

"We come to the island," she said breathlessly.

"So I see," he told her, but he saw nothing at all at that moment, nothing but her eyes.

"Shouldn't you be—"

"Do you know, my lady, that you are one of the most beautiful creatures ever to walk this earth? Perhaps you do know. You are not a woman who lacks confidence."

Her breath came quickly. Her lips were dry and she moistened them. She strained against his firm hold upon her upper arms, but he did not release her. Her gaze wavered, then returned to his. "What do you want?" she cried.

He smiled slowly, assessing her. "I'm not quite sure as yet. I think I've decided that I could tame you. Perhaps I shall not ransom you at all. Perhaps I shall take you with me and have you reside with me forever."

"Don't tease me!" she pleaded, her eyes very wide upon his as she sought some truth from him.

What did plague him? he wondered. His fingers bit more forcefully into her arms. "Indeed, why should you think that I tease you, Skye Kinsdale? We pirates revel in debauchery and conquest. It would be most natural to return the ship . . . but not the maiden."

He lowered his lips as he spoke until his words fell like a warm breeze upon her parted lips. Then his mouth formed to the sweet curve of hers. She gasped but he drew her closer, seized by the dark power of a sweeping desire. Her lips were sweet; the clamor of her heart was sweeter still. He plundered her mouth with his tongue. He ravished and he laid bare. He tasted her until drums beat explosively in his head, and he knew that he would lose not only control, but his very soul in the bargain.

His lip moved from hers. He seared a trail down her throat with the damp heat of his parted lips, teasing her flesh with the tip of his tongue. He swept her collarbone, and the rise of her breasts above the haunting décolletage of her gown.

She had been still through it all. Then, as his kiss touched her breast, she let out a shriek of rage. He no longer held her with force, and she wrenched from him, shaking, wiping her lips with the back of her hand as if she had tasted evil.

It was less than complimentary, he decided wearily.

"Bastard!" she screamed, and she flew forward, her fists flailing. He barely protected his face and beard, catching her clawing fingers in the nick of time and bringing her back into his hold.

Damn her, he thought, then, and damn himself, for his desire for her remained, or perhaps it burned more fiercely. She was energy there in his arms, she was the power of the sun and the rhythm of the sea. She loathed him so . . . but it had taken her a long, long time to protest against the intimacy of his kiss, and she seemed ablaze. Was it hatred? Certainly, but it was a passionate hatred, alive, searing. It caused her to sizzle, to tremble, to stare at him with eyes afire. She swept into the very core of his being, heating him anew with her fire. In silence he swore against himself, and he swore against her.

He was captain. He could do what he chose. He was a pirate. The dread pirate Silver Hawk. He could sweep her across the room to his bunk, tear her clothing asunder, have her, sink into her, die within her . . . and it would but enhance his reputation.

He was losing his mind. He struggled with his heart, with his soul, and with the searing piece of his anatomy that was sweeping away his senses. Then he smiled at her, crookedly.

"Good, Lady Skye. Your kiss is good, your lips are sweet, your body is sound. You would not make a bad companion for the while, except that your temper is quite a thorn. But then again, perhaps your father or Lord Cameron will offer a high enough price for your head. No woman is worth too much a sum of silver or gold. And you do seem to lack experience."

"Oh!" she cried, and swore again with vengeance. Her eyes snapped and sparked their luminous aquamarine and he was ever more tempted by her.

"Milady, I have not heard such language from the rogues who sail with me. Take care. I may well tame you yet."

She spat out an explicit oath, struggling fiercely.

"Maybe you sit too easily today. Perhaps you need to be reminded that my touch is not always so gentle and tenderly given."

"Gentle!" she gasped. "Tenderly given!" But she went still then, her eyes very round, her features ashen. She had not forgotten their encounter the day when she had wreaked havoc upon his tableware.

No, she had not forgotten, nor did she sit so easily yet. Skye gritted her teeth and kept her eyes hard upon him. She fought no more, for she was suddenly certain that the words were more of a warning than she could imagine, that he was truly at some brink, as if his temper burned on some very short fuse. But oh, she longed to hurt him! How she longed to have the power to taunt and humiliate! She despised him with every breath within her, she was infuriated. . . .

With herself, as well as with him.

She stood so still before the very onslaught of his lips. She did not hate and decry his kiss, she felt it, she savored it. She allowed it! He startled her so, he took her so quickly. . . .

There was no excuse, for in her heart she knew that she had allowed it. Fascination had held her still, and a simmering curiosity had swept her into its grip while his heat had seeped into her, leaving her without sense or reason and scarce able to breathe.

He was a pirate, a cur. Then what was she, she wondered with humiliation, that she could so easily crave his touch, rather than despise it?

She stiffened her shoulders and raised her chin. "Do it!" she snapped out. "If you intend to rape me, then do it now! Let's end this torment!"

A single dark brow shot up and his lip curled into a rogue's smile, a quick, handsome smile that caused a new shimmering to take hold deep within her. She would shame him! She would make him feel less than a man, and surely he would leave her be!

"Pardon?" he said politely.

"I said do it! If you intend—" He stared at her so boldly! The words began to falter on her lips. "Do it! I have had it with this constant torment!"

"You're inviting me to rape you?" he said pleasantly.

"Yes! No!" she cried in dismay, and it didn't matter at all, because suddenly he did sweep her off her feet, and with long strides he bore her toward the waiting bunk where they had lain together so many nights now.

She fell upon her back, and he was over her. Her heart thundered and her breath came too quick and panic seized her. She hadn't shamed him in the least!

"No!" she cried, struggling fiercely. But his thighs, hot and strong as steel, locked around her, and laughing, he grabbed her wrists. She tossed, she writhed and arched, until she realized that her movement brought them into close contact. She railed against him with a new assertion that he was the absolute worst of the sea slime, but then she realized that he wasn't moving anymore at all, that his bold rogue's smile still touched his features.

"Alas! And I thought that I had disappointed you!" he cried

passionately. "How would you have it now? Clothed, or unclothed. It can be done either way, I assure you. Shall I rent and tear fabric? How shall I manage this?"

"What?" she gasped.

"Ah, such a quandary, my dear love!" He adjusted his weight, straddling over her firmly. With one hand he pulled her wrists high atop her head, leaving the other free to taunt her. He touched her cheek and she twisted her head, trying to bite him. "Ah, careful, love!" he growled out, his smile fading, tension riding high within his features as he lowered his face close to hers once again. "Careful, careful love!" Then he cupped her breast, the heat of his hand defying the fabric that lay between his hand and her flesh. She spat out an oath and he laughed, taking his leisure, amused as she writhed and thrust against him. "Shall I take it slow, my dear? Tease and taunt and relish every movement you make against me?" His fingers found her nipple and she gasped and swore again, yet felt a rush of color flood her cheeks as she felt the peaks of her breasts grow pebble-hard to his touch. It was not the man, it was not an attraction, it was surely a response just like—

"Stop!" she hissed.

"How *shall* it be? There's fast, there's brutal. I could thrust you up against the wall and lift your lovely thighs about me and have done with it all in a matter of minutes!"

He no longer stroked her breast. His weight shifted again and he was leaning atop her, his fingers tugging upon the hem of her skirt and bringing it high against her thighs. His touch roamed intimately against her and she cried out, squirming to escape him, yet bringing herself intimately against his touch. Her cry suddenly changed to one of desperation as she felt the total heat and power and strength of the man. His heart was thunder, his pulse ticked mercilessly. She had perhaps asked for rape, and he now seemed obliged to have it all as she had challenged him.

"Please . . . !"

"Please? Please shall I continue? Shall it be rough and tumble? Or shall we try seduction?"

She closed her eyes, gritting her teeth, and trembled suddenly. "I shall see you hang!" she whispered.

She heard a curious sound. She opened her eyes carefully. He was laughing again, watching her. "You are a challenge, love. A definite challenge." He leaned close to her. "But I promised you once, lady, that it will not be this way, though I am ever more convinced that the time will come when we will lie together."

His face was so near, his whisper touched her. His eyes sought out hers with such a startling silver glimmer that she felt her protest die within her throat. She wanted him away, and that was all. For whatever else he might be, the Silver Hawk was an exceptional man. Honed and muscled and bronzed and fine, and able to awaken her from a maiden's innocence. She could deny it, but it was true.

Even though he had told her that no woman was worth much in silver or gold.

Yet he was going to let her go, she realized. He was not going to rape her. He had never intended to do so. He had merely meant to taunt and torture and tease her and provide himself with vast amusement.

"Oh!" she cried, squirming furiously against him again. "I, sir, will never come to you!" she promised him. His eyes flickered a silver warning and her voice fell to a quiet tone, but still, her words did not falter, and she was glad of it.

He said no more but released her and climbed off the bunk. He walked to his desk and searched through some papers there, speaking to her with his back to her. Skye lay still for a moment, afraid to move. Then she rolled to the edge of the bunk and sat there, smoothing back her hair and keeping a very wary eye upon him.

"I will be gone for some hours, probably late into the night. You will not be alone." He swung around suddenly. "New Providence is a dangerous place. Keep the drapes closed while we are here. Do not seek the deck, for no man will take you there."

She did not respond to him. He spoke to her sharply, very sharply.

"Do you understand me?"

Her eyes flashed angrily but she answered him very sweetly. "Why, Captain, your every wish is my command."

"Lady, trust me, you do not begin to know the depths of my temper, but I promise that you will know my wrath and know it well if you do not heed my warnings."

"What is there to heed!" she cried, leaping to her feet. "You will lock me in here, and your men will not let me out! Why bother to threaten me!"

He strode the few steps toward her, pulling her back into his arms. His lip curled as she jerked upon her wrists to free herself from his touch. He shook her suddenly, fiercely. "I know you, my love!" he said curtly, his eyes meeting hers as her head fell back and her hair cascaded around them both. "I know you, and I am never quite sure how I should be dealing with you. Warnings are no good—only threats seem to avail."

She stamped on his foot as hard as she could. For a moment she was vastly pleased, for the taunting smile left his lips and his face paled with the pain. Then she screamed, for he quickly sat down upon the bunk, dragging her along with him—over his knee.

"I've thought all along that you really need a good thrashing!" he swore.

"No!" Skye screeched, straining to raise herself from his lap. She bit his thigh. His hand landed harshly upon her posterior section and she cried out, tears stinging her eyes with the humiliation. She twisted around in time to see his hand rise again. "Stop, please!"

"You bit me! You stomped on me, and then you bit me! Apologize!"

"I can't!"

He was about to pull her skirt up for more intimate contact with her flesh. Crimson, Skye squirmed her way from him so that she fell to the floor at his knees. She stared up at him, dazed. "Please, stop!"

"Apologize!"

"All right! I'm sorry that I bit you!"

She lowered her head, despising herself for having apologized to a pirate. He stood up, and she saw his boots as he walked by her.

"I'm sorry I bit you!" she cried out, adding softly, "I wish that I could have boiled you in oil."

He was back beside her, lifting her chin. The silver in his eyes danced and the devil's smile was back upon his lips, so sensual that she trembled with warmth even as she swore that she hated him.

"I cannot wait to return," he told her very softly. "We can explore all of these secret yearnings of yours."

She opened her mouth to reply, but he had already turned away and was gathering his papers again. He swung back to her, his eyes narrowed. "Behave, Skye. I am warning you." His long strides brought him to the door. He swung about and stared at her hard one more moment, and then he turned to leave. She never heard the doors close with such a shattering force before.

Despite his warning, or forgetting it, Skye leaped up and raced to the window seat at the port side of the ship which faced the island. She hesitated there, wondering why he was so determined that she not open the drapes, then she set her hand upon the material, just to peek out. She shivered slightly. They were close to the shore, and she could see a great deal very clearly. All manner of persons lined the docks! Fishermen hawked their catches while a curious array of men and women walked the streets. Two scantily clad women looked down from a shanty balcony to beckon laughingly to a tall lad below. Barrels lined the steps before the thatch-roofed dwelling. Arm in arm, a man and woman lumbered along, then fell, drunk, upon each other in the street. Dandies strutted about in brocades and velvets. They wore knee breeches and silver-buckled shoes and silken hose and scarves and magnificent plumed hats. And yet some of these very dandies walked with near-naked seamen. They wore eye patches, and many a man had a stump for a leg.

She gasped suddenly, realizing that the finery was most probably ill-gotten gain. These were not gentlemen that she observed, but pirates, and probably the very worst of the lot. The Silver Hawk had come here to do business.

Just as the thought passed her mind, she drew back quickly, letting the drapery fall.

A longboat was moving out, away from the ship. The Silver Hawk was within it along with a dozen or so of his men. She had no desire to be caught by the man. She did not know quite what he would do to her, but she did not care to discover what it might be. Not after everything that had just passed between them. He would do anything, she thought. Dare anything . . .

He would come back. To her. No matter what she did. And she did not know how long she could bear the emotions and sensations that he brought raging within her.

She inhaled deeply, thinking of the island.

The lure of the place fascinated her. She waited impatiently, biting her lip, until she was sure that the longboat had reached the docks. Then she looked out again.

A second longboat had left the pirate ship. There were a good forty or so of the Hawk's men going to shore. She didn't think that he sailed with a crew of more than fifty or so. Few men would have been left aboard.

The Silver Hawk must have believed that no man would molest his property in the pirate haven.

Skye drew the drapery once again. The sun was setting, and the shantytown did not appear so tawdry or so dangerous. Someone was lighting flares to line the docks and the distant beach.

The longboats had reached shore. Someone came up to the Silver Hawk, offering him a silver horn to drink from. There was suddenly a burst of revelry upon the shore and men crowded around him.

She let the drapery slide back into place. A slow, burning heat had set fire deep inside of her, and she longed to leave the Hawk's cabin. Leave this atmosphere dominated by his presence. Her cheeks flamed as she remembered his words that he might decide to keep her. Then he had told her that no woman was worth much in silver or gold.

Perhaps all pirates felt that way. Somewhere here she could strike a deal. She could promise a sailor a huge quantity of money for her safe passage to Williamsburg.

But she couldn't even leave the cabin! she reminded herself. She was locked in. But she wasn't alone. Someone was with her. She knew it. Robert Arrowsmith? She hoped fervently that it was that young man left behind to guard her.

She was being absurdly reckless! she warned herself. She was waltzing into danger. The island was not populated by gentlemen. It was inhabited by cutthroats and rakes. They might not offer her help, but only the gravest danger!

But what danger could be greater than this she already faced? Lying with a man who threatened her with much more than the sins of the flesh as night after night passed by. Oh, indeed, he threatened her very belief in herself, he threatened her dignity and her pride, and assuredly, her very soul.

She leaped to her feet and paused a bare second. Then she hurried to the door and knocked strenuously upon it.

She would see him hang! she swore to herself. Indeed, she would see the Silver Hawk dance from a rope, so help her God!

The pub was called the Golden Hind in honor of a man that many of their brotherhood deemed to be the greatest pirate of them all, Sir Francis Drake. It sat far back from the market; to the left lay the sands of the beach and to the right were the docks where a man could purchase almost anything he desired. A ship could be repaired here, knives could be honed, weapons acquired. Flesh could be bought as easily as a fillet of fish, and even a murder could be negotiated if a man so desired. But there was honor among thieves, for the men here had their own twisted code of ethics, and upon the island, a pirate's property—stolen though it might be—was sacred.

Usually. But private wars did arise.

And this night, since his adventures with One-Eyed Jack, Silver Hawk knew he might be called upon to defend himself. He had, however, made his intent to take the *Silver Messenger* clear, and so he was the man with the right to the spoils. Jack was the offender, and a man was expected to slay an offender.

Tonight the Golden Hind was in raucous full swing. Fiddlers played upon a dais, rum flowed freely, and it seemed that the best names in the business were all in attendance. An up-and-coming man who was rumored to hail from Bristol—Edward Teach, who was known more notoriously as Blackbeard—held court at a far rear table. A man nearing forty, or so the Hawk determined, he was known for being ruthless, though not so deadly as the late Captain Kidd. Anne Bonny, her youth fast fading, sat nearby with her own grouping of louts. Whores freely strode about, pocketing the loot tossed about by the drunken pirates.

William Logan, a lean, mean bastard with blackened front teeth and a steel claw for a right hand, sat at a table with a few of his henchmen. A dark-haired whore perched upon the arm of his chair, but Logan gave her little attention. He stared broodingly at the Hawk.

"There's one to give us trouble," Robert Arrowsmith murmured as he entered at the Hawk's side.

The Hawk shrugged and took his place at a center table along with his men. He frowned, noticing that a man hastily entered the establishment and came up to William Logan, stopping by his side and speaking hastily. It disturbed the Hawk, though he wasn't sure why. Some sixth sense of danger sounded an alarm, but he held his ground.

What was going on? The question would have to wait.

Captain Stoker, sometimes called the "governor" of the island, sat before him and his men. He was an older man, bearded and graying, but he was built like an old Saxon warrior, and had a body to reckon with in a fight. He was grave as he spoke to the Hawk.

"There's some as don't like the idea o' Jack bein' dead, and you know that rightly. We're not out to murder our own number, Hawk, and that's a fact, it is."

The Hawk leaned across the table, skewering a piece of roasted lamb from a trencher in the center. His eyes met those of Captain Stoker. "Jack was well aware that the *Silver Messenger* was mine. I laid claim to her back here in March, the very day we learned that she had set sail from England!"

"Jack spoke of it first—"

"Jack mentioned the ship, sir. He was interested in the Spaniard, *La Madonna,* out of Cartagena, at that time!"

"Still—"

The Hawk slammed his knife, meat and all, into the table, and stood. "Listen to me well, me hearties!" he called, his voice ringing out. The music ceased. In seconds, the room came silent. Every man and woman looked at him, some with trepidation, and some, the Hawk knew, like Blackbeard, with interest. Some would respect his stand, and some would whisper behind his back. "One-Eyed Jack is dead, that is a fact, and that he died by my sword I do not deny! But I did not seek his death, he desired the fight, for he disturbed what he knew to be my intention, my prize. He died in combat with me, and me alone. He died by the very rules we all know here within our hearts. If any man here—or woman"—he interrupted himself, bowing to Anne Bonny—"cares to dissent with my words, I am ready to listen. Face me now, for whisperers will know my wrath!"

A fist slammed against the table. William Logan stood. The Hawk faced Logan. They had grappled once before, in this very room. Logan had wanted an English ship, and the Hawk had seized it first. They had dueled here with cutlasses.

And Logan had lost a hand before Captain Stoker had stepped in to end it all.

Logan wanted blood now.

"The ways that I sees it," Logan said, "Jack was already aboard the *Silver Messenger.* He had claimed the ship for his own. He had done battle, and he had taken the prize."

The Hawk planted a boot atop a bench and leaned forward casually. "He knew the prize was mine. The ship was not secured when I came aboard. Jack could have given way, and sailed clean and free. He chose to fight. And he died."

"So you're saying, Captain Hawk, that one of our brotherhood has the right to another prize?"

"It was my prize."

"His prize—that you seized from him."

"The overfine logic is yours, sir."

"What's logic?" a drunken whore whispered, and hiccuped.

Logan bowed low to the Hawk. "Logic, sir! As you will have it!" He turned, and with his men in tow, he exited the establishment.

No one else moved for quite some time. Then a young pirate, an Englishman, rose and spoke quietly. They said that his name was Richard Crennan, but whether that was true or false, no one knew. Men left their homes to seek their fortunes, dreaming of riches. Most of them thought to return to their homes one day, and so they seldom used true names, or gave out true facts regarding the towns from which they had hailed.

The Hawk liked young Crennan. He was a gentleman pirate, so they said, and hailed from a good family somewhere. Like the Hawk, he made money on his hostages, and disdained murder.

"I say that this matter is well and done!" Crennan called out. He raised a pewter mug. "We all know the Silver Hawk. He laid claim to the *Silver Messenger* out of England, I know well, for I was here, in this very room, when he did so. He did not betray our articles of brotherhood! He fought a fair fight. I say, gents, that that is that!"

"Here, here!" came a voice. It was Blackbeard, the Hawk saw. The man was a bloody cutthroat, but a strong ally nonetheless.

Hawk turned to Anne Bonny. "Madame, I crave your opinion?"

She smiled. Once, he thought, she had been a young thing. With dreams similar to those dreams that haunted other young maidens. He did not know what had drawn her here.

"I saw, Captain, that you have presented yourself well. The matter is done, and the facts established."

"I thank you, Mistress Bonny!"

He sat again. The proprietor made an appearance again, bringing wine and bread and more lamb to the table. "Hiding out lest there be trouble, eh, Ferguson?" the Hawk inquired, amused.

"Captain Hawk, I tell you, the roof is thatch, since you fine sirs do continually see fit to duel and set fires. My tables are ramshackle, easily replaced. My hide, though tough, is not so easy to replace, and so, good sir, yes! I disappear at the slightest hint of trouble."

The Hawk laughed and poured more wine for Captain Stoker. "Ease up, Cap'n! The matter is settled now, and peacefully at that."

"Logan will not let it lie. Already, he seeks to carve your heart from your body, you know!"

The Hawk waved a hand in the air. The musicians began to

play again. A harlot shrieked with glee as a seaman poured a trickle of wine into the valley of her breasts. Laughter rose, and the night was made merry once again.

The Hawk picked up a pewter goblet of wine. "He will simply never have a piece of me, Captain, you needn't fear."

"I fear this warfare among us, for it will bring destruction down upon us."

Robert Arrowsmith glanced quickly at the Hawk. "How?" the Hawk asked with an easy smile. "Why, I hear tell that the governor of North Carolina is in league with a certain one of us! A man to be bribed, so they say. We, in this our Golden Age, shall reign forever."

Stoker shook his great head broodingly. He shrugged. "In the Carolina waters, perhaps, we find a certain safety. But in Virginia that damned Lieutenant Governor Spotswood seeks us out like bloodhounds!"

"So they say."

Stoker smiled, finding some amusement in the matter. "He will have to intrude upon Carolina to destroy us, though, eh?"

He started to laugh. The Hawk glanced at Robert, and then he started to laugh, too. He patted Stoker strongly upon the back. "Aye, Captain, he'll have to do just such a thing!" He sobered. "Now, to business, sir. I need canvas, needles, coffee, and fresh meat. And rum. Can you see to it all?"

Captain Stoker raised a hand, calling to one of his clerks. A little man hurried to them with an inkpot, quill, and paper, and sat down to take the orders.

For the moment, peace and laughter reigned.

It was not Robert who had been left aboard the ship to guard her. When she slammed upon the door, it was soon opened, but it was opened by a huge, burly Frenchman.

"Mademoiselle!" he cried, looking at her warily. He was like Samson out of the Bible, she decided. He had a head of dark curls and warm brown eyes. His size was intimidating; his eyes were not.

"Monsieur! Forgive me! I feel so ill of a sudden. I must have some air!"

"Ah, but my lady! *Sacrebleu!* The captain would have my head. You are to remain here."

"Ooooh!" she started to moan, doubling over. "I feel so very ill, I must have air. . . ."

"D'accord! I will take you out. Come, lean on me!"

She offered him a sweet, pathetic smile and leaned heavily against him. He led her out to the deck. She inhaled deeply, gasping, bringing in air. This was easy. Much, much easier than she had imagined.

He brought her to the railing. She leaned over, clinging to him, gulping for air. She also looked around herself. The ship was almost empty. She looked up. There was a man in the crow's nest. She looked across the water. There were still men upon the dock. Someone was pointing their way. She felt a shiver seize her. Night was coming on quickly. Darkness was falling. Perhaps this plan of hers was not so well advised.

She looked down. The ladder was still in place from the deck to the water, and a longboat waited there, tied in place should it be needed. The temptation was too great to be resisted.

"Mademoiselle! Speak to me, are you better?"

The Frenchman's attention was entirely for her, and he was desperately worried. She felt a twinge of guilt, but ignored it. She sank down upon one of the barrels near the rail. "Oh, monsieur, I am much better, truly!" she said. He was by her side. She offered him a flashing smile, for it was then or never.

She reached down and drew his cutlass quickly from the scabbard that laced around his waist. Before he could move, she had brought the point to his very chin.

"Monsieur, forgive me, but I will be free this night!" she told him.

"Mademoiselle!" he said, and he tried to move. She pressed the point against him, drawing blood, and he went still. "Now, come, sir!" she said softly. "We will take the longboat to shore. If you cross me, I will skewer you through. I will do so unhappily, for you appear to be too kind a man for this life you have chosen, but I swear that I will gladly slice you open, nonetheless."

He said nothing. She pressed her point still further.

"Am I understood?"

"Mais oui, mademoiselle—" the Frenchman began, but he broke off as the sound of an explosion suddenly burst through the night.

Skye leaped to her feet, backing away from the Frenchman. There was a huge thud and she screamed as she saw that the sailor in the crow's nest had fallen to the deck, his shirt crimson with the spill of his blood.

"Mon Dieu—" the Frenchman said, ignoring her and spinning around to see from where death had sprung.

A man was halfway over the railing. He tossed a still-smoking pistol to the deck and drew forth a second flintlock weapon, aiming it their way.

He was a hideous soul, Skye thought, her heart hammering. He was dark and surly; a scar marred his right cheek. He wore a hat pulled low over his forehead, but it did not hide his eyes. They were pale and cold. He smiled, and his mouth seemed a black cavern, and his teeth looked awful and fetid. The leer gave him such a bearing of cruelty that she trembled.

Then she saw his left hand, or the very lack thereof. A deadly-looking hook protruded from his coat sleeve.

He aimed his pistol straight at the Frenchman. Without a sound or a word of warning, he fired.

Skye screamed with horror as the Frenchman went down in a pool of blood. She stared at the fallen man, frozen.

The hook-armed pirate crawled aboard. She had the Frenchman's cutlass. She needed to lunge quickly and fight. She needed to make the attack. It was her only hope. She raised her sword.

The hook-handed pirate looked past her, allowing his smile to deepen. "My pet, but you are sweeter than gold!" he said softly, and then he nodded.

Skye swung around, but too late. She barely saw the man who had come up behind her. There was a blur, and then nothing more. She was struck upon the head, and the world faded as she fell. The last thing she saw was the blood seeping over the deck. Then it all went black.

She heard the sound of waves lapping nearby. She became aware that she was rolling backward and forward herself, and that oars were striking against water. She opened her eyes. Darkness still surrounded her and she realized that she was wrapped in a suffocating, rough wool blanket. She struggled to free herself from its confines. The blanket fell away and she faced the pirate with the hook again. He aimed his sword with deadly accuracy against her throat and she sat still, watching him. "So the Silver Hawk sought the *Silver Messenger,*" he mused. "I do wonder if you were the prize he sought all along. He was careless to let you be seen, my love. Very careless. Had Brice here not seen you peeking through the window, I'd never have thought to find you. And then, my dear, you came straight to the deck, making the whole thing so very easy for me. I do thank you." Behind her, his accomplice continued to stroke the water with his oars. She said nothing, and he idly picked up a golden curl with the point of his sword. "My dear, I am so very pleased to have found you! Not only shall I have my opportunity to slay the Hawk now, but I shall enjoy you as I'm sure you can't even begin to imagine."

"Over my dead body!" she whispered vehemently.

He leaned toward her. "Yes, my dear, that is quite possible, too."

Skye quickly changed her tactics. "I'm worth a fortune. If you keep me safe and return me—"

"I'm so sorry, my dear. This is vengeance, not finance. Brice! Row more quickly. I would not have the Hawk leave the Golden Hind before I can show him that I hold his prize."

He was deadly, Skye realized with a sinking heart. He was cold, as if no blood flowed through his veins.

And he was revolting; from his fetid breath to his icy eyes, he made her skin crawl. She had sought to flee one knave only to stumble into the arms of a monster. Her teeth chattered.

She wanted to die.

She leaped to her feet suddenly, praying that the boat would tip. She could swim, but she would rather drown than go any further with the horrid monster who sat before her.

"Grab her, Brice!" he roared, leaping to his feet. The longboat teetered precariously. It careened over.

She pitched downward into the warm, aquamarine sea. They were almost to the dock. If she could just swim . . .

But she could gather no speed, for her skirts were dragging her down.

A hand grabbed her hair, tugging painfully. She screamed, and drew in water. Coughing and sputtering, she fought only to breathe. She was being dragged along through the water. Light wavered before her eyes. She was wrenched upon a wooden dock, surrounded by voices and kissed by the balmy warmth of the night. She closed her eyes and opened them.

And stared into the evil glare of the hook-handed pirate.

She spat at him, struggling to rise. He swore, and tossed a new blanket over her face. She was being smothered again, but she could still fight with her limbs, kicking and scratching.

But she was dragged up and cast over his shoulder and held there forcibly.

"Don't fret, my dear. You will see blood run soon enough," he promised her.

They drank, they laughed, they ate. The whores flirted, and they laughed at their antics. A buxom blonde promised Hawk the finest night of his life, and he told her that her words were a challenge indeed, but all the while he was thinking of another woman. One who was young and fresh and radiant and possessed the most glorious eyes.

And somehow she was able to touch him in a way he had never imagined. Touch him with her innocence, and yet evoke the most pagan and sensual thoughts that had ever come to plague him, to burn him. The whore whispered something, and he laughed. Then his laughter faded as the front doors to the establishment were suddenly cast wide open again.

He leaped to his feet. The whore fell to the floor, ignored. His hand lay upon his sword hilt where it rested within its scabbard upon his hip.

Logan had returned.

And he wasn't alone. He swaggered into the building, a blanket-draped, struggling figure held over his shoulder, his pistol raised in his free hand.

"Hawk!" he called. "You say it's just to seize one another's prizes? Well, sir, I have seized one from you, and in honor of our late brother, One-Eyed Jack, I demand of the brotherhood that this prize shall be mine in your stead!"

And with that, he cast his struggling bundle upon the floor, wrenching the blanket away.

To the Hawk's eternal horror, the Lady Skye Kinsdale appeared, scrambling frantically to her feet, pausing only when she saw the assemblage of rogues before her. Her hair was a tousled sunburst, damp and curling to her face and shoulders. Her gown was ragged, drenched, and torn, and her beautiful eyes were wide and brilliant with horror. She stood before them like a shimmering star in the horizon. Disheveled, she was still the lady, tall and straight, her pride radiating from her in the beautiful colors of life that separated her from the riffraff that filled the room. Her very beauty separated her from it all.

She was, indeed, a prize.

God in heaven, how in hell had she come to be there? the Hawk wondered in fury. He had to save her, he determined.

Just so that he could throttle her himself!

She spun to flee suddenly. Logan pushed her forward. Laughter broke out. A seaman rose to stop her when she lunged anew. And then another man rose, and another, and she was nearly encircled.

It was time for him to step into it. She lunged anew, and he left his table. The next time she lunged, she fell to the floor at his feet. She was quick. She braced her palms against the floor to rise, then paused, seeing his boots.

She looked up. Her eyes met his. She inhaled and gasped. He did not know if she trembled to see him, or if the dazzling liquid in her eyes was meant as a plea to save her. His heart leaped and careened to his stomach. They were in deadly danger now.

She had betrayed him somehow. Despite his threats, his words of warning, she had betrayed him.

He smiled icily. "Well, milady, do not say that you were not warned!" he whispered furiously. But there was no more that he could do then.

Logan had drawn his cutlass, and was stepping toward him.

VI

Skye watched in deep dread as the Hawk stepped over her to meet the instant clash of Logan's steel.

With a gasp she swiftly rolled to avoid being trampled. She came up beneath a table, and with a certain, horrified fascination, she watched the fighting men.

It was a fair fight; one well met. They might have engaged in a macabre dance, so graceful, yet so deadly, were their movements. Their left arms remaining behind their backs, they met and clashed, and parted again, their swords ripping the very air, so that it seemed the night itself whispered and cried. Cheers rose within the room, some claiming for Logan, some for the Hawk, and all of them urging on the fight with merriment and blood lust.

The men broke apart. Logan jumped upon a table. Leaping into flight, the Hawk followed behind him. The table crashed to the floor. Wine and ale spilled freely and pewter clanked upon the floor. Skye's hand fluttered to her throat, for she saw no movement. If he had died, then it seemed that she had best pray for death. What madness had brought her here? she wondered. But her thoughts were fleeting, for both men were upon their feet again. The duel was reengaged.

A hand clamped upon her shoulder of a sudden. She choked upon a scream as she was dragged to her feet.

She looked into the eyes of a man with thick dark hair, a stocky build, a sharp, cunning gaze, and the faint sign of pockmarks beneath the heavy growth of his beard. He wore a scarlet frockcoat with golden epaulets and fine soft mustard breeches. He hauled her up against him. She struggled fiercely, seeking to bite him. "Hold, lassie!" he warned her. "I'm not your enemy!" Swinging her before him, he called out to the fighting men. "Gents of the brotherhood! Cease this ghastly foray and listen! This fight is no longer over Jack, nor, I daresay, was it ever! Logan, you would have him dead. Hawk, you would have the woman. Let's put a price on her head. That's our business, is it not? Gaining riches? So what is she worth, gentlemen? In gold?"

"Here, here!" someone else cried, laughing. "Is it open bidding, then? I'll give a hundred pieces o' eight, Spanish gold, the best o' the lot!"

"One-fifty!"

"Two hundred!"

"A thousand gold doubloons!"

"A thousand!" It was the Hawk. He stared down the length of her, then looked to her captor. "Nothing that lies 'twixt a maiden's thighs could come so dear!"

"Dear me, and not hers!" chortled one of the whores, who waltzed by Skye, tweaking her cheek. Skye kicked her furiously. The woman screamed out, lunging toward her.

"Cease!" the Hawk yelled, catching the whore. She turned to him with huge dark eyes and her painted features, a pretty thing despite her paint, young and buxom.

"She kicked me, Hawk! Why, I'll claw her eyes out, I will!"

"She's not that easy, Mary, trust me. And she is to be ransomed, so keep clear of her, eh?" Gently, he thrust the whore far from himself, and far away from Skye.

"Is the bidding open again?" someone called.

"Aye, and think on this. She's a feisty piece of baggage!" the dark pirate called out.

Skye stared about herself in dismay. The Hawk was lost to a clang of steel once again while the others were all having a rollicking good time discussing her life in terms of the highest sum. The pirate holding her had a cutlass at his waist. She eyed it as another bid rang out. She itched to get her fingers upon it!

"A thousand! I've said a thousand! Someone top that, me friends!"

Skye heard something like the roar of a furious lion, and she saw that the Silver Hawk had come to the center of the room again, staring at her and her new captor, Teach, as Hawk had called him. "She is not public property, Teach! I took the prize, the prize is mine, and I will slay every man jack here who attempts to tell me otherwise!"

"What?" the pirate Teach said in dismay. "Why, I'd had in mind to bid upon this morsel meself! Can she be worth so very much then, Captain Hawk?"

The Hawk's eyes raked her with a careful disdain. Even there, before all others, the gaze seemed to strip her of her clothing, to lay her bare and naked before them all. A sizzle of mockery touched his eyes. "No woman is worth so much," he said, "and this one screams like a banshee and lies like a log. The equipment is there, but alas, she lacks the talent to use it."

She gasped out loud, despising him, despising the way that he had made her feel. She hated the cold steel in his eyes, and she hated the humiliation he caused her. Snickers of laughter rose up softly at his suggestion of their intimacy. "The point, sir," Hawk continued, "is that the prize is mine! What is mine, I shall keep!"

"But if she is of little use—"

"She will draw a good ransom."

"I would pay that ransom."

"Neverless, sir, I have begun a certain . . . er, contact with the lady, and I would continue where I have left off."

"You said—"

"Aye, Blackbeard, but I believe I could train her and tame her, and for the very measures, I would keep her now in my possession until I have chosen to make other arrangements."

Blackbeard! Skye shivered, aware then that she was being

touched by another of the most notorious pirates in the Caribbean.

"Perhaps this could be settled with Captain Logan if you were to pay him the ransom," Blackbeard suggested.

"I'll not take money!" Logan cried.

"And I'll not buy back what is already mine!" the Hawk claimed.

Watching him in fury and amazement, Skye suddenly screamed. Logan had wasted little time, but had come up behind him, his sword raised and ready to swing in a wide arc. The Hawk ducked just in time, else the arc would have severed his neck and sent his head flying. The Hawk swirled about, striking out.

"Logan, you backstabbing refuse!" the Hawk roared.

"This is a fight!" Logan snarled back. "Not a bloody mincing court of civil law!"

The Hawk caught Logan's cutlass with his blade; the sword flew and clattered. The Hawk stepped back, but one of Logan's men leapt into the fray, charging for the Hawk.

"The plate!" A heavy-jowled man behind Skye and Blackbeard called out. "Save the plate!"

Skye quickly understood why. The fight was no longer one-on-one, but a melee. Men leaped about to join in with roars and cheers, and steel was soon clashing about the room.

"Look at this, at what you have caused!" Blackbeard hissed in her ear. "Alas, the law does not catch men, but mere women send them to their dooms. Perhaps I should let them all battle it out, mam'selle, and spirit you away myself."

She did not know if he taunted her or spoke the truth. The room had become terribly warm. Now screams arose, and injured men fell from the fray, crashing upon tables, falling to the floor.

Blood ran, mingling with the wine upon the sand and dirt.

Very likely, they would all long to slit her throat when it was over.

Skye acted on desperate impulse, reaching swiftly for the man's cutlass and jerking it from his hold. She wagged the sword beneath his nose. "Leave me be, sir, and I will leave you be!" she cried out.

"Why, a fighting maiden. Girl, give me back that sword!"

She shook her head. Blackbeard yelled out. "Mr. Clifford! Toss me a sword!"

A sword flew his way. He grinned at Skye. "Now give me that weapon, girl!"

She refused and he thrust toward her blade. She parried him with swift skill, but knew that his strength would be great.

"Blimey!" he cried. "She knows how to use it!"

Skye wanted no more of the man known as Blackbeard. She counted on her speed to bring her through the crowd of rioting men. At first, no one thought to strike her, only to stop her wild flight. Then, as more and more of the sailors came away from a brief encounter with pricks of blood upon their persons, cries of warning went up.

Three men came toward her.

There was a stack of wine barrels by the door. Skye instinctively tossed them over. They cracked and spilled, and it seemed that the earth was soaked with it.

"Dear God, dear God, I am ruined!" called out the proprietor. A straw-haired harlot in totally disreputable undress shook a fist toward Skye. "You've cost us all, girl!"

Skye ignored her, looking to greater danger. She was backed against a wall then, and more and more men were coming her way. They laughed no more. Their faces were grim.

"Get behind me!" she heard. White-faced, she dared to look around.

The Hawk was coming her way, fiercely challenging every man who sought to approach her. She was amazed again at the deftness of his swordplay. He leaped upon a bench and soared forward, taking with him three of her attackers. He spun about and caught one man at the knees, leaving him screaming, slicing a second man through the arm, and catching a third at the throat.

She nearly missed an opponent, watching him. She came to attention just soon enough and ducked a blow that struck the wall. Hawk was beside her then. His weapon, she saw, had taken a beating. The steel had cracked.

"Give me the sword!" he commanded her.

She stared at him, her eyes growing very wide. Did it matter? She had caused this fray. She had brought him to arms against his comrades. He had claimed that she wasn't worth any fortune in gold, that he would keep her just because he already had her. He was surely furious with her, and might very well plan to torture her near to death once he had his hands upon her.

She could not give her sword away.

Men were approaching them quickly.

"Give me the sword!" he roared once more.

Of course, if she didn't hand him the sword, they might very well perish at that very moment.

He lunged for it. She gasped, but released the steel to his grasp. He stared at her with a promise of fury, then turned to the sailors now ready to assault. He raised the weapon against them, and steel began to clang again.

He moved forward, maneuvering himself and Skye away from their disadvantaged position against the wall. Skye saw that they were slowly joined by the Hawk's men. She didn't know them all, but she suddenly realized that she was being shielded behind the Hawk and Robert Arrowsmith. They were fighting their way to the door.

Slowly, the attackers began to fall away. Only a few remained when they reached the entryway.

The Hawk paused, reaching into a pocket within his frockcoat. He drew out a number of gold coins.

"Mr. Ferguson! For the damage done, sir!" he shouted. Then he said to Robert, "Watch my back, Mr. Arrowsmith!"

"Aye, aye, sir!"

And with that, the Hawk grabbed hold of Skye's arm. He dragged her along the primitive road with him in a raw fury. They were not far from the sea. She could smell the salt and feel the breeze. The Hawk's men now raced behind them, like a giant wave, seeming to pitch them ever forward. She could still hear shouts of rage and fury from behind them. What had happened to Logan? She didn't know.

She stumbled.

"Move!" the Hawk shouted to her. Grasping his arm, she tried to do so. She apparently did not move fast enough for he swept her up into his arms. She struggled briefly. "I can walk—"

"By God, I should let them have you!" he thundered out. Caught by moonlight, his eyes glittered with a striking, chilling silver. She caught her lower lip between her teeth and went silent. He wasn't looking at her anymore, he was running with her held taut in his arms. "The longboats!" someone cried. "We're there! All men to the oars, and quickly."

Their boots fell heavy against the dock as they raced down to the longboats. Skye was tossed heavily within the first. The Hawk quickly landed by her side. He dropped his borrowed sword while his men crawled in with them and picked up the oars. Reaching to his waist he drew out a long flintlock pistol. Staring at him, Skye had not seen the shirtless man with the knife between his teeth reaching up to her from the water. The pistol flared. The man cried out, and the knife fell from his teeth as he crashed into the water.

The Hawk cast her a chilling stare. Her eyes fell upon the sword as the longboat shot away from the dock. Fear made her think to lunge for the sword. His booted foot fell upon her fingers before they could wind around the steel. She cried out and her eyes met his again, and this time the hostility in them ran deep, and far colder than she could have ever imagined.

"Aye, mistress! I should have left you to them!" he hissed, sinking down beside her.

Shouts were arising from the dock. The contingent from the tavern had followed them down to the sea.

"Are they coming, Mr. Arrowsmith?" the Hawk called to his man.

"I'm not sure, Captain. They seem to be hovering at the moment, sir, and nothing more."

The Hawk's eyes were upon her again. Skye felt them boring into her. She shivered with a dreadful cold. She looked to the shouting rogues upon the dock, and to the man beside her, and then to the water. The dark depths seemed absurdly inviting that evening.

His hand clamped hard upon hers and she started, meeting his fiery gaze. "No, milady, I think not! I did not haul you from that menacing crowd to lose you to the sea!"

She sat still and tried not to shiver. His eyes remained upon her. "What happened?" he demanded curtly. "What has come of Jacques DuBray and the men left with you."

She started to shake her head, unable to speak. His fingers dug into her damp hair, wrenching her head back. "What happened?"

"Jacques—the Frenchman is dead."

He swore violently, staring at her with a greater hatred. "A good man, and dead, on your behalf, milady! You still have not told me what happened!"

His hold upon her was fierce. His men, setting their oars upon the sea, also stared at her. In the darkness she could feel their eyes condemning her as the longboat skimmed the water, bringing them ever closer to his ship.

"Tell me!"

"Logan came! He came from the shore and snuck up on the ship. The man in the crow's nest saw him, but Logan shot him before he could cry out an alarm. Then he came topside and shot the Frenchman."

The Hawk swore violently. His hand fell from her hair and he looked toward his ship.

None of the men on the docks seemed to be coming in pursuit, Skye saw. She shivered, feeling very, very cold. The sea breeze seemed to glue her wet clothing to her and the little discomforts made her ever more wretched as she wondered about her fate.

The figurehead of his ship loomed into view. Skye had never noted it before. It was the proud figure of a woman, one of the Greek goddesses, she imagined. The breasts were bared, and a crown rode the head. Soft carved curls fell over the woman's shoulders and her face was strong and beautiful.

It was a fine and artistic piece of work, Skye thought. Of course. The ship had surely been seized.

Her teeth were chattering. Her mind was wandering to all sorts of avenues, because she was afraid.

The longboat came shipside. The ladder awaited them, hanging there in the darkness of the night.

"I shall go first," the Hawk told his men. He rose, clutching the rope, shimmying quickly upon it. He paused, pulling a knife from inside his boot, looking to Robert. "Mr. Arrowsmith, see to Lady Kinsdale."

"Aye, aye, sir!"

Skye sat in silence while the Hawk disappeared over the portside hull of his ship. She heard the water lapping against the longboat and felt the eyes of his men upon her. She had endangered them all.

I am your prisoner! she wanted to shout out to them. *Had you let me be, I'd have offered you no harm!*

But she didn't open her mouth. She waited in silence, and then she realized that they were all waiting with anxiety, and she, as well as the men, was worrying about the Hawk.

Worrying about a man who would probably flay every inch of her flesh from her bones . . .

"All clear!" he called suddenly from far above them. She nearly screamed, she was so startled. He held a lantern far above his head, and in the night he watched her, his eyes nearly fathomless within the curious shadows of his face.

"Come along, Lady Kinsdale," Robert told her gruffly. Numb and frightened, she obeyed, reaching for the ladder. She faltered nearing the top of the rope. The Hawk reached down to her, dragging her over the hull of the ship. She nearly fell. He held her up and pulled her against him.

The men climbed aboard the ship. The Hawk shoved her toward Robert. "See that she is locked in," he said briefly. Robert took her arm and started toward the captain's cabin.

She turned back, opening her mouth to speak. She didn't know what she meant to say and words caught in her throat. He was watching her. Watching her by moonlight, his hands upon his hips, his face now in the shadows.

Then he turned away from her.

Robert swung open the doors and thrust her into the darkened cabin. He didn't pause. He slammed the doors and bolted them without a thought.

The darkness closed around her.

Skye wrapped her arms around herself and closed her eyes tightly and sank to the floor. She tried to fight it. With all of her heart she tried to fight the fear that was overwhelming her. She felt as if the walls moved, as if they came around her, as if they would close upon her.

They wanted to hurt her, she reminded herself. Hawk and all his men were bitter against her for the havoc and death they believed she'd caused. She needed to be still, to be silent, to pray that they would forget her here within the cabin. . . .

Logic did her no good. The fear was not a rational fear, it was not something that she could control. The night seemed so black; she could not breathe, she could not see, she could not help the sensations that spilled upon her. Sweat broke out upon her brow and goose bumps rose all over her skin. It was sweeping over her, wave after wave of awful, terrible and primal fear. . . .

She wasn't aware at all of what she did. In total terror she cast back her head and started to scream as if she were encountering the very demons of hell.

The door burst open. Dimly she was aware of the light. Even more dimly, she was aware of the figure of the man silhouetted there within its glow.

He moved quickly, coming down upon the ground beside her. She didn't know how long she had been in the darkness, ensnared within the web of fear. She was aware that he held her, but she shook violently still. He rocked her, but she stared into the night with open eyes. His arms came more tightly around her and he lifted her, holding her close as he strode quickly about the room, lighting the lanterns.

He sat with her upon the bunk. He whispered to her, and she didn't hear the words, but the cadence of his voice worked its way into her heart. Slowly, the icy chill left her. She ceased to shiver, and shook only in an occasional spasm. She blinked, and then she was able to close her eyes, and then she leaned against him, sobbing softly.

His fingers moved over her hair. "It's all right, it's all right. I am here," he whispered.

Perhaps that was the very moment when things would forever change for her. No matter what was to come between them in the future, whether fear or anger or hatred burned in her heart, she would not be able to forget that moment.

"What is it?" he murmured. "What is it that you fear more deeply than death?"

"The darkness," she said softly.

"What of the darkness?" he said.

But that she could not answer, and he did not press her, but sighed. His muscles constricted suddenly as if he would move. Her fingers wound into his shirt. His own closed around them. "I told you that it was all right. That I am here."

He eased her fingers from him and stretched her out upon the bed. She bit into her lower lip, letting her lashes shield her eyes. He strode across the room and she heard the clink of glass. A moment later he was back, lifting her head. He teased her lips with the snifter of brandy and she swallowed. He crawled to the back of the bunk, leaning against the paneling and bringing her head down upon his lap. He sipped the brandy himself, then lifted her head once more, and this time she swallowed deeply. The brandy burned throughout her. It warmed her. She gasped and fell back again, her lashes heavy over her eyes.

He studied her, staring down at the perfect oval beauty of her face and the softness of her skin, ashen then. Even her lips remained pale. He traced them with his finger. Her eyes flew open. Glistening turquoise, they held fever and torment. Her lips trembled slightly. "I am sorry about your Frenchman," she said softly. "He was kind."

"I am sorry, too. He was a good man."

"He was a pirate," she said gravely. "At least, now, he shall not come to hang."

"As I shall?" he demanded softly.

Her lashes fell upon her eyes once more, covering them. "As you shall!" she whispered. But she did not say the words with venom, just with a terrible certainty.

The Hawk twirled the remaining brandy in its crystal snifter, watching the swirl of amber liquid. He smiled with a certain irony, then sighed and sat back. He needed to be on deck. He did not care to test the reefs by darkness—many a careless captain had lost his vessel and his life upon the deadly coral—and so they needed to keep a sharp guard until morning. Perhaps the trouble was over; perhaps it was not. He would wait until the morning to see if the business deals he'd negotiated with Stoker were still valid. Then he would ride the outgoing afternoon tide and hurry for Bone Cay.

He did not want to leave her, he realized.

His fingers fell upon her hair again. It was tousled and still sticky from her bout in the sea. It was still beautiful, still the color of a sunset.

She did not move beneath his touch. He waited a few moments longer, then eased her down upon a pillow. He rose carefully and walked back over to his desk. He poured out another two fingers of brandy and swiftly swallowed it down.

He stared at her pensively, then he forced himself to come about and return to his deck, and his command.

When Skye awoke, daylight was streaming into the cabin. The draperies were drawn far back.

She rose stiffly. She could feel the dried salt upon her body and her hair.

The ship was moving.

She leaped out of bed and hurried to the windows. Looking out, she saw that the ship sluiced swiftly through the water. They were leaving the island of New Providence behind.

Even as she sat upon the window seat, staring out, the door burst open. She swiveled quickly to face the Hawk as he entered the cabin, eyeing her as he carefully closed the door behind him. She almost offered him a wavering smile, but it faded before it ever came to her face. His tenderness and care of the night before were gone. She faced a cold taskmaster that morning, one who seemed without mercy.

He did not speak. He sat behind his desk and rubbed his bearded chin, staring at her.

"We have left the island," Skye said.

"Aye, milady, we left the island. You, mam'selle, made my position quite untenable there."

She rose, her fingers clenching by her side. Did he want her to feel guilty? By daylight, she was able to fight. "Sir, you have made my position quite untenable!"

"Have I?" he asked her. Dark lashes fell over his eyes, then his searing silver gaze swept her once again. "So untenable, mam'selle, that you would have preferred Logan?"

"Logan, One-Eyed Jack, the Silver Hawk, Blackbeard, pirates one and all."

He pushed his seat away from the desk and stood, walking around to lean upon the edge of it. "I was able to complete my business this morning despite your antics, Skye. Supplies were delivered to the ship along with a few offers. One fool fellow is still willing to pay me a thousand Spanish gold doubloons for you. Perhaps I should oblige him."

She gritted her teeth. "Perhaps you should."

"Tell, me, mam'selle, are you worth it?"

"What?"

"Are you worth a thousand gold doubloons?"

"According to you, sir, I have no more worth than any other woman, and as I saw last night, the tavern was crawling with women. Of course, I daresay that things do also crawl upon those women, but then, what is that to one of your . . . persuasion."

He crossed his arms slowly over his chest. "I may well have saved your life, you know."

"And I may well have saved yours."

He burst out laughing and came toward her, pulling her into his arms. "So you saved my life, did you?"

She pressed against his chest, seeking to free herself. "I cast you my sword—"

"You cast me your sword! Why even in the moment of greatest distress, I had to snatch it from you! Imagine, milady! I offer my throat to a dangerous murderer on your behalf—I find myself at odds with every man in the brotherhood—and you have the audacity to claim that you saved my life!"

She pressed more firmly against him. His smile faded. "We have just cast Jacques and Hornby to their graves within the sea, milady."

She swallowed, lowering her lashes. Her palms remained pressed against him. "I am your prisoner. I must attempt escape—"

An oath of such vehemence escaped him that her eyes flew to his. "You would escape me—into Logan's arms? Tell me, do I beat you? Starve you? Why is it, mam'selle, that you would escape to a man who would treat you with total disregard and violence?"

"Let me go!" she whispered feverishly.

He did not let her go. He fingered a lock of her hair, and then he moved against her, his lips searing her throat and touching her shoulder. She gasped, startled by the touch, stunned by the sensation.

He stepped away from her suddenly, and his eyes were bright. He swept his hand from his head and gave her a sweeping bow. "Perhaps, mam'selle, you are worth a thousand gold doubloons," he told her.

Her hand fluttered to her throat. His gaze swept her up and down in a fashion that left her feeling naked and afire inside. Then he arched a brow and scratched his bearded chin.

"Not as it stands, I think. Dear woman, you do, decidedly, need a bath."

With a vicious oath, she threw the pillow from the window seat at him. He caught the pillow, smiling.

"For your entertainment? No!" she snapped.

"We'll arrive at Bone Cay at nightfall," he told her softly. "Home."

"Should that please me?" she demanded.

"It pleases me. And who knows? Perhaps I shall seek to determine whether you are worth the trouble you have cost me."

"You, sir, have caused *me* the trouble!"

"Worth a thousand gold doubloons," he murmured.

"My father will pay—"

"Ah, but has he the purse?"

"If not, then my fiancé will pay. Lord Cameron is one of the wealthiest men in the Virginia Colony."

"But I do believe that he is aware of your feelings toward your impending nuptials, mam'selle. And, alas, all men are not so eager to pursue vixens who despise them."

"I do not despise Lord Cameron," she said coolly.

"Don't you? Well, I am sure that such words would truly warm his heart! Lady Kinsdale, this is enchanting, but you must excuse me. We come ever nearer Bone Cay, but I fear that Logan is either so enamored of you or hostile toward me that he may seek an engagement upon the sea. I am needed."

He bowed deeply and turned to leave her. At the door he paused and turned back, and amusement curled his lip. "I shall send men with the tub and water."

"You needn't. I rather like the way that I am since it does not please you!"

The smile stayed upon his lips. "Lady Kinsdale, I am giving you a direct order."

"And I—" She broke off, for he was returning to the room. He sat upon the edge of the desk, waiting. "What are you doing?" she cried.

"If you cannot obey a simple order, then I shall stay to assist you."

"You just said that you fear an attack!"

"Let Logan come with his guns blazing! If this is how you will have it be, then this is one war that I will wage first." He raised his voice. "Robert! Mr. Arrowsmith. I need you!"

Skye stared at him and knew that he meant every word, no matter how dramatically each was spoken. She stamped a foot upon the floor. "Go!" she breathed in fury. "Go! I shall just live and breathe, Captain, to obey your slightest order!"

He smiled. "Good," he said pleasantly, and jumped down from his desk. He turned at the door, and she saw the sizzle of amusement in his eyes, and she realized that more than anything, he taunted her. He'd offered the bath for her comfort, and not his own entertainment.

He had come to her against the terror of the night.

He was her enemy. Her deadly enemy. But he was a curious man, and she could not deny his courage, his determination. . . .

Or his strange tolerance and his even stranger tenderness. In her greatest hour of need, he had offered comfort.

"Mam'selle—" he said, nodding as he opened the door to leave her.

"Wait!" she cried.

He paused, a brow arched. She lowered her eyes.

"Yes, mam'selle?"

"Thank you."

"Thank you?" he repeated, amazed.

"For the lights," she whispered.

It seemed that he paused a very long time. "You are most heartily welcome, mam'selle," he said at last. Then he left her, and the door closed.

Robert came with coffee and rolls, and then he and a number of sailors trudged in with the hip bath and water. She felt the men watching her. Blue eyes, green, brown, and hazel, they all fell upon her. Old men, young men, thin and ruddy, they stared at her as they came and went. They despised her, she thought.

But when she dared to look up, she did not think that they hated her so. The last man to leave the cabin bowed her way. "You fought well last night, Lady Kinsdale!" he said. He smiled deeply. "A lady, and ye dared take Blackbeard's own sword against him!"

"Out, Rodgers!" Robert Arrowsmith commanded gruffly.

"Aye, sir, aye! Good day, Lady Kinsdale."

The door closed. Skye let out a long, uneasy breath.

She stood still for several seconds, then turned back to the window seat and stared out to sea. Would Logan really come for them? She shuddered. She had lied so deeply to the Hawk. She knew he was a better man than any of the others. A man to be respected.

And . . . were he not a pirate, she would have admired him.

As the long afternoon waned, Skye dozed in the window seat. She was awakened by a loud blast of one of the ship's cannons. Jerking up in terror, she stared out at the sea.

They had slowed their pace to a mere crawl and she could just see the shore. Far to her left stretched white sands and long grasses. To her right she saw towers, high brick towers rising on either side of a slender channel. They approached that channel.

She sank back, her heart thundering. Home, the Hawk had called this place.

A cannon fired in answer from one of the towers. Skye lay still as she felt the ship move through the channel. Then she bolted up again as she heard laughter and words of welcome.

They had come to rest against a long wooden dock, and the plank was being lowered. Men were teeming off of the ship, being greeted by their fellows. . . .

And by their women.

Skye gnawed her lip, straining to see. Many of the sailors were being hugged and caressed by women, old women, young women, pretty young barefoot girls, and somber-looking matrons.

There was a whole community here! she thought. Bone Cay. It seemed that the Hawk ruled his own little kingdom. The Hawk! There he was himself, tall, lean, and striking in an elegant black frockcoat and knee breeches. A small blond woman yelled something and he laughed to her, picking her up in greeting, swinging her about. He set her down and she stared up at him adoringly. Another sailor joined them, and another woman. Skye experienced a strange searing sensation that brought a flush to her features. She swallowed tightly against the pain. She hated him, she wanted nothing to do with him, and she was glad that he was back to his beloved mistresses.

She started, falling back from the window as the door opened. It was Robert Arrowsmith.

He bowed gravely. "Milady, if you will accompany me, please?"

"Where are you taking me?"

"To your room within the castle."

"The castle?" she inquired imperiously.

" 'Tis what we call the house, milady, for it is made soundly of stone, a fortress if you like. You will be safe there."

"I will be a prisoner there."

Robert paused. "A safe prisoner, mam'selle."

She accepted his arm, eager to quit the ship but determined that he would not know her mind. He led her from the cabin and across the deck. The sails were furled now, and the deck was silent and still.

Robert Arrowsmith led her over the gangplank. A hush fell over the dock. Men and women stared at her, and she stared in turn. Robert led her through the crowd that thronged around the ship.

The people gave way, parting to give them an open path.

Then she saw that the Silver Hawk was still there. Indeed, he awaited her. He sat mounted upon a huge white steed, his plumed hat low on his head.

Skye paused, ignoring the pressure of Robert's arm upon her.

"Come, Lady Kinsdale!" the Hawk shouted to her. "Welcome to the Hawk's Nest! Do hurry along."

"I'll not!" she shouted defiantly. It was the gravest pleasure to humiliate the man in turn.

But he was not humiliated. He cast his head back with a thunder of deep laughter, and she was left to gasp as the white horse thundered down upon her. She stood her ground.

She should have turned to flee.

She should have . . . but she did not. And upon his snow-white stallion, the Silver Hawk seemed to fly on the wind. And leaning from his seat, he plucked her from the ground, sweeping her before him, and racing toward the fortress that rose ahead of them.

And still the deep husky sound of his laughter rang against the coming of the night.

VII

They did not ride far. Skye had just dug her fingers into the stallion's mane when she saw tall stone walls rising above her. The wind swept by them and the sandy earth churned as they came upon a set of wrought-iron gates, opened in expectation of the master's return, or so it seemed.

The horse unerringly turned and brought them through a courtyard to a high rising porte cochere. The Hawk reined in, setting Skye upon the ground. He touched his plumed hat. "Milady, my house is yours," he said simply.

Smiling, he turned the horse around. He led the animal around the side of the house. Skye watched him go, and then paused, staring about herself in ironic dismay. No one was near her; she was neither chained nor confined. But she had probably never been more of a prisoner, for there was absolutely nowhere to go. The Silver Hawk had chosen his base of operations well. The island was surrounded by coral atolls and shoals, deadly to the unwary sailor. His harbor was protected by the deep, natural U shape of his island. The channel was protected by the towers with their massive guns. It would take an army to come in here and clean out his rogue's den. And for a prisoner, there was very simply nowhere at all to go. The island was his. The people who lived upon it were his.

And she was his, she reminded herself. Worthless—or not worth any great sum, or so he had said. But still, his prize, and as such, he had fought for her, and he had kept her. And he had brought her here.

She shivered suddenly. Not because it was cold, and not because she feared him, but because she was afraid to be there, upon the island with him. She knew not why.

She turned about and followed the handsome brick path to the door of the imposing structure. She shouldn't be afraid. This was where she would wait for her father or her fiancé to rescue her. The Hawk would surely grant her some privacy here. It was a huge domicile.

She lifted her hand to knock, but the door opened before she could and to her surprise the Silver Hawk stood within the door frame. She frowned and he quickly arched a brow. "I left Samuel in his paddock, milady. You did take your sweet time to enter."

"Samuel?" she murmured. "Not the Silver Wind? Not the Hawk's Messenger, or some such. You named your horse Samuel?"

"Sam for short. He much prefers the abbreviation." He reached out and caught her hand, drawing her into his fortress. The entryway was in shadows, but she could see his eyes, smoke gray now, and haunting. "I'm sorry if I disappoint you, but I'm afraid that I was just a lad when Sam was born, and therefore I named him quickly. He's twenty-three now, and I'd not disturb his tranquillity with a change of name to suit my fancy."

"Twenty-three?" Skye said. The huge, sleek animal looked to be a young horse. "He has aged well."

The Hawk smiled slowly, and to her great distress, Skye felt her heart quiver as he drew her close. "I take very good care of all living creatures within my domain, milady. Alas, I tried take good care of you, but you are forever fighting my efforts."

"Perhaps, sir, it is because I am not your property to be cared for. I am neither pet, nor beast of burden, nor—yours."

A smile touched his lip. "Well spoken, milady, but then that is part of your appeal."

"Ah! But still a woman, and worth only so much!"

"Your worth is still debatable," he said. The words were simple and light, but the silence that followed them was not, for she felt both the warmth of his hands and the heat of his appraisal, and it seemed that a lingering question hung upon the air. She flushed and pulled from his grip, spinning to see the entryway.

It was grand. It was huge, with doors leading to rooms on either side. The walls and ceiling were paneled, and then lined handsomely with weapons of warfare, cutlasses, rapiers, scores of hunting rifles and muskets and brown Besses.

"Impressive," she muttered.

"Every man and woman on the island knows where to come in case of attack."

"And every one of them shall die with you?"

He shrugged. "They are here by choice. I force no one to live here."

"You have forced me."

"You, milady, are visiting, and naught more. Come along. I shall show you the rest of the house."

He took her hand into his own. To the right was a library with a guest bed, to the left was the butler's pantry—complete with butler. The man stood so silently awaiting their arrival that Skye gasped to see him living, alive and well. He was tall and strong of build, white-haired and immensely dignified. "Mr. Soames," the Hawk said in introduction, and Mr. Soames bowed to her very gravely. "What you need, he will give you."

"With the greatest pleasure, milady," Soames said, and bowed.

He might have graced the finest English manor! Skye thought, and she wondered how on God's good earth such a man had come to work in a pirate kingdom.

"All the pleasures of home," she murmured softly.

"What was that, Lady Kinsdale?" the Hawk said. She was

certain that he winked to the butler, and that the butler winked in return. It was all a joke perhaps.

No, it was not joke. The cannons upon the protective towers were no joke. The skill of the Hawk was hardly amusing to the men he had robbed of ships and plunder.

Soames excused himself and closed the door upon his domain. The Hawk was staring at her. "Well?"

"Quite remarkable."

"The house itself is remarkable, don't you agree? But not so difficult to construct as you might imagine. Brick makes wonderful ballast. I was able to have this all brought within the span of a few years." He walked her along the hall and paused, pushing open a set of doors. A long, claw-footed mahogany table stretched before them. It would seat at least twenty people, she thought. "The formal dining room."

"For those 'state' occasions?" she taunted.

"For negotiations," he corrected. "Your very worth might well be negotiated right here, milady."

"With whom do you negotiate?"

"No man fears to come here if he is invited, Lady Kinsdale. Your fiancé is well aware of the truth of those words. There is no safer haven upon the seas than this."

He drew her out and closed the doors. Pointing toward the rear of the house, he told her, "The ballroom, milady. And occasionally we do have balls."

He barely let her see the long room before he was whirling her around again and pulling her toward the stairway. It was big and broad with a velvet runner. A manservant polishing the banister bobbed to her and saluted the Hawk. "Sir, 'tis good to see you home, sir!"

"Mr. Tallingsworth, Lady Kinsdale. He, too, will be delighted to see to your every comfort."

"Yes, milady," Mr. Tallingsworth said.

She nodded skeptically and the Hawk continued to lead her upward. The second floor, too, seemed to stretch endlessly. He did not attempt to show her the length of it, but rather paused to the right side of the stairway, pushing open a door.

It was his room, she knew instantly. The dominant furniture within it was a huge four-poster bed in a dark walnut. Full-length windows lay open to the breeze coming off of the sea, making the room cool despite the heat of the day. There was a huge desk on the other side of the windows, and there were chairs and a daybed in front of a marble-manteled fireplace. In the center of the room was a fine cherrywood dining table, far more intimate than the large table downstairs.

"Your personal domain?" she inquired. She knew that he was watching her as she studied his room.

"Umm. Through here," he said, and he took her hand, leading her to the back of the room. He opened a doorway there and they entered a second chamber, not much smaller than the first. But whereas the larger room had been beyond a doubt decorated for a man, this room was softer. It might have been decorated to resemble a lady's chamber at Versailles. The delicate, white furniture appeared to be of French design. The drapes at the windows were sheer and trimmed with gold thread, and a gilded mirror hung over the fireplace. There was a card table and a huge wingback chair before the long windows, and the dressing table came complete with a set of silver combs and brushes. The chamber looked almost like a bride's room.

"I'm to stay in the room next to yours?" she said. She was not afraid of the situation. At least she did not think that she was afraid. She had spent nearly a week aboard ship in the arms of the man and he had not, in any serious way, brought harm to her.

Indeed, he had come to her time after time, a bastion against the terrors of the night. She might well miss the security and warmth of his arms. . . .

Never! she assured herself hastily. Never . . .

He smiled. "The door locks."

She cocked her head, meeting his eyes with a cynical smile. "And will I be able to lock you out, Captain Hawk?"

He did not answer right away, but took her hand within his. His fingers stroked it and his lips touched the back of it in the lightest caress. "Milady, locks lie within the heart or soul, and not upon the material earth."

He released her. "If you'll excuse me, I've things to attend to. I shall join you for supper, but it will be a late repast, I am afraid. Your belongings will be brought to you."

He paused because she was smiling. He arched a brow. "What is it, Lady Kinsdale, that you find so amusing?"

"You."

He stiffened. "Oh? And why is that?"

"Your manner, sir. You have dragged me about like a deer carcass at times, and now you are unerringly polite."

"One never knows—does she?" he said lightly.

Shivers danced along her spine as his eyes met hers. No, she never knew. He kept her off balance at every moment. He made her furious, he made her afraid, and then he would whisper to her or touch her and give her sweet comfort. This week he had become her very life, and every other moment before he had swept upon her from the sea paled and faded before him. But it was true; she never knew. She never, never knew. What would the evening bring? Laughter or fury. Would he treat her like fine porcelain, would he drag her mercilessly into his arms . . . ?

She backed away from him. He said no more, but turned and left her, going back through his own room. The door closed.

Skye sat upon the bed and trembled. How long would she be kept here in this prison? She was not cast into any dungeon, not beset with hardship.

This was far, far worse. . . .

She leaped to her feet and hurried to the door that connected her room to his.

Apparently the door locked both ways, for she had been locked out of his chamber. Curious, she hurried to the hallway door. To her surprise, that door swung open to her touch. She stepped out, and then back in.

What was it of his that he did not want her to find? She wondered. She wandered to the windows and pondered the question.

She was a captive, she thought, in a most curious place.

He did not return for supper that night. Her trunks were delivered to her, all of them, and she saw that nothing of hers had been molested. Her jewels were still among her belongings, along with the finest of her gowns—velvets and brocades, gold-threaded linens, silks and satins, all were there. They were delivered by Mr. Tallingsworth and another man, under the direction of Mr. Soames. Later, Robert Arrowsmith came to see her, informing her that the Hawk would not return, much to his regret. Mr. Soames would see that supper was delivered to her room.

Skye thanked Robert Arrowsmith, keeping her eyes lowered. She was alarmed to discover that it was much to her regret, too, that the Hawk would not be returning.

Robert had been given careful orders, she thought. He walked about the room lighting lanterns until all was aglow. She thanked him quietly, and he left her.

She slept well that night.

In the morning she awoke to the sounds of laughter. Carefully opening her eyes, she gasped in astonishment. The pretty Irish lasses, Tara and Bess, were standing before her, and looking none the worse for wear.

"Bess! Tara!" she cried, pushing up in amazement.

Tara plopped a tray upon her lap. "Aye, Lady Kinsdale!" A shimmer of tears touched her eyes. "We're so grateful to ye, lady! Ye stepped in ta save us, ya know."

Skye blinked. "I didn't save you from anything! We're captives of a pirate. They dragged—"

"They dragged us into the second mate's cabin, and treated us with more kindness than many a mistress I've known," Tara said. Skye stared at the girl. She was very young, barely sixteen, but she spoke with a startling wisdom.

Skye's eyes narrowed. "You were not . . . you were not bothered in any way?"

Tara shook her head. "Not at all. Oh, we were deeply afraid when the commotion began at that other island! I thought that someone would come to burst down the doors! But nothing bad happened to us, and then we were brought here!"

"And it is paradise!" Bess cried.

Nibbling upon a piece of bread, Skye eyed her suspiciously. Her brow arched. "And how do you know that this is . . . paradise?"

Tara stared at Bess and shrugged. "Why, we've seen much of it, milady. Near the dock there's a few fine houses and stores and the like. Any seaman who chooses to do so may build himself a home. There's a freshwater lagoon inland, and deep into the cove there are soft sand beaches protected by rocks and shoals and the water is the most beautiful color you'd ever want to see, milady!"

"Oh?" Skye murmured.

Tara flushed crimson. "There's a man. A Mr. Roundtree, milady. He took us riding there in his little pony trap when we arrived."

"A man?" Skye said. "Oh, Tara. A pirate!"

Tara shrugged, then lowered her head in shame. She looked at Skye then with a sheepish smile. "Milady, there's even a chapel here! And a minister from the Church of England."

Skye swallowed some coffee then offered the tray back to Bessie. "I see. And when Mr. Roundtree was finished showing you this paradise, he took you to church services?"

Bessie flushed radiantly this time. "Well, no, but Lady Kinsdale, he did point out the chapel to us."

"A pirate's priest," Skye muttered. "What next?"

What next indeed?

Having given back her breakfast tray, she pattered to the pitcher and bowl left upon a small stand and washed her face, appreciating the coolness of the water against her flushed skin. While she toweled her skin she decided to test her freedom. She turned back to the girls. "Bessie, would you find my riding habit? I should like to view this—paradise."

Bessie and Tara obligingly set to work. It was fun to have them back. They chattered nonstop, and even if their chatter was all about Mr. Roundtree and his friend, Simon Greene, it brightened her spirits tremendously. That the girls were alive did not surprise her, for she knew that the Silver Hawk was not a bloodthirsty murdering pirate.

That they were happy as larks did startle her, however, for she could not forget those first moments when the Hawk had wrested the ship from One-Eyed Jack, claimed her for himself —and cast the girls to their fate among his men.

The Hawk was, indeed, a most exceptional man.

Dressed handsomely in a riding suit of brown velvet, Skye left Tara and Bessie. Her skirt was full and sweeping with yards of fabric, while the jacket much resembled a man's frock coat. She ran down the stairway, seeing no one, and when she came into the front hall, she heard voices. There was a group of men in the dining room, she realized. She headed for the doorway, but before she could peek in, Mr. Soames appeared, closing the door behind himself. "Good morning, Lady Kinsdale," he said.

"Good morning, Mr. Soames."

"Was your breakfast satisfactory, milady?"

"It was perfect, Mr. Soames." She smiled. There was something about the way that he guarded his master's door that reminded her that this was no English manor. "I would like to ride, Mr. Soames. Would that be possible?"

"But, of course, milady. We wish to afford you whatever pleasures you desire. Come with me, please, I will take you to Señor Rivas. He is the horsemaster here at Bone Cay, and will be your delighted servant."

They left the house by the rear and came instantly to the stables, whereby Skye learned how the Hawk had made it back to the house so quickly the night before.

They entered into the shadows, but Skye quickly saw that there were at least twenty stalls, and that the stables were kept as neatly as the Hawk kept his ship. A tall, lean, dark-haired man stepped forward. He was Señor Rivas, and Mr. Soames quickly left her in his care. Skye realized that she was waiting for someone to leap out and stop her, to tell her that it was an absurd joke and she was insane to think that she might have the freedom to ride. But no one appeared and Señor Rivas drew a dapple gray mare from a stall and saddled and bridled her. He led her from the stables and to a block so that Skye might mount easily, then he stepped away. "Good day, Lady Kinsdale. Enjoy your ride."

His soft Spanish accent again reminded her that this was the New World, and that she was in a most uncivilized part of it at that. Spaniards and Englishmen mixed easily enough here now, for Spaniards and Englishmen had become pirates together, preying upon one another. The wars might be over now, but piracy was not.

Certain pirates were flourishing!

Skye turned the mare toward the docks and rode back the way that she had come. Barefoot children upon the sandy streets greeted her with bobs and curtsies. Small craft lay moored by the docks, too, and fishermen dragged in nets full of fish. Near the Silver Hawk's sleek dark pirate ship Skye paused. Some of the crew remained upon her, repairing rents in sails, unloading cargo, scrubbing down decks, running new lines. She watched for several moments. Men saluted her, but none of them spoke to her, and none questioned her. She turned the mare about at last, and in a fit of aggravation, set her to galloping.

She raced with the wind past the fine brick walls and the pirate's house. The land was nearly flat; sand and scrub fell away beneath her, and then the foliage began to thicken and it seemed that the trail began to rise over a mountainous terrain. At length, she reined in. She heard a rush of water, and she wandered further along a pine path and then came upon a startling and glorious sight. A deep blue pool lay before her with the water splashing over pebbles and rocks, and falling from a cliff high above in dazzling spurts of silver foam.

Skye dismounted from her horse and walked along the water's edge on the clean, hard-packed sand. She did not sit, but stared over the water. Flowers surrounded the small pool with a burst of color, which followed the route where the water trickled into a brook and disappeared into the trees. It was, she thought, a startling paradise.

Standing there, Skye at last looked across the water to the shore beyond. Her hand flew to her mouth and a gasp escaped her. He was there, the Hawk, upon his white horse, watching her from the foliage. He had not been hiding; he merely sat so still atop the snow-white stallion that she had not seen him in the profusion of color.

He lifted a hand to her and urged his mount forward. The white stallion stepped into the cool water without hesitation. The water rose higher and higher, past the stallion's flanks, and still he proceeded without fear. Like his master, the stallion moved purposefully. The water began to fall away, and the magnificent creature rose out from it, bearing the Hawk ever closer to her. She looked at the man. He was wearing a loose white shirt, black breeches, and his boots. His hat lay low over his eyes, the plume dancing, shadowing his eyes and whatever secrets lay within his heart. He looked like a true rogue, reckless, careless, ever the adventurer.

He came toward her, and she did not move, but held her position upon the shore. Still in the shallow water, he dismounted several feet from her. He was silent, watching her. She heard the soft music of the water as it cascaded from the cliffs and danced below in the sunlight. The breeze was light and soft and cool, and just whispered a tropical cadence as it rustled through the flowers and foliage.

For the longest moment, for eternity, Skye felt that her eyes were caught by his, and that his soul laid claim to her own. Locks lay upon the heart, he had told her. Not upon the material earth. Perhaps it was true. Perhaps there was no way to guard herself from the man.

He stepped back suddenly, casting a foot upon a rock, crossing his arms over his chest. "Good morning, milady," he said, his rakish gaze sweeping the length of her and breaking the curious spell. "How do you find this place?"

"A prison, sir, for all its beauty."

"I see," he murmured. "Well, perhaps I have not had the time to show it to you properly. This is a place of most exquisite beauty. And unique, although much of the island of Jamaica is similar."

"Why is this island so unique?"

"Why? Ah, Lady Kinsdale, this island is mine. That in itself makes it unique."

He caught her arm, drawing her forward. "This water is fresh, not brackish. We never want for pure sweet water to drink. See the cliff and the flowers, and the radiant burst of color. This is soft here, while not a mile away lies the tempest of the ocean. Storms rage here, wild and free, embroiling the ocean. Yet the reefs protect us, for only an accomplished sailor would dare to risk my shores!"

He stood beside her, his arm touching hers, and she felt

keenly how very much alone they were, the delicate rhythms of the moving water and the whispering wind their only company beside that of the waiting horses. He smelled of cleanliness, of soap, and of polished leather, and beneath it all, she felt a haunting pulse, the essence of the man, calling upon something within her that had little to do with life as she knew it. In a place like this, it was easy to forget the boundaries she had always known.

Easy to forget innocence.

She pulled away from him, crying out hoarsely. "Why are you always here? Always near me! I came to ride alone, and you are here! I never turn that you are not there, endlessly, always, there! Leave me be! I cannot abide you! Don't be polite, don't be courteous! You are a pirate, sir, and I despise you!"

She flung around in such fury that she startled the mare. Skye set about to leap upon her, but the creature snorted and reared, frightened. Her hooves rose high, scraping the air. Skye watched in fascinated horror as they danced above her.

"Skye! Damn you!"

He was upon her in an instant, bearing her swiftly up and out of the way. The speed and the force with which he moved sent them both flying down to the soft sand.

The mare's hooves struck the earth, just inches away. Sand blew past them. Skye strained to sit up, but he was over her, his eyes on fire, his arms holding her tightly. Muscles clenched and unclenched within his face and throat and shoulders, and he railed against her. "Why, lady, are you always such a fool! You would cast yourself into any danger in order to get away from me! So you would not have me courteous, for I am a pirate still. Then, madame, let me play that pirate, and be damned with it all!"

"Bastard, let me up!" she cried. "You should have—"

"Aye, I should have! I should have given you free to One-Eyed Jack, and I should have let Logan take you and be damned with you then. Blackbeard could have been plagued with you as his prize, and I damned well should have let the horse mar your beauty forever, that you might haunt no other man with your glory and your fire. But you would have a pirate, lady, a rapist, a rogue, and never a gentleman. Then let's have it, for, lady, I am done skirting the thorns of your temper!"

She opened her mouth to scream and gasp in terror, for she had never seen him so angry. No sound left her, for his mouth ground hard upon hers with a punishing power. His tongue ravished her lips and teeth, forcing them apart. She gave way to breathe, and then felt the startling warmth as he filled her with the heat and lightning and intimacy of his kiss. She longed to fight, to twist. She had no power to do so. His fingers curled within hers, his weight bore her down upon the earth, and the passion and the savagery of his assault were stunning. She lay there and felt the ground, and it seemed to tremble beneath her. She heard the soft sound of the water, but it was no melody within her ears, it was a rush, a flow, a cascade. It mingled with the searing flow of her blood. She did not fight . . . she felt his lips, and the hardness of his body. She felt the sun, and the taste of the man, and the tempest of him.

And felt that tempest sweep into her being.

His hands were upon her, stroking the length of her, fire through fabric. They touched the bare flesh of her thighs, and she gasped, unable to breathe, for his lips burned their fiery path against her throat. They fell to the rise of her breasts, and still she did nothing but stare at the sky above her, beset by soft, flowing clouds. She felt the sun, but the sun had lost its heat, for fire burned deep, deep inside of her. It came where his lips seared her, where his fingers stroked her flesh, where the very hardness of his body drove her down to the earth.

His fingers tore upon the ribbons at her bodice, and the fabric gave way. Her breasts spilled above the bone of her corset and his lips found that tender flesh as his hand cupped the mound to the hungry desire of his teeth and tongue. A molten, demanding tug raked upon her nipple, and then it was laved by his tongue. The sweet, blinding sensation ripped into her like cannonshot, firing throughout her body. His beard teased her bare flesh with ever-greater intimacy.

"No!" she cried out suddenly, but he had seized her mouth again. She struggled, but fell limp as languor overcame her.

The very earth continued to tremble. Perhaps it was not the earth. The trembling came from deep within her, a beat, a pulse, a sweet yearning need to know more. . . .

She was not a prisoner. Her hands were free and they were upon his shoulders, and it did not occur to her that he was a pirate, only a man, and a man who had shielded her against all enemies. Muscle rippled beneath her fingers, and in this strange paradise with the water rippling around them and the tropical breeze a tender touch upon them, he was all that she had ever desired in the deep secret shadows of her heart. The scent of him filled her; the force of his passion swept her into netherworlds where nothing mattered at all except for the sleek animal grace of him, and of his touch.

Suddenly he wrenched away. He stumbled to his feet. His back to her, he looked up at the sky. "God damn you!" he raged at her. He jerked around, caught her hands, and pulled her to her feet. "What would you have of me?" he shouted.

She jerked away from his touch, horrified that it was he, and not her own protest, that had put a stop to what they'd been doing. "I wish that you would leave me be! I wish that I could be away from this place!" she cried, wiping her mouth with the back of her hand. She could not erase the feel of his lips. She felt his eyes upon her, burning still, and she realized that her bodice was askew, her breasts bared and spilling forth. She blushed deeply, but she did not lower her head and fought for whatever control she possessed. Still her hands trembled as she brought her fingers to her laces. He tore his eyes from her breasts and looked directly into hers. "You will be gone soon enough, I swear it!" he told her heatedly.

She turned from him, running toward the offending mare. The frightened beast skittered away. An oath burst forth from him. "Don't ever run from me, you little fool. You would never manage it, and in each of your attempts you are hurt or cause havoc!" He caught hold of the mare's reins and brought her around. He reached for Skye's waist.

"I can manage, leave me be!"

"You cannot manage."

He set her firmly upon the horse. She picked up the reins

and stared down at him. "I think, Captain Silver Hawk, that you are running from me."

His eyes narrowed. "Lady Kinsdale, I will never run from you, I swear it. I've tried to leave you be, as you so ardently wish. And even when you singe my soul with the heat of your flame, I do back away. Don't try me again, lady. In this battle I tell you, the gentleman is surely giving way to the rogue within me, and if next tempted, the pirate will prevail."

Hot shivers ran down her spine. She jerked the reins from his hand, nudged the mare, and turned to race away from the lagoon, and from the haunting, bitter laughter that played upon the air in her wake.

Skye returned to the stable in a tempestuous mood. She left the mare to Señor Rivas, and walked hurriedly into the house, ignoring Mr. Soames, who came to greet her by the stairway. She raced up to her room and slammed the door hard, then sent the bolts hammering into place at that door, and at the door that connected her room to the Hawk's. She paced the room in deep agitation, then glanced at the connecting door again. The lock wouldn't mean a thing to him if he wanted to reach her. A lock? Why the man fought battles upon the sea and had seized her very ship! What was a lock to such a man. . . .

A lock lay within the heart, or within the soul, or so he had told her. No man could hold the key to such a lock, unless it was given to him, and freely so. And this the Silver Hawk seemed to know, and know well.

She stiffened suddenly, aware of a door slamming below. The Hawk had returned, too, and it seemed that he, too, was not in the best of humor. His shouting could be heard throughout the house.

Skye raced to the hallway door. She could not make out the crisp words, only that it was his voice, deep and vibrant, commanding. She heard his footsteps upon the stairs, and then the door to his room opened and slammed, and she stood dead still, her hand cast to her throat. He would come to her then. He would ignore the door that lay between them, he would come to her in anger, seize her. . . .

Seconds ticked by. The door slammed again. The Hawk was gone. She breathed a deep sigh of relief and cast herself across the bed, then stared up at the canopy. Surely, he had business to attend to. And he had broken away, not she. . . .

She flamed with humiliation. He wanted her gone. This would not go on much longer. Perhaps, say what he might, he had his own sense of honor. She was his cousin's betrothed, despite the fact that that cousin be distant, and born on the right side of the sheets.

Betrothed . . .

She had no wish to meet such a man! Not when her lips remained swollen and her flesh burned from another's touch.

She sat up, pressing her temple between her palms. God help her, she did not know herself anymore.

She leaped from the bed and threw open the door to the hallway. Mr. Soames had said that he was there to serve her. Well, she wanted to be served. "Mr. Soames!" she called down the stairs.

"Milady!" Within seconds the elderly gentleman had climbed the stairs to reach her. "I'd have some brandy, if I may, please," she told him.

He arched a brow in surprise that she should ask for spirits, but quickly lowered his brow again. "Yes, milady," he said, and was quickly gone. She paced again as she awaited his return. He arrived with brandy and a single crystal glass upon a silver tray. She thanked him, and waited for him to leave.

"The Hawk will have supper with you, milady. He will knock for you at eight."

"Will he? You must tell the Hawk that I do not care to have supper with him," she said.

"But, milady—"

"You have heard me, Mr. Soames, and you have said that you will attend to my every wish. Well, I wish you to tell your master that I will not have supper with him."

"Yes, milady."

With no further display of emotion or opinion, Mr. Soames bowed to her and left her side.

She liked the brandy. It soothed her spirits and eased the tempest in her soul. She stared broodingly out the windows at the startling blue beauty of the island. Bone Cay. Such an ugly name for such a striking piece of paradise.

The day grew warm and she opened the windows to feel the breezes. She cast aside her jacket and tried to cease her endless pacing. What would his reaction be? He had come back in a state of anger to demand that she attend him for a meal. Would he accept her refusal with a casual shrug?

The afternoon was waning, but her spirits slowly rose and her confidence returned in direct proportion to the brandy she consumed. He would not break the lock; it would be against his very peculiar code of honor.

Feeling hot and sticky as sunset neared, she called down to Mr. Soames again. He ran back up the stairs. She asked him sweetly if she might have a bath. He stared at her blankly, and she knew that sending a half-dozen servants with a tub and water would be a hardship on him as head of the household staff at this particular hour of the afternoon. She wasn't terribly sorry. She didn't care to be there. If they didn't care to have her there, then they would hurry to see that she left. The Hawk had said that she would be gone soon. He had said it with a vengeance. Surely, Mr. Soames would help see to it that he kept that vow!

"I should like it very quickly, Mr. Soames!" she told him as innocently as she could.

"I shall do my best, milady."

"Perhaps you could send my own young lasses along, and spare your own staff."

"That won't be possible, milady."

"And why is that?"

"Well, they're at the fish market, milady."

"The fish market?"

"They wished to stay busy, and you had given them no word that you might require their service. . . ." His words trailed away. He had given the girls leave to go, she realized. She smiled. She had no rights here—except those given her by the Hawk, and it was the Hawk she longed to annoy.

"Whenever you can manage, Mr. Soames," she said very sweetly.

She was quickly obliged. Very little time had passed before

Señor Rivas and one of his young grooms dragged up a brass tub, and then a stream of servants—household and estate men, so it seemed—arrived with water. She thanked them all charmingly. Mr. Soames himself came with towels and rose scents and a thick sponge. "If you require anything else . . ."

"Not a thing. Just my privacy," she said.

"Yes, milady." He bowed his way out. Skye stared after the closed door, suddenly sorry for making the elderly man miserable. His master had already screamed at him, and now poor Soames had the sorry task of telling the Hawk that his female prisoner had no intention of obeying his commands for the evening.

Her guilt faded away as she cast her clothing off in disarray. She had consumed way too much brandy, and she knew it. She didn't care. It had eased her torment, it had made her almost cheerful. Content and relaxed, she crawled into the tub. She coiled her hair on top of her head and lazily rubbed the sweet-smelling rose-scented soap over her body. She smiled. There were benefits to being the hostage of a prosperous pirate. He did supply the finest in luxury accommodations, fresh from Paris.

She set aside her sponge and soap and leaned back, basking in the warmth of the water. With one eye barely open, she saw that the sun was setting, sinking into the horizon beyond the windows. The colors of the coming night were breathtaking, strident red, shocking gold, so very bright, so very deep.

She allowed her eyes to close. It was so easy, so gentle, to be there. The water was warm, near tender in its touch. Her head was so delightfully at ease. . . .

She was aware of shadows upon the rippling bathwater, then she was aware of nothing at all. Then she thought that she dreamed, for she heard a fierce pounding, and it was as if her name was being called from a distance.

There was a sound of thunder, stark, strident. Skye bolted up just in time to hear wood crackle and split, and to hear the Hawk slamming into her room, the door falling flat to the floor. He stared at her, his hands on his hips, his eyes on fire.

She parted her lips and tried to speak. He sounded as if he was strangling.

"My God! I thought you were dead!"

"You said I might lock the door—"

"Did you hear me! I thought that you were dead! I knocked, I shouted!"

"I—"

She slipped within the tub, nearly going under. He exploded with a furious oath, and she heard a new thunder. It was the sound of his footsteps, falling upon the floor. Then his hands were upon her, wrenching her up, and into his arms.

She soaked him. Water sluiced from her body to his own, and dripped onto the floor. He paid no attention to it, but stared at her sharply. Alarm swept through her, as shocking as his hands upon her.

She struggled against him. "I did not care to come to dinner!" she cried.

"But I commanded that you should."

"I do not dine with thieves, with gentlemen rogues. Your manner does not save you from the truth! I will not sit to eat with a courteous—"

"Sea slime? Gentleman rogue, milady?" his eyes, flashing fire, fell upon hers. "This night, lady, I am no gentleman rogue, and a rogue at the very least. You wish a pirate, you expect one—"

"Put me down, Hawk!" she cried, her panic growing. The soft brandy blur was deserting her. She was naked, and his touch upon her bare flesh was an excruciating sensation. She was in his arms, and he was vibrant, burning with the heat of anger. He was a flame that seemed to consume everything, her will, her heart. She had to escape him, to stand outside that flame. She did not so deeply fear his anger; she feared the tempest within him that so seduced and beguiled her.

She pressed fully against his silk-clad chest. "Now! I demand it!"

He shook his head slowly. "You do not like to be treated with courtesy, not by a pirate, so you say. Well, take heed then, lady. This night you have the pirate, the demon, the monster, the rogue. And trust well, lady, that this night, the rogue will have you. If you have thought to cry for mercy, now is the time to do so, milady."

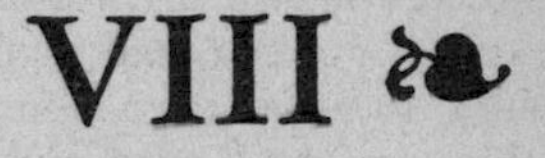

VIII

"Perhaps we *should* dine first," Skye said softly.

He stared down upon her. "What?" he shouted in exasperation.

"Dinner!" she whispered desperately, meeting his silver gaze. "You wished to have dinner. It's . . . it's all right with me."

He was still stiff with anger, as hot and radiant as a winter's fire, but as hard as stone. "You're drunk," he said.

"What?"

"You're drunk!"

"I am not! Ladies of good breeding do not get drunk, sir!"

"I shudder to suggest, Lady Kinsdale, that your breeding is anything but the absolute best, so I must beg to differ upon the principle itself. You are drunk."

"Tipsy, perhaps."

"Sodden."

"Sir, you drive me to drink," she said woefully. Her fingers curled about his neck as she held him tightly rather than fall.

"I drive you to drink, lady! My God, but a sane man would

have left you upon the sea!" He cast her down suddenly and with such vehemence that she gasped, for she was certain that her bones would shatter upon the floor. They did not, for he had come to the bed and cast her upon the soft down mattress. Like silver daggers, his eyes flashed upon her. "I drive you to drink? Lady, you would drive the very saints to despair!"

He whirled around and she clutched nervously at the bedclothes, dragging them around her. He seemed as explosive as a keg of powder, and though she had a reprieve, she wondered what his next action would be.

He wrenched open one of her trunks with a vengeance. Silks and satins and velvets went flying about. Then he tossed a soft green satin garment her way. She reached for the fabric as his footsteps cracked and thundered upon the floor and on the shattered door. "Dinner, milady, is already served."

For the longest time she lay there, her hand at her heart, feeling the frantic beat. He was gone again. But not far. He stood away from her, through a doorway that could no longer be closed or locked. It had never meant anything anyway. He had always known and she was discovering that the barriers lay within herself.

And within him.

Skye lay very still. Night was coming quickly. It would not matter, she realized. If darkness fell, he would come back to light up the night for her, whether she did or did not rise. If she stayed just as she was, she would need have no fear. He would not touch her, nor would he let blackness descend upon her.

She rose quickly, glancing nervously to the open doorway. She could not see him. She scrambled into the gown he had left her, a satin dinner gown with a laced bodice, high collar, and sweeping train. She came to the dresser, observed her pale image within the mirror, and mechanically picked up the silver brush he had provided and swept it through her hair. The golden locks fell like waves of sun and fire upon her shoulders. The high collar of the gown complemented the deep cleft of the bodice. Her eyes were grave then, for the tender embrace of the brandy was fast fading away, and it seemed that very much lay at stake that night.

Impulsively she turned from the dresser to dig about in her trunks. She found a delicate gold necklace with an emerald pendant that was surrounded by a sunburst of diamonds. She hooked it about her neck and it fell far below her throat to touch the valley of her breasts.

She walked over to the open doorway and paused there, watching him.

He stood by the windows, and seemed as pensive as she. The drapes were open, the breeze blew in. He looked the gentleman then, the striking young gentleman, more lordly than any man she knew, lost in thought, tall and undaunted against the coming night. He held a silver goblet in one hand. Across the room, Skye saw that the small dining table was laden with a meal, with silver flatware and fine plates upon a white cloth. Candles were burning, casting a gentle glow over the table.

"Lord Cameron comes for you any day now," Hawk said without turning to her.

"How can he?" she murmured. "How can he even know that I am here?"

"I sent your ship, the *Silver Messenger,* close in to Cape Hatteras as we traveled south. Her signalman sent messages to a merchantman. The *Silver Messenger* came here this afternoon, and my man assures me that his messages were received, and answers were sent."

"That is . . . good to hear," she said softly.

He turned around suddenly and his eyes swept over her from head to toe. They lingered upon the emerald that lay between her breasts, but he did not mention it. He bowed to her. "Milady, you wished to dine?" He indicated the table. She walked to it and he was quickly behind her, pulling out her chair. He poured her wine in a goblet before taking his own seat. The candles glowed softly between them, flickering occasionally, for the table lay before the open window, and both the colors of the sunset and the coolness of the twilight breeze rushed softly in upon them.

"Shall I serve you, milady?" he asked.

Skye nodded, sitting back, her fingers curving over the arms of her chair. She watched his dark head and the fine, brooding line of his features as he dished out food from the servers. She wasn't sure what touched her plate, for she studied him so earnestly. He caught her gaze at last. She flushed and picked up her wineglass. But she continued to study him.

"What? What now, milady?" he demanded acidly.

And she smiled very slowly. "What manner of pirate are you, sir? I sit before you unmolested. In my jewels." She leaned forward, fingering the emerald. "It's worth a small fortune, Sir Silver Hawk. Of that, I am sure you are aware."

"Perhaps, lady, I will receive a small fortune for your safe return."

"Perhaps." she murmured, but her smile remained. He swore softly and tossed down his serving implements. "Lady, I tell you, I am at the end of my resources. I am past being driven to mere drink, and I hunger for far more than dinner."

She picked up her fork and idly touched her food. She was scarcely hungry herself. She tasted some delicious fish, and steamed fresh carrots and potatoes and sweet toasted bananas. She could eat very little. Nor did he pay much attention to his food. He watched her, and a deep, dark tension remained with him. His brow continued to knit and a scowl played upon his lip beneath his mustache.

"He will come here?" she said. "Lord Cameron?"

"Aye."

"He will feel safe?"

"He will know himself safe."

She shoved about a piece of fish with her fork. He leaned toward her. "What is it, milady?" he snapped. "Who do you think you are, what sweet nobility sets you so confidently upon this golden crest of disdain you would cast down upon others? I am a pirate, yes, but you scorn a member of your own society, a man who is willing to sail a tempestuous sea for an unwilling bride?"

Her temper rose and her first impulse was to slap him. She smiled instead, holding her silver goblet, tracing its rim with her fingers. "I am my own mistress, sir, and that is all."

He sat back, his eyes narrowing. "And what precisely does that mean, lady?"

"I—I am graced with my own mind, sir. My mother"—she

hesitated just briefly, swallowing—"my mother died when I was young, and I quickly ran my father's affairs. He sent me to school in London, and neglected to tell me about a promise given at my birth!"

"So the promise is not your concern."

"No."

"You do not choose to honor your father?"

"Not in this." She set her wine down and spoke to him earnestly. "One would think, sir, that daughters were created as slaves, to be cast to the highest bidder."

His eyes were smoke, concealing his thoughts. "Perhaps he cares for the security of your future."

She lowered her head suddenly. "He knows so little about me."

"About your fear of the dark?"

Her head jerked up like a marionette's. "I don't care to discuss any of this with you."

"Why not? Perhaps I can help."

"Help!"

He shrugged, sipping more wine. "He is a cousin, distant at that, proper, stoic, and all those gentlemanly things. I do know something of him. He is sailing to retrieve you. He is no ogre."

She smiled, touching her dangling pendant. "You are the ogre, right?"

"Don't test me," he warned her sternly.

"I have tested you time and again," she said softly. "You have proven yourself, sir."

"Have I? Lady, please, my mettle is in shatters. I promise you this, if I hold you again, I'll leave no questions in your mind as to my true nature."

She did not reply, but continued to smile. He reached over suddenly, grasping her wine goblet. He set it down upon the table with a small clunk. She arched a brow to him.

"I think you've had enough. How do you feel?"

"I feel very well. I dozed in the tub merely because of its comfort, and though I did consume a great deal of brandy, I did it throughout a very long day."

"Oh. Is that so?"

"It is."

He watched her for a long moment, his hands folded upon the table. "You are well and sober now?"

"I am, sir."

He stood and caught her hands, pulling her slowly up from the table and into his arms. She should resist. Something languorous stole over her with the gentle touch of the breeze. Draperies fluttered and the soft fragrance of the tropic night whirled around them. The moon had risen as the fiery colors of sunset gave way to shadow, and then darkness. Candleglow was soft, and gentle as the ethereal beams from the moon falling down upon them.

"Run!" he told her softly. "Run away, and embrace the darkness, for you enter here into greater peril." He clutched her hand and brought it to his chest, against his heart. "Feel the beat, lady, feel the pulse. Suffer the tempest, for I have been like a man long damned. Don't take comfort in my presence, and don't trust in my justice or honor, for by my justice you would lie with me now, and as I have warned you, what honor a rogue possesses ever dims within my heart. Run from me now, lady. And swiftly."

It was fair warning, and well she knew it. Her palm and fingers lay over an erratic pulse, and a wall of vibrant, living heat. They pressed so close together that a fever danced throughout her and cast her into a field of sweet confusion far greater than any spirit could bring. She wanted him. Shameful, horrid, and illicit as it might be, she wanted him. That such feelings should rage within her heart left her aware that she could be no true lady, but in the night breeze, she could not care. This world was real, and he was a beacon, shining ever more brightly to her tempest-tossed soul. Codes and society could not matter here, all that had meaning were the earth and sky, the breeze, the primal power of the man.

She parted her lips to whisper, but knew not what she would say. Rescue came for her any day now, blessed rescue to her home, to a land of safety. To a lord, a man of the peerage, the betrothed who would give her the proper place in society, a gracious home, wealth, servants, security, all that she could desire.

Her security lay here, she thought. And the wealth to be found in the arms of such a man were all the riches she might come to desire.

"Go! Go now, I warn you!" he growled to her.

She pulled away. She stared at him, thinking there were so many things that she would say to him, but none of them were things that words could convey. If she stayed, she would be damned. She turned and fled through the doorway, then paused, gasping, the tempo of her heart staccato, the very breath and soul of her in torment.

She did not think anew. She did not reason, nor pause to think that the morning light might bring regrets. She came back to the doorway and looked in once more.

He had come back to the window. He stood there, a tall and silent man, a powerful shadow in black silk shirt and breeches and boots, formidable and striking against the glow of the moon. She must have made some small sound, or else he sensed her there, that she had so swiftly returned. He came about, staring at her. She could not see his eyes, his features. She cried softly and raced toward him on her bare feet. She cast herself against him, and his arms swept around her with a staggering hunger. His lips found hers.

Captured there in the moonlight in his arms, she dared to kiss him in return. His tongue tempestuously seared her lips to plunder her mouth. She welcomed it, and daringly tasted, met, and matched his forays with her own. A sweet-honeyed surge burst forth from within her, swirling within her belly, rushing to fill her limbs. She sought to touch his hair, to tease it at his nape, to feel the power of his shoulders and arms, to come ever closer.

She gasped when his lips lifted from hers, and she stared up at him, framed as they were in the moonglow, in the windows opened to the night. He stared at her the longest time, and his ragged whisper rode hauntingly from his flesh. "You cannot run anymore," he said.

"No," she whispered, and her lashes did not flutter, nor did her eyes fall from his. His hands were upon her shoulders. Her lips parted in a soft gasp as he tore upon the fabric there and her gown swirled to a very soft heap of silk upon the ground. And still he stared at her, for the moonglow danced eloquently upon her body, outlining the firm fullness of her breasts and defining the dusky rouge peaks, touching shadow at the slender ribbon of her waist, glowing full on the flare of her hips. The moon seemed a master of temptation in itself, finding shadow again in the haunting juncture of her thighs.

A deep, guttural cry came from him, startling her, causing her to tremble. Then his hands were upon her again, pulling her close. She felt the fever of his mouth upon hers once more, and clung to him, stunned by this new ferocity of passion, yet willing to ride the soaring force of it. She met his lips again and again. He sought her mouth and tongue over and over, breaking away, finding her warmth once again. His hands began a bold foray upon her. As their lips met in searing fire, he stroked her shoulder and her breast, rounded her naked hip. His fingers grazed her belly and drew with startling purpose to the golden nest between her thighs.

She flinched, startled, but he drew her closer. He whispered against her lips as he explored her further. She gasped and shuddered, so weak that she fell against him as his touch surged intimately inside of her.

"I cannot, will not, let you go," he muttered.

She did not wish to be let go. She burrowed her head against him and she was swiftly swept off her feet and carried to his massive bed. Lying there without him, she was briefly cold, but he quickly returned to cover her with his warmth. His lips seared her all anew. He touched her with shattering liquid heat in intimate places, bringing gasps to her lips as he possessed her breasts with his touch and teeth and tongue, covering her belly with the ardent sweep of his mouth. The liquid fire was outside of her, and then inside of her. Sensation came to rule the night, for each new touch was shocking and evocative beyond measure, and she was barely able to register the one before the next began.

She knew that he was a practiced lover, and that did not matter to her. Not then. She knew, too, that a woman was seldom so carefully cherished with both tempest and tenderness when initiated into the realm of senses. He was with her because he had desired her, and tonight he could let hunger rage, for he had shown her long ago that he cared for her fears, and for her soul.

He moved from her, and she realized that he hovered over her, seeking out her eyes, his own ablaze with tension. Lightly he touched her breast, keeping his eyes upon her. He drew his fingers low over her ribs against her abdomen, down to her thighs. Her lashes fluttered. "No," he told her softly, and she lifted her gaze to his again as he invaded her more intimately. She drew her limbs together as the flame touched her features, but her body surged against his touch of its sweet desire and he laughed with sheer pleasure and triumph and his lips seized upon hers. "Moonglow," he told her. "Thank God, lady, that you crave the light, for I hunger for the very sight of you, and would die tonight for this touch!" His lips covered hers. In tempest and abandon they traveled to her breast. To her belly, ever downward. Brazenly he touched her. She cried out loud in stunned protest, writhing against him, reaching for him to draw him against her. He left her, stripping away his garments. And then it was he who was covered in the moonlight, and she was dizzy with anticipation, warmed by the beautiful bronze glow of his shoulders, frightened by the masculine force of him.

He did not let her know fear. He teased her no longer, but fell upon her with purpose, parting her thighs to his desire, cradling her gently into his arms.

The pain was astounding, wrenching her from the web of sweet desire that had wound within her. She cried out, she bit into his shoulders, she slammed against him and shrilled away in fury, tears stinging her eyes. He ignored her, holding her. Moving, moving against her. Thrusting harder and harder and tearing into her. "Pirate, bastard, rogue!" she choked out.

"Sea slime," he responded with a tender understanding, and she nearly laughed, and then the sweetness overrode the pain and she was astounded anew at herself. She had never known a hunger so great; she had never wanted so desperately. Her form shifted and writhed and arched on his own. She stroked his flesh and felt the constriction and heave of his muscle, and the ever-greater fury of his force. She swirled with it, she soared, she reached. Then it seemed as if the entire world exploded deep inside of her and that nothing had ever been so rapturous in her life. She was wrapped in clouds, cocooned among moonglow and stars, seared by the sun. Darkness nearly claimed her, the breath left her. She died, she thought. She touched the sun, and so she died.

She did not die. She closed her eyes perhaps, passed out, perhaps. But she did not die. She shuddered again and again and hot rapture tore through her. She opened her eyes to discover that she had not even left the earth, but lay within the bed still, drenched and slick, entwined with the Hawk. He lay atop her still, and quietly within her. He had not ravished or raped her or used violence against her in any way. She had come to him.

He pulled away from her, coming up on an elbow, smoothing the tangle of her hair away from her face. She wished suddenly that she did not so strenuously fear the dark, for she would have liked to hide her face in the shadows then.

"Regrets?" he asked her.

"No." Well, perhaps one, for now that ecstasy had quietly given way, she was sore and amazed at her own lack not only of virtue, but of anything resembling restraint.

"I warned you," he reminded her.

She nodded uneasily. She turned against him, burrowing against his chest. "Please, leave it be."

He touched her gently, letting her lie against him. She suddenly imagined that love was a grand and magical thing, for it was, perhaps, even more wonderful to lie against him so, to feel the ripple of his muscles and his soft touch upon her as he held her close. This seemed an even greater intimacy.

As did his easy stroke. He did not touch her then to enflame her, but just to idly feel her flesh and soothe her. He rested his bearded chin atop her head and sighed deeply.

"What shall you do now?" he asked her.

She shook her head against him, not knowing what he meant.

"Well, my love, you go to your betrothed. What shall you tell him?"

"The truth."

"The truth?"

Angry, Skye pushed away. "Tonight . . . this is not the truth. The truth has always been there, as you have been so quick to tell me! I will not marry him. I will not honor some silly pact made between his father and mine. He does not wish to marry me, either!"

"But he comes for you."

"What is this!" she charged him, pulling away, suddenly longing for her clothing and eager to be far, far away from him. Something terribly momentous had happened in her life. He had taken from her all that a woman had of her own to truly give, not so much the physical side of innocence, but the very heart of it, too. "Is your cousin your best friend that you must care for his concerns so deeply?"

"We are not friends at all. We are enemies. We respect one another and leave room for negotiation, but he would slay me in the open waters, and I would slay him in turn."

"Then leave me at peace! I shall deal with my own life." She tried to pull away in a sudden fury. He leaped atop her, smiling his buccaneer's leering smile, and pinning her beneath him. "Get off!" she insisted, flailing against him.

"No, lady, I cannot! And I gave fair warning. Forget the future, and answer to the sweet whispers of the night!"

"Nay—"

But her protest meant nothing. His lips seared hers, his body burned against her. She felt the hard swell of his sex and she gasped and strained to free herself, but he sank into her, filling her, and making her one with him. Tempest could not rise so swiftly again! she thought, and yet it did. Soaring, sweet, thundering, savage, it rose like a summer storm, brought her to a sweet and shattering climax, and cast her down softly and incredibly to earth once again. He gave her no quarter and no mercy, now that he possessed her. Still holding her, still entwined with her, he rose above her.

"Say the word, and I will rescue you from the trap of your betrothal. I will say that my hostage is not for sale, but my property and mine alone, now and forever."

She gasped, stunned by the ferocity of his words.

"I—I cannot!" she cried. She could not! She had discovered ecstasy here, and perhaps she had discovered a man of startling temper and curious honor upon the savage seas, but she could not stay here! Her mind would work but little then, but she knew that she could not be his mistress. She could not stay here.

"So you would marry Lord Cameron!"

"No! Yes, I mean that I could not stay here!" She could not, ever. Not while her father lived. As angry as she might become with him for charting her life, she adored him. He was all that she had in the world. All who really loved her, who needed her. Just as she needed him, and his love.

His eyes were fierce, they were silver, they probed her, they went past her nakedness and tore into her soul. "You little hypocrite!" he told her. "You deny the man, but you would have his position! You would dine at the governor's mansion and walk the streets in splendor. You cannot manage without your silks and velvets and jewels—"

"How dare you judge me!" she screamed, tearing at his chest. Suddenly she longed to escape him with such a fever she could scarce bear it. "It is not Lord Cameron! I tell you that I will not marry him—"

"You will not?" he taunted.

"I do not owe you an explanation!"

He wrenched back, still angry, and she wondered at the force of his explosion. He fell down beside her and she quickly sat up, searching for her gown to wrap around her nakedness. His eyes were scathing, telling her that she was a fool to cover herself from his eyes, ever again. She was furious with him, and furious with herself. Holding the covers tightly, she determined to get away from him. She leaped to her feet. He rose, too, not coming after her, just watching her with his feet firm upon the floor, his arms crossed over his chest.

"And where are you going now, milady? I told you that you could not run any longer."

"I am going back to my own bed."

"Ah, but it is my bed, too, milady!"

"Nevertheless, you are not in it!"

She strutted through the doorway, regally clad in his bed covering. But she had scarce crossed the threshold into her own room when darkness descended upon her. The lanterns were not lit; he had not come there, for she had been with him.

God! How she despised the weakness! She claimed herself to be her own mistress, but the suffocating fear of the darkness came at her with talons to tear against her every time.

She cast her hands over her face, shuddering. Then she felt his hands upon her, gentle and tender. He lifted her, covers and all, into his arms, and strode with her back to his room, to where the candles flickered softly, and the moonglow bathed them once again.

"When I am with you," he promised her softly, "I swear that there will always be light."

She slept then, in his bed, in his arms. Her last waking thought was that he had become her light, a searing sun ray, ever fierce against the darkness, ever strong against the night.

In the morning he was gone.

Skye slept very late, and when she awoke, she was alone. No one came to disturb her.

She left his bed to return to her own room, stepping upon the splintered door. Daylight did bring thoughts of the night crashing down upon her, but in truth she did not regret what had happened between them, although the consequences of what might come of it seemed to lie heavily upon her. Though she lived on the hope that she would elude her betrothal, breech of promise would not be smiled upon by many, and her father's position could well be jeopardized. No one could force her into anything.

But neither could she let her father be ruined.

Then, of course, there was the danger of the man himself. Were she to conceive a child . . .

She would not, she told herself hastily. She had no good reason to believe that she would not, but thought that God could not leave her with a pirate's child.

She had washed and dressed when this thought struck her. She cast herself back upon the bed and imagined that she held the Hawk's infant and watched while the pirate captain was led to the gallows on a spring day and hanged by the neck until dead. She shivered uncontrollably, hugging her arms about herself. He could die. He would die if he persisted in his dangerous calling!

There was a tap upon the door. She murmured uneasily, "Come in!" and Mr. Soames appeared with a breakfast tray. He was wonderfully impassive. He didn't even gaze toward the broken door. "The captain says if you've a mind, Lady Kinsdale, you might wish to meet him down by the lagoon this afternoon. He has business this morning, but will come soon after. He wants you to know that it will be his deepest pleasure."

"His deepest pleasure? Or his command?" she asked lightly.

"Milady, I am but a messenger—"

"Of course. Well, then, thank you, Mr. Soames, for the message."

He nodded uncomfortably and set her tray down upon the card table.

She didn't bother to ask about Tara and Bessie. They seemed to be making their own way upon the island, and making it well enough.

And besides, she reflected, with heart fluttering madly, she had every intention of riding out that afternoon.

She did. She waited until the sun rode high in the noon sky, then she went back to Señor Rivas. He saddled the same gray mare for her, and she rode slowly toward the lagoon.

When she arrived, he was not there. She looked anxiously about and saw his snow-white stallion grazing up the slope past the far bank. The water skipped and danced from the cliff, dazzling beneath the sun.

Skye dismounted and neared the water's edge. She let the horse nibble upon the plants there and sat upon the sandy slope. She edged nearer, feeling the water. It was cool and fresh.

Then her eyes rose slowly, for she discovered the Hawk's whereabouts.

He rose up out of the water. It sluiced from his body, the droplets catching the sun and burning like studded diamonds in the heat of the day. He was naked and bronzed from head to toe and he approached her with swift determination.

She came to her feet. She meant to speak, to say something. No words came to her.

She thought about the sun, high overhead. She thought about the breeze, and the gurgling waters of the brook. She could not shed her clothing here. She could not lie here, in the sand, in the soft grass.

He came closer to her. She could not speak, nor did he bother her with words. He slipped her riding coat from her shoulders, letting it fall to the grass. Then he spun her about, adroitly slipping each of the tiny hooks that lined her back. His fingers slid beneath fabric to touch her bare shoulders, and her gown fell low over her breasts and down to her waist. He lowered his head, and his lips and beard, wet and cool, touched her flesh. His tongue rimmed her shoulder and she started to shiver.

"I . . . I cannot!" she stuttered.

He spun her around. "You can," he assured her, and found her lips. His fingers fell upon the ties to her corset as his lips ravished and seduced. Her breasts were suddenly bare, and the sun warmed them. She was sinking down into a pile of her own clothing, and his weight and warmth were covering her.

He did not take her then. He touched and teased her and watched her as he slipped away her shoes and hose. She felt the fresh air touch her and she shivered and he drew her to him. They rolled upon the soft grasses, and he smiled as he caught her above him. "This is my domain, Lady Kinsdale, and none may enter here to come between us."

She smiled slowly to herself, enchanted by the beauty of the lagoon and by his whisper. There was some sweet madness there, and the excitement of it filled her. She could not be here, not so, not with him. She could not play in such a primitive Eden, laugh to the music of the bubbling water, dare to feel the breeze upon her flesh.

Her hair tumbled down upon him, covering his shoulders. His laughter faded and his eyes grew dark, and then he drew her head down to his, and his kiss entered and filled her, touching upon the newly lit flames of passion that stirred in her heart and body. His touch raked over her. He lifted her atop himself and she cried out in startled surprise as they came together instantly as one.

Sun touched her, whispers touched her, the trees and leaves shuddered over her. She felt the earth beneath her and the ragged breath of the man and her own reckless and abandoned cries as a sweet rush of satiation burst upon her. She felt the sand at her back and the tickle of the grass and the hard brush of male hair against her belly and thighs.

She felt his arms.

"Perhaps I will not let you go," he warned her. "Perhaps I shall do with you always what I will."

"You cannot," she told him firmly.

" 'Tis my domain," he reminded her. He lifted her high into his arms and she cried out in protest. "Wait! Where are you going! You cannot think to walk about like this!"

"I am not going far," he said, striding out into the water.

"Put me down."

"I will do as I choose with you, remember?"

She tossed her head back. "You will not do as you will with me, Captain Hawk. I will not allow it!"

"Oh?" He smiled with a sensual curl taking hold of the corner of his lip. His pirate's silver gaze sizzled. He dropped her flat, and she pitched into the cool fresh water.

She burst up, sputtering and protesting, and laughing. She tried to drag him under but she hadn't the strength. He caught her and brought them both beneath the cascade of the cliff, and then, as the cool water raged over them, he kissed her. A fervent flame beat against the cold. She felt his hands upon her breasts, between her legs, and she clung to him, stretching her fingers with sure fascination over his shoulders and back and hesitantly down to his buttocks.

It was madness. . . .

She cast her head back and his kiss consumed her throat until his mouth moved to close over her breast. He swept her beneath him and they came near shore, and as the cool water rushed over them, he made love to her there.

She felt the earth more keenly, never knew a touch so acutely, never imagined that a woman could know a man so completely. When she lay at rest, she had never known such a peace. He held her still, and the sun beat down upon the two of them and the water rushed over their limbs.

The sun created dazzling currents in the lagoon, and Skye narrowed her eyes against them. She spun a daydream as he held her, idly stroking her arm. Her father would come to this place. The Hawk would cast aside his buccaneer's ways and a pardon would be found. This madness could go on and on, forever. She could feel his strength and delight in his husky laughter and the fierce demand of his passion and desires. . . .

"What are you thinking?" he asked her.

"That you are a pirate," she said softly.

He stiffened. "A rogue—in a rogue's domain, milady."

"The seas will be cleared one day!" she said fervently.

He shifted, rising above her upon the sand. "That, milady, will take time. When your pious Lord Cameron comes for you, you must not travel the seas again. Do you understand me?"

Her eyes widened. "If I must do so—"

"There is no reason for you to do so."

"I am my own mistress!" she reminded him passionately.

"Are you? You forget yourself, lady. If I chose, I could keep you here. No man could storm this fortress. No pirate would think to come against me, and it would take the combined forces of several royal navies to destroy here. If I commanded it, you would stay."

She lay beneath him, trembling. If he chose, he could do so. She touched his cheek and whispered softly, "I am here because I knew no force from you. No man can force desire, sir. You said yourself that the lock upon the door did not matter, for locks lay within the heart. You could break the door, but you knocked gently upon my heart, and entered through there by the gentle care you gave me."

"And tell me, lady, shall I remain there, when you have gone on to a husband."

He mocked her. She bared her soul to him, and offered her heart. And he mocked her.

She pressed against him, maddened that he had the strength to hold her to his will. She tilted her chin proudly, but again, could not forget the hard naked feel of him against her. "I am my own mistress, sir."

"I shall miss you when you are gone, with all of my heart, Lady Skye. Tell me, will you miss me?"

"I think—quite highly of you," she said primly.

He laughed, and nuzzled her earlobe with a fascinating tenderness. "For sea slime, that is."

She met his eyes, silver with his laughter, touched by the charming rogue's curl of his lip. His arms were so strong about her. I have fallen in love with you! she thought with the deepest dismay and despair.

"You don't—you don't need to be sea slime forever," she told him.

"Alas," he said huskily, "there you are wrong, my dear, dear Lady Skye. The die has been cast."

Suddenly the natural quiet of the lagoon was split asunder. The sound of a single cannon rent the air.

The Hawk looked up. Some fiery light touched his eyes, and when he stared at her again, she thought that he did not know her at all.

She frowned. "What was that?"

He did not reply. He groaned deeply and shuddered and bent to take her lips. He kissed her deeply, and then more deeply. He held her fiercely, and still his lips assaulted hers with abandon. As if he drank from her to take his fill. As if he could not move away.

He moved sure and fleet, bringing his body against hers, and making love to her with a savage determination. She could not protest the driving force of it, for his hunger was so very deep, drawing upon the passion he had created within her. The day ceased to be, the fire of it was so swift, and so complete.

It was his world, his domain. He ruled here.

He had commanded her from the beginning, she realized. He had wanted her, and she had come to him, and in these blinding moments, it mattered not at all. He loved her with the force of a wild sweeping storm, he touched her as if his hands could hold the memory of her from everything. His palm closed upon her breast, and then his mouth, even as his body moved with arrogance and demand, knowing that he would stoke the flames with her. He reached to her womb, to her soul, she thought. His whispers cried out to her, and it was as if he cast the very force and life of himself into her, welding them into eternity. She rode a gale at sea, she thought, dangerous and beautiful. Or a fire storm. So very explosive . . .

She clung to him, and rode out the tempest, for her body gave so thoroughly to the impetus of his thrust. The sun upon their bodies was as radiant as the heat within them, the very ground beneath her back reminded her that this sweet and volatile binding of a man and woman was as old as the earth, as necessary. . . .

She cried out with the force and beauty of the shattering climax that fell upon her. He cast back his head, muscles tensed and the whole of him glimmering bronze with a sheen of perspiration, and cried out hoarsely. He fell upon her, and the raging force of him swept deep, deep inside of her like a liquid portion of the sun. She shuddered and fell back into his arms, awed and amazed anew, and certain that he would hold her then in tenderness.

He did not. He fell back against the earth, and a fierce oath exploded from him as he stared bleakly up into the powder-blue sky. He rolled and bounded to his feet. He stared down at her for a long moment. Her eyes were teal-blue and puzzled, her hair a damp splay of sunset over the earth.

He reached for her, offering her his hand.

"Get up," he said curtly.

She looked at him, hurt, her temper sizzling. "I do not obey commands, Captain Hawk."

"Don't you? We shall see."

"Shall we?"

He smiled, pulling her to her feet. His jaw was taut, his features strained as he spoke.

"The cannon, milady, is a signal. The ship has come, Lady Kinsdale. Your betrothed has come for you, slightly tarnished as you may be. I shall be heartily interested in the details of your nuptials."

She slapped him with such speed that he did not catch her until too late. Then he dragged her back against himself and bruised her lips with the hot demand of one last kiss. She jerked away from him, horrified. She would never, she thought, forget the mocking fire that burned so silver and so fierce within his eyes.

He turned away. She stared after him, blinded by sudden tears. "Wait!" she cried to him, and he turned back to her, and she wasn't even aware of what she did when she pitched herself into his arms.

He was stiff, cold. Then he held her more tightly and smoothed his fingers over her hair. A long, shuddering sigh escaped him and he kissed the top of her head. Then he freed himself from her hold and led her to the pile of her clothing. "Come, we must return before someone comes to look for us. No doubt, your fiancé is most eager to meet you."

IX

"Milady, it is time."

Skye stood quickly at Robert Arrowsmith's words. She had been sitting restlessly in her room for what seemed like hours. It had not been so long, of course. At the lagoon the Hawk had helped her into her clothing—either the gentleman or the rogue until the very end—and then he had taken her into his arms one last time and cast upon her lips a kiss that would remain with her into eternity. She could still touch her mouth and feel the passion and pulse of it there now.

"You can stay," he had told her.

She shook her head desperately. She longed to tell him about her father, that there was more. That she could not bear to wait for the day when they would come and tell her that the Hawk lay dead. Nor could she bear to awaken and discover that there were many more women in his life, that he took them when he chose, and that they fell too easily to his rogue's smile and silver eyes, fell, just as she had done. . . .

"*You* can make me," she had whispered.

His laugh was curt and bitter. "Can I? Ah, yes! Demand a

sum of Lord Cameron that is so high that all the nobility and honor of his fine house cannot pay it! Is that what you wish?" He brought his fingers to her lips. "Once you promised me everything. I brought you from the darkness of your dreams, and you promised me everything. And that is what I would require." They stared at one another, and he smiled wistfully and touched her cheek. "Perhaps we will meet again. I have never learned from you just what demon it is you fight in the darkness. I enjoyed slaying the dragons of your dreams, and I would have put them to rest forever, had I the power. Adieu, love." He dropped her fingers to her side. He brushed her forehead with his lips.

Then he disappeared into the water and crossed the lagoon, and she didn't think to turn away when he arose again, striking and noble in countenance and bearing. He had dressed with swift, deft movements and leaped upon the snow-white stallion. He looked her way and lifted a hand high.

Then he was gone, and she rode back alone.

"No hurry, milady!" Mr. Soames told her. Negotiation would take some time. That was well, she thought, for her hair was still sodden and dusted with sand as was her riding attire. A bath was in order and Mr. Soames did not mind at all; he suggested it.

And so it was, she thought when she was done, hair shampooed, her body newly attired in bone and elegant green muslin and brocade, that she would meet her betrothed in cleanliness of garb, even if she did not remain so pure in body or spirit.

She had no wish to meet this man! she thought. Reckless thoughts of breaking free upon his very deck filled her mind. Dreams of what went on below filled her thoughts. The Hawk would refuse to take ransom for her, claiming her for his own forever. And she might then protest this paradise, but remain in his arms nonetheless. . . .

It was a foolish dream. She could not bear not to see her father. He grew older with each passing year. He was precious to her, and he was surely worried and anxious beyond measure.

She stared down at her lace-gloved hands. They were trembling. A feeling of sickness surged in her stomach. She had to get out of here. She would forget. She was Lady Kinsdale, the very proud daughter of Lord Kinsdale, and she did not—by choice!—associate with pirates.

Aye, by choice, she had touched the Hawk, and been touched in turn.

By the time Robert came to the door, telling her, "Milady, it is time!" she felt as if they had come to take her to the executioner.

"It's time?" she repeated.

"Lord Cameron awaits you aboard his ship, the *Lady Elena.* He wishes to sail with the tide."

She swallowed quickly, trying to betray no emotion. "Will I see your master again?"

"I do not know, milady. Come along, please. Men will come for your trunks."

She left her room behind. Mr. Soames was waiting at the bottom of the stairs. She thanked him for his services and felt more and more like a maiden walking to the headman's block. She was being rescued, she reminded herself. Lord Cameron would expect her ardent thanks and appreciation.

Robert took her outside. Señor Rivas was waiting with a small pony trap to take her down to the dock. Robert helped her into the vehicle, then joined her. "I will see you safely to the *Lady Elena,*" he said.

Skye looked back to the house. She stared up to the window at the master's bedroom. She thought that she saw the drapes fall back into place. Was he watching her leave?

She turned away from the window, feeling the fool. He had amused himself with her, then accepted payment to rid himself of her! She should despise him so very fiercely.

Tears welled within her throat. She knew that she would not shed them. She stiffened her shoulders and reminded herself that she was her father's daughter, and that she would not fail or falter now.

Before them lay the docks. She saw the two tall ships there, both tall and proud. The *Lady Elena,* and the *Silver Hawk.* She had never realized before that the pirate had drawn his name from his ship. She looked at the beautiful figurehead, a silent sentinel.

The *Lady Elena* lay with a woman's figure upon her bow, too. It was an Indian, Skye thought. An Indian maiden with long flowing hair and buckskin dress. What a curious choice for Lord Cameron, she thought.

The docks were busy. Men loaded supplies aboard the *Lady Elena;* seamen scrubbed deck and knotted rope. Skye saw all the hustle and bustle as the pony trap came to a halt and Robert Arrowsmith helped her down. Señor Rivas tipped his hat to her and Skye smiled, telling him good-bye. Then Robert led her along the broad plank that stretched from the dock to the *Lady Elena.*

She was a larger ship than the *Silver Hawk,* Skye thought. She seemed to carry fourteen guns, with a narrow and high-rising hull. She would be a fleet ship; if not quite so swift as the pirate ship, she was more heavily armed and could probably fight well upon the open sea. Lord Cameron was a merchant, she knew. His fields were filled with tobacco and cotton and corn, and his ships endlessly plied the routes between the mother country and the New World. He armed himself very well against pirates, she thought. And yet her father had thought that he had done the same, and still the *Silver Messenger* had been taken.

"There he is!" Robert said suddenly.

Skye's heart slammed hard against her chest and her breath seemed to catch within her throat. Her palms were damp. She was not afraid of Lord Cameron! she assured herself. But she was nervous about this first meeting. She did not yet know what she meant to say or do, or how she would manage her life from now on. Thoughts of this meeting had been difficult enough before she had come to know the Silver Hawk; now it seemed a travesty.

"Where?" she murmured uneasily.

"There," Robert said. "At the helm. He speaks with Mr. Morley, his quartermaster, and Mr. Niven, his first mate."

"He captains his own ship?"

"Always, milady, if he is aboard."

She could see only his back and his form, and nothing of his face. He was dressed in a fine fawn-colored brocade coat and soft brown knee breeches. His shirt was white beneath his waistcoat, laced and frilled, spilling from his cuffs and neck. He wore a cockaded hat with eagle plumes above a full powdered wig. He was a tall man, and seemed able.

"Milady?" Robert said.

She realized that she stood there, upon the plank. Robert took her hand and led her forward and helped her to leap down to the deck.

"Milord! Milord Cameron!" Robert cried.

The man paused, passing his ledger to the mate on his left. Robert urged Skye along, bringing her up the four steps to the high-rising helm. She stared downward, carefully holding her skirt lest she trip upon the stair.

"Milady, let me assist you."

The voice was low and well modulated. The hand that touched hers was gloved in soft leather. She accepted the assistance, and looked up slowly.

A startled gasp tore from her lips.

He was nothing like the Silver Hawk, nothing at all. He was clean shaven and his powdered wig was neatly queued, and he was dressed totally as the lord. He was young, and his features were striking and clean cut and strong.

It was his eyes . . .

Only his eyes . . .

They were the same as his distant cousin's, so very much the same. Silver-toned and arresting, perhaps more so on this man, for the very white of his powdered wig made the darkness of his lashes and brows all the more striking.

He arched a brow, stiffening at her look. "Milady, be not afraid! I am Petroc Cameron, sworn to defend you, and not that heathen cousin of mine. The eyes, I'm afraid, are an accident of birth. The resemblance has always been a matter of distress to me, but never so much as now, as it causes you discomfort!"

Discomfort . . . he did not know the depths of it!

"Sir!" she managed to murmur.

"Milady . . ." he said. She thought that there was warmth

to his whisper. He held both of her hands and studied her swiftly. "You are well?" he said anxiously.

"Very."

"Thank God for that," he said, and turned to his men. "Mr. Morley, Mr. Niven, I give you my lady Skye. Skye, all and any of us are at your service, and we will strive to erase the horrors of the past days for you."

She could not speak. She nodded to Lord Cameron's mate and his quartermaster. Mr. Niven was young and blond and blue-eyed, and though his smile was as grave as the circumstances, his eyes were merry, and she thought that she might like him very well. Mr. Morley seemed more staid and strict; he was bewigged like Lord Cameron, and solid in posture.

"Mr. Morley will see you to your cabin, milady," Lord Cameron told her. "I will be with you as soon as possible; I'm afraid that I must now see to our embarkation."

She nodded, turning around to say good-bye to Robert. She would miss him.

Robert was gone. He had left the deck without a word.

There was a touch upon her elbow. She turned again to see Mr. Morley standing there, a grave expression upon his heavy jowled face. "If you'll come with me, my lady?"

She nodded vaguely, but she had no desire to leave the deck. The plank was being pulled, and seamen were climbing into the rigging to half-hoist certain sails to catch a steady breeze and move them carefully down the channel. Small boats—the *Silver Hawk's* small boats—came to the bow, preparing to guide the *Lady Elena* away from the treacherous shoals.

"Milady?"

"Mr. Morley, I should like to stay on deck."

Mr. Morley shifted uncomfortably from foot to foot. "Lord Cameron has ordered that I take you to your chamber."

"I will not be ordered about by Lord Cameron, Mr. Morley."

"He thought that you would despise this island, this place of your imprisonment, and would be eager to see your last sight of it."

She smiled sweetly and with a tremendous guilt upon her

heart. "I sail away, Mr. Morley, and the breeze is fresh and sweet."

The *Lady Elena* moved away from the dock. A command was shouted, and men scurried about. A sailor paused before Skye, bowed his head to her in flushing acknowledgment, and said, "Beg pardon, milady?"

"Oh, of course!" she murmured, and stepped aside. He cast his weight against the rigging for the mainsail, seemed to dangle upon it, and shouted for aid to pull up the canvas. Another of his fellows came along, and between them, the huge mainsail rose above them.

"Come, milady, please!" Mr. Morley urged her.

She sighed, but could not leave the deck. She pushed past him and hurried to the hull, looking backward to Bone Cay.

She saw a figure upon the pirate ship where it lay at berth, quiet and restful.

Sunset was coming on. Sunset, and the tide. The island and ship and channel were bathed in color. Red draped beguilingly over the ship, the sand, the men and women milling upon the dock. She looked from the rise of the island to the outline of the house and walls back to the dock, and to the ship, an elegant lady in the sunset. Then she blinked back a sudden surge of tears.

He was standing aboard his ship, she thought. The *Silver Hawk* was floating there. The *Lady Elena* pulled swiftly away, but still, she knew that it was he. He stood tall upon the deck, his arms akimbo, his legs well spread apart as if he rode the waves, even though the ship lay at dock. He was dressed all in black, from his sweeping hat to his booted feet. The plume and brim fell well over his eyes, shielding his face from her view.

But it was he, she thought.

He lifted his hand to her in a final salute.

To her horror, a cry tore from her throat and she spun around to a very startled Mr. Morley. "Please! I'm ready. Take me from the deck to my quarters, now, please!"

She was half-blinded, she thought. He caught her arm and led her, and without him she would have tripped over the cleats and rigging. They came to a narrow passage of steps, and Mr. Morley warned her that she must take very grave care. She scarcely heard him.

They stepped below, and he led her quickly to the aft, throwing open a chamber door there. The cabin was huge, with windows stretching around the hull for her pleasure and ease. There was a large bunk, elegantly covered in white linen, and secured tight to the wall. There was a screen for her privacy, rows of books, a washstand and pitcher and bowl, a circular window seat, and a mirrored dressing table. It was all beautiful, all elegant, all well fit for a lady, one who was honored and cherished.

She could barely glance about herself.

"Thank you!" she told Mr. Morley.

"Lord Cameron will be with you soon. Supper will be served in his cabin as soon as we are clear of the shoals and reefs."

"Thank you. I shall look forward to our meeting." She dreaded their meeting with all of her heart. At the moment, though, she wished only to be free from Mr. Morley.

He bowed deeply to her and left. Skye swiftly closed her cabin door and cast herself down heavily upon her bunk. Tears suddenly fell swiftly and forcefully down her cheeks, and she found herself swearing aloud. "Damn him!"

Oh, but she had been a fool! To fall for a pirate, a knave, and now discover that her heart remained twisted within his callous hands.

What had she desired? she asked herself. To live with a pirate? To lose her father forever? To wonder day after day if the rake she had sold all honor and pride for would return from his latest venture? No! One day he was destined to hang, or he would die upon the sword of another, like Blackbeard or Logan. No . . .

But she didn't want to be here. Not aboard this ship. Not with the gentleman lord who had come to rescue her.

Her tears abated slightly. She needed time, and distance, she told herself. She needed to see her father, to cast herself into his arms, to cry her heart out and tell him that her world had been turned over, and she needed to learn to understand it, and herself.

It was going to grow dark, she told herself uneasily. And the Silver Hawk was no longer with her, a beacon against the night.

She rose, wiping her eyes. She saw no lanterns about the cabin, no candles. Beneath the washstand, though, she found a decanter of brandy. There were pewter mugs beside it but she did not bother with such a nicety. She pulled the stopper and drank heavily. The brandy burned throughout her. She felt somewhat better, somewhat stronger.

There was a knock upon her door. She threw it open and stared at the young man there in stunned surprise.

"Davey!"

It was the young, sweet lad from the *Silver Messenger.* She reached out and touched his shoulders, assuring herself that he was there. A smile of pleasure swept across her features. "Oh, Davey, you are alive and well!"

"And have been, Lady Skye," he assured her, flushing and grinning broadly. "He was not a cruel master, milady."

She gasped, drawing him into her cabin. "Tell me! Where have you been? What has happened?"

"Why, we've been at sea, milady. In your father's ship. We weathered the storm, then held off Hatteras. They were sending messages, I believe. We met with Lord Cameron's ship on the open water, and those of us who had been captured and sent to the hold were passed on over."

"Were you cared for, Davey?" she asked with a frown.

"Aye, milady, a surgeon was sent down to the lot of us. The Hawk, he said, did not care to see any seaman in chains, so if we promised good behavior, we were free. We were even brought on deck for good, fresh air. It was not so loathsome a time, milady." He paused, looked at her searchingly, then flushed. "And you, milady? I prayed for you daily. Are you well?"

She swallowed. "Aye, Davey, very well, thank you."

He nodded and flushed again, and stepped away from her. "I came to see if you might require anything, milady. Lord Cameron would probably not take too kindly to my talking with you."

"Lord Cameron has no right to tell me who I may or not

speak with, Davey," Skye said flatly, standing. Then she paused, startled, and felt a peculiar sensation sweep along her spine. Her lips parted into a soft gasp, for she realized that the man had come up behind Davey, and stood, filling the doorway behind the lad.

Davey swung about, and whitened.

"Is your duty here done then, lad?" Lord Cameron inquired.

"Aye, sir!"

"Be gone with you then, son," Lord Cameron said, his eyes not upon Davey but looking over the young man's pale head, and finding Skye's. She started to tremble. She hated that silver color, and hated that he could appear so like the Hawk. . . .

And so entirely unlike his black-sheep cousin.

"We have left the shoals and reefs behind us, Skye. I have come to take you to dinner."

She folded her hands together tightly. "That is very kind of you, Lord Cameron. This is all . . . very kind of you. I do, however, find that I am very weary. If I could—"

"Lady Skye! I shall not keep you long at all, I promise. And I could not dream of allowing you to take to your cabin without a meal. I understand your distress, but please, I insist. You must come to dinner."

There was a note of steel to his voice. Like his distant cousin, he was accustomed to command. What was it with these men? she wondered irritably.

"Sir—"

"Milady," he said firmly, and offered her his arm.

She hesitated, then accepted, for short of total rudeness, she had no other choice, and whatever his feelings in the matter, he had risked life and limb to come for her.

He drew her arm within his and led her just down the hallway to the next door. "My cabin, milady. And should you need them, Mr. Morley and Mr. Niven share quarters just across. There are more officers down the hall, and the seamen's quarters are the deck below."

She nodded and tried to smile. When he pushed open the door, she entered quickly, eluding his touch. She looked around quickly and found it to be a more practical than elegant place, though all seemed to be in the best of taste. His desk was heavy and finely polished and heavily laden with charts. Warm velvet drapes fell over the windows in a deep sea blue, matching the simple coverlet that lay over the bunk against the far wall. A table had been brought to the room. A snowy white cloth lay atop it and a complete silver setting, and handsome plate with soft flowered designs.

Lord Cameron closed the door to his cabin behind him and walked behind one of the handsome high-backed chairs, pulling it out for her.

"Milady?"

"Thank you," she murmured, sliding into the chair.

He did not join her. He walked over to his desk, to a decanter there. "Wine, my dear?" He turned about to face her with a curious smile. "Or have you already been indulging?"

"What?" she gasped, staring his way. There was a look of steel about him that made her think that she had underestimated the man.

"Forgive my very bad manners, milady," he said apologetically. She avoided meeting his gaze. She could not bear to see the color of his eyes.

"You are forgiven."

"You have been through an awful ordeal. You are certainly entitled to—indulgence."

How did he manage to make the word sound so frightfully decadent?

He came to the table, setting a glass of deep red wine before her. She was tempted to grab it and swallow down the liquid in an instant. She could not let this man so unnerve her! He was no pirate, she reminded herself, but a lord of the peerage. He was sworn by honor to certain behavior, and she need not fear him.

She did not fear him. She picked up her wineglass and sipped upon it and forced herself to meet his eyes. "Yes, it has all been quite an ordeal."

He drew back his own chair and sat opposite her. "I heard wonderful things about your valor, Skye."

"Did you?"

He nodded to her gravely. "The crew rescued from your father's ship told us how you battled the pirates in defense of the Irish maids. They say you fought unbelievably well. They say that you won."

"I know something of swordplay."

"Yes, your father told me. You do not know something of it; you know it very well."

"Yes."

"So you bested the first pirates."

"Yes."

"But not the Silver Hawk."

Despite herself, she felt her eyes fall. "No."

He was silent, silent so long that she wished she could scream or meet his stare boldly and brazenly and shout out the truth of it all.

"But he did not injure you?"

"No, Lord Cameron, he did not injure me."

"Skye! We are soon to live together as man and wife. My given name is Petroc, a whim of my mother's, and those who are close to me call me Roc. I would hear that name from you."

She smiled stiffly and felt a chill sweep over her. As last she could meet his eyes, for he had ceased to plague her about her adventures. "Roc," she murmured obligingly.

"It sounds well upon your sweet lips, milady."

"Tell me, sir," she said, sitting forward. "How is my father."

"Well and good," he assured her. "He will meet us at Cameron Hall."

"Cameron Hall?" she said with dismay.

"What is wrong with that, milady?"

"Nothing. Why, nothing, of course. I had just thought that we would sail for Williamsburg."

"Ah." His dark lashes fell briefly over his eyes. He stood and moved away from her, sipping his wine and idly pulling back one of the drapes. It was nearly dark beyond the light from the cabin, Skye saw.

He dropped the curtain. "Williamsburg has vastly changed, you will discover. Governor Spotswood has moved into his new manor, and it is all but complete. He has hosted many an elegant ball there. The magazine is complete and filled with muskets and swords for the militiamen. The Bruton parish church has been rebuilt since you were home, and more and more merchants flock to the town daily. Even coming from London, my dear, I believe that you will be impressed with the growth of our capital city."

"I'm sure I shall."

"Not that we shall be so very close to Williamsburg."

"I beg your pardon."

"Cameron Hall, milady. It is a good three hours down the James. Closer to Jamestown, but on higher ground. We do, of course, come into the city now and then. You will not be so completely isolated."

She felt as if the bars of a new prison were falling quickly shut upon her.

"I wonder, milord—"

"Oh, you needn't fret so uncomfortably, milady. I have already heard that you are opposed to the marriage."

She stared at him, her eyes flashing. "Well, milord, I have heard that you, too, were opposed!"

He inclined his head, smiling. "Ah, but that was before I sailed the seas for you, milady!"

She flushed, and swallowed down the whole of her wine after all. Lord Cameron quickly stood, taking her glass to refill it. She watched him walk away. He was a tall man, too, with a long back and broad shoulders. She imagined that beneath his finery he was well muscled and toned. She shivered suddenly, and did not know why. He was unerringly polite, yet she sensed that his temper might be great when provoked.

"Milord—"

"Roc, Skye. Please, you must be comfortable with my given name."

"Roc—" She paused, gritting her teeth. He came around, facing her. He placed her wineglass down before her again and moved away, this time perching upon the corner of his desk. He waited expectantly. "Roc, I do with all my heart appreciate your trouble and valor in coming so swiftly to my rescue. And the expense, of course—"

"The expense?" He arched a brow.

"The—the expense," she repeated, faltering. "The ransom! I'm sure that he charged you dearly for my return."

"Why, not at all, milady."

"You are too polite and generous, milord."

"Not at all. I tell you the truth. The pirate didn't charge me a single farthing for your return."

She gasped out loud, coming to her feet. "He what?"

Lord Cameron's dark lashes flickered over his silver eyes. "Why the distress, milady? We paid for the seamen, the ship, and the maids, but you, my dear, were returned to us through goodwill."

"He did not even charge you for me!"

His brow flew up. She quickly tried to hide her distress, falling back into her chair, swallowing down her second glass of wine.

"I repeat, my dear, he did not charge for you."

She lowered her head quickly, but there came a knock upon the captain's door, and Lord Cameron quickly answered it. "Thank you, Mr. Monahan," he said, directing a hefty sailor with a huge serving tray to the table. "My dear, this is Mr. Monahan, the cook's assistant. Mr. Monahan, my Lady Skye."

"Lady," Mr. Monahan said, bowing deeply as he set the tray down with a flourish. He lifted the silver cover from the serving plate. "Pheasant, milady, stuffed with nuts and cornmeal and raisins. I hope that it will be to your pleasure."

"I'm sure that it shall, Mr. Monahan," she said sweetly. Then there was silence as Mr. Monahan prepared the plates. Skye waited uneasily until he was gone and cast a gaze toward Lord Cameron. Her heart catapulted when she discovered that he was staring at her deeply and intently. The cabin was too small for the two of them. She longed to escape him. She desperately, desperately needed to be alone.

"Do you feel ill?" he asked her when Mr. Monahan had left them. He took his place opposite from her.

She shook her head. "I—I'm fine." She wasn't fine. She didn't feel well at all. She picked up her fork and played idly with her food.

He was still watching her, paying no heed to his food. "The

governor intends to clean out the pirates, you know. Lieutenant Governor Spotswood, that is. He is bold man, adventurous and determined. Where other men in power turn their heads, he stands strong. He will see all the pirates swept from the seas, skewered through or brought to trial. Then they may hang from the neck until dead."

She set her fork down.

"Skye, whatever is the matter?"

She shook her head, then she stared at him. "How can you be so callous? The man is your cousin."

"Cousin!" He shuddered. "Several times removed, milady, I do assure you. And lady, after all that has been done to you, I would think that you would rejoice to know that the scourge will be cleansed from the sea. Can you find the likes of pirates pleasant? Logan and his crew? The late One-Eyed Jack? Mr. Teach?"

"Of course not! I find them despicable. It's just that—"

"What?"

"You spoke of one who is your own blood, that is all."

"Barely, milady."

"Even your looks—"

"An accident of birth, and I don't care to be reminded of it."

"But you do know one another! You negotiate and speak, else I could not be here so swiftly."

"Bone Cay is the safest of the pirate havens, and the Hawk is perhaps the most dependable of the buccaneers; no more, milady. Aye, we speak. We come to agreements, that is all."

She lowered her head, still feeling queasy. "There is a precedent," she murmured.

"Pardon?"

"Sir Francis Drake," she said, and then she realized that she was repeating words she had heard from the Silver Hawk.

"Yes?" Lord Cameron arched a brow.

"He—he was a privateer. Men set sail against the Spanish, and even when we were not at war, Elizabeth turned her head while her Englishmen ravaged Spanish ships. When the Stuarts came to the throne, the mode continued. We created these men. And now they flourish. But where does the line come,

Lord Cameron? Some were privateers, sanctioned by their governments. Some are cutthroats, and some simple thieves."

"Simple thieves have been known to hang. Trust me, the pirates will do so, too."

"Including the Silver Hawk?"

"I shall escort you myself to the execution."

She was silent. The pheasant was delicious; she had no appetite. The wine churned in her stomach.

"Let's not speak of this, milady. The past is over; you are safe with me. You do seem well. You were not harmed? In any way?"

A dark flush came quickly to her features. The question, she knew, was far more intimate than the words alone could convey.

"I was treated well enough," she said. She folded the corners of her napkin together in her lap. What did he know? Why did he stare at her so probingly, with his unusual eyes of silver, as riveting as the Hawk's? He could know nothing! she told herself.

"You're quite sure?" he asked.

"I was well treated!" she repeated.

"Tell me about it."

"What?" she gasped.

"Tell me what happened. I am most anxious to hear, and the governor will want information, too."

"I—"

"The ship was seized first by One-Eyed Jack and his men, is that right?"

"Uh—yes."

"But then the prize was stolen from one pirate by another, is that right?"

"Yes."

"The Hawk, of course, instantly knew your value."

"Yes, yes, of course."

He stroked his chin. "How strange. He then decided to release you, asking nothing for you." He leaned forward. "So you came to know him well."

"Well enough."

"And you were imprisoned separately from the others?"

"Yes."

"Where?"

The rapid, spitfire questions had her reeling, feeling deeply on the defensive. She leaped to her feet, allowing her chair to fall back. "Stop! I do not care to speak about it longer!"

"But you were treated well!" he reminded her.

"Lord Cameron!" She stared at him with all the icy reserve that she could summon. "I do not care to speak of it anymore! Not now, not ever! Governor Spotswood will seek out his pirates, and he will slay them all, no doubt! But I cannot go on tonight, do you understand me, sir?"

He came around, righting her chair. His hands fell upon her shoulders and she was startled by the strength of him. He spoke softly, his voice low, well modulated. He was a lord, a gentleman, yet more than ever she had the feeling that he was not to be underestimated, that a simmering anger lay deep within him, and that if it rose to the surface, it would be dangerous indeed.

"Sit, milady. I have not meant to distress you."

"I am not distressed."

"I am grateful to hear that. We will speak no more of it for now. The future lies before us, and we should not speak of the past."

She raised her eyes to his. "I am grateful, Lord Cameron. I am very grateful for your presence here, for the fact that you came so swiftly to my rescue. I will not marry you."

He arched a brow.

"You will not marry me?"

"No."

"Your father gave promise."

She shook her head impatiently. "I know, sir, that you did not wish to marry me—"

"Perhaps I have changed my mind."

She gritted her teeth. "I have not changed mine."

"I don't think that you understand. My will is very strong."

"I don't think you understand. I promise that my will can be of steel when I so choose."

"You cannot change what is."

"But I do not want—"

"You insult my family name, milady," he said pleasantly, but his eyes flashed their silver warning.

"This was a fool's bargain made by two doting fathers when we were just children. I was an infant. You cannot hold me to this." She pushed away from the table and stood. "If you will excuse me now, sir, I am very exhausted."

He stood, too, and came around the table, blocking her way to the door. He did not touch her, but he watched her, and she didn't know if his silver eyes danced with humor or fury.

"I'm afraid that I cannot excuse you as yet, milady."

"Oh, and why is that? Truly, Lord Cameron, you are not displaying the manners of a good gentle peer in the least!"

"My apologies, milady. But there is something that you must know before you quit this cabin."

She tossed back her head with her most imperious manner. "And what, pray tell, Lord Cameron, is that?"

"Only this, milady. Protest comes too late."

"What are you talking about?" She frowned. A certain dread came to settle over her. She longed to flee before he could speak. There would be no way. She could not barge past him. He was too tall, towering against the door. His shoulders, for all their elegant apparel, were too broad.

"I'm afraid that by the law, we are legally wed."

"What?"

"Your father was quite concerned even as you set sail from the English shore. We were wed by proxy the day you left London behind. You see, my dear, whether it pleases you or not, it is done."

He waited, allowing the words to settle over her. She was silent, stunned. Her father could not have done such a thing to her!

He sighed deeply, but spoke with a frightening edge to his voice.

"Madame, you are my wife, and that is that."

She shook her head, disbelieving. "No!"

"Yes."

"I will fight it."

"I will not allow you."

"You must! You cannot love me! You must let me go."

"No."

He said the word with such finality that she found herself shivering.

But then he stepped aside from the door, opening it for her. He bowed deeply. She stiffened, and walked by him. He caught her arm briefly.

"I will never let you go," he said. "You will become reconciled."

"I will never become reconciled. We will be wretched!"

"Then wretched, my love, we will be." He released her, bowing deeply. "Good night, my love."

The door closed, and she was left alone in the hallway.

X

Skye stormed down the corridor to the door to her own cabin. She cast it open to step inside, and when she did, the darkness surrounded her.

She leaned against the door, swallowing, closing her eyes. If only!

If only One-Eyed Jack had never spotted the *Silver Messenger,* if only the Silver Hawk had not come behind him. She had been mistress upon the *Silver Messenger,* her father's ship, and she had never needed to fear the darkness there, for she had always been surrounded by lamps and candles. Now, no matter what her feelings for the man, no matter what lay between them, she would have to go with him. The clammy hand of terror was already upon her. If she did not move swiftly . . .

She moved away from the door just as a tap came upon it. It opened, and she saw that Lord Cameron stood there, a lamp in his hands glowing cheerfully against the darkness. "Milady," he murmured, bowing to her and handing her the light.

Unnerved, she felt her fingers tremble as she took it from him. "How did you know!" she gasped out.

"It is my ship. That is why I knew that there was no lamp here," he told her.

He had known that there was no light, not that she was terrified beyond reason of the darkness.

"And," he added, "your father has warned me that you do not care for the darkness."

"Oh," she murmured, lowering her lashes. Drat father! she thought. What had he been doing to her? Giving away her every secret, and selling her, body and soul! "Er . . . thank you," she managed. Still, he hovered there in her doorway. Darkness hid his eyes and his features and she sensed him on different levels. Perhaps the Hawk had made her more attuned to the body. She felt the heat and energy of his presence, and breathed the scent of him. He smelled of very fine leather and good Virginia tobacco in a subtle and pleasant way. He was not at all, as a man, repulsive.

He was her husband, or so he claimed, she reminded herself, and was seized with a fierce shivering. He had given her a separate cabin, she quickly assured herself. He would not fall upon her, he would not demand his marital rights.

But perhaps he would!

He stepped through the doorway and looked about the cabin. "Is everything to your comfort?"

"Everything is fine!" she cried with vehemence. He looked her way, a smile curving into his lip. "You are very nervous, milady."

"I have been greatly unnerved by your comments."

"You mustn't despair." He came closer to her. She backed against the wall, turning her head from his, terrified that he meant to touch her. She had fallen from the arms of one charming rogue to another, she thought briefly, one a pirate and one a lord, and both far too arrogant and assured.

His knuckles grazed over her cheek. She barely held back a scream, and a soft gasp escaped her.

"You are my wife," he said.

"I am not your wife!" She stared at him again, her eyes sizzling. "And don't be so sure that all the pirates shall hang! I have come from London, sir, and I am far more abreast of certain news. I was in the mother country when Queen Anne died, when they reached over to Hanover for King George. The rights for trial upon men such as Hornigold and Blackbeard and—and the Silver Hawk—must come directly from the monarch. No new commissions have been granted by King George as yet. It was my understanding—"

"My dear lady, do tell me! Just what is your understanding, and from where do you draw upon it?"

"I do read the papers, Lord Cameron. And there was a great deal of talk in high places about the king offering a pardon to what pirates would surrender and swear an oath by a certain date. Perhaps these fellows will surrender, and there will be no need for murder."

"Murder! You call the death of a pirate murder?"

He spoke with a certain ferocity, but she sensed that he was smiling beneath it. Was he laughing at her? Was he furious with her? She didn't know.

"Bloodshed, Lord Cameron."

"You are opinionated."

"Yes! I am most opinionated, and very brash and outspoken, not at all ladylike, and surely not possessing qualities that you might want in a wife!"

"Ah! So you admit that you are my wife!"

"No!" she cried, alarmed, pressing ever backward against the paneling. She tried to straighten, to stand firm. He was a gentleman, a lord. He would not seize her, would he? "No! Why in God's name are you doing this! I had thought you opposed to this barbaric treatment of marriage, of—"

"I have discovered myself quite pleased—Lady Cameron," he said very softly. Chills swept along her spine. There was something about his speech . . . the soft, low, deeply modulated tone and cadence of it reminded her of the other. She was suddenly desperate for him to leave. She would have said anything just to be free of his presence then.

"Milord—" she whispered, but it was not necessary. He did not touch her, he moved away from her.

"There is ample oil for the lamp to burn until daylight," he said softly.

Then he left her, closing the door behind himself.

Skye remained against the paneling for a long time. Then

she slowly exhaled and, in time, pushed away from the wall and sank down to her bed. She lay there fully clothed and thought wretchedly of the morning, and of the night that had passed before. She could not forget the Hawk. She could not stop thinking of everything that had passed between them, and she could not stop feeling as if her very heart bled. She could not love such a man; she could not even care for him! But she did. Heat washed over her with memory. Yet how carelessly, how callously, he had cast her aside! He spoke of money and ransom endlessly, yet she had, in the end, been worthless to him. He was a pirate; she had been a whim, an adventure, and the adventure was over now.

The adventure was over. . . .

And a tall bewigged stranger with silver eyes was telling her that she was his wife!

It was too much. Too much. She longed then for nothing but home. For Williamsburg. For market square with its endless fairs, for the bowling green where she had often played and laughed with the other children. Williamsburg, with her planned and beautiful, broad streets. With the College of William and Mary, her endless bustle of students and scholars, her law debates, her fashionable and tawdry taverns . . .

It was her home. It was where her father had built his house, just down from the governor's mansion begun when she had been a child. Alexander Spotswood had planned much of it himself. When she had been very little, she had watched the construction with him, and he had tousled her hair with affection. "See, child, the entry will be here, and I, your lieutenant governor, will greet most guests here. But if you are very important—and of course, Skye, you shall be that!—you may come up the steps and I will greet you in the hallway above. See here, I have shown your father. We will have the most fashionable leather to cover the walls in the hall. Then my bedchamber will be here, and our guests will be here. And as I've told your father, we will have the most fabulous wine cellar."

Home would be a haven, she thought.

But she was not going to be brought home. Lord Cameron was taking her somewhere down the peninsula to his Tidewater plantation. She swallowed fiercely, watching the lamplight waver over the walls of the ship.

He meant to keep her there. At some godforsaken manor in the wilderness. Surely, it would be horrible, it would be swampland. By summer the insects and heat would be unbearable.

She shuddered and reminded herself that she planned to fight Lord Cameron to the very end. A rising anxiety engulfed her. Could she fight him? There would be no help for her when she tried to fight a lord, a powerful landowner. No one would help her, for anyone would think that she was daft, trying to fight something so very right and proper.

Then there was Lord Cameron himself. . . .

She shivered, wondering how he would feel if he knew the truth about her. He would loathe her, she thought.

Perhaps . . . perhaps he would loathe her enough to disavow her. To annul the marriage himself. Proxy marriage! They could not do that to her, could they?

Perhaps . . .

But then again, perhaps, if he knew, he would show her no deference. He would hate her, but he would show her no deference at all. He would not leave her at peace in this cabin.

She turned over and tried to close her eyes, tried to find oblivion in sleep. It eluded her for a long, long time. Nor were her dreams restful. She imagined him coming to her. . . .

The Silver Hawk.

He came as he had come to her from the lagoon, rising up with the water sluicing from his body, coming to her with firm purpose, reaching for her. His eyes blazed, and suddenly he was not her lover, but the man who claimed to be her husband.

His arms closed around her and she struggled, but he was dragging her down, deep down into the sea. She heard him whispering to her, and she didn't hear the word. Then suddenly it came clear.

"Whore!"

She awoke with a jerk. She was fully clad and the light was

bright around her and she was alone. She lay back, shivering. She did not sleep again that night.

Tara and Bess, cheerful and chattering, came to serve her in the morning. Skye was quiet, allowing Bess to talk on and on with grave excitement about the pirate's island while she brushed and braided her hair. Tara set up a breakfast tray for her, complete with fresh eggs, brown bread, and strong, sweet tea. The girls were excited, she knew, because they were heroines. They had survived an ordeal by fire, and when they spoke about the Bone Cay, they had a rapt audience among the young sailors. Skye kept a grip upon her tongue, determined not to ruin their happiness when she was bitter and frightened of the future herself.

Because a pirate continued to plague her dreams, and because Lord Cameron entered in upon them in moments of intimacy.

When her clothing had been straightened, her hair done, her cabin neatened, Bess asked permission to go on deck. Skye freely granted it.

She remained within the cabin herself for a long time, hoping to avoid Lord Cameron. But the walls seemed to close in upon her, and she soon came topside. He was at the helm. She stood far across the deck from him with crew and rigging and sails between them. He bowed to her, his hands upon the heavy wheel. She nodded curtly in return and came portside, staring out over the water. The day was beautiful, the water was very blue, and the sky was light and powdery. She could see a distant shoreline.

"Florida," he said softly behind her. She knew his voice, it was so like the Hawk's. His breath touched her nape and feathered along it. She turned. He wasn't looking at her, but at the land that lay off the hull of the ship. "A treacherous land, beautiful, and inhabited by all manner of creatures. It's fascinating." He smiled at her at last. "I have always loved it."

Something about his smile drew a response from her. "I have never seen it."

He shrugged, leaning over the helm. "Ah, but you've lived

in London, and to many in our fair colony, London constitutes all of the world."

"And don't you feel that way, Lord Cameron?"

"More than anything, I love Virginia," he said, and she felt the curious intensity in his voice. He leaned against the wooden railing at the hull and studied her as he spoke. "I love Virginia, and Cameron Hall, and the acres that surround her. The house sits high atop a hill, and from the windows and porch you can look far down the slope and see the James flowing by. You can see when storms roll in and watch as the sun rises. You can see the ebb and flow of traffic upon the river. She runs deep. All manner of commerce come to us. Tenants work much of the land, and all of them come to the docks to send their produce to England, to buy their ribands and baubles and fine dish and plate and materials. The grass upon the slope is so green and verdant that at times it appears blue. The summers are hot, but the river sweeps away much of the heat. The winters are never too cold. It is endlessly beautiful."

"It sounds as if you speak of a paradise," she said softly, the last word catching in her throat, for she had found her own paradise, and that on a tropical isle with bright wildflowers and endless heat and the glow of the sun upon the earth. He could not know the secrets of her heart, she thought, and yet he looked at her with a slow, rueful smile that seized her heart. "Paradise? Perhaps. It is a realm we create ourselves, isn't it? Separate unto each and every one of us, and found where we choose to seek it."

She turned quickly from him, watching the shoreline.

"They say that there is endless treasure buried there, upon the sandy shores," he mused. "They've all played there, the buccaneers. Once it was Captain Kidd. Now Hornigold and Blackbeard and others." He looked at her once again. "Blackbeard and Hornigold have been wreaking havoc along the Carolinas this fall. Blackbeard fought a fierce battle with a ship of the Royal Navy. He is vastly admired among men. They stand in awe of his daring."

"Do they?" she murmured.

"It will be something to see, if this pardon proclamation of yours comes through."

"I imagine it will," she murmured.

"Thank God, my dear, that your adventuring days are over. Soon you will be at Cameron Hall . . . forever."

She looked to him quickly, and the gaze he gave her with his subtle curl of a smile sent rivulets of sensation coursing down her spine. Damn those silver eyes of his! The simple words seemed to carry the most satanish, underlying threat. Or promise. Or warning. It was a warning, she realized. On this ship, she was somewhat safe from him. But when they came to his house, his precious Cameron Hall, things were destined to change.

"Forever, sir? I think not. My father will be there when we come in, will he not? I must protest vehemently all that has been done without my consent."

"Nothing was done without your consent."

"But it was."

He shook his head gravely. Still she thought that he was enjoying her discomfort. "You signed all the appropriate papers when your father visited you in London."

"I—I did not!" she said, but her words tripped and faltered as she wondered just what she had signed. She had been arguing with her father, and therefore not paying much attention to what he required of her. Some of his holdings were in her name, too, for various business reasons. She often signed papers, and she had always hated to be bothered with the details of them. Especially in London, where so very much was going on at all times.

"We will see, milady," he said softly. He turned from her, heading back toward the helm. His absolute assurance ignited her fury. "Wait!" she demanded.

He turned back to her, arching a brow expectantly.

"You can't mean to keep an unwilling bride, Lord Cameron! Surely it would be far beneath your dignity."

He doffed his hat to her, bowing neatly. "Madame, I do intend to keep my bride, willing or no. Good afternoon, milady." He turned and walked again.

"Wait!" she cried again.

"What?" he demanded.

"I—I can't!"

"You can't what?"

She had to tell him that she couldn't possibly be his wife, but he was some distance from her then, and she didn't feel like shouting such news across the whole of the ship. He waited with definite exasperation. She moistened her lips, about to suggest a certain privacy, when suddenly the seaman atop the crow's nest shouted down to him. "Ship to the starboard, sir!"

Cameron turned around without another glance her way, striding with assurance and grace to leap up to the helm platform. "My glass, please!"

Skye, forgetting their dispute, raced toward him, lifting her skirts to hurry up to the helm. He ignored her, facing starboard. The seaman atop the crow's nest cried down to them. "She's changing her colors, sir! She was flying the English flag —now she gone a-pirate!"

"Gunners to your stations!" Cameron called. He brought the glass to his eye. "It isn't Logan," he muttered. "Nor Blackbeard, nor Hornigold . . ."

"Do you know them so well, sir?" Skye taunted softly.

"Blane!" he called to the hefty seaman at the wheel. "Bring her about sharp. We'll pretend to run, then ram straight toward her, all guns blazing then. Understood?"

"Aye, sir!"

He drew the glass from his eye, startled to see her beside him. "Go below," he told her curtly.

"No!" she said, backing away from him.

"I have ordered you—"

"You will not order me, sir! I have been through this before, and being ordered below will not save me, that I know well! Give me a sword, if you would be helpful, for I might defend myself where others might fail."

His eyes went very narrow and sharp, and for several seconds she did not see the anger blazing within them. "Mr. Blair, I shall return promptly!" he announced. He handed his glass to a seaman and took a step toward Skye. Too late she cried out in alarm and sought to escape him. Hands of iron set upon her, plucking her up.

"Sir! How dare you!" she protested in wild fury. She thundered her fists against his back to no avail. He came quickly to the steps leading below and ducked to bring her under. He walked the corridor with long even strides, ignoring her shouts and her fists. At her door he cast her down. It was daylight; there was nothing to fear. It was a test of wills that went on between them now, and they both seemed to realize it. Pretenses were stripped away as they stared at one another. How she hated those silver eyes! So like his cousin's in so many unfortunate ways. Their spark meant anger, and atrocious determination.

She didn't speak, but simply cried out in rage, casting herself upon him as if she could dislodge him from the doorway. He caught her wrists and pinned them to the small of her back. He was too like the Hawk! she thought in a growing panic, for his body was tall and heated against hers, too close, too masculine. She twisted savagely within his grasp, having no desire to meet his eyes. "Let me go!" she commanded him.

"Never, dear wife," he returned. She lifted her eyes to his. They were fire and smoke, a shield of secrets, and suddenly very dark as tension overcame him. His lip curled just slightly. He bent his head and his lips touched down upon hers, encompassing them, savoring them. The probe of his tongue parted her mouth and consumed her very breath. He touched all of her. The very movement, swift and deep and ravaging, seemed an ungodly insinuation of more. . . .

She writhed to free herself. She screamed deep within. She twisted free from him at last, twisting and shaking and appalled that he had been able to touch her so easily.

And appalled that he had touched her so deeply. She was trembling, she was hot and cold.

And all the things that she had learned in the arms of the Hawk were surging forward to wrap around her, and whisper softly to her of a desire that could exist.

Lord Cameron freed her suddenly, pushing her away. "This marriage may not be such a travesty, milady. I would love to explore it further, but I am afraid that pirates knock upon our doors. Will you excuse me?"

She cried out in fury, wiping her mouth with the back of her hand, wishing she could wipe the sight and sound and touch of him from her memory forever. Footsteps pounded overhead of them. The crew was preparing to go to battle.

"I must leave you—"

"Damn you! Leave me a sword!"

"So that you might use it against me later?" he mocked.

"Are you afraid that I might use it too well?"

He laughed, reached to his scabbard, and tossed her his sword. She meant to threaten him then and there and demand her freedom, but he was too quick for her, dodging behind the door and bowing deeply. "I should love to oblige you, my love, but I'm quite afraid that we are under attack. You will excuse me!"

The door slammed sharply, a lock twisted. Skye charged it, but too late. With an oath she slammed hard against it. He was gone, she knew, but she turned around to scream to the door anyway. "Men! You think to lock me in for protection, but if you fail, then the rogues will come so easily for me!"

There was no reply. She fell upon her bunk, holding his sword. It was rapier sharp. She bit her lip, and then she found herself hurtling across the cabin on the floor. The ship had come about at a startling, reckless speed.

Crushed amid her petticoats at the door, she stumbled to her feet just in time to fall again as the roar of the ship's cannons exploded all around her.

She came up and hurried to the window. She pulled back the draperies and gasped, for they were fast coming broadside against the buccaneer. The ships came together with a mighty crunch. There was an awful screeching sound as grappling hooks were tossed, and then the cries of a dozen men went up as they leaped from the rigging to the deck. The clash of steel could be heard above all else.

Skye scrambled for the sword and held it tight. She coughed, and her eyes started to water, and she realized that smoke was entering her cabin through the doorway.

She screamed, and hurled herself toward the door. It was not yet hot. She could still escape.

The door flew open. Young Davey stood there, his freckled face pale. "There's fire below, milady. They're fighting it, but I'll take you closer topside—"

Skye brushed past him. "Closer topside! I'd rather die by the sword than burn to death any day!" she assured him, starting along the narrow hallway.

"Milady, wait!" Davey wailed, scurrying to get before her. "All is under control, the rogues are just about bested! The ship is captured, she is!"

Skye ignored him and hurried up the steps, rushing up atop the deck. The air was not much better here, for it was thick with black powder from the cannons. She blinked, trying to get her bearings in the smoky shadows. She could hear no clash of steel; the day had gone silent, quickly, completely.

"Welcome, milady!"

Hands were upon her so suddenly and completely that she screamed, her wrist nearly crushed as a giant hairy paw fell upon it, shaking Lord Cameron's sword from her hand. She was jerked back against a burly, unwashed body and held tightly. A touch of sharp steel came against her throat and she gasped, then barely dared to breath. A long knife lay against her neck, and the slighted movement might well sever her very life.

"Lord Cameron, sir!" The man's laughter rang out. "Lookee what I've got here, sir! Perhaps this changes things just a bit, mee-lord! Now listen up, and listen real good! You want the girl back? Well, if you want her, you pay heed to my words. My men and I will nonchalantly return to our ship. I take her with me. When we're free of you, I'll send her back in a longboat with one of your own mates. What do ye think about that?"

There was no answer. Skye stood dead still as the powder began to clear.

Lord Cameron was perhaps twenty feet away. The deck was, indeed, filled with men in various positions. Bodies lay upon the deck, but mostly they seemed to be the pirates who had gotten the worst of it. Lord Cameron's men knew how to fight.

The rogues had not surprised them; they had surprised the rogues.

She didn't allow her gaze to linger about the ship; it fell upon Cameron. He was coatless now; he had fought in fawn breeches and a white shirt. There was a small nick upon his cheek where a sword had touched him briefly, but other than that, he did not even seem to be breathing heavily. His one foot rested upon a coil of rope, a cutlass dangled from his right hand, and a pistol was gripped idly in his left. He smiled as he faced the pirate.

"Mr. Stikes," he said in answer to the pirate. "You are a rank amateur, sir!"

"Your pardon!" the pirate roared. He jerked upon Skye. "Amateur, indeed!" He started to laugh. "Drop your weapons, man, or she's mine, dead or alive, your choice!"

Roc Cameron shrugged casually. "She's a great deal of trouble."

"I'm what!" Skye cried out, gasping in amazement.

"What?" the pirates exploded in unison.

"You heard me!" Lord Cameron called out, ignoring Skye and addressing the pirate. "She's a great deal of trouble."

"Rumor has it that she's your wife!"

"Aye, my wife, and my headache!" Roc complained, adjusting his weight. "Go ahead! Take her. She's yours."

"Dear God!" Skye cried out in amazement. The scurvy coward! He meant to let her be taken by the likes of this man.

"Take her! If she was worth a halfpenny, she'd not have come topside in the midst of this! Take her!"

"Take her!" the pirate cried.

Cameron sighed. "All right. If you must, let her go."

"You're mad! You are absolutely mad!" the pirate said. "Back off! Just back off, I'm taking her with me!"

Skye felt that the grip upon her had been released just the slightest bit. He started to drag her forward. She came closer and closer to Petroc Cameron with his clean-shaven, hard aristocrat's features and smoldering silver eyes. Stikes drew by him.

Skye spat at Stikes. He flinched, startled. His eyes narrowed further as he wiped his face. They were straight before Cameron then, two feet away. The pirate Stikes began to speak. "Now listen to me, your lordship, one move—"

Roc Cameron moved. Skye stared aghast with horror as he drew his pistol upward with a startling speed, aimed, and fired.

The explosion of the bullet rent the air, and Skye was temporarily deaf. She screamed with horror, and she could not hear her own scream, but she felt the blood that sprayed from the pirate and onto her person, and then she was dragged down by the weight of the falling pirate. He fell, stone dead, atop her. She glanced at his face, and saw that it mostly gone, and she started to scream again, hysteria rising within her. She felt the body torn away from her, and she kept screaming.

Suddenly and rudely she was wrenched to her feet. She faced Cameron. His shook her fiercely and she gasped, ceasing to scream at last.

"Why, he's killed him! 'E's bloody killed Stikes!" someone shouted. Cameron continued to stare at her, and she stared back. Someone moved behind them and he swung around just in time to raise his cutlass and slay the cutthroat who had leaped toward him at Stikes's death.

There was movement again all about them. Skye dove for the sword that Stikes had knocked from her hand. Rising swiftly, she looked about herself, but she was safe. Cameron had her behind his back, and he was warily watching the men before him. His own crew had things in hand once again. There was silence. Slowly Cameron lowered his sword. "Mr. Blair! Take ten men. Put the rogues into the hold on the pirate ship. You'll take them straight to Williamsburg."

"Yes, sir!"

The danger, it seemed, was over.

Or else it was just beginning.

Skye stood braced against the mainmast as Cameron turned her way again, looking her up and down with a sweeping distaste. "You were told to stay below."

"There was a fire—"

"Davey was sent to bring you forward, not topside."

"I did not care to burn—"

"And how will you care, madame, when the lad receives a dozen lashes for failure to obey orders?"

"You wouldn't!" she gasped. But he would, she thought. A cold fury burned in his eyes. She stiffened, feeling the blood of the pirate upon her and longing for nothing more than to strip away her stained clothing and scrub the terror from her flesh. She raised her chin, frightened now for Davey, who was so ready to defend her always, no matter what punishment it brought upon him. She spoke as coldly as she could and with all the scathing dignity she could muster, hoping to shame him. "If you must mete out lashes, Lord Cameron, don't hurt an innocent boy. It was my fault, not his. Bring your whips against me."

"As you wish."

"What?"

"I said, as you wish. You or Davey. Someone must take the blame."

He turned from her as the body of the dead pirate was dragged away. They both stared as it was hoisted overboard. Then she stared at him again in amazement and shock.

"You wouldn't! You wouldn't dare tie me to the mast and bring a lash against me!"

He smiled very slowly. "With the greatest pleasure, milady."

Amazed, she gasped.

"Sir!" His attention was distracted as a seaman came to him, saluting sharply. "The fire is out, and it did no damage except within the hold. It is safe below."

"Very good," Lord Cameron said.

"Mr. Blair is prepared to toss the grappling hooks."

"Fine. Call the order, and we'll break away. I shall be at the wheel with all haste."

He turned back to Skye, but she had already intended to push past him. He stopped her, bringing his sword tip to her throat. She stood still, her chin raised, her temper soaring, and the whole of her quivering with outrage. His sword remained within her hand. She did not lift it. She intended to keep it within her own possession.

"This matter will wait," he said softly. His sword fell and she flinched anew, for his fingers came to her cheek, touching a spot where the blood of the pirate marred her pale flesh. "I'll see that you are brought water to bathe."

"You needn't bother—"

"Yes, I need bother," he said simply. "Do you need an escort, madame? Or can you manage on your own? I am afraid that I am growing shorthanded, so I would prefer—"

She swung away from him. At that moment, she was only too eager to reach the haven of her own cabin.

She hurried beneath the deck. The smell of smoke had faded away, and gunpowder no longer turned the air to gray. She heard commands shouted, and the heavy footsteps of men as they ran about. At the foot of the steps she paused, clutching her heart. She closed her eyes and listened. A mast had been hit and sailors hacked away at the wood and the canvas sail to cast the damaged pieces overboard. Other men raced about to raise the mainsail higher and catch the wind as they shoved away from the pirate vessel.

She made her way down the hall and hurried to her own cabin. She slammed the door. Once inside, she keenly felt the blood upon her. She started to tremble anew. Cameron! He had been so cold and cool and so damned competent! He had mocked and taunted, and she had been certain that he had meant to send her merrily upon her way with Stikes. But that had never been his intent. He had saved her with a swift and deadly cunning.

She sank down upon her bunk, but then she could not bear the clothes she wore. With a cry she rose and tore her gown in her haste to strip it away. She stood in her shift only, shivering, when there came a knock upon the door.

She grasped the coverlet from her bunk and wrapped it around herself, then threw the door open. It was not Davey who stood there or any man she knew. It was a graying and brawny seaman who carried a heavy brass tub of water. "Lady Cameron, may I?" He indicated the cabin, where he would set down his heavy load.

"Don't call me that!" she charged him.

He shrugged and came through the doorway, setting down the brass pot. There was a sponge within it and steam rose high. It was a small bath, but she could just stand within it and sponge water over herself, and she could not help but long to do so.

"There you be, Lady Cam—" He hesitated with another shrug. "There you be, milady."

"Thank you," she told him. He left her. She stripped off her shift and found the sponge and soap within the water. She scrubbed herself as if she were covered in mud, and still she could feel the blood. She did so again, and again, until the water grew so cold that she stood there shivering.

There was another knock upon her door. She hastily dried and slipped into her shift and dragged the coverlet about herself again, then drew open her door. The graying seaman was back with a fine fluted glass dangling from his sausage-sized fingers and a bottle in his hand.

"Dark Caribbean rum, milady. His lordship thought as how you might need a swallow."

"His lordship is so right," Skye muttered. She heard the closing of a cabin door just down the hall. His lordship! She trembled, thinking of the man. Her temper burned, and her pride.

"Aye, and he'll see you soon, he says."

"Will he?" she muttered, and the shivering seized her again. Why was this man here? Why was he serving her? "Where is—where is young Davey?" she demanded.

The brawny man shook his head most sorrowfully. "Preparing to repent his ways, milady, if you know what I mean."

"No!" she gasped. He couldn't have! Cameron couldn't have taken that poor boy and lashed him for her appearance on the deck!

But he could have. She remembered the cool way that he had goaded Stikes and wrested her from the pirate, and she was convinced that the man calling himself her husband could do anything at all.

She forgot her state of undress and pushed past the seaman, heading down the hallway. She didn't knock, but shoved open Cameron's door and strode inside.

He was seated behind his desk. His legs were lifted upon it and he rubbed a sore muscle in his calf, wincing as he did so. Startled, he turned her way. His eyes quickly narrowed.

"You bastard!" she hissed.

The seaman came up behind her. "Sir, she slipped by me! I'm sorry, milord—"

"It's all right, Mr. Whitehead. My wife is invited to join me in my cabin whenever she wishes." He smiled pleasantly, lifting his legs down to the floor.

"I am not visiting you in your cabin," Skye announced.

He arched a brow pleasantly, and stood. "That will be all, Mr. Whitehead."

"Yes, milord."

The burly seaman left them. The door closed sharply behind him. Skye realized that she was standing there barefoot and in her damp shift, with her bedcover upon her shoulders. She suddenly regretted the fury and impulse that had brought her here. Still, Davey had risked much for her. She would not allow him to be hurt.

"Where is Davey?" she demanded.

"Davey," he murmured. He came around his desk and sat upon its edge, watching her as he calmly crossed his arms over his chest. "Davey?"

"Davey! My man! He was a sailor aboard the *Silver Messenger,* and came into your service that way. You know exactly who I am talking about! And if you have offered him any harm—"

"Ah, yes, the lad! The one who deserves the stripes upon his back."

"He deserves nothing of the sort! I told you that it was my fault, my choice to come topside—"

"And did you realize, madame, that in coming topside you risked the lives of every man aboard this ship, not to mention your own?"

"You were quick enough to cast me to the wolves, milord!"

"Never, milady. There was not a single second when I did not prepare to slay the rogue."

"Then—"

"You endangered us all. Stikes was an amateur, madame. His crew was small, his vessel was faulty. We had bested him from the time that he raised his pirate colors over the flag of England."

"Then—"

"But you, madame," he interrupted again, his voice low and soft and still full of menace, "you could well have risked it all. To a man my crew would lay down their lives on your behalf. To see so much blood spilled unnecessarily would be a sorry crime before God. Discipline is mandatory upon a ship, especially in these waters. Davey must learn not to be conned by the wiles of a woman."

"He was not conned! I forced my way by him!"

"He should have suspected the trick."

"It was no trick!"

"Nevertheless, madame, your appearance on deck in the very arms of the pirate was disconcerting—"

"Disconcerting, indeed!" Seething, she approached him. She forgot her state of undress and the coverlet fell to the floor. Skye did not heed it as she slammed her fist upon the desk at his side. "Disconcerting! Well, then, sir, you should have let the pirate take me, trouble that I am! He was an honest rake, at that, while you! You claim to be a gentleman, a champion of justice! And you take that poor young boy—"

"Or yourself in his stead, madame."

She straightened, realizing how very close she had come to him and, at the same time, realizing her drastic state of undress. She had not dried thoroughly and her shift clung to her damp skin, outlining her breasts with a startling clarity. His eyes fell upon her with both amusement and fire and she tried to push away from the desk, determined to reach the coverlet. He caught her arm, dragging her back before him.

"Is it all bluff, milady? Tell me, are you willing to suffer for the lad? Is all that you say a lie or a taunt? Should you be stripped down to the bare truth of it all."

"No, it is not a lie!" she gasped, jerking upon his wrist. "Do it and be done with it! Call out your ship, if you so desire, and drag me in your chains! I will not protest!"

"No?"

She cried out, stunned, when he suddenly whirled her around, ripping the fragile material of her shift from her back. She fell to her knees, clinging to the damp material at the front of her shift, holding it to her breasts. What manner of man was this, she wondered, to behave in this fashion?

She stumbled up, ready to fight him on any level. But even as she held tight to her clothing and her dignity, he came behind her. The soft rush of his breath touched upon her bare flesh just as his arms wound around her, bringing her close.

"Nay, lady, I would not think to mar that beautiful flesh, ever, nor would I allow another man to bring harm to it!" She froze, then trembled fiercely as she felt the searing pressure of his lips against her naked back, blazing a trail of sensation to her nape and to her shoulder. "Nay, lady, I would not seek to harm you."

She swallowed, sinking swiftly into some netherworld. If he held too tightly to her, she would not be able to fight free.

But again, his words brushed against her earlobe, provocative in their sensual cadence.

"Lady, fear not. Your lad is below deck, punished with bread and water for the night, left alone, but well and unharmed, merely to reflect upon the foolishness of ever trusting a beautiful woman. Now, madame, as to you . . ." He paused, and it seemed that a fire ignited deep within her, flooding her limbs, causing her to tremble all anew.

With fear, with anger . . .

And, she realized with a startling horror . . .

With anticipation.

XI

Petroc Cameron strode across the room and plucked her coverlet from the floor. He returned to her, sweeping it around her shoulders while she stared at him in stunned silence. "As for you, madame, perhaps you would be so kind as to return to your own cabin. It has been a trying afternoon, and I've work to attend to."

Blankly, she stared at him. He smiled slowly. "Did you really think me so cruel? It's just that it is a very serious situation when a pirate flag flies, as you well know, and I must confess, my heart leaped to my throat when that ruffian had his filthy fingers upon you. Davey is a good lad; he will learn to be a fine sailor. And now, my love . . ."

She was silent still and he caught her arm, leading her to the door. He did not leave her in the hallway, but went with her down the few steps to her cabin. Someone had come back and cleared away the small tub, and several lamps burned brightly upon the dresser. He opened her door, bowed deeply, and left her, and she had still to say a single word.

He was a curious man, indeed.

She sat down upon her bunk, either bemused or completely in shock. In a while she curled up on it, drawing the covers high around her and shivering.

Perhaps she shouldn't have burst upon the deck so. It was just that she had not wanted to be trapped in the smoke and fire. It might have spread. A fire on shipboard was a frightening and serious matter. She walked right into the arms of the pirate, just as she walked straight into Logan's arms when she had been the Hawk's prisoner off of New Providence. . . .

She curled up and thought about the Hawk, and tried hard to cling to his memory. It was fading, and she could not allow it to do so. Fading . . . and becoming combined with the reality of his cousin. Her husband.

She burned suddenly where she lay, thinking of Cameron's intimate kiss. It had been no gentle caress, but something fierce and demanding. She thought of his casual display of disdain topside when the pirate had held her. Take her, she is trouble, he had said.

And he had bared her back, but not to the lash. Rather to the searing tenderness of his lips . . .

She tossed about. He could call himself "Lord" Cameron, but he was hard and could be callous. The tenderness was a facade, for they were already well cast into battle. She would not remain married to him—no, she would not accept that she was married to him! She would not. She owed him gratitude, perhaps, but no more.

She had just dozed when another seaman brought her dinner upon a silver tray. It was a delicious fresh fish seasoned with green peppercorns. She was weary and discouraged that night, though she knew not why. She didn't bother to dress for dinner, but cast aside her torn shift and donned a nightgown made of fine linen decorated with tiny embroidered daisies. She tied the delicate laces at the bodice and sat down in her nightdress and froth of covers to eat. The rum he had sent earlier sat upon the dressing table, and she dared to sip it. It was so potent a brew that her lips quivered before she could swallow, but she did manage to imbibe some. It burned down to the very heart, blazing a path from her throat to her stomach. She did not sip much, but she was glad of what she tasted, for it allowed her to lie down again and seek to sleep. In the midst of the night she dreamed of the beguiling paradise lagoon upon Bone Cay. Her lover rose from the water and came toward her, but with each step the man was different, depending on how the sunlight dappled on his naked shoulders. At one moment it the Silver Hawk, claiming her affections with gentle demand. Then the light would change, and it would be her lord husband, noble and imperious and bold and undaunted, and she would not know whether to run and to scream, or to wait until he came to her, and open her arms to him.

She awoke with a jerk. Her lamps were burning low, so she knew that morning was almost with them. Arising, she heard a soft oath in the hallway. Was someone coming her way?

She slipped out of bed and found Lord Cameron's sword upon the floor where she had left it the previous night. Footsteps were coming to her cabin. She leaped back into bed, carefully bringing the razor-sharp weapon along with her. Her heart thundered.

Her door was cast quietly open. For the longest time she lay there, barely daring to breathe. She opened her eyes a bare slit, allowing her lashes still to shield them. She feigned sleep, but looked to the doorway.

It was Lord Cameron. His white wig neatly queued, his shoulders broad upon his tall frame. He watched her in silence.

As she waited, he entered, closing the door. He came her way. The cover had slipped from her shoulders. She nearly screamed when he moved his hand to pull it more fully upon her. She could not help her eyes from flying open and falling upon his with grave alarm.

"There is nothing, madame. I apologize for disturbing you," he said softly, his words a breath of air in the night.

"You've no right in here!" she murmured nervously. He did not touch her, he just stood over her, and inwardly she came alive with hot, cascading shivers.

"I've every right in here, but we won't dispute that tonight. We'll come home soon enough."

"My home is Williamsburg."

"Milady, your home is a beautiful place upon the peninsula. Sweat and tears and blood went into the founding of it, and I do not take kindly to your insults."

"I've not insulted—"

"But you have. Good night."

She was not about to let him turn away. She sat up, drawing his sword from her covers with a blue flame rising in her eyes. She was quick and expert, bringing the tip of his own sword against his throat before he began to realize her intent.

"Skye—"

"No! No!" she admonished, holding the blade at his throat while she came up upon her knees and faced him. She dug slightly, forcing him to raise his head. It was her turn to smile. "Sir, I have had it with beginning and ending these conversations. Shall we go back to the beginning? You have no right here. You and my father played some trick and you think then that I am married. Well, I dispute that fact, so you do have no right here! Now, sir, you have rescued me from the grip of not one pirate, but two. However, sir, I find you little better than either of them! You fought today with the same sizzle of conquest in your eyes, and you are every bit as arrogant and disdaining of social custom as your cousin! I did not set out to make your life miserable, sir—you stumbled into my life!"

"I beg to differ. Your father—"

"My father!" She prodded the sword closer to his throat, forcing him to cease speaking. "My father! What is this about my father? Are you not a man, sir? Have you not heard the word 'no'?"

She pressed against his throat. He did not seem to care. His eyes grew narrower by the second and they seemed to blaze like the North Star. "Madame, there is nothing that I do not do by my will, and by my will alone. But I honor my father, and so I chose to honor his vows. If you have a disagreement about our present relationship, feel free to bring it up to your father, but know this! By the law you are my wife. By temperament I am afraid that your very hostility has made me bound and determined to keep what is mine. You are at my mercy, madame, and you'd best remember it!"

Skye laughed with sheer delight. She had him at the disadvantage; he was the one with the blade of honed steel against his throat, and he still thought to threaten her.

"I should slice and dice you!" she whispered.

"Yes, you should. And immediately," he said calmly. "Umm. I daresay that your best move would be to do murder this very second, because otherwise you will live to rue this moment with all of your heart."

"I don't think so. I think that you will leave my cabin this very second."

"Not without my sword."

"That will be difficult. I hold your sword."

"No, you do not."

Maybe he knew that she could not really murder him; maybe she had not been threatening enough, or maybe she had been so thrilled with her own moment of triumph that she had fallen prey to his speed and daring. He simply took the blade with both his hands and thrust it from him before snatching the hilt from her. And he did it with such speed and reckless bravado that the blade lay against her breast before she could so much as blink.

He smiled pleasantly. "I hold my sword, milady, as you see."

Skye sank down upon her haunches, keeping a very wary eye upon him. His smile remained. So did the blade. He very calmly drew it through the laces of her gown. Its honed edge slit the delicate ties soundlessly and effortlessly, and her gown spilled opened. His eyes fell upon her in the lamplight, but gave no clue to his thoughts. She could not have known if he desired her, or despised all that he saw. He moved the material away from her breast with practiced ease—the razor-edged blade did not so much as scratch her flesh. To her dismay, her body responded in an alarming fashion. Her breasts swelled, her nipples peaked and hardened. Her breath rasped too quickly and he surely saw the rise in her pulse as it beat against her veins. She saw his eyes then, and the satanic mischief in them. "Bastard!" she hissed to him, and shoved the sword away. With deep throaty laughter he allowed it to fall.

She clutched her bodice together. "This was a good gown!" she snapped to him.

"Since it is my duty to see you fed and clothed, I shall replace it, madame. May I say that it shall be well worth the cost."

"You may not!"

"Poor rogue who captured you, milady! So this is why the Hawk let you go without demanding a single farthing!" Chuckling softly, he turned. Had she been blessed with any good sense whatsoever, she would have let him go.

Good sense seemed to be the least of her virtues at the moment. Skye vaulted from the bed to slam against his back with both fists flying. "You are not amusing, and you are not my husband, and I absolutely insist that you—"

She broke off, for he had whirled around, and he held her very tightly in his arms. The sword had fallen to the ground, where he ignored it. He didn't speak for several seconds; she had gone dead still, for she sensed in his hold, in the heat of his body against hers, that now, more than ever, she had gone too far. He held her in a grip of steel, he held her without moving, barely breathing. Then at last he whispered very softly, "Unless you wish me to prove you my wife in every way this very night, this very moment, press me no further!"

She did not. She allowed her head to fall back and she watched him with a certain awe, trembling and trying not to do so. Her bodice gaped open and she felt the tremendous burning pressure of his body heat against her breasts. She could feel his hips, flush to her thighs.

She wanted to die. Shame and humiliation rushed into her, bringing a rose red flush to her cheeks. She did not want both men; she hadn't wanted either man, but the one had taught her about passion and the sweet dark secrets of desire, and now this stranger with the same silver touch seemed to be beckoning her anew. She could not allow it; she could not bear this of herself.

"Please! I am sorry, let me go!" she said.

He breathed out in a rasp, slowly releasing her. His fingers brushed her bare flesh as he brought the straying folds of her torn bodice together.

Then he turned again, and Skye was only too grateful to let him go. Alone at last, she sank back to her bunk, curved her legs taut to her stomach, and shivered anew. What in God's name was she going to do? She could not marry him; she could not be touched by him. . . .

She might well be carrying a rogue's child, she reminded herself.

And with that thought she leaped up once more, and drank down several swallows of the deadly potent rum.

In his own cabin Petroc Cameron—captain of the *Lady Elena* and once master of his own destiny—sat and imbibed more than a few swallows of rum.

He sat at his desk and slammed down the bottle and swore with a startling velocity, then tossed back his head and drank even more deeply.

Damn Spotswood! Damn Blackbeard and Logan and Vane and every pirate who had ever sailed the Atlantic and Caribbean. "And most of all," he muttered aloud, "damn the Silver Hawk! Damn him to a hundred thousand different hells!"

He fell silent then and leaned his head back against his chair. The rum began to work its easing magic, pulling the pain and the tension, the ache and the desire, slowly from his constricted muscles, ligaments, and extremities. He closed his eyes, but he could not close his mind from the memories of her, nor could he cease to breathe in her scent, to imagine the silky softness of her flesh beneath his fingers, beneath his lips.

He could not forget her hair, spilling like sun rays over her breasts, wild and free and tempting him to touch. He could not forget her vows, or how like the Caribbean waters her eyes were, blue green, fascinating with their depths, their ever-changing color. . . .

He could not forget her form, and more than anything in the world, he wanted to drag her back into this cabin and feel her beneath him on his bunk that very night. Let the world be damned! Let any man come and blow them straight out of the water, he would sink and die happily, having her in his arms. . . .

She was his wife. He had the right.

The right . . .

But he had destroyed it all himself. In a surge of passion he had condemned himself to this hell, and so he would burn within it. He had no other choice.

He touched his clean-shaven cheeks and the nick where a blade had caught him that afternoon in the skirmish with pirates. He grimaced, duly noting that a bit closer and the blade might well have ended his days. His fingers ran down to his throat, where he could still feel the point of his sword. It was a mistake. He could see her face all over again, the fire in her eyes, the sweet triumph. She was always proud, he thought. She did not know how to surrender, no, she simply did not surrender, not even when she was bested. Even when he had wrested his throat away, even when he had slit the delicate ties to her gown, her eyes had battled him still. And surrender had lain within his own heart, for he had wanted with all of his heart to reach out and touch, to feel the fullness of her breast within his palm.

He swallowed more rum, groaning aloud. Had he any sense, he would keep away from her. He would bring her to Cameron Hall, deposit her there, see to business, and strike out again as soon as possible. Had he any sense. Sense did not always remain with him. One sight of her and he was challenged back to battle again. He could not leave well enough alone, he had to keep testing her.

He wanted the truth from her.

No, he wanted her. He wanted her with all the fire and flame within him, and he found it increasingly hard to endure the hell of his own creation. He could not seize her; he could not drag her here. He shouldn't have kissed her; he shouldn't have touched her. He should not be sitting here now, thinking of her. Of her hair brushing his naked flesh, of her eyes, liquid with passion, of her hips, moving beneath him. He should not. The hell was his, and his alone.

He would burn. . . .

With his bottle of rum, he thought wryly, and with his dreams.

During the next day it seemed that Lord Cameron quite purposely avoided her.

Davey was out and about again, and only slightly subdued

as he served her. She was glad to have him and Bessie and Tara with her as she watched the ever-present shoreline.

The next day he did speak to her. He came to her where she stood by the railing, looking out. "North Carolina, madame. We near Virginia, and soon the Chesapeake Bay and the James River." He paused, and she felt his eyes falling over the length of her. "And Cameron Hall," he added.

"How nice. I shall see my father quickly, I imagine."

"I imagine that he will be at the house. I saw Spotswood before I sailed. He knew that your ship had been seized, and that I was to claim you from the Hawk. I am sure that he has had your father come to my home."

"We shall settle things quickly enough," she murmured.

"Perhaps," he said simply. He pointed to the shoreline. "Inlets and islands," he murmured. "Spotswood finds the government of North Carolina to be sorry indeed. But then he commands a fine militia himself. And he is a military man, you know."

She lifted her chin. "I know the lieutenant governor, Lord Cameron. I grew up not far from his new mansion."

"You haven't seen it yet, complete."

"No."

"It's a fine manor. His balls are famous." He smiled recklessly, widening his eyes like a rogue. "Be a good girl, and I shall take you to one."

"Behave, sir, and I shall see that you are still able to walk to reach one!"

He laughed softly. "Lady, you threaten so swiftly and so fiercely, when it is like a sparrow against a hawk!"

She looked away quickly at the word "hawk." Roc grated his own teeth, looking to the shore. "Madame," he said bluntly, "you will never best me. Cease to try, and we shall get along, I am sure. Truly, my every desire is to see to your comfort."

"My comfort—upon your bed!" she spat out, then flushed furiously, and looked about for someplace to escape him. She could not believe that she had said the words! He was laughing at her again, but his brow was arched and there was a cynical note to the sound. He came close to her.

"Tell me, my love, what do you know of such things?"

"Nothing!" she cried, and pushed away from the rail. She looked to the shore. "Father—er—Father says that Alexander is very suspicious of Governor Eden. He says that his government is not just poor, but perhaps corrupt. That he lets pirates seek safe havens in his waters—for a price."

"Many men have a price."

"Tell me—do you?" she demanded quickly.

He shook his head very slowly. "No, milady. I have my faults. I suppose you would say that arrogance is among them, no doubt."

"And a certain lack of humility?" she suggested sweetly.

"Maybe. But I cannot be bought. Not for any price. Remember that, milady. If you ever seek to—negotiate."

He turned away. She was left alone at the rail, shivering despite the balmy warmth of the day.

When she awoke the next morning, they were sailing the Chesapeake Bay. She quickly dressed and ate, and came topside, and by then they were coming down the James. There was tremendous energy and motion on board as seaman trimmed and drew in sails.

"Oh, how lovely, milady! Don't ye think so!"

She turned about. Arm in arm, Bessie and Tara were staring at the shoreline. There eyes were rapt, and Skye realized that this was a dream for them. They had left behind poverty and cramped spaces in the Old World, and they were looking to the New. She smiled, for they stood arm and arm, and in awe. Skye smiled at the two of them. "It is something indeed," she said agreeably.

She glanced to the helm. Lord Cameron himself was at the wheel, navigating the river. He did not look so much the seaman as the aristocrat. He was extremely proper in his queued wig, elegant brocade frockcoat, blue satin breeches, fawn hose, and silver buckled shoes. A dark velvet ribbon tied his queue while he wore an eagle-plumed three-cornered hat. Skye was not close to him, but yet she could sense the tension and energy about him. He stood so straight; he rode the ship so well. He looked to the land.

Then she felt him turn to her, as if by instinct. He stepped briefly from the wheel to bow to her.

Skye looked quickly back to the shoreline.

Not much later the order came down that a cannon should be fired.

Lord Cameron had come home.

Skye saw the house first. It was impossible to miss, for it sat high atop a hill. Built of brick, it was both elegant and imposing. Tall pillars seemed to reach to the heavens, and the whole of the building was surrounded by a broad, sweeping porch. There were outbuildings all around it, making it appear more like a small village than a residence. The house seemed massive, and perhaps even more so because of the bounty of land that surrounded it. The hill commanded the area with majestic deep green grasses rolling down from it all of the way to the river and the docks. On either side Cameron Hall was surrounded by trees. Far beyond, she could see the fields.

"My great-great-grandparents claimed it from wilderness."

Startled, she swung around. The captain had left his helm to come by her side. "Jamie Cameron came as a lad first, sometimes exploring with John Smith. In 1621 he came over with his bride. There was a wooden palisade then, and his first home was built of wood. They were attacked by the Indians during the massacre at Easter in 1622. Jassy was kidnapped by the Indians."

Skye smiled, looking his way. "Sir, I am well aware that we have pushed the Indians far inland. Are you trying to frighten me?"

"Never, my love."

"I assume that your relative was rescued?"

"Of course. We Camerons love to rescue damsels in distress." He pointed upward to the house. "You can see the main hall, there. That was the first section built. King James died, and Charles the First came to the throne. Then came the English Civil War. Eion Cameron went home to fight as a Cavalier. He died there battling Cromwell's men. Some of our English holdings were lost, England was under the 'Protectorate,' and even our holdings in Virginia were in jeopardy. But then Cromwell died and good Charles the Second was invited to return to take up his crown. Eion's son went and retrieved his body and his property. Eion is buried upon our slopes. His son, another Jamie, added on the east wing." His grin deepened and he leaned toward her. "James the Second came to the throne upon his brother's death, and Jemmy, Duke of Monmouth, Charles's favorite bastard child, tried to take the throne, damning his uncle as a papist. Alas! Jemmy went to the block, and it's quite possible that his uncle did not blink an eye. Still, he was rumored to be handsome and gallant, and he had many supporters. Many of them came here, to Cameron Hall. There are secret passages within the walls, and tunnels run away to the sea."

"Ah! So the Camerons are known to harbor criminals!"

"Criminals? Never!" His eyes sparkled so that she discovered she had to smile in turn. "No criminals, madame, just those with visions different than some. Those passionate, and sometimes foolish, in their loyalties. There was little danger when he harbored Jemmy's revolutionaries. You see, James the Second did not last long upon his throne. William of Orange was a dour fellow, so they say, but extremely bright. With James's daughter Mary he started his own bloodless and 'glorious' revolution and between them and their very proper and Prostestant ways, they took the throne. And they were a tolerant pair. Alas, poor Mary died quickly, and then William, and then Queen Anne wore the crown, and now it is a German from Hanover. Meanwhile, over here, at Cameron Hall, we merely battle Indians and mosquitoes and disease, and we set sail from our coasts to battle the Spanish each time our reigning monarch declares us to be at war. We watched Jamestown burn, and burn again, and my father was delighted when they moved the capital to Williamsburg."

"And you, Lord Cameron, what do you delight in?"

It was a leading question; one she shouldn't have asked. He took her hand and kissed it slowly, meeting her eyes. "My love, I don't remember. Since I have seen your face, I delight in your presence."

There was a wicked gleam about his eyes. Skye snatched her hand away. "I believe, Lord Cameron, that since you have seen my face, you have delighted in taunting me!"

He bowed gracefully to her. "That, too, Lady Cameron. That, too."

He turned and strode back to the helm, shouting out orders as he did so. She did not miss his smile of amusement, despite his quick motion. He knows! she thought furiously. It was almost as if he knew the very truth of her heart, and taunted her mercilessly for it. She gritted her teeth and stared toward shore. The ship was coming about at the dock. She could see a throng of people there; it was like a holiday. Barefoot sailors cast ropes to the dock and the ship was soon brought to her berth. The sails were all furled and men worked to coil the rigging. Wives called to husbands, children to their fathers. It was a fascinating and colorful display. Tara and Bess were silent, in awe of the commotion. Skye was quiet, wondering at her future. She stared up the slope to the house. Her father would be there. And this fiasco would come to an end. She would go home and see her friends in Williamsburg. Mattie would be there, keeping house. Skye would be her father's hostess, planning parties and engagements with Mattie, discovering the gardens again, walking to the governor's new mansion for afternoon tea. It would be all right. She would pitch into her life with energy and fervor, and she would forget the pirate Silver Hawk, just as she would forget his noble cousin.

That was not to come so quickly, though. The plank was being stretched to the dock and Lord Cameron was coming her way once again. "My love?" He took her elbow, not allowing her to refuse his touch.

"I am not your love!"

"Come!" he commanded swiftly.

She had little choice. "Wait until I see my father!" she threatened him in a whisper.

"I wait with bated breath, madame," he assured her.

They stood upon the plank. Lord Cameron paused, smiling his charismatic smile. A cheer went up, and cries of welcome. He silenced them all. "My bride, Skye, Lady Cameron!" he announced. More cheers went up. Little urchins struggled from their mother's skirts to see her. Scarves were waved high in the air.

He led her across the plank and to the dock, and there he

started making introductions so swiftly that her head began to ring. "My love, here's Mary, the rector's daughter. And Jeanne, his wife. Mr. Tibault, and Mr. Oskin—they are our tenants, my love, and farm the northern acres of the hundred. Mrs. Billingsgate—" He paused, brushing an old woman's face with a quick kiss that sent her to flushing like wildfire. "Her late husband sailed with me. She runs a wee store here at the docks for the men and their wives. She brews tea and ale and makes fine, sweet biscuits!"

Mrs. Billingsworth bobbed quickly to Skye, still blushing. Her eyes fell back to her lord, adoringly. He did have his charm, Skye admitted, and it seemed that his people were all a bit spellbound by it. He was a popular master.

"Ah, the carriage!" he said, and pulled her forward. With every step, there were more rapid introductions. She nodded here and there, meeting people whose names she would never remember. Everywhere she was greeted with warmth, and nowhere did she manage to say that she was not Lord Cameron's wife, nor would she ever be so.

He brought her to a handsome coach that would have been wonderfully appropriate for a fine English estate. The Cameron coat of arms was emblazoned upon the doorway. A footman opened the door while a coachman drove the fine team of four dapple grays. Skye entered the coach and he quickly followed her in. She sat back. It was luxurious indeed. A whip cracked in the air, and the horses started off. The ride was smooth, the upholstery was deep and cushiony and in an elegant teal velvet.

But even this ride had its price. He was watching her.

"What is it, madame, that dissatisfies you so?"

Skye moved against the door because he was leaning too close to her; his eyes were dark and probing, and she was suddenly afraid. He could be a brooding man, silent or eloquent as he chose. His temper could be great, she knew, soaring like flash fire before it became carefully leashed once more. "I don't know what you mean," she murmured. How long could this ride be? They were so near the house.

And he could be, at times, so like the Silver Hawk. He could reach inside of her. He could tease and evoke the same fevers, and make her feel as if she gasped for breath, as if she could forget the past, or remember it all too well.

"What is it, madame, that you do not like? My pride in my home is exorbitant, perhaps, but it is still one of the richest estates in all Tidewater Virginia—in all of the colony, I imagine. There is a certain prestige to be discovered here. The house has every luxury available, madame. We are a seafaring people, and acquire all manner of fine imports. Our table is always bountiful. So what is it, madame, that you do not like about being Lady Cameron?"

She smiled very sweetly. "*Lord* Cameron!" she told him, and turned quickly to look out the window. She did not know if she had ignited his temper, and she suddenly did not care to discover the truth of it if she had.

She heard his soft laughter, but it came with an edge. "We will see about that," he promised her.

"Aye, we shall!" she agreed.

The coach came to a halt. The door was swung open by the footman, whom Lord Cameron quickly thanked. Then he reached for Skye. She fell against him as he lifted her from the carriage to lower her to the ground. His eyes touched upon her. "Indeed, we shall see!" he promised her.

She was dismayed to discover that her heart raced frantically. Quickly she lowered her eyes and disengaged from him. He took her elbow, leading her quickly up the steps to the porch with its massive Greek columns. Doors to a massive hallway with a polished wood floor lay open to them and a very correct butler in handsome livery awaited them.

"Peter, how goes it, man?"

"Well enough, sir. A bit o' the gout in my leg, but that is all." The man swept a low bow to Skye. "We welcome you, milady, with all of our pleasure and very best wishes!"

Petroc Cameron stood away, and as Skye looked into the wide hallway, blinking against the sunlight, she saw that the household servants were all arrayed to meet her and offer her best wishes. She met the groom and the cook and the upstairs maids and the downstairs maid and the head groom and his staff. She smiled graciously, and seethed inside. She would not stay! And with every passing moment, she felt as if ties bound ever more tightly around her.

When she came to the end of the line, she discovered that her husband had disappeared. The butler Peter was waiting for her. He bowed again, offering a pleasant and eager smile. She thought that for all the very proper dress and appearance of the servants, things were very different here. Cameron was a lord, but he was a colonial, too. A Yankee, like herself. It was not England. Servants, tenants, and masters all depended upon one another, and so the lines of society were far less rigid here. Peter, she thought, was more Roc Cameron's friend than a mere servant. And he was eager to please her for his master's sake.

"Milady, if you'll be so good as to come along, I will show you to your room."

"Fine. Thank you. But, Peter, where is my father? Lord Cameron said that he would be here."

"Lord Kinsdale has not yet arrived, milady."

"Oh," Skye murmured, disappointed.

"If you will, please . . ." Peter indicated a graceful and sweeping stairway. She followed him along it, looking about. The manor was truly fine and gracious. The hallway loomed beneath her, while a fine gallery stood above her. She followed the curve of the banister and came at last to the landing, another hallway, leading to the main room, and to the two wings of the house, east and west.

She paused in the hallway. It was a portrait gallery, the type made popular during the reign of Elizabeth I. There was a fine array of Camerons portrayed there, beautiful women, handsome, provocative men.

Too many of them with the haunting, silver eyes! she thought, and shivered. They could be so much alike. The Hawk could just as easily have his portrait hung here as the rightful Cameron heir. Shave him and queue him neatly and dress him fashionably and—

"Milady, this way, please."

He took her through the hall to a more narrow corridor leading into the west wing. There he cast open a set of double doors to a large chamber.

Skye stepped inside.

The room was huge and handsome. Paned windows reached near to the floor on the far side, looking out upon the James River and the beautiful slope of the land. Skye walked to them first, and instinctively murmured with delight. Then her murmurs and delight faded as she slowly turned around to look at the room.

It was dominated by a huge four-poster bed with handsome blue velvet draperies. Far to the right were bookshelves, and far to the left was the fireplace with several wingback chairs brought near to the hearth. There was a huge trunk at the foot of the bed, and there were matching armoires in the two rear corners. Across from the fire and facing the windows was a large oak desk, and closer to the sunlight was a small round table covered simply in white linen. An open doorway led to a dressing room. Skye strode to the doorway and stepped through, bracing herself against the shadows there. There was a washstand and a pitcher and bowl and beyond it a huge brass hip tub and a necessary chair. To the far rear of this smaller room was a rack hung with coats and apparel.

Men's coats, men's apparel.

She stepped out from the dressing room. Her trunks were already arriving here. She didn't speak, but looked around once more. It was the master's room, beyond a doubt. It faced the river, and it caught the river breezes. It was a handsome and masculine room. It offered every amenity and elegance, but it retained something of a manly air.

"This—this cannot be my room!" she protested to Peter.

Peter, startled, looked her way. "Milady, this is Lord Cameron's room, of course. He instructed me to bring you here, Lady Cameron."

"But I'm not really—"

She broke off, not willing to argue with his servants. It would get her nowhere, she realized. Her trunks were already arriving, carried by grooms and houseboys, who all bowed to her again with shy and welcoming pleasure. If she protested, they would merely think that she had gone mad.

Her fight was with Lord Cameron. She had to stop him from this madness, and no one else.

She clenched her fists to her sides and approached Peter. "Where is your master, Peter."

"He's busy, Lady Cameron—"

"I did not ask you that. Where is he?"

"His office, milady. But I would not—"

"No, Peter, you should not—but I would, and I will interrupt him," she said sweetly. She left Peter and the servants and the wing behind, coming out upon the portrait gallery and clutching the banister to scamper down the length of the stairway. She felt all those pairs of blue and gray and silver eyes following her down to the landing in the lower hallway.

In his office . . .

She pushed open a door to the left and discovered the formal dining room. Swords crossed over the fireplace, the table sat at least twenty, a Persian rug lay over the floorboards and beneath the table, and the Cameron coat of arms covered the far wall. Windows looked out upon the sloping lawns of the estate.

Skye slammed the door and went on. The next one entered to a music room with comfortable chairs and a beautiful rug and molded and corniced ceilings. She slammed that door and went on, discovering a parlor decorated to the Sun King's tastes. She slammed that door, too, and hurried across the hallway. She shoved open the first door and discovered Roc Cameron behind a massive, polished desk. There was a huge globe on the floor nearby, and every shelf there was lined with books. Again, it was a masculine room.

He had shed his coat and wore only his breeches and fine laced shirt. He pored over correspondence, a frown on his face that faded when he saw her standing there. He laid down the letter he was reading, and waited. He did not invite her in. He didn't even speak.

For a moment she panicked. She had rushed here, she had torn apart the house, and she wasn't even sure what she intended to say.

She should have just run, she thought. She should have very sweetly agreed to everything, and when the servants had all disappeared, she should have run for the stables and stolen a horse. She didn't know the peninsula well, but he had said that it was three hours to Williamsburg. Surely she could find her way!

"Are you coming in? Have you something to say? Or have you come merely to stare at me?"

"No, of course not."

Skye came in, closing the door behind her. She strode to his desk, then discovered herself tongue-tied. She pushed away from it and paced, then suddenly sat in the leather chair before his desk.

"You have put me in your room," she accused him.

He lifted his hands and shrugged. She sensed that a smile played beneath the bland and innocent stare that he gave her. "You are my wife," he said.

"I dispute that."

"You may dispute the sun, but when it rises, it is still daylight."

She slammed a fist against the table. "You said that my father would be here."

"I expected him, yes."

He was telling the truth, she thought. He seemed as puzzled as she that Theo had not yet arrived.

Skye sat back. "If my father were here," she told him with narrowed eyes, "you would not attempt to put me in your room!"

"Madame, if your father were here, and his father, and his father's father, I would still put you in my quarters. You are my wife."

"But—"

"I left you be upon the ship, milady, out of the delicacy of the situation. We are home now. Upon terra firma. I weary of the waiting, madame."

She stiffened, leaning back. He meant his words. She could not be his wife!

And unless she did escape him that very afternoon, there seemed little hope for it. Her stomach catapulted. He would discover her a liar in the very worst way. What would he do to her then? What could he do, except release her . . . ?

And yet, she didn't dare chance the discovery. Nor did she think that she could bear his touch. She dreaded it; she felt the heat of it too keenly. She didn't know if she despised the man, or if she was fascinated by him beyond all measure. The tempest living inside of her was unbearable.

"I can't!" she said suddenly, certainly.

"Can't?"

She leaped up from the chair, walking about the room in a state of agitation. Could she say what she intended about the Silver Hawk? What difference would it make? If the Hawk were ever captured, he would hang pure and simple, and her words could not make him die any more or less thoroughly.

For a moment, though, it seemed as if her heart itself sizzled, for she was betraying something. It was love, she thought, for indeed, despite her later anger, the tenderness and care of the pirate had drawn upon her every emotion. She had, indeed, loved him with care as well as passion. Now she betrayed that very love, but it seemed she had little choice.

"I cannot be your wife because . . ."

He sat back. "Because . . . ?" he prompted.

She turned her back to him, looking to the windows. If she was going to die, she might as well do it dramatically, wholeheartedly.

She dropped her head in abject shame. "I cannot come to you as your wife. Ever. I am not what I appear to be. I—"

She broke off.

"He—he raped me!" she claimed.

"He what?"

The chair fell back as Lord Cameron jumped to his feet in indignity. He came behind her, grabbing her shoulders, spinning her around. "He—what?"

She kept her head lowered, willing a glaze of tears to her eyes. Slowly she let her head fall back. "He is a pirate, you know! Scourge of the seas. A deadly, horrible rogue."

"And he—raped you?" Lord Cameron repeated.

"Yes!" she cried, breaking away. He allowed her to go. She sat upon the edge of his desk.

"My God," he whispered in what she was certain to be raw fury. "He used horrific force against you? He dragged you—my very wife!—beneath him. Horribly and cruelly against your will?"

"Of course!"

"My God!"

She kept her head lowered. She brushed her cheek as if to take away tears of shame.

"You did not tell me!"

"I could not—I could not speak of it at first. But now you have to know so that you need not be saddled with me, or with this farce of a marriage. Lord Cameron! I free you to find a proper and innocent bride."

"How ghastly!"

"Yes!"

"How very deplorable!"

"Yes!" She dared to turn, looking up at him at last. Shadows seemed to have fallen over the room, and she felt the silver probe of his eyes deeply upon her. She leaped up, lowering her head once again. "I shall see my things are moved. I will sign anything necessary to free you—"

"No, my love," he said very softly.

"What?" she gasped. He came toward her, taking her shoulders. Her head fell back. His eyes sizzled, and she wondered at his thoughts. "Your—honesty—is commendable, my love. But can you truly think so poorly of me? You are my wife, sworn to me before God. I will not cast you from my side, no matter what your generosity. So, go, my love, back to our room. When my business is done, I will join you there, and most gladly still!"

In disbelief she stared at him. His eyes danced in lamplight and shadow. He lowered his head slowly to hers, and she was too amazed to move. His mouth covered hers with passion and fire, his lips molding tight to hers, his tongue probing and ravaging past all barriers with fervent demand. Warmth filled her, as shocking as the invasion that seemed to fill the whole of her body. Laps of flame seemed to lick within her stomach and all along her spine, and spin and swirl to the very heart of her desire at the juncture of her thighs.

She wrenched away from him, gasping and desperate, despising herself, despising the very passion he could elicit and evoke within her. He watched her, his hands on his hips, his eyes knowing.

She backed away from him, trembling.

He smiled, and she felt as if she faced the very devil.

"Go to our room, love. To our bed. I will follow you swiftly, I swear it."

She wanted to deny him; she wanted to rage and tell him that she despised him completely.

But it wasn't the truth, and so she said nothing.

She no longer wished to fight; only to run.

And escape.

XII

Skye turned swiftly and fled.

Outside Lord Cameron's door she knew that she had little choice left but to run. Where in God's name was her father?

She fled up the stairs and back to his room, frantically digging through her belongings until she found a skirt and jacket more serviceable than the gown she wore. She changed nervously, ever watching the door lest he should appear. He did not. Leaving all of her belonging behind, she left the room. She sped down the stairway, then backed against the wall, certain that she heard Roc Cameron talking with Peter. She ducked into the dining room, her heart thundering. Footsteps passed by on the hardwood floors. Their echo dimmed. Skye thrust open the door and checked out the hallway, then tore through the hallway and out to the porch.

The outbuildings stretched before her.

She had no difficulty locating the stables, for the building was large and impressive and the painted doors were open to the afternoon sun. She hurried along the path until she came there. A young groom, raking up hay, paused and bobbed her way.

"I need a mount, please, Reggie, is it?"

He smiled his vast pleasure and quickly nodded. "We've Lady Love, she mild and sweet—"

"Oh, no!" Skye allowed her eyes to flash with laughter. "I ride very well, Reggie, and would have a fleet mount to show me much of the property while it is still daylight."

"There's Storm then, milady. But he's Lord Cameron's stallion, and a wild one at that." His gaze was skeptical, and she felt sorry for the lad. He had long obeyed one master, but now he had a mistress, too, and he didn't seem to know if he should bow to the wishes of the one or worry about the other.

"Storm!" Skye said sweetly. "Wonderful. Reggie, fetch him for me, please, he sounds perfect for what I have in mind!"

Her smile convinced him. Reggie quickly returned with the animal in question. He was gray, and huge, prancing with his every movement and watching her with deep, dark wide-set eyes. He was one of the most handsome horses she had ever seen.

Except for the white, she thought. The great white animal she had seen upon Bone Cay. The Hawk's horse.

She bit her lip, unwilling to think further. She glanced nervously to the house, hoping that Lord Cameron's correspondence was holding his attention. She smiled a dazzling smile to young Reggie. "Thank you. Reggie, you are swift and sweet, and I promise that my husband will know how kind and helpful you have been."

Reggie, blushing furiously, brought the horse around to the mounting block and Skye quickly mounted upon him. She glanced around uneasily, getting her bearings. Northeastward along the river, and she would reach Williamsburg. Three hours, he had said.

Skye glanced anxiously toward the powder blue sky. She prayed briefly that the daylight would hold for her, then she gathered up the reins and nodded to young Reggie. "Thank you!" she cried swiftly, then she turned the huge horse about and swiftly nudged him. It was not difficult now, for a great sweeping drive beneath trails of oak led toward the main road.

She leaned against the stallion's neck, whispering to him. "Storm! Go! Race as you like, it cannot be too fast for me!"

The animal could race, she discovered. Earth thundered and tore beneath her, the trees and the world spun by. On the main road she loosened her rein and gave him his lead, ducking low against him and becoming as much one with him as she could. He was wonderfully powerful, and his muscles tautened and relaxed, tautened and relaxed. The wind whipped her face, and she loved it, for it was cool and fresh and it seemed to cry to her of freedom. She was nearly home. To her home. Away from the pirate, and away from the lord.

She let the stallion run for a good twenty minutes, then she pulled him in, afraid that she would injure such a noble beast. She still passed small wooden and thatch-roofed houses, farmhouses, and acre after acre of rich and verdant fields. Cows and horses grazed upon fields on the one side, and the forest stretched out on the other, deep and green and dark. Once, these had been the lands of the great Powhatan Confederacy. Now, there were few Indians left. War and disease had ravaged them, and the white man had pushed them ever further west.

Skye shivered anyway. Like the darkness, the thought of Indians never failed to bring new terror to her soul. She longed for courage but it was not to be hers.

She looked upward. Shadows were beginning to fall. She closed her eyes for a moment, beginning to feel dizzy. The daylight was fading fast, far more quickly than she had expected. When night came, it would come completely. She would be here, in the forest, with the darkness all around her. . . .

But she would not be caged, she assured herself. She would not be contained with the darkness in close quarters. A moon would rise, and stars would rise, and it would not be so awful.

"And I will have you!" she told Storm. His ears pricked as she spoke. "You handsome thing, you, I will not be alone. I will be free, and I will be fine. . . ."

Her voice faded away as she heard a rustling from the foliage. She looked toward the river and assured herself that there were other manors there, that Tidewater Virginia was coming to be very well populated. Indeed, her father's friend from Daniel Dridle's tavern, Lord Lumley, lived out here somewhere. She was not alone.

Shadows came deeper. She reined in, watching as the sun sank quickly to the west. There were no glorious colors of night, not that evening. Twilight came, shadowland, and then darkness.

Something rustled behind her in the brush. Panic seized upon her, pure and simple, and Skye dug her heels into the stallion's flanks. The animal took flight.

Skye's hair whipped before her, the stallion's mane flew back. Suddenly, a branch slapped against her, and she realized that they were no longer on the road, that the horse had raced into the thick and never-ending green darkness of the forest.

"No!" she shrilled, pulling back. And then she realized Reggie's hesitation in giving her the huge stallion, for she quickly discovered that the horse was more powerful than she. Desperately she tried to rein him in. She was a good rider, more than competent, she had ridden her entire life. It was just that the horse was stronger than she, and at the moment, every bit as panicked as she by the darkness.

"Storm!" she cried in dismay. The foliage tugged and tore at her clothing and scratched at her hands and face. She ducked lower, wondering when the horse would plow straight into an oak and kill them both. "Whoa, boy, whoa . . ."

There was another rustling sound. The horse reared straight up. Skye tried to hold her seat, but it was impossible. She screamed, letting go, frightened that he would fall and roll upon her. She hit the ground hard herself, and though stunned, she rolled into the brush, anxious to avoid the huge thrashing hooves of the stallion.

He fell to earth, rose and flailed the air, and fell back to the earth again.

Then he took flight, leaving her breathless and defenseless and totally alone in the darkness of the forest.

For several long moments she just lay there, paralyzed with fear. She heard the crashing sounds as the stallion rode away, far, far away from her. She began to hear the little rustlings all around her.

"Damn you, horse, oh, damn you!" she cried out softly. Her hands lay over her heart and she stared up at the sky, willing the moon to become more apparent.

There were insects all about her, she told herself. There could be snakes. She lay in the brush. She needed to move.

Carefully she stretched out her limbs. None was broken, and she closed her eyes and breathed quickly, then opened them to the night once again. She could not give way to fear. She could not!

She stumbled up and dusted the fragments of leaves and trees and dirt from her bodice and skirt.

The road! She needed to reach the main road, and walk swiftly, and not think of the darkness or the forest. She whirled around and looked up. There was a moon out. It offered a gentle glow. It was not so horribly dark. And there were stars in the heavens, too. She would be all right, she would be all right.

That way. She twirled around very slowly and repeated the words out loud. "That way. The road to Williamsburg is that way." She started to walk, tripping over fallen branches, feeling the slight sob in her each and every breath come just a little bit louder. The road was not that way at all. She was going deeper and deeper into the forest. An owl screeched over her shoulder suddenly and she screamed aloud, falling to her knees, breaking into sobs. She simply could not bear the awful darkness, not alone.

She fought for control and listened to the night. What, besides the horrible owl, lurked in the forest? The Indians were all gone—oh, God, please, it was true, they were gone, they were all gone!—but perhaps there were bears. Brown bears with long claws and a deadly hatred for men and women. . . .

What had ever caused the Camerons to come to such a godforsaken place! She hated it. She would never leave the city of Williamsburg again once she found it, she would never, never leave it again. But she had to find it first; she had to find it.

She stumbled to her feet. Her hand came to her throat as she heard movement behind her. She went dead still, the blood draining from her face, and listened. A bear. It had to be a bear, moving slowly but certainly, and with stealth. She opened her mouth to scream, but no sound would come from her. She turned blindly and started to run again.

Something was after her. Something in the darkness. It was stalking her, quietly, slowly, seeking her out. . . .

Then there was nothing.

Silence . . .

There was silence, but no, the forest wasn't silent at all, it was just that the rustling was drowned out by the rush of fear in her ears, by the awful pounding of her heart. The forest was not silent at all; it was alive with sound. She was being pursued. She was no longer quietly stalked, she was being pursued.

She lost her bearing and spun in a circle. She started to run again and realized then that the sounds were growing louder. She was racing toward the beast that was pursuing her in the night.

Suddenly she screamed, throwing up her arms to cover her face as she dashed from the trees and straight into the path of a running horse.

The horse reared as its rider jerked back with ferocity. The animal went up high on its hind legs and then crashed over backward into the brush. Someone swore furiously as the animal stumbled up. Skye screamed again as the horse went thrashing by her into the woods. She turned to run again herself.

It was not over; it had not ended. Blindly she turned to run, aware that the forest was still alive, that she was still being pursued. Recklessly, desperately she ran. The branches touched upon her hair like spidery fingers, pulling it. Tree roots seemed to come alive beneath her feet, reaching out to trip her.

And clouds fell over the moon. As if the very heavens laughed at her, dark clouds covered the moon and cast her into deeper, greener darkness.

Then a shrill cry to split the very earth burst from her as hands seized upon her. She was falling, falling hard upon the earth in the darkness, fighting wildly and desperately against the thing that stalked her in the night.

"Skye!"

She couldn't register her own name, nor did the man above her mean anything to her at all. She beat out and kicked at him vigorously, unaware that he swore softly, irritated and alarmed. She knew only that she was losing the battle. He straddled her hips, pinning her to the earth, and then he captured her flailing hands, and they were pinned down to the earth, too.

She screamed in terror and frustration, thrashing even as she was held.

"Skye!"

The clouds drifted away from the moon just as he said her name again. Spiderwebs seemed to fall away from her vision, and reason came slowly back to her.

Roc Cameron, taut and solid, straddled her. She stared at him, and slowly, slowly exhaled. It was no beast, just the man who claimed to be her husband. She might have been better off with a tusked boar, she thought briefly, but that thought quickly faded. She might fear his temper upon occasion, but it was so different than her absolute terror of the darkness.

"Skye!" he repeated, and she went very still, swallowing tightly, staring at him.

"What in God's name were you doing?" he demanded.

"Me!" she cried. "You stalked me, you scared me to death, you—"

"You, madame, nearly killed yourself running into my mare. After not only having deserted me, but having stolen my finest mount in the process."

"I didn't mean to steal him. I would have returned him."

"And yourself?"

"I am not yours."

"You are."

"That's debatable."

"I say that it is not," he told her softly.

She opened her mouth to argue with him anew, but at that very second another treacherous cloud chose to close over the moon. Darkness fell upon them and all that she could see was the startling silver flame of his eyes. She started to shiver.

He lifted away from her and she was stunned to find herself

clinging to him. He freed himself from her grasp. "Hold, my love. I will build a fire."

He was true to his word, and prepared with a striker and flint. She sat shivering by a tree while he gathered up tinder and logs and arranged them to his satisfaction. He struck hard with his flint upon the striker and drew sparks, and in seconds his tinder had caught, and soft flames began to rise, higher and higher. His face was caught in those flames, and then the glow fell over them both and lit up the darkness of the forest.

He had changed to come for her, she noted. He looked like a woodsman. Gone was the elegance of his customary attire, and even the more casual garb he sometimes wore upon his ship. Tonight he was clad in simple buckskin and cotton with a homespun cotton shirt beneath his jacket. His hair was still queued, but he had eschewed his wig. Despite his clean-shaven cheeks, she had never seen him look more like the Silver Hawk than he did that night, alone with her in the forest.

She started to shiver all over again, but then it had little or nothing to do with fear. She hugged her knees to her chin and watched him, her eyes wide with the night.

He came over to her and drew her gently close. She protested his touch, then gave in to it, leaning against him.

"Why did you come after me?" she asked him. "I would have been all right—"

"All right? Like hell, madame! I found you because Storm came tearing out of the woods. You're not even heading in the right general direction!"

"That's because I got lost. I would have found—"

"You were in sheer terror before you ever came thrashing into my horse. And now we're both stuck out here because that stupid mare will run like the blazes home and Storm will break his tether to follow her back. Leave it to a fool stallion to go racing after a female."

"Just as you run after me?"

He gazed at her sharply. She was too weary, and still trembling too fiercely, to seek a fight. He smiled slowly. "Just as I race after you, milady." He paused, finding a tousled tendril of her hair to smooth back. "Why did you run?"

"I had to," she murmured simply.

He left her standing, finding another log to set upon the fire. For the longest time he was still, tall before her. She had tried to escape him, but now he was her barrier against the night, and she was glad of him there. She spoke softly. "I—I needed to find my father."

He cocked his head for a moment, listening to something. Then he came back beside her. "I am worried about your father myself. I would have taken you first thing tomorrow morning to Williamsburg by carriage."

"Tomorrow morning," she murmured uneasily.

He reached out, touching her cheek. "You were in such horror of me that you were willing to brave the darkness rather than my touch?"

A flush came to her features. She drew her face from his finger, lowered her eyes. "No . . . I . . . no."

"Then?"

"I—I—"

"You're lying."

"I'm not. I don't know what to say to make you understand. I—I don't hate you."

"Well, we've nothing here," he murmured, drawing to his feet once again. "I brought food in my saddlebags, but that is gone now. We can snare something if you like. And there is water nearby. I can hear the brook."

"You can?" She tilted her head, listening. She could hear nothing.

He nodded. "Trust me, madame. I was not bred to the city. I can hear the water plainly."

"How close?"

"Very close."

He reached down to her. "Come on. I'll show you."

She rose as he helped her. Despite herself, she looked longingly to the fire. "Don't worry," he told her. "We will not let the flames get too far behind us. You will see the light."

She cocked her head with disbelief, a rueful smile tugging at her lips. "Couldn't we . . . walk toward Williamsburg?" she asked him.

He shook his head. "It would take us hours and hours afoot, and with these clouds, it is a dark night indeed."

"You intend that we should stay here—in the forest?"

"We will be safe. The fire will burn throughout the night."

They had left the fire behind then, but he was right, she could still see its glow. He wouldn't leave it too far, she thought; he would not risk the forest in flames. He knew his way here, just as he did upon the sea.

"Hold up," he told her softly, stopping before her. He had her hand. She came around beside him and saw that the flames and the moonglow just touched upon the water. It made a slight bubbling sound as it ran toward the river.

"Oh!" she murmured, thinking that it looked delicious. She knelt down by the water's edge and cupped handfuls of the clean clear liquid to drink. He came to his knees beside her, throwing it over his face, drinking as deeply as she. When Skye was done, she fell away from it, lying upon the mossy slope. It was all right. The moon was freed from the clouds. Stars shone. She could feel the coolness of the brook, and the warmth of the fire.

And he was with her. She was not alone.

Not alone at all. He lay at her side upon an elbow and idly chewed upon a blade of grass. He watched her intently, she knew. He dropped the blade of grass and touched her cheek. She did not draw away.

"Why the darkness?" he asked her softly.

She flushed. "No one knew of it at all," she murmured. "Except for Father and Mattie, and Gretel, my housemaid at school."

"Why?" he persisted.

She shook her head, lowering her lashes and flushing. "It's so silly really. Not silly, but frustrating that I cannot get over it. It isn't a reasonable fear. It closes in upon me and I begin to panic, and then I have no control at all."

"Why are you so afraid?"

She hesitated a moment longer and then sighed. After all that she had brought upon him, she probably owed him something so simple as an explanation. "Father owns a lot of land," she said. "He had property up in the northern country."

"Iroquois country?" he asked her.

She nodded. "I was very young then. No more than five. My mother was supposed to have been very beautiful. She was no great lady, but a colonial tavern wench, and my father defied his own parents and tradition to marry her, she swore that she would love him all her life, and follow him to the ends of the earth." She hesitated a moment. "She was warmth and beauty and energy. I will never forget her."

"You loved her very much."

"Yes. Yes . . . well, she followed Father when he came to see this northern land in Iroquois country. Father was out with his surveyor; Mother and I were in a little cabin alone. We had only one servant with us, and Mother was singing and humming, as happy as a sparrow not to have to remember her manners and that she was a lady. Then suddenly she quit humming, and she shoved me into a little trapdoor where they stored wine and ale in the summer to chill it. It was very small, and it was black, and it was made of earth, and the smell of dirt was stifling."

She hesitated, gasping for breath, finding it difficult to breathe all over again. She hated the weakness, hated to betray it to anyone, but he knew about it. Her father had married her to him without her consent. He had surely warned him about the darkness, and had Theo not told him, she knew that this man would have discovered it on his own.

"What happened?" he persisted.

She shook her head. "She warned me not to make a sound. Then I heard noises as if the whole place had caved in, and then I heard her screaming. I peeked out. I saw the Indians coming for her. Perhaps they wouldn't have hurt her; perhaps she fought too desperately. I fell back against the earth, terrified at the sight of them. They were painted; a war party. I didn't see anymore. I just kept hearing the screams. Then they found the trapdoor. One of them was looking in at me, laughing. He was bald and painted with a thatch of hair, and his hands were covered with blood when he reached for me. Father came back and shot him. He fell on top of me, and the door closed and we were locked in the darkness together with his blood streaming over the both of us. I suppose that it wasn't that long before Father dragged us out, but it seemed like forever."

"And they killed your mother?"

She shook her head. "She took her own life rather than let them capture her," she whispered. "She—she loved Father. That's why I cannot understand why—" She broke off, not wanting to say anything bitter when he was being so decent to her, and when she was pouring out her heart to him.

"You can't understand why he forced you to marry me?"

"I can't understand why he would force me to marry anyone." She stared up at him hopefully. She had never really spoken to him before, not with any sincerity. Not as a possible friend. "Roc, please tell me, this thing cannot be legal!"

He shook his head. He seemed almost sad, as if she had his sympathy. "It is legal," he said. She fell back against the earth. "Why is it so horrid. I am not a monster."

"I did not say that you were. I just—" She hesitated. "I cannot make you understand."

He was quiet for long moments. She heard the brook as it gently danced alongside them. She felt the fire, warm against the flesh on her face. She was absurdly comfortable, and not at all afraid of the night anymore. He was there, beside her.

"Tell me, did you fall in love with my rogue cousin?"

"Of course not!" she argued, jumping up. "He—he was a pirate. I—I told you—"

"Ah, yes. He was cruel and horrible and forceful. You must despise him terribly." The same cloud that came to cover the moon dropped enigmatic shadows upon his eyes. He looked up at her curiously. Words caught in her throat. "Of . . . course."

He smiled suddenly, reaching out to her. "Come back here. Lie down. It's comfortable upon the earth, and I will just hold you until morning."

"I—I—" she stuttered, but she had no choice, for he wound a foot about her ankle and jerked upon it and she came sprawling down to the earth. She sputtered in protest, but he halfway rolled atop her, laughing, and then he pulled her against him upon the soft mosses. "It's all right," he said softly. Her head rested upon his shoulder. His hands held her close to his body.

His long hard frame curved around her back, like a living wall of security.

She smiled, curiously thrilled by the words. She didn't need to face him, and so she closed her eyes.

"Umm," she murmured. "You were ready to hand me right over to a pirate for being trouble."

"You are trouble," he agreed.

She did not dispute him. She closed her eyes, and slept in the wilderness, content to do so with him near.

As daylight came, she dreamed, and yet it was real. There were sun rays breaking through the leaves and trees, and she could hear the tinkle and melody of water.

The lagoon . . .

She lay by the water, with the Silver Hawk. She could feel the warmth of the sun and breathe the fragrance of the earth.

She could feel her lover's hands upon her, stirring and provocative as they had always been. She could feel the heat of his breath at her nape and the tender stroke of his fingers over her breasts. She could feel the length of his body, hard and as hot as molten steel.

She lay there in her web of melody and sound and sensation, a dreamer in her distant paradise. His hand shifted, slipping beneath her shirt. His fingers stroked a fantastic dance upon the bare flesh of her thigh, and formed over the soft tender curve of her derriere. She murmured, and she would have turned to him to cast her arms around him, but he held her still. His touch was no longer gentle but demanding as his hands latched firmly upon her hips. Then she gasped, startled by the searing steel rod of his sex thrusting deeply into her. "Shh!" his whisper came to her, and he held her tight. The world erupted into life and vibrance and sweet fury. He moved against her with the force of the wind and waves, with the driving, undaunted tempest of a storm at sea. It swept her by surprise, but it enwrapped her completely in its splendor. It raged within and around her, and it left her crying out softly, reaching for the sunlight, reaching ever higher for a grasp of rapture. It exploded upon her, as sweet as silken drops of sugarcane, filling her limbs, her body, her very center with warm liquid ecstasy. She trembled and felt him, groaning and shuddering, and holding her fast one last moment as his body surged into hers, seeming to touch the length and breadth of her in one sweep of magic.

Then he fell still. His hand rested upon her naked thigh, exposed beneath her skirts.

She opened her eyes and heard the delicate sound of the brook. She looked up and saw the trees, and she felt his limbs entangled with hers still, the life and pulse of him within her still. . . .

He withdrew from her, and she felt him adjust his breeches; she felt the buckskin next to her naked rump.

It was no dream.

She turned with fury to face her husband. His eyes were open, lazy silver daggers that touched upon her with satisfaction and pleasure and masculine triumph.

"Oh!" she screamed, wrenching free her skirts from beneath him, struggling and scrambling to her feet to right her clothing. He rested upon an elbow, completely and respectably clad. "How could you!" she sputtered.

The cloud fell over his eyes. "How could I, madame? Indeed, how have I waited this long?"

"But you knew—" She broke off.

"I knew what?"

"You knew that I wanted no part of you!"

"Oh?" His casual air left him as he sprang to his feet, lithe and agile as a cat. His hands upon his hips, he faced her. "I beg your pardon, wife. I did not hear you scream in protest, nor feel your hands upon me in any fight. Would you like to know what I did hear, what I did feel? Just this, milady. Soft sweet moans coming from your lips. The jut and rhythmic sway of your hips against my own. A lush sweet cry of pleasure escaping from your lips."

"You did—not!" Skye protested furiously.

He arched a brow in stunned surprise. "This was deadly force?"

"Yes!" she cried too quickly. His eyes instantly narrowed and his voice took on the gravel of demand.

"Is this something like the force that the awful and despicable pirate used against you?"

She gasped aloud and stepped forward, slapping with all the strength that she could muster. He allowed her hand to fall across his face, but then he swept her hard against him, threading his fingers into her hair with a cruel grip and setting his lips upon hers with fire and determination. She struggled and squirmed and fought him and he held her still to his pleasure, coercing in his touch as well as demanding, filling her with his fire until it burned between the two of them and she went limp in his arms, lacking the power to fight him any longer.

He broke away from her and his tongue just teased her lips, then his mouth fell against her eyelids in a gentle touch. He lifted her chin and whispered, "The next time, milady, I will make sure that there is no mistaken identity on your part beforehand. The kiss will come first. And you will face me with your eyes open, and you will whisper my name."

"There will not be a next time!" she cried.

"I say that there will be."

She shook her head, no longer fighting his hold, but suddenly and fiercely close to tears. "I cannot make you understand!"

"No, you cannot, I fear, my love."

"Don't you see!" she demanded desperately, and the tears did spill over her lashes. He frowned, as serious as she, taut and straight with tension. "What?" he demanded.

She wrenched away from him, turning aside, and spoke in a broken whisper. "I will not be able to bear it, and neither should you, if I—if I carried a child now. I would not know if it belonged to the pirate or the lord, and still, sir, I should love it! And you would despise me . . . don't you see?" she repeated.

He was silent for a long, long time. She turned at last, and was stunned by the anguish that seemed to touch his features.

The look was quickly gone. He reached out to her, and then his hand fell away. He sighed, then bowed to her.

"Milady, I will not disturb you again," he said quietly, and then he turned away from her. "Come on. Williamsburg should not be more than a few hours' walk by daylight."

XIII

Roc Cameron paused long enough to drink deeply by the spring, dousing his head in the cold waters. Skye longed to sink within the water, but she did not, sipping it in silence and cooling her heated face with several splashes of it.

He waited for her quietly. The fire had long since died away, but he kicked the scattered ashes, dusted his hat upon his breeches, and proceeded toward the road. She followed him in silence. Even when they came upon the main road, she hovered slightly behind him. Exhaustion seemed to weigh heavily upon her heart. She could not forget the night, or the dark secrets she had given away during the length of it. Nor could she forget the morning. She knew him better than she had known him before, and still she did not know him at all. Perhaps she could escape him still, and perhaps she didn't really want to escape him at all. He intrigued her, and fascinated her, and he could evoke wild fires within her. If she could just forget the man who had come before him . . .

But that didn't matter now. He had admitted that he was

worried about her father, too. They did not head back toward his estate, but hurried along the road to Williamsburg.

She paused to pluck a pebble from her shoe. He waited for her, frowning. "Do I walk too fast?"

She shook her head. "No." Then she admitted softly, "Perhaps, just a little."

His dark lashes fell over his eyes for a moment, then he reached for her hand and took it within his own. "We needn't travel so swiftly," he said, and started out again. They had not moved far then when he paused once more. She looked at him curiously. "There's a carriage coming. Mine, I hope."

It was his carriage. It came around a corner and Skye saw the family crest upon the doors. She looked at Roc and he offered her a rueful smile. "I should hope that they would have come looking for us. I can almost guarantee that Storm followed that mare all way home."

Perhaps Storm had followed the mare, but now he obediently trailed behind the carriage. Peter sat by the coachman; he leaped down from the driver's seat as he saw the two of them, his face splitting into a relieved grin. His affection for his master was so apparent that Skye felt her heart warm and shimmer slightly. There was, perhaps, much about the man to draw affection. His voice could ring with steel and he could command with the finest of captains. He was a seaman of worthy measure. He knew his own mind and seemed determined to his own will.

And he was young and striking, with his silver-eyed charm and reckless ways. He could make her laugh, she thought, and he could also make her tremble with excitement and desire.

"Milord, milady! And glad I am to see the two of you!" Peter called out, hurrying to them. "When those horses came back with the dawn, we were deeply worried."

"No harm done anywhere, Peter," Roc said. "Minor spills and mishaps, but we're most heartily glad to see you, too. Peter, we've a need to reach Williamsburg, and quickly."

"Yes, milord." He opened the door of the lovely teal carriage for them. "Williamsburg, and quickly!" he cried to the driver, who nodded gravely to Roc beneath his low-brimmed hat.

Skye paused, wondering if she hadn't seen the man before. Then she forgot him as Roc urged her into the carriage with a prodding hand upon her derriere. She moved in quickly and sat, gnawing upon her lower lip. He sat in his own corner, ignoring her then. When she glanced his way, she saw that his eyes were dark and brooding and a finger of fear touched upon her heart. He was worried, too.

"What's wrong?" she asked him. "Where could Father be?"

"At home, perhaps? Thinking that we should come to him?"

She shook her head. "You know that isn't so. Where could he be?"

"I honestly don't know."

He reached out as if he meant to take her hand and squeeze it with assurance. He stiffened his fingers instead, and his hand fell flat. "We shall see soon enough."

The carriage stopped in another few minutes and Peter came around to the door. "We're on the outskirts of the city, sir. Am I to go direct to the governor's house, or Lord Kinsdale's?"

"Lord Kinsdale's," Skye said over Roc's shoulder. She glanced his way as he watched her. "Just in case Father is there."

She parted the drapes as the carriage set to motion again. Her heart leaped. Williamsburg had changed. They were passing the Bruton parish church, and it had been built anew. They turned, and she saw the governor's mansion, complete now, rising at the end of the broad greenway with grace and elegance.

Children were playing, men were hawking their wares. Slaves were working in the gardens, and upon a pile of bricks before a white house a fifer was idly playing a tune. She sat bolt upright. There, halfway down the street, lay her own home. Two-storied, whitewashed, brick-trimmed, with a picket fence about the small yard.

The coachman knew his way. He drew up before the house. Skye didn't wait for anyone to come to her. She leaped down from the carriage and tore through the fence, ran up past the steps, past the flower beds, and burst through the doors.

"Father!"

She heard footsteps from the parlor and headed that way. A tall black woman with strong handsome features came hurrying toward her. "Mattie!" she said with pleasure.

"Skye!"

They came together with a fierce hug. "Child, child, child, it is so good to see you! Safe and sound and home at last. Your father was so very worried about you—"

"Where is Father?" Skye asked hopefully, pulling away. Mattie was looking over her shoulder to the parlor door. Roc stood there now, watching them.

"Lord Cameron," Mattie murmured, bobbing him a small curtsy.

"Mattie," he acknowledged her. He stepped on in. He was comfortable in her parlor, Skye thought with a touch of resentment. "Where is Lord Kinsdale?" he asked also.

"It's a terrible thing, Lord Cameron!" Mattie said. She pulled away from Skye and walked to the elegant rosewood liquor cart and poured out something. Skye assumed it was a brandy for her.

Mattie walked straight past her and handed the glass to Roc. He nodded his thanks and drank down the brew. She looked at Skye. "I'll get tea on right away, and something for you to eat."

"Mattie!" Skye wailed.

Mattie shook her head miserably. "He's gone run off and been captured by those louts, he has!"

"What?" Skye gasped, looking quickly to Roc.

"The *Silver Messenger* come into the river about a week ago. You know your father, Skye. He went about ranting and raving and saying that he had to come for you himself. Well, he's so anxious to go off to sea to find you or meet you or just wear off steam, that he decides to hire himself a new captain out of one of the taverns. Turns out he hires himself a pirate! It's the government down in Carolina, that's what Spotswood says it is. Those slimy sea creatures go into North Carolina, then slip on up here. When we catch 'em, we hang 'em! It's just that we don't catch them all. . . ."

Skye fell into one of the elegant little Louis XIV chairs before the fireplace. She covered her face with her hands, remembering the carnage when the *Silver Messenger* had first been taken by the pirates. A great trembling shook her, and silent tears began to fall down her cheeks. He was all that she had in the world.

No, she had a husband.

A stranger . . .

She needed her father. She loved him, and she needed him desperately. The old fool! Why had he left?

He had come for her. He had wed her to Roc Cameron, but he hadn't even trusted in Roc. He had been impulsive—like she was herself. He had cast care and reason to the wind.

"Has there been a ransom demand as yet?" Roc asked.

Skye looked up hopefully.

Mattie shook her head. "A man come back off of the *Silver Messenger,* a decent man, I assume, for he went to the governor with his tale. The ship is taken, and Lord Kinsdale is prisoner in the hold, and that is all I know for the moment."

A sob escaped Skye. Mattie sank down by her, taking her into her arms. "Don't fret, they won't hurt him, I'm certain. The governor has ships out—"

Skye leaped up. "The governor. Perhaps he knows more!"

She swept past Mattie and Roc Cameron and came out to the street again. She was travel-stained from her night in the woods and tears made dirty tracks down her cheeks, but she didn't care. She ran down the length of the palace green, near hysteria. She loved Theo; she adored him. Even when they disagreed, he would puff up his cheeks and eventually see things her way. Even if he had cast her into marriage against her will . . . He had worried about her unduly, all of these years. He had wanted a fine house for her, a bastion against the world. He hadn't even wanted her to travel to England, but his position had meant that she should be well trained in the fine arts of feminity, and so he had given in.

"Skye!"

She paused, leaning against a tree. She didn't stop because she had been summoned, she stopped to gasp for breath. Roc was coming behind her.

"Skye, wait!"

She turned around and ran again, approaching the gates to the mansion. Armed guards stood before them. They blocked her way with their brown Besses when she would have burst through the gate. "I have to see the lieutenant governor!" she cried.

"And who might you be, miss?" one asked her skeptically.

Hands fell upon her shoulders. Roc had caught up with her. "Lord and Lady Cameron, and it is most urgent."

"Oh, milord! It is you. Lieutenant Governor Spotswood is in." The guards moved away. "He was preparing to ride to your estate this very morning, milord."

"Well, then, we have saved him some trouble," Roc murmured. His hands remained fast upon her shoulders and he steered her through the gate. His words sizzled angrily against her earlobe as he bent to whisper to her. "Now, milady, I know that you are upset, and in private I have promised you certain concessions, but if you think to burst away from me like that again, I'll take a horsewhip to you." To emphasize his words, his hand fell hard upon her rear anatomy.

She gasped in surprise and fury. The guards all turned their way. Roc smiled charmingly. "Horsefly!" he said.

"Horsefly, my—"

"Come, love. We're far from properly attired to visit the lieutenant governor, but it seems now that we shall visit anyway!"

Even then the front doors opened and Spotswood's butler bowed low in greeting. "The lieutenant governor will see you upstairs, Lord Cameron." If the butler thought anything of their strange attire, he did not betray it. As Roc pushed her through the entryway she suddenly gasped, looking at the layout of the mansion, at the arms upon the walls, at the size of the hall and the stairway.

"What?" Roc demanded tensely.

"Bone Cay," she murmured.

"What?" he repeated suspiciously.

"Bone Cay. The—the Silver Hawk's house there. It greatly resembles this one."

He fell silent. Skye did not glance his way. Maids were polishing the floor. The butler hesitated, awaiting them.

"Come along," Roc murmured, urging her forward.

Upstairs they came straightaway to the grand reception room with the fine leather wall covering that was of such pride to Spotswood. The lieutenant governor was at tea, finely dressed and wigged and ready for his day. He stood, expecting them, a fine porcelain cup in his hands. "Ah, Skye, my dear!"

He set his cup upon a table and hurried toward her, taking both her hands tight in his and studying her anxious eyes. "I am so sorry, dear, to greet you after these years with such sorry news!"

"Is there nothing else that you know, sir?" she asked.

Lieutenant Governor Spotswood looked over her head to Roc. Irritated, Skye squeezed his hands. "Sir, please . . . !"

He squeezed her hands in turn, and his gaze returned to hers. "I believe that he is alive and well, my dear. I told him that he should wait patiently and all would prove to be well. But he could not be patient, he determined to set to sea, and set to sea he did, with a rogue for his captain."

"Do you know the pirate's name, sir?" Roc asked.

Spotswood nodded slowly. "A seaman managed to escape the ship and swim to shore. He came instantly to my house, bringing the news."

"And?" Roc persisted.

"The man's name is Logan. Captain Logan. We hear tell that he has sailed with Hornigold and Vane. Do you know anything of him?"

"Logan!" Skye cried. Logan, she repeated inwardly, feeling the blood rush from her face. Logan, cruel, reckless, careless—and hating her greatly, she was certain. What would he do to her father?

She shivered, remembering the hook upon the man's arm where his hand should have been. She remembered his narrow face, and his total lack of mercy. She remembered his fury when the fight had broken out, and how he had demanded her as his prize.

"You know this pirate?" Spotswood said to her intensely. She looked into his eyes again and nodded. She trusted him; he would do what he could. Some found him controversial;

Skye had always cared for him greatly. He had been born in Tangier, on the east coast of Africa, when his father had been stationed there for the Crown. He was an adventurer himself, she thought, a man quick to rise to a challenge, determined, and vigorous.

"I know—Logan," she murmured. She was striving for control but a huge sob shook her anyway. "I am afraid that he will kill Father."

"Tea!" the lieutenant governor said. "You must have some tea, and something to eat. Then a long wash with hot water, and a good night's sleep. Sleep will make the world look brighter."

"I must do something!" she cried.

"Perhaps—" Spotswood began, but Roc cut him off with a startling fury. "Sir! Would you cast the girl into danger all over again when she has just been brought from it? I will take the *Lady Elena* and go after this Logan."

His hand was upon Skye's shoulder again. He pressed down, causing her to sit. "My love, you will do nothing! You may remain here in Williamsburg, or you may return to Cameron Hall, but you will not set sail again." He bowed low to them both. "Sir! I am going to order my servants home, to see that the *Lady Elena* is readied for sail."

"I shall see to breakfast, Petroc," the lieutenant governor called after him. He smiled to Skye. "It will work out, Skye, I am quite certain."

Her troubled eyes fell upon his. "Sir! You do not know this Logan. I have seen the man."

"Have you?"

"On the island of New Providence."

"Hmmph! That den of iniquity will soon be no more. There will be proper government there, and soon, I swear it!" He handed her a cup of tea and winked. "There's a touch of honey and whiskey in the brew, Skye. Steadies the hands, on an occasion such as this. So you know Logan."

"Yes!"

"As fierce a man as the Silver Hawk?"

Skye lowered her eyes, shaking her head. "A far, far different man than the Silver Hawk! Logan is cruel and horrid and the Hawk—"

"Yes, my dear, tell me. I am boundlessly interested in these rogues!"

"Logan is cruel," she repeated simply. "The Hawk is not."

"They say that Logan is sailing the islands and shoals of the inland waters just south of our own colony, in North Carolina. It might take one rogue to find another." He came close to her suddenly, coming down upon one knee and looking past her shoulder to the hallway. He was anxious, Skye realized, that her husband not return.

"They say that your Silver Hawk is in Virginia."

She gasped, winding her fingers into her shirt. "So—why—why haven't you seized him, arrested him. Surely, you plan on hanging the man!"

"Too slippery, my dear. I cannot come near him, not as yet. I haven't the force, or the power. He could well disappear into the night, and that would be that. But I have heard rumors that there is a tavern near Jamestown way, but on the peninsula, by the waterfront. All manner of rogues congregate there, milady! I have heard that the Silver Hawk is among them, just arrived last night."

"Why are you telling me this?" Skye whispered. Suddenly, like Spotswood, she was looking over her shoulder, lest her husband should return. Her heart began to beat quickly. A startling new hope began to build within her.

Lord Cameron was a worthy seaman.

The Silver Hawk was . . . indomitable.

"You were his captive for many days?" Spotswood said.

She nodded, feeling that the blood was drained from her face.

"And he was gentle with you?"

"Er—yes," she murmured.

"Then perhaps you could pay the one rogue to go after the other! Let him help us first, then he can hang in his own time!"

"Sir—"

"Shush! Your husband is returning."

He is not my husband! she longed to shout, but he had once told her that she could not change truth by denying it.

And she was also shivering and trembling within, besieged by a tremendous guilt. He had been honorable in all things. Perhaps not. There had been last night. Last night he had not been so honorable; he had been a man, and the man who claimed to be her husband. He had touched her and awakened her, and maybe it hadn't been his fault that she had dreamed of another, and that their images had combined.

She could not go to the Silver Hawk. She was Lord Cameron's wife. She could not seek out a rogue. . . .

But her heart was beating frantically. When Roc Cameron left her, she knew that she would ride herself, and try to find the pirate king. Her father's life was at stake.

Roc Cameron's long strides beat against the hardwood floor. Spotswood called to a servant and asked that a meal be served to them there. Roc came behind Skye. "I have sent Peter homeward. I will find your father, Skye. I swear it. I will bring him home safely, no matter what the trial and cost. Believe in me."

Skye thought that Spotswood watched them with a curious light to his eyes. She flushed, for Roc's declaration had been passionate, and his touch upon her was tender. She didn't know quite what Spotswood knew about their relationship, but she found herself looking uneasily to her lap. She meant to betray her husband.

"When will you leave, Petroc?" Spotswood asked him.

"I'll see Skye settled in her home tonight, and ride out in the morning."

"The morning!" Skye cried.

Roc's silver eyes fell to hers. "Yes. What is the matter with that?"

"Just that—just that you should leave earlier! You should leave today. Perhaps Logan takes Father further and further away. Time is of the essence—"

"Skye, they can only load and arm and supply the ship so quickly. I will see you safe this evening, leave by the dawn, and sail with the tide. It will be all right, I swear it."

Food was brought to them. Spotswood began to question her sharply about the time she had spent in New Providence. There was little she could tell him. Her time there had been so brief. Yet both men listened to her with rapt attention, and when she caught her husband's eyes upon her, they were bright with a startling fire.

What could she do? she wondered in dismay. If he would not leave, then she could not escape him to find the Silver Hawk!

When the day waned to twilight, Roc rose and told Spotswood that they would take their leave. Skye nervously arose with him. He took her hand and bowed to Spotswood. Skye murmured something, aware that the lieutenant governor was watching her. He thought that she should go for the Silver Hawk. That's why he had told her what he had.

He would gladly hang the Hawk, but later!

She nibbled nervously upon her lower lip as Roc led her from the governor's mansion and outside to the palace green. His hand was upon hers and she trembled, torn between guilt and a growing affection, and a slowly rising desperation that he should leave her.

"What is the matter with you?" he asked her suspiciously.

She shook her head, lowering it. "I am worried about my father."

He paused, catching her shoulders, drawing her close. "You mustn't worry!" he told her kindly. "You mustn't. I swear that I shall not fail you."

She smiled, startled to feel that tears were hovering on her eyes. He held her against him. She heard the sound of the children playing, of the leaves rustling over their heads. It seemed so peaceful, and he held her so gently. As a husband might. As a lover.

She inhaled and exhaled quickly, pulling away. "I'd like to get home. I'd like to have a bath."

"Of course," he told her.

By nightfall she was up in her own room and in her own deep tub with a froth of French rosewater all about her. She leaned back her head and breathed deeply and felt steam rise above her.

He was across the hallway from her. In one of the guest bedrooms. She had not told him that he must go there; he had chosen the room. He had said that he would not disturb her, and he was a man of his word.

A man of his word, and more.

The steam about her seemed to swirl within her. She remembered his whisper, and his touch, and it seemed that the very heat of the steam swept deep inside of her. She flushed, wanting to forget. It was so wrong to feel this way. It had to be, after what she had come to feel for the Hawk.

She was going after the man to help her—and never to come close to him again. She could not do so. She was married to Lord Cameron. Truth, whether she denied it or not.

And truth . . . because in the fireglow and green darkness of the forest, he had taken her into his arms, and their marriage had been consummated there. She would never escape it now.

Not her marriage . . .

She had to escape her husband. That night, she had to escape him. How? she wondered desperately.

She shivered, despite the heat of the water. She could not betray him so. He had been too decent to her.

She had to leave, and leave that very night!

She never quite knew her intention when she stood in her bath, the scented rosewater dripping from her, to reach for her bathtowel. It was a huge cotton sheet of material that smelled freshly of the sun. She wrapped it around herself and stepped into the hallway. Downstairs, she could hear Mattie humming softly. But no one would ever disturb her up the stairs. Mattie would come if she called. If not, Skye knew, she would be left undisturbed.

She clutched the towel to her breasts. For long moments she stared at the door, then she knocked upon it. She did not wait for an answer, but shoved it open and entered into his room.

He had been lying upon the bed. As she entered, he bolted up.

He had bathed, earlier, Skye knew. He had gone out to the barn, and they had brought him pails of warm water there. He was barefoot and bare-chested, and clad only in a pair of soft bleached buckskin breeches. He looked at her, startled, reaching for a linen shirt that lay across the bed. His action amused her somewhat. He had been so ready to touch her in the night, to make intimate demands upon her. Then he shielded his own chest with a startling modesty.

His actions did not help her cause, she thought, and she was already rueing the rash impulse that had brought her here.

"What is it?" he asked her. The room was dim, his voice was husky. Strange, but the lack of brightness did not bother her here. She felt safety, knowing that he was near. No . . . she felt very alive, knowing that he was near. She dared not admit that it had been easy, easy to come here.

The damage was done! she cried inwardly. It had been done last night. And if this ever ended well, then she would be his wife in all truth, and she would make it up to him, God help her!

She stepped closer. "I . . ."

"What?" He came out of the bed. She remembered briefly from the fleet seconds in which she had seen them bare that his shoulders were broad and fine and his skin bronzed and sleek. She remembered his touch, and the strength and demand of it, and she wondered briefly if she hadn't discovered him to be very fine, and if she hadn't lost a corner of her heart to his raw demand and vehement, sometimes tender care. Perhaps she had. In the dim light she found that she had no voice, and she could not think of the words she wanted to say.

"You're trembling," he murmured.

It was not without some astonishment that he said the words, for he was amazed that she should be there.

He had been a fool to touch her last night. He should keep a far greater distance than he did. But when she had lain so close to him, and when his hands had found her nakedness in the night and her soft moan had been his response, he had cast caution to the wind. He had never meant to take her. Her distress this morning had struck deep into his heart, and he had never felt more the knave.

But now she was here.

Fresh from her bath. Her eyes wide and luminous and nearly teal in their glazed color. Her features so fine and delicate and so hauntingly feminine that the sight of her trembling lips brought a rush of heat stabbing into his groin. Desire rose, and pulsed hard against his breeches, and still she stood there, silent.

He strode around the bed to the side table where he had brought a bottle of Mattie's best dark rum. He poured out a portion and came before her, bringing the glass to her lips. She swallowed, and winced slightly as the fire of the rum rode through her.

"I . . ."

"Yes?"

"If it is truly your desire . . ."

He waited, but her voice had trailed away. "Yes?" he prompted softly.

She took another sip of the rum, moistening her lips. Her hair spilled all about her, touched by candlelight. It glowed with the red fury of fire, it cascaded like sunlight. He longed to thread his fingers through the length and mass of it. He longed to feel the fiery tendrils fall softly over his naked shoulders and chest. . . .

"Yes?" he repeated.

"You have been very kind."

"Have I?"

She was still faltering. "I appreciate all that you have done for me."

"You are my wife," he said softly, standing back to watch her curiously. The length of him had come alive. The pulse and need rushed to fill his limbs, and his heart, and his soul. Warnings called out to him, and he ignored them. Let her speak! Let her come to him, or run, for he could not bear to keep his hands from her a moment longer. He wanted to rip away the towel and drink the sweet scent of rose dust from her flesh.

"That's what I'm trying to say."

"What?" he demanded sharply.

"I've been trying to say that . . . if it is your desire despite all that has happened . . . if you wish to have me for your wife, then, milord, I am yours."

Her words hung softly upon the air for long moments as he tried to believe them. This sweet wild thing, this creature of temper and beauty and tempest, was coming to him.

She lifted her arms and dropped the towel that covered her. She stepped from it and stood before him in naked perfection, her flesh so gently kissed by the glow of the candlelight that touched the room. She was exquisite. Her hair did not touch his shoulders, but streamed over her own. Her breasts rose with coral peaks, full and tantalizing, beneath the caress of her swirling gold locks. Strands of red and gold cascaded all the way to her waist, and curled over the curve of her hips and buttocks.

He caught his breath. For one long moment he was unable to move.

Then he cried out hoarsely, casting the rum glass into the fireplace and sweeping her into his arms. He carried her swiftly to the bed and laid her upon it. The candles glowed on the table. He looked down at her and her eyes were passionate slits, teal and shadowed by the lush fringe of her lashes. Her lips were damp and parted as if they awaited his. As if they invited his touch . . .

But he did not bring his mouth to hers. Not then.

His lay low against her, fascinated to touch her. His hands curved over her breasts while his tongue teased the taut skin of her abdomen. Slight sounds escaped her, and he continued to touch. He rose against her to bring her breast deep into his mouth, and he withdrew to watch the nipple harden and the color deepen. He stroked the length of her, and felt the surge of her body, and still he did not touch her lips. She reached for him, but he eluded her, and buried his face against the sweetness of her body again. He moved lower and lower again, taking all of her with his sweeping caress. He parted her thighs and heard a startled sob escape, but he gave her no quarter that night; he longed to seek from her all that she had to give. He watched her for a moment, and her eyes were closed. They opened slowly, and when they met his, he lowered himself between her legs. He teased her inner thigh and stroked her flesh with the searing heat of his tongue. She gasped, writhing to escape so great an intimacy, but she was his, and he knew it. He touched her with that sweet stroke where and how he would, and her fingers curled into his hair while a breathless series of whispers and sobs and incoherent words tore from her lips. He brought her to the very brink of passion and then cast her over the edge, savoring the constriction of her beautiful form, and at long last, coming to her lips, there to swallow down the cries of pleasure that rose.

He did not hesitate a moment, but untied his breeches and drove deep within her welcoming warmth. She lay still, just trembling from all that had been before. He moved against her with the care of a master artist, seeking to elicit all emotions, all desires, and all needs. And when she rose again to the sure blaze of sensation, he at last gave over to his own desperate need. Hungry and afire, he took her with a fierce and driving force, and it seemed that the sun rose in his heart and vision, only to burst and explode all around him. There was no woman like her. None with her slender, provocative form, none with the perfect fullness of her breasts, not with her wild blaze of hair, her startling teal eyes.

No woman could love as she, caress a man so, part her lips so. Drive him to absolute heights with the thrust and sway of her hips, with her whispers, cries that touched the wind, that brought him to heaven.

She created . . . paradise.

She was his wife. She had said it. He had claimed her.

And he loved her. Deeply, and forever.

He fell beside her, pulling her close. For long, long moments they were silent. They were together, softly trembling with aftershocks of the explosion of the sun.

At long last he gently moved his hand over her bare breast, watching a golden curl fall from it. She buried her head against his throat and reached out a finger tentatively to touch his shirt.

"You're still dressed!" she whispered reproachfully.

He hesitated. "Umm," he said noncommittally. He saw his own fingers upon her flesh and he drew them away, holding her tightly. He should not even let her see his hands so, he thought. A smile teased her lips. Of all women to fear the darkness!

Darkness could hide so many sins.

He drew up the covers, but she was watching him pensively. She seemed very nervous. He leaned against her, and a shudder swept through him. He was about to leave her again. It might have been easier if she hadn't come so close to him. If she hadn't given him, freely, and willingly, this ecstasy.

He touched her lip. He stared into her beautiful eyes, and he remembered how he had fought the very idea of marriage.

This was no cross-eyed bride.

She was everything to him. She had been, from the very beginning.

"I love you," he told her.

She inhaled sharply, her eyes widening. Then they widened even further, and she whispered, "I—I think I love you, too."

"You think?"

She twisted away. He longed to pull her tight again. He knew that she was remembering a different man, a pirate, in a faraway paradise of her own.

He hated himself at that moment.

He longed to speak to her.

But he could not.

He pressed his lips against her hair and held silent for long moments. Then he whispered again, "I do love you, Skye Kinsdale Cameron. You have become my very life, and I swear, my love, I vow myself to you, now and forever."

She lay silent. He turned away with a sigh, tying up his breeches. He rose from the bed and walked over to the table, picking up the rum bottle and swallowing down a long draft.

They would have this night, he determined. He would have to leave her in the morning, and by God, he would return with her father. She would be his wife then, in every way, for every day and month and year that came to follow.

But until then, he would have this night.

Something like a sob seemed to escape her. He turned around and saw that she was rising, too. Naked and graceful and beautiful and sleek, she walked his way. Her head was lowered. She came to stand in front of him. Her hands fell upon his chest. She leaned against him, kissing him, letting the wet warmth of her tongue blaze through the linen of his shirt.

"I will honor you, I swear it!" she cried softly.

He frowned, for her tension was so great, then his frown faded, for the lap of her tongue against his flesh was so arousing. Her fingers moved against his shoulder, her body was flush against his. She had indeed given herself to him that night, in so many ways.

In so many ways . . .

He moved to sweep his arms around her, but she slipped away and idly picked up the rum bottle.

"I'll get you a glass, love," he murmured.

She shook her head, and her teal eyes were luminous with a glaze of tears. "It will not be necessary," she said.

She slipped back into his arms. She drew him down to her embrace, finding his lips with parted mouth, meeting him with a wild abandon that swept away his very thoughts. . . .

Then a shattering pain burst upon his skull.

Darkness came in upon him, and wavered back. Liquid spilled over him as he crashed down to his knees. He managed to look up, and into her eyes. He saw the broken rum bottle in her hands, and he managed to swear at her in a single gasp.

"Bitch!"

Then he fell, heavy and flat. She cried out, but stepped aside, and his weight came down full upon the floor as the blackness of oblivion came surely to claim him.

XIV

Roc came back to consciousness very slowly.

Pale light flickered by his eyes.

He smelled like the scurviest of taverns. He moved his hand, and winced, feeling broken glass beneath.

Then he heard a soft chuckle and saw a handsomely buckled shoe with a well-turned masculine calf attached to it. He groaned aloud, allowing his eyes to fall closed once again.

"Come on, my boy, up, up!"

Wincing, he sat, and cast Spotswood an angry glare. "What are you doing in my room? And why is it—sir—that you seemed to have known that you would find me in this state."

"Truthfully, Petroc, I did not know how I would find you at all, but it was imperative that I see you now, so I came as quickly as I saw your wife leave."

"Leave!"

He bolted up, shaking his head, desperate to clear it. "Blast that wench! I have chased her over half the seaboard and through forest and glen, and I swear, sir, that I am about to keep the lady in chains. Dammit, where has she gone now?"

"Why, to find the Silver Hawk, of course," Spotswood said complacently.

"What?"

"I believe that I've sent the young lady off to find the Silver Hawk. In fact, I know that I have."

"Why!" Roc exploded incredulously. "Damn you, sir, but what have you done to me now?"

"Petroc, wait, listen!" Spotswood pleaded vehemently. "We've worked at this for years now, and you must know the rationale of what I've done. A tremendous favor, and that's the God's own truth, sir, and I swear it. Think—"

"Think!" Roc groaned and clutched his head and sank down to the bed. "Think, eh? Sir, it has been bad enough. I returned from my last adventure with the woman who is my wife, afraid to put my hands upon her, afraid to come too near her! Now you think that I must go out and change roles again! Her husband was going for her father! I was going, I would have sailed today with my legal and legitimate crew and a ship that docks safely upon the James—"

"Robert Arrowsmith has the Hawk's sloop ready and waiting on the river. You need only don your whiskers—"

"Don them! They were real last time." Roc rubbed his clean-shaven chin, gritting his teeth. He'd had time to grow a fine set when sailing for New Providence and the Tortugas in the hopes of claiming the *Silver Messenger* and his bride. This time he would have to play with theatrical hair and sticking gums. He didn't care for the idea, but in one respect, the lieutenant governor was right—it might be far better for the Silver Hawk to set sail against Logan than for Lord Petroc Cameron to do so. No other pirate would come to his assistance if they knew him as Lord Cameron, but if a battle or skirmish came about someplace, he might find assistance as the Silver Hawk. Everyone knew about the "relationship" between the two men, and therefore it was easy enough to play the act before men and women who did not come too close—

Playing an act before one's wife . . . one's mistress, one's lover . . . was nearly impossible.

He had envied the Hawk. Until this very evening, he had longed to be his alter ego once again, the man who could freely shed his clothing before Skye and not fear that she'd find some scar upon him that would tell her beyond a doubt that he was, indeed, his own "cousin"—the sea slime, the scourge of the seas, the rogue.

The man to whom she had willingly and so sweetly given her love.

He stood up suddenly, his temper soaring. The wretched little adventuress. She'd seduced him to betray him—him! her lawfully wedded husband—to go off to find a rogue. Perhaps the acting would not be so heinous after all.

"You, sir, sent her after the Hawk?" he inquired darkly of Spotswood.

"It was necessary, Petroc."

"Alexander, did it occur to you that you might have warned me?"

Spotswood shrugged, a twinkle in his eye. "Petroc, I didn't think that a mere wisp of a girl could take you by such complete surprise. I was most interested in the results myself. When I remembered how you fought the marriage vows—to that poor cross-eyed lass!—I thought that surely, the man will be strong against this, his despised baggage of responsibility. Then lo and behold, the great Lord Cameron of the Camerons of Tidewater Virginia falls prey to a trick older than time."

"Hmm." Roc crossed his arms over his chest and nodded laconically to Alexander's amusement. Perhaps he did deserve the man's laughter.

Skye deserved a lot more.

And she was going to get it.

"You've put me in a horrible position, you know."

"Alas, Petroc, this has been in the works these four years now!"

"I should have told her the truth," Roc murmured.

"You can't. Not yet. Not until you return safely to these shores. Not until you can make her understand. You promised me to uphold the secret, Petroc. I need you! I need the Silver Hawk. It is my only way of knowing what goes on in the Caribbean, and down in North Carolina, beneath my own nose. You cannot tell her yet."

"I didn't intend to tell her—not yet," Roc murmured. What

role was she going to play herself this time? The Silver Hawk was longing to touch her again. Touch her . . . as she touched and seduced him this night.

Lord Cameron was dying to throttle his beautiful bride, the lady willing to trick and seduce him to seek assistance from another.

"You need to hurry," Spotswood said. "I let her slip away just as I came. She'll take some time to question some of the men in the town taverns, then they'll send her down to the river's edge, and to the Blackhorse."

"The Blackhorse? Why, 'tis full of river rats!"

"Umm. And a place where the Silver Hawk has been seen before, and may appear again. I'll send down. Peter should be below with the Silver Hawk's apparel." He paused, looking back. "It really was necessary, Petroc. You do know as well as I that the Silver Hawk will command the respect of the rogues in the area. They will not come together against him, while they might pool all their resources to send Lord Cameron down to the bottom of the sea."

"Yes, it was necessary." He touched his temple and winced. "I'm not sure about the headache, though, sir. Perhaps you could have warned me, and she could have just slipped out unnoticed."

Spotswood lowered his head, a subtle smile playing on his lips. "I don't know. Maybe the way she left was necessary, too."

He turned around and left.

Roc crossed his arms over his chest, pensively awaiting Peter's arrival with the things he would need.

Maybe her departure had not been necessary, but perhaps it had been well worth the price of a headache. She had come to him, and she had given the promise of a sweet tomorrow. . . .

Right before she had clunked him on the head to leave him.

Maybe it really wasn't such a bad thing that she was going to see the Silver Hawk again after all. They had a bit of reckoning to do, all three of them: the Silver Hawk, Lord Cameron—and Skye, Lord Cameron's lady.

* * *

"He's going to catch up with you any minute, young woman. Any minute!" Mattie moaned. She looked over her shoulder, past the lamplit main street and toward the palace green. Mattie was absolutely convinced that Skye had dragged her on a fool's mission. Any minute indeed her young mistress's husband—enraged husband, now, surely—would come tearing out of that house and down the street, seeking his wayward bride. Mattie did not want to be in the path of his anger, nor did she think that Skye really wanted to meet his fury, either.

"Mattie, that's why we need to hurry!" Skye said. "Now come along."

Mattie groaned and hurried along beside her Skye. It had been her choice to come. She wasn't happy about Lord Cameron lying on the floor in a pool of rum, but she hadn't been able to endure the idea of Skye running off alone. She had practically raised the girl, and Skye's years in London hadn't lessened the affection they shared.

Skye was heading on toward the next tavern on the street. This one wasn't as reputable as the others where they had gone to seek information, but Mattie still felt as if they were safe. This was Williamsburg. It was Lieutenant Governor Spotswood's city, and there would surely be some good men about to know that Lady Skye Kinsdale had been married to Lord Petroc Cameron—and that to touch her or cause her harm could well mean death at that man's able hands.

Mattie hurried along beside Skye against the quiet of the night. As they approached the tavern, a shadow stepped out from the trees by the side of it. Mattie gasped, pulling Skye back against her side. "Lady Cameron!" a voice called softly.

"Sh! Don't give no stranger in the shadows your name!" Mattie warned her.

"Yes!" Skye said, stepping closer.

The shadow backed away, lifting a hand.

"No closer, milady. No closer."

"Then what do you want?"

"I hear you've been prowling about tonight, asking what

ships lie in the James, seeing if any man knows about a pirate. A rogue ship, out in the river."

"Yes! Do you know about her?" Skye stepped forward again in her excitement. The man blended against a tree. The streets were always lit well by lamps, but the trees afforded such deep secretive shadows that the lamps could help little against the night.

"Stay where you are!" the voice commanded.

"Let's get out of here!" Mattie urged her in a whisper. "Let's go home. Please, child! You can be the fine lady wife, kneel down by his side, and pretend it was an accident—"

"An accident!" Skye whispered in turn. "I struck him over the head with a rum bottle—by accident?" She shook her head. "Mattie, no! I must find the Silver Hawk. He can save Father."

"Hey!" called the man from the shadows. "Are we negotiating here or are we not!"

"We're talking—" Skye said quickly, coming forward.

"Stand still!"

"I'm standing still," Skye promised, stopping. Mattie hovered unhappily just behind her. The breeze stirred, sweeping unease along her spine.

"I'll tell you where to find the Silver Hawk."

"Where?" Her heart thundered quickly. Perhaps she was on a fool's errand. She was coming to know Roc Cameron well, and he would not take kindly to her betrayal. Maybe she should run back and throw herself upon her husband's mercy. Maybe it would be much, much better than leaving the one man behind to seek out a rogue and enter into a world of tempest and temptation. She clenched her jaw, realizing anew that she was coming to love her husband. To love the man that she had betrayed. She had to move forward. Her father was out there, Logan's prisoner.

She almost screamed aloud with the thought, and she cast her guilt from her shoulders with a shrug. "Where!" she cried out to the man in the shadows.

"Not so fast, milady. You wear an emerald around your neck. I will have it."

"What?" Skye murmured. Her fingers came to her throat

and she realized that she still wore the emerald pendant she had found among her things at Bone Cay. She had worn it the first night that she had been with the Silver Hawk. She had worn it when she had cast aside all else, all clothing, all inhibitions. . . .

Her fingers closed around the pendant. She carried gold to give to the Silver Hawk. She could afford to give this man the pendant.

She snatched it from her throat and started to cast it forward. "Wait!" the voice cried. "Come forward, and drop the pendant."

"No!" Mattie called out. She stepped forward, taking the pendant from Skye. "I'll drop it, and if this man is a reputable liar and thief, then he'll have his pendant and you'll have your information, child."

Skye would have protested casting Mattie into danger, but Mattie gave her no chance to do so. She hurried forward to the tree and cast the pendant down as the shadow slunk back. Mattie sniffed her opinion of the man loudly, and came back to Skye.

A hand reached down and scooped up the emerald.

"The Blackhorse Tavern. It's south on the river. Speak softly and subtly, and you'll find the Silver Hawk." The shadow turned from the tree and went racing toward the rear of the tavern. Skye followed after him and found him leaping atop a sleek bay horse. "Wait! Wait, please! I still don't where this tavern is! I—I haven't followed the waterfront that often—"

She stopped, gasping. She recognized Robert Arrowsmith, the Silver Hawk's first officer aboard his pirate ship. "Robert!"

"Milady!" He doffed his hat to her, then swore. "Come! Come with me now!"

She didn't have time to agree or disagree. He urged his mount quickly forward and reached down to her, sweeping her up before him on his mount even as the bay pranced and prepared to bolt.

"Skye!" Mattied shrieked, coming after her.

"Tell her it's all right," Robert warned her.

"Mattie! It's fine. He's a—friend."

Mattie's tense and worried features as they rode into the night gave Skye a second seizure of guilt for the evening. Mattie would understand, surely. Mattie loved Theo Kinsdale as much as Skye did. But she would worry. She would worry horribly.

And worse. She would go back to the house and arouse Lord Cameron and then Roc would come riding for her. She swallowed as the wind lashed against her face. It was going to be dark along the road.

She couldn't fear the darkness, for there were worse dangers in the offering that night. Roc Cameron might well come for her, determined to kill the Silver Hawk. And if he did, it might well be her own fault—because she had told her husband that she was no innocent bride and that the Hawk had behaved in a foul and abusive way and seized her innocence away. . . .

She couldn't think about it. Robert would take her to the Hawk, and when she reached him, she would explain that they had to run, and quickly. He was a fool for being in Virginia anyway. Governor Eden of North Carolina might suffer pirates, but Lieutenant Alexander Spotswood of Virginia did not. The Hawk had to flee Virginia, and since he did, he might as well seek out Lord Theo Kinsdale and reap the benefits of the gold that Skye would so gladly pay.

The gold only! she thought with vehemence.

Gold . . . and nothing of herself.

She shivered, remembering the day not so long ago when she had lain in the pirate's arms beneath the sun. When she had felt his dark beard brush her naked flesh along with the searing rays of the sun. It was so easy to remember.

Easy to remember the first night, the very first night. He had warned her. . . .

And she had walked into his arms anyway, of her own free will.

That was before! she vowed to herself. Before she had come to know Petroc Cameron. Before she had discovered that she could love him. Before this very night, even, when she had come to him knowing that she would leave him, and determined to love him first. It was before the soaring splendor of his passion.

She trembled suddenly, and it was not the darkness of the night that brought her fear. Robert rode behind her, and though the lamps of the city were fading behind them, the moon was very high. There was light.

And she was learning not to fear the darkness, to fight the panic of it. Roc Cameron had done that for her, she thought. He had drawn the venom of the past from her soul. She had spoken about it to him, and she wasn't afraid. Roc had taken the words from her, while the Silver Hawk had taught her that there could always be a beacon against the darkness of the night.

The Silver Hawk . . .

She loved her husband.

She had fallen in love with the pirate king first, and though his memory had faded away only to combine with that of the man she had legally wed, she was both dreading and anticipating her meeting with the pirate. What would his memories be?

What would his demands be?

Could she sell her soul to come to him again, if that should be his price?

"Are you cold?" Robert whispered behind her.

She shook her head. "No. I am—I am anxious to see the Hawk. Are you certain you know where he is?"

"Yes."

She hesitated, thinking how kind Robert had always been to her. He was here in Virginia, and she had to be glad. But she dreaded the future for him. "Robert, you shouldn't be here!"

"The Hawk dares anything."

"The Hawk is not in Williamsburg."

Robert chuckled softly. "Sometimes it is necessary to come close to the flame of the fire, lady. Surely, you know that."

"You came to Williamsburg to spy," she accused him.

"Aye, milady, I did."

"If they catch you, they'll hang you."

"They'll never catch the Silver Hawk."

"But—"

"I am Robert Arrowsmith here, milady, good citizen of His

Majesty's colony of Virginia. I am safe." He hesitated. "Are you all right? We are almost there, another twenty minutes."

They no longer galloped, but Robert moved the horse along at a quick trot. The moon beat strongly upon the road, but she was touched. Even Robert considered her fear of the darkness.

"I am fine," she murmured, twisting to seek out his eyes. "But my husband might come after me. Robert, I would not have him come upon you. . . ."

"Is his temper so bad then?"

"He would slay a pirate, surely."

"But you would defend me?"

"I would, for you were always kind."

"And tell me, milady, what of the Hawk himself? Would your husband seek to slay him, or await a hanging?"

She started to shiver again. She could not imagine the Silver Hawk and Lord Cameron coming together. One of them would die, and she would not be able to endure the outcome of it.

"Hurry, Robert! Race the night, for we must get the Hawk and leave Virginia. We must!"

"We!"

"Yes! My father—"

"I know about your father, milady. But there will be no 'we.' I'll talk to the Hawk with you on your behalf, and I know that he will set sail. But he will not take you. You will go home."

She would not go home. She could not go home, not now. But she didn't tell Robert that—it was something she would have to worry about later.

Robert turned his mount eastward toward the river, nudging the animal's ribs, and sweeping them into a fast lope once again. She liked Robert so much! Skye thought. She felt warm with him, and assured that he would carry her to the Hawk.

Even if he had stolen her emerald!

It was all right. It was all right to race with him through the night, leaning low against the flying mane of his bay horse, feeling the wind and the gentle wash of the glowing moon upon her. It would be all right. . . .

"There! We're coming up on the Blackhorse now!" Robert said, reining in. "Stay with me, milady, do you understand?"

Skye nodded. She was glad of his presence, for she did not like the appearance of the tavern.

It stood just off the waterway and the docks, a rickety place with broken windowpanes and faulty steps. Dim, misty light issued from the open doorway and windows, and raucous laughter could be heard.

Robert dismounted from the horse, reaching up to help her down. Skye drew the hood of her navy mantle close over her forehead and slipped her hand through his arm as he led her toward the doorway.

It was not a place for a lady.

It was a complete den of iniquity, she thought, and her heart hammered somewhat as she thought of the Hawk. How dare he come here when she might need him! It was not a place where any decent woman would want to be.

"Milady?" Robert said to her, watching her curiously.

"Shall we?" she murmured.

He helped her up the rickety steps and through the open front doorway, and there they paused.

The main rooms were heavy with smoke and they stank of ale. Even the standing room by the bar was crowded, and all manner of men—and women—were there. The smell of humanity was terrible here. The men were old and young, but all of them had a look of dust and dirt about them; they were neither clean shaven, nor did they seem to have a decent beard among them. One fellow at the bar wore an eye patch and a white queued wig, but his wig was askew and his brawny shoulders seemed about to split the shoulders of his elegant mustard frockcoat. A stolen coat, no doubt, Skye thought.

Nearby at one of the tables a group of seamen in linen shirts and caps frolicked with a single, buxom, dark-haired wench. One fellow slipped his hand straight into her bodice while she kissed another, then laughed uproariously. She bit into the coins handed to her by the both of them, then laughed, and kissed them each, in turn.

Robert cleared his throat.

"The Silver Hawk is here?" she said.

"Aye, milady. He is a pirate, you know."

She thought that Robert's eyes were twinkling. "A pirate, a rogue, and he'll hang!" she agreed. She cried out as one of the men from the rough wood table rose, grinned a drunken grin, and lunged toward her. Robert stepped forward and his fist shot out and the man fell flat to the floor. "She's come to see the Hawk!" he warned the others. "Make way—she's here for the Hawk!"

Men and wenches stepped aside and Robert led her through the path of them toward a dark and narrow stairway in the rear. Skye felt eyes boring into her. The men coveted her gold, or her person, Skye thought. The women would have gladly robbed her blindly of her clothing.

But Robert was at her back. And he had announced that she had come for the Hawk. None of them would touch her.

"This is awful!" she muttered.

Robert passed ahead, catching her hand. She saw his eyes, and he flashed her a smile. "As I said, milady, the Hawk is a pirate."

"Umm. And welcome to his ways."

"You mustn't be . . . jealous, milady."

"Jealous! I assure you, sir, I am not jealous!"

"Umm, well, begging your pardon, milady, it did seem at the end that you and the Hawk had settled . . . er . . . well, certain of your difficulties. But you must remember, and I warn you kindly, that he is a rogue and a fiend."

"Oh, is he? Thank you for the warning, Robert. I might not have noted that on my own!"

They had come to the top of the stairs. Robert smiled, and with a broad shrug he cast open the door there. He prodded Skye into the murky light of the room, then closed the door behind her.

Slowly, her eyes adjusted to the light in the room. She heard a soft giggle, then she stared with amazement and a slow simmering rage.

Robert had brought her to the Hawk, all right!

"Lady Kinsdale! Why, no, 'tis Lady Cameron, is it not?"

She stood dead still, collecting her wits and control as she stared at the Hawk. He lay bare-chested atop the bed, with a beautiful redheaded wench curled nearly atop him. The girl watched her with amusement; the Hawk watched her with interest. His hand rested lightly atop the redhead's hair, and he seemed not at all distressed to have been found so by Skye.

"Aye, 'tis Lady Cameron," she murmured, pushing away from the door. If the sea slime meant to unnerve her, he would be surprised. She would never let him know that her insides were afire, that she had thought that he had come to care for her because he had taken her with such passion and such fire. . . .

She was not jealous! He was a fiend, a beast, a pirate! Robert had warned her.

But she had spent all that time on the road here wondering what she should do if he demanded her love in payment for service. Demanded her love! The rogue had a string of women in every port.

The sheets were drawn to his waist. He folded his hands over them and cocked his bearded face to the side. "Far be it from me to question a lady, madame, but what are you doing in such a place? Did you miss me so, then? Were you anxious to come back?" He didn't wait for an answer, but teased the redhead at his side. "If Lady Cameron is anxious, then you must hurry away, Yvette."

"I've come on business!" Skye snapped.

"Oh. Oh!" He pretended that it was a very grave matter, narrowing his eyes. Skye shivered suddenly, fiercely. Now she shivered because his resemblance to her husband was so great. Cousins! They were near to being twins. If she had not seen the both of them at the same time on the day that she sailed away from Bone Cay, she could easily think that they were one.

Well, the Silver Hawk had been bred on the wrong side of the Cameron covers. She had seen the portraits now at Cameron Hall. This Cameron had the eyes, if not the name.

"Sir—" Skye began, but he interrupted her, turning to the redhead.

"Yvette, love, this is business." He gave her an affectionate pat on the rump, and Yvette arose, dragging one of the covers along with her. She wrinkled her nose Skye's way.

"That's business, Hawk? Eh, is she paying you then, love, for the servicing?"

Skye nearly gasped, but determined that Yvette was a whore, and she was a lady. She smiled sweetly instead and strode very calmly for the washbowl. Within a blink of an eye, she had tossed the contents of it over Yvette's red head. The girl cried out in shock and rage.

"Eh, Hawk—stop her, or I will!"

Yvette lunged across the bed for her. The Hawk reached out for Yvette, capturing her wrists. Sodden, she fell against him and he laughed. "I cannot kiss and tell, Yvette, but if Lady Cameron needs a word with me, then for"—his silver gaze shot to Skye—"then for old times' sake, I must listen."

"You're a very scurvy son-of-a-bitch, sir," Skye said sweetly. She watched as Yvette arose, looked her way with menace, then smiled to the Hawk.

"See you later, love."

"You'll see him on a gibbet, I'm sure," Skye said pleasantly. Her eyes remained upon him. Yvette slammed the door.

The Hawk smiled deeply and patted the now empty spot on the bed beside him. "Care to join me?"

"Never."

"Ah, Lady Cameron, but you lie!" he taunted her, his silver gaze wide. "I can make you want me, you know."

Skye lifted her brows with imperious disdain. "No, you cannot, Captain Hawk. I do not come where refuse has lain."

"Refuse?"

"Trash, rank trash."

"Do you refer to the girl—or to me. Wait, wait, don't answer that. She must be rank trash, since I am merely sea slime."

Skye carefully ignored him, remaining very straight, her eyes smoldering. "I have come on business—"

"Wait," he interrupted her sharply, his gaze narrowing upon her. He sat up further, winding his arms around his legs as he watched her. "We have not finished with this first business yet."

"Aye, sir, but we have finished!" she insisted softly.

"I remember the very day that you left me, madame. The

warmth and the woman. Where has she gone? Where is the warmth."

"Iced over, I'm afraid, Captain. Now if you would just—"

"You would not lie where refuse had been," he repeated pensively. "So you will not crawl in beside me because another has warmed my bed, is that it?"

"Time is of the essence here!" Skye said irritably. "All right, no, you stupid, stinking, stupid knave, I would not so dirty myself. Are you satisfied? May we get on with it?"

He shook his head, his eyes insistent upon hers. "You didn't mention your husband, madame. Isn't marital life bliss? I had thought to hear you cry that you could not betray him—not that you would not play where another lass had tarried."

She inhaled sharply, hating him with her whole heart. He had thought of words that should have come to her lips, should have been wafted there on wings from her very soul. She stayed stiff and still and silent, praying that she showed no emotion. "My reasons, Captain Hawk, do not matter. Let's let it remain sufficient that it shall not come to pass."

"Skye, Skye," he continued mildly, casting off his sheets to rise from the bed stark naked. Skye tightened her jaw and turned about, determined not to see him. He was taunting her, he wanted reaction, and so help her, she would not give it to him.

She had to react; she had no choice. He came around behind her, catching the hood from her head and pulling it back to display the length of her hair. "You're forgetting, Lady—Cameron, that I am a pirate. And we all know what pirate's do to their women!"

Skye emitted a sharp sound of displeasure, stepping quickly away from him. Fear crept along her spine. She spun around, desperately wondering how to elude him. She moved to the left and he smiled slowly, his hands upon his hips, everything about him bold and brash. Like a cat with prey he stalked and played with her. "Bastard!" she hissed.

"Sea slime!" he corrected.

She turned about again and he followed her. He no longer played. He caught hold of her arm and sent her flying to the bed, then sprawling down upon it. She cried out, flailing at him wildly. He ignored her flying fists and feet, leaping roughly astride her and pinning her there.

His eyes were alive with silver sparks. "Alas, I am a pirate. And you, my love, are in my power once again. And now that I have you here . . . ah, I retaste every sweet morsel of all that ever lay between us."

"Quit this and get up!" Skye insisted with bravado.

"I am a pirate, madame! Forceful and brutal. I can wrench you into my arms—"

"You have already done that!"

"I repeat! I can wrench you into my arms and force you beneath me. Brutally, terribly, I can ravage and rape you. Isn't that what one expects of a pirate?"

Her eyes went very wide as she desperately tried to read his mind and his reason. His naked body was a blaze of fire against her, burning through her cloak and gown, corset and bone and petticoats. She didn't want to tremble beneath him, but she was afraid. She didn't think that she had ever seen him this fierce, this taut. This demanding, seeking something of her. She swallowed tightly, looking up at the living steel of his eyes, feeling the force of his muscle and flesh against her, the wrought-iron pressure of his fingers lacing around her wrists.

He did mean to rape her, she thought. He was not the man she had known at all. He meant to have her, and brutally.

Just as she told Roc that it had been . . .

"Stop it! Please, stop it!" she whispered to him. She trembled from head to toe.

Some of the fever left his eyes. He bent low against her. His lips brushed hers, his beard and mustache teased the softness of her flesh. She would have twisted away but his kiss was so gentle, so light, baby's breath. Then he stared down at her again.

"You must listen to me, please!" Skye said. She wanted to hate him so thoroughly. She could never let him touch her again, but she despised herself as well. When he came near, there was warmth, there was fire. She felt alive.

She loved her husband! she cried to herself. But her husband was so very like this man.

"Talk."

He still sat above her, impervious to his lack of dress. Skye sought out his eyes. "I need your help. And my—my husband could be right behind us."

"Oh?"

"My father is missing. He isn't missing—I mean, I know where he is. He was anxious to see me, and when the *Silver Messenger* returned here, he outfitted her with a new captain. It turned out to be Logan. Logan has my father. Please, I need you."

"I've heard about it," he told her.

"Then . . . ?"

"You say that you think that your husband might well be on his way after you?"

"Yes."

"Why. Where did you leave him?"

"What does that matter to you? I tell you that time is of the essence."

"I am curious. If you want my help, answer my questions."

"You haven't told me if I will get your help or not!"

"Talk!"

"Oh, you are a fool anyway! Spotswood will hang you if he finds you here."

"And your husband will slay me."

"Of course!"

"I might well slay him." He fell down by her side, rested upon an elbow, staring at her with fascination again. She rose quickly, leaping out of the bed, returning his glare.

"Don't be so certain, Captain Hawk. I have seen him in action, and he is a bold, brave fighter."

"Oh?" His brows shot up with surprise. "I thought you were determined to rid yourself of the excess baggage of your betrothed—your husband, that is—the moment you touched shore."

"None of this is your concern."

He smiled, enjoying her, enjoying himself. He rolled over, staring up at the ceiling. "So, madame, it was not so awful then. You lay with him and came back to me, furious that I should have another in my bed. Were your expecting my undying devotion. Should I have pined away while you slept with my illustrious cousin?"

Skye snatched up his black breeches from the floor and tossed them along with his boots upon his naked belly. He grunted from the pain and stared up at her, still smiling.

"Your temper, love! Marriage had not improved it."

"Are you going to help me or not?"

"I don't know. I'm still thinking about it."

"I will pay you."

"Of course, you will pay."

"I have gold."

He cast his legs over the side of the bed and slipped into his breeches. Standing, he tied them, then sought about for his hose. His bronze chest glimmered in the candlelight, rippling muscle defined and fascinating.

He sat again in a chair before the mantel and donned his hose and boots and buckled his black knee breeches. Skye watched him in silence all the while. She waited. Then, exasperated, she repeated herself. "I have gold! Are you going to help me or not?"

He stood and found his light linen shirt upon the foot of the bed. He drew it over his head, then looked at her with a slow lazy grin and a long, cunning assessment. "I have a lot of gold already, madame. I am not just a raping, plundering, murdering sea-sliming pirate, but I am a very successful raping, plundering, murdering, sea-sliming pirate. I don't really need your gold."

"You have to help me!"

"Why?"

"Because, because . . ."

"Because you're a damsel in distress?" he suggested. He came toward her, taking her hands, keeping his eyes upon her as he kissed both sets of her knuckles. "Ah, because I was the first lover you had ever known! Women have soft spots for such things, don't they?"

She jerked her hands away from him and lashed out at him. He caught her fists and, laughing, drew her against him. He held her tight and met her eyes.

"Let go of me!" she said.

"You came to me."

She didn't know if he referred to the night now, or if he talked about that night in a different lifetime in his paradise at Bone Cay. The night when the tropical breezes had swept through the windows.

"Please, let go of me." She hesitated. "Whether you help me or not, you mustn't stay around here, don't you know that? Spotswood—Spotswood knows that you are here."

"Does he?" The Hawk seemed unalarmed.

"Yes. He'll hang you."

"I do not need gold."

"Please, you must—"

"Ah, yes. I must."

"And you must hurry. My husband—"

"Why, madame, didn't you go to your husband with this request? You told me yourself that he was brave and bold and competent."

"But he is not a pirate!"

The Hawk's lashes fell over his silver eyes, hiding his thoughts from her. "Not a pirate, you say?"

"No," she murmured.

His arms tightened around her. "But what if he were?"

"He is not! You can find Logan, I know that you can. Roc could fight him, but he could not negotiate. He could not draw upon support from others in a battle. Please . . ."

He still held her too tight. She could feel the length of him, hard, determined.

"I do know where Logan is," he murmured.

"What?"

"I know where he is. I heard of it when I arrived here."

"Then—oh, my God, please! Help me."

A slow, cynical smile curved into his lip. "For payment, madame, always for payment."

"Of course, I told you, I have gold—"

"And I have told you, I do not want your gold."

"Then—"

"I want you, milady."

Skye gasped. "But—"

"You, milady. I have named my price. I will have you. Just

as I had you upon Bone Cay. Scented softly from the bath, sweet and seductive, your hair a sunset blaze about your naked shoulders, and most of all . . . your will agreeable to the act, your heart and body not just willing, but eager."

"I—I can't!"

He smiled and released her, turning away. "That is my price, and my final offer. Take it or leave it."

She stamped a foot furiously against the ground. "I cannot pay such a price! I'm—I am married now."

"Now you think of such a thing!" he said. "You were married at the very time we lay together before."

"I did not know it then."

"You knew you were betrothed."

"What does it matter! I cannot pay this price."

He shook his head, still smiling, as he picked up his black frockcoat and pulled it around his shoulders. He found his scabbard and buckled it around his waist. He set his hat atop his head and found his pistol to shove into his waist.

He tipped his plumed hat to her.

"Then, adieu, milady. I will take your advice and vacate the premises." He strode past her toward the door.

"No!" Skye cried out.

He turned around and arched a brow to her slowly.

"I'll—I'll pay."

"You will?" He waited. "And what of your ardent husband?"

"It is none of your concern! I said that I will pay."

"Perhaps it is every bit my concern."

"What?"

"Never mind," he said swiftly. He strode back into the room and took her hand. He turned it over and planted a kiss on it. Then his eyes met hers. "Our bargain is made, milady."

"Yes."

"I will collect upon the payment, come what may."

"Yes." Silver chills raced along her spine. She had made a bargain in hell, she thought.

What of her ardent husband?

She couldn't think of him now, couldn't believe in him or dare to believe in love. Her father's life was at stake. Was another night spent in the arms of a pirate a small enough price for life?

No . . . for it was betrayal now.

The Hawk was staring at her, as if his silver eyes read her thoughts, and her very soul. He kissed her forehead, then took her hand.

"Come, lady. Our deal is made, and our bargain sealed. I will deliver. . . ."

"And then payment will be made."

XV

The Silver Hawk cast open the door to the hallway. "Robert! Robert Arrowsmith." he called.

Robert could not have been far away, for he came instantly to the door. "Aye, Captain?"

"Give the order to our own men below that we must get to the longboats and onto the ship. We sail out tonight."

"Aye, sir!"

"And when the warning is given, come back to me. You may escort Lady Cameron back to wherever it is that you found her. Deliver her to the lieutenant governor with my compliments and suggest that he might wish to keep her somewhere out of harm's way."

"As you wish, sir," Robert agreed.

"What!" Skye cried out.

"Go," the Hawk told Robert. Robert saluted, and left them. The Hawk turned back to look at Skye. "You're not coming, milady. You know that you cannot possibly come. You must go back to your husband and your home."

"My father—"

"I will find your father. I will give you my word."

"But—"

"I will not put your life at risk again. Were your father not so impulsive as to seek you when others were better at the task, we would not be here now. There is danger aboard a pirate ship. You should know that well."

"Not when one is under the captain's protection!"

"But you know very well that one captain can be killed and another man take his place. You know full well that the sea can rage, and cannons fire. I will not take you with me."

"But . . . but what about your reward, Captain Hawk, your payment?"

He shrugged. "I have given you my promise that I will find your father and restore him to you. I will take your word that you will give payment, when payment is due. Your promise will be sufficient."

"My promise—"

He came back to her, a curious smile curving his lips. She didn't think to walk away; she was touched by the silver fire in his eyes and the wistful curl of his mouth beneath the mustache and beard. "You made a promise to me once before," he said softly. "Do you remember?"

She started to shake her head, suddenly frantic to be free from him. Sweet warmth filled her.

She might have stayed with him. Once, if it had not been for her love for Theo, she might well have cast caution and society and propriety to the wind. She might well have stayed with him upon his paradise while the world be damned. She had cared so very deeply. And now with his touch upon her . . .

"Do you remember? Darkness had fallen and you defied me and all danger to escape the night. And you promised me anything, anything at all that I could desire. To give to me all. You later retracted the promise—you had given it to a pirate. But you did not retract, in truth, and I will never forget the time that you gave me the innocence, the trust."

"You never forget?" she whispered. "Except when you bed with whores?"

"Never even then," he replied. "You tell me, milady, do you think of me when you bed with your husband?"

She pulled from him quickly, lowering her head. She had made new vows in her heart. She had sworn that when this danger was over, she would never fight her legal lord and husband again. She would live with him at Cameron Hall, and love him for all of her life.

If he wanted her still, after what she had done. Perhaps this time he would not forgive her.

Her heart seemed to tear within her chest and she wondered if he could understand what she had done. She was afraid to return, she realized, and she wondered not only who she loved the more, the pirate or the lord, or, at the moment, who she feared the more. In the whole of her life no man had had such power over her; now she was storm-tossed between two men, ever battling, and seldom leaving the fray without some wound.

"I love my husband," she said softly.

"What?"

He came up to her, spinning her around to see her face. His gaze was as sharp as his snapping voice, full of demand. Her eyes widened with surprise at his manner, but just then the door burst open again. Robert Arrowsmith had returned. "The men are heading to the longboats and await you. We'd best hurry. It seems that someone has spied a group of the lieutenant governor's militia coming our way. I can leave the lady in their care, and find you as you sail."

"Fine," the Hawk said. He turned, captured her hand elegantly, and kissed it with courtly finesse. "Milady, I stand forever at your service. My promise is my vow, as I am sure that yours shall be."

His eyes sought hers quickly, and then he was gone. She was left to Robert's care.

"We should leave now, and quickly," he told her. "The word is out that Spotswood's men approach. This place is coming alive with scurvies afraid of capture and hanging. I must leave in safety, and see to my own continued life, if you don't mind."

She shook her head, certain that she never wanted Robert Arrowsmith to hang. She dreaded returning to Williamsburg, and even more she dreaded returning to her husband. Perhaps there was some way to explain why she had rendered him unconscious, but she was certain that she could not make him understand a promise such as the one she had made to the Silver Hawk.

She could never explain it. But then, neither would she ever be able to forget it.

"Milady?"

Robert offered her his arm and she took it and they hurried toward the stairs together. Once there, they were brought up sharply.

The Hawk's men were gone, but many another knave was not. They awaited Robert standing in a circle at the foot of the stairs. He paused, shoving her behind him.

One fellow with a gold tooth and straggling dark hair stepped forward, grinning broadly. "Why, 'tis Mr. Arrowsmith of the Silver Hawk's sloop, is it not? Alas, while the Hawk's away . . ."

"What do you want, Fellows?" Robert demanded darkly.

Fellows lifted his hand, rubbing his thumb together with his forefinger. "What is it that we always want, good Master Robert? Gold, son, and that's a fact." Jeering, he pointed a finger behind Robert toward Skye. Nervously she pulled her hood further down upon her forehead. "There's rumor in the common room that the Hawk was visited by a lady . . . and that the lady was none other than the Cameron bride. She's a pretty thing, ain't she? Nay, lads, more than pretty. She's a beauty true and rare, and that's a fact. She's a ticket out of here to any man. She's a very fortune in gold—"

"Let me by, Fellows. She's been given the Hawk's safe passage, and that's a fact."

Fellows cocked his head. "Why, the Hawk's gone, Master Robert. 'E's gone after Logan, so I 'ear, and this time, I daresay, they will kill each other at last. I fear the Hawk no longer."

"Don't you, then?"

The voice thundered across the room and all assembled at the foot of the stairs turned quickly to the doorway. The Hawk wasn't gone at all, not yet. He was standing in the doorway with his greatcoat over his shoulders and his sword drawn. He lifted his hand, beckoning to Fellows. "Come, sir, let's discuss this with our steel, shall we?"

"Get the girl!" Fellows bellowed out.

It was quickly apparent that he did not intend to battle the Hawk, not when a roomful of men stood between them. Some loathsome young man with filthy hands and rum-coated breath lunged toward Skye. She screamed, hurrying up toward the top of the stairs. Robert came against the young man, not reaching for his sword but jabbing his fist into the lad's jaw. The young man went down, and then Robert drew his sword.

"Get her out!" the Hawk raged to Robert across the room.

Robert shoved her upward. They were quickly pursued. Robert dueled with agility and grace, but he had no less than three opponents at a time.

"I need a sword, Robert!" Skye called.

"A sword, milady?"

He lunged at an opponent. The man gasped, clutching his skewered middle. He fell forward, and his sword fell to his feet.

Skye could not take the time to look upon the ugly death with horror. She plucked up the enemy's sword and swept her skirts behind her, anxious to parry their attackers along with Robert.

"Me! My hearties, 'tis me you must fight!" the Hawk cried, coming further and further into the room, battling all who came his way with a startling ferocity and trying to draw opponents from Robert and Skye.

He was strong, Skye thought, yet his brilliance at swordplay lay in his grace. No sword could touch him, for he could leap above the steel. No man could surprise him, for he would suddenly soar atop a wooden table and leap down upon his attacker.

"Come!" Robert urged her.

They fought to the top of the stairway. The Hawk fought his way closer and closer to them, and then he was suddenly beside them, his steel bathed in blood. They entered into the hallway, then he pushed open the door to the room where they had been. He shoved her inside, then Robert, then entered himself.

"The bed!" he roared to Robert.

Between them they shoved the bed against the door. Swords and knives hacked against it. It would burst open soon, Skye thought, in a bare matter of seconds.

The Hawk was already across the room and to the window. He picked up the hearth chair and sent it shattering against the murky panes. He jerked the dirty drapes down and wrapped them quickly about his wrist, shoving aside the broken glass. Then he turned to her. "Come on."

"What?" she demanded incredulously. "We're on the second floor, Captain Hawk. You—you and Robert can jump. I cannot!"

"You can!" Robert assured her. "You will be all right. It's our only chance. It—"

"Oh, for the love of God, Robert! We have to go!"

Skye screamed as the Hawk suddenly strode to her and swept her up and brought her straight to the window. He did not pause, nor could she begin to fight his movement or his speed.

He meant to kill her! He meant to cast her straight out of the window!

He did just that, tossing her instantly. She screamed for all that she was worth as she fell and fell into the night, then her scream was silenced and her breath was swept away as she landed hard upon a stack of hay. A body fell near hers, and then another. She tried to scramble up. She couldn't breathe. She couldn't believe that she was alive.

Skye pushed herself up at last.

"Go, Jacko!" the Hawk called out.

And Skye fell again, flat on her back, as the hay wagon that held her jerked forward. She tried to struggle up again, but the ride was rickety and so swift she could barely move. Fingers curled around hers. "Lie still!"

The wagon came to a halt. The Hawk and Robert leaped down, then their driver, Jacko. The Hawk reached for Skye, lifting her up, and she recognized Jacko from her days aboard the pirate ship. He bowed to her with a broad grin. " 'Evening, milady!"

They stood upon the dock. Skye could hear the lap of the

water. "My God, how did you know to double back?" Robert demanded of the Hawk.

"I didn't like the look on some of the men's faces as I left," the Hawk said briefly. "Jacko here thought to borrow the wagon and head around back to the windows, for which I am eternally grateful."

"We have to move," Jacko said. "Any minute now they shall discover the room empty, and the bulk of our men have headed out. They'll have to run themselves, with the militia coming. We've got to reach the ship, and quickly, Captain."

"What about Lady Cameron?" Robert asked.

The Hawk looked her up and down and then issued an exasperated sigh. "She comes with us. We've no choice. I cannot send her back, even with the militia coming. There are no guarantees." He caught Skye's arm and jerked her up against him. "Madame, I have said it before, and I say it again. You are trouble!"

She jerked away, her fingers still tight about the sword she had plucked from the slain ruffian. "You pirated my ship, Captain Hawk! Bear that in mind, sir! Had you lived an honest life, we'd have never met!"

"That thought could, indeed, make a cutthroat repent, milady. I shall bear it in mind. Now, let's go!"

He stepped toward her and she was afraid of some fight, but he merely swept her up into his arms and took another step with balanced precision into the darkness beneath them. She muffled a cry of alarm, for they had merely come down into the longboat, and Jacko and Robert were following them. The men quickly picked up oars, and they slid away, silently, into the night.

The Hawk leaned toward her suddenly. She was shivering; she had grown very cold despite her cloak.

"Milady, I dare not light a lamp. Will you be all right."

She nodded. His eyes remained fixed on hers.

Suddenly the soft sound of the oars dipping against the water was drowned by the shouts and fury that emanated from the tavern. "Company comes!" Jacko laughed.

"Ah, and I fear too late!" Robert said, pleased. Skye quickly looked back toward the land. The rogues from the tavern were spilling out to the stretch of land before the docks. They raced for their boats, but even as they sought the water, an explosion of shots was heard on the air.

"The militia," Robert murmured.

"They'll be taken?" Skye whispered.

"Aye, lady. Those known for their deeds will face trial and hang. There will be a few of the notorious among them. Those not known by face or name will be set free."

"The Silver Hawk would be known," she whispered.

"Aye, lady, the Silver Hawk would be known." He offered her a wry grin, and she trembled inside. Freedom had loomed before him while death had lain behind him and he had still come back. He had come back for her.

"Will we make it?" she said.

He lifted his oar. "The ship lies just ahead."

"You thrive on danger!" she accused him.

"Ah, but I do appreciate my neck, my love!" he assured her.

They fell silent again. Skye looked back. Horses raced along the shoreline. Boats were slipping into the river, men fought fiercely on land. Shots rang out; steel clanged.

The light began to fade in the distance, and the noise, too.

They knew the river here well, these pirates, Skye thought. They navigated in the near darkness. Silence and darkness enveloped them. Skye began to shiver.

The Hawk ceased to row. His hand stretched out to hers, his fingers entwined over them. "It is all right," he assured her softly. His warmth swept into her. She nodded and swallowed. Her throat was dry. Her heart was wretched.

"It will not be so long," he promised her.

It was long. She knew that his ship could not have been so close, that he must have hidden her carefully in some inlet. Still it seemed that they traveled long and hard before they at last saw a beacon in the night.

"The ship," Robert murmured.

"Aye, she awaits us," the Hawk said. "Is Mr. Fulton at the helm, ready to set out?"

"Aye, Captain. That he is."

The longboat moved up by the ship. The ladder was cast

over the portside, and the Hawk helped Skye to her feet. Shivering, she clung to the rope rigging and climbed.

He was quickly topside with her, then Robert, then Jacko.

"Take Lady Cameron to quarters," the Hawk said.

"Wait!" Skye cried. Did he think to take her into his cabin again? She had to make him understand that he could not.

"I cannot wait!" he cried impatiently. "I'm captain here, madame, and I sail at your request, hounded my the militia on your behalf. Robert, take her!"

He turned away, heading toward the helm. Robert seized hold of her arm, and she knew that no matter how the man cared for her, he would obey the Hawk.

"Milady, come, please."

He tugged upon her arm, gently, then more insistently. "Now, milady."

"Damn. Damn him!" she cried out, hoping that her fury would reach the Hawk. But he had already dismissed her. He stood atop the platform and shouted out his orders. The anchor was drawn; men were rushing to the rigging to hoist sails.

Robert led her along to the Hawk's own cabin. She bit her lip. He opened the door and thrust her inside.

The fire burned in the stove. Lamps were lit. Warmth and light surrounded her.

The cabin had not changed. Not a bit, since she had been within it last.

"I cannot stay here!" she cried to Robert.

But he ignored her and pulled the door closed behind her. She heard him slide the bolt outside, and she knew that there was no fighting the circumstances.

She fell down upon the bunk, exhausted. It had to be nearly dawn, and there wasn't a thing in the world that she could do at the moment.

She dropped her sword, doffed her cloak, and stretched out upon the bed. Her mind raced and her heart ached and fits of trembling seized her again and again.

At last she stood up and went straight to the Hawk's liquor supply. She downed a good portion of rum, recorked the bottle, and staggered back to the bunk. She fell down upon it again.

And that time, she slept.

In the morning she awoke alone.

She had feared the Hawk throughout the night, but he had not come near her. As she rose, she realized miserably that she did not fear his force, but her own response.

Robert came, quiet and subdued, bringing her breakfast and water with which to wash. He watched her intently. "It was not your fault," he told her. "The Hawk's not pleased at all that you're with us, but don't be alarmed by him, it was not your fault."

"Thank you, Robert."

He smiled to her encouragingly. "Robert, if a pardon comes through, is there any possibility that you will forswear your ways and sign loyalty to the king?"

She thought that his smile deepened, but he quickly lowered his lashes and she could not see his eyes any longer. "I will do whatever the captain does, madame."

"Is your loyalty so fierce, then?"

"It is." He hesitated. "He nevers betrays a trust, milady. He has said that he will lay down his life for you—he will do so then. I will lay down my life for him. That is how we all feel, all of us sailing with him. And that is why he is feared and respected." He paused, as if he longed to go on. Then he shrugged. "The door is open, milady, you are welcome topside."

"Wait, Robert!" she pleaded. He stopped, and it was her turn to pause as a crimson flush climbed over her face. "Robert, where did he sleep last night?"

Robert's gaze swept over her, and he smiled secretively. "In the officers' quarters, milady. Is there any other way in which I may serve you now?"

In the officers' quarters . . .

He had given her his cabin in privacy. Was he waiting to collect his payment, the honorable rogue to the very end? The thought made her shiver, and then she remembered her husband left lying upon the floor, and she wondered where Lord

Cameron had spent the night. A fierce surge of trembling rose within her and she had to sit down upon the bunk. Roc . . . could he forgive all of this? Would he disown her, or beat her? Or both. Such behavior would lie well within his rights for all that she had done.

And gave promise to do in the future.

She didn't know who she hated the most then, Lord Cameron or the Hawk. She didn't know who she feared more.

And she still didn't know who she loved more.

"All you all right, milady?" Robert asked anxiously.

"I'm—I'm fine, Robert. Thank you."

"There's nothing I can do?"

She shook her head slowly. When he was gone, she picked at the food that he had brought her, then she quickly washed, brushed her hair, and came topside.

The sails were mostly drawn in, and they traveled slowly and very close to shore. Dangerously close, Skye thought. She could see land to the starboard side. She looked to the carved platform and to the helm and saw that the Hawk was there, navigating his own ship that day.

Skye smiled to the men she passed upon the deck, and they smiled in turn or tipped their hats. Once, she had been in terror of these men, she thought. Now they were her allies.

Her friends.

She couldn't dwell upon such curious twists of fate. She hurried by them and up the platform.

The Hawk was in a black open-necked shirt and black breeches and his dark head was bared to the day. He nodded to her gravely when she came his way.

"Did you sleep well, milady?"

She nodded. "Did you?"

"Alas, I whiled away the night in dreams."

"I thank you for that, Captain Hawk," she said softly. He glanced to her, then looked up toward the crow's nest.

"Jacko!"

"Aye, Captain?"

"Is she clear?"

"As clear as fine crystal, Captain!"

"Robert! Mr. Arrowsmith!"

"Aye, Captain!" Robert was quickly with him, bounding up the steps of the platform from the far deck.

"Take the wheel, sir, if you please."

"As you please, Captain!" Robert agreed.

The Hawk stepped away, offering Skye his arm. She hesitated, then took it, glancing wryly toward Robert. "I wonder if His Majesty's ships of the Royal Navy work so smoothly," she murmured.

"I wonder," the Hawk agreed pleasantly. He led her starboard side, where the sea breeze touched her face and lifted her hair. "I've a few lady's things aboard," he told her. "We had not anticipated your arrival, and so little was prepared. What I have will be sent to you by afternoon." He leaned against the rail, watching her intently. "I know your penchant for bathing, milady, and would not deny you the pleasure."

She flushed slightly and turned to stare out at the coastline. "I want nothing of your ill-gotten gain, Captain," she told him.

"Who says that what I offer is ill-gotten gain?"

She glanced at him sharply, and then her color deepened. "I want nothing belonging to your whores, either, Captain, thank you."

He smiled, staring out on the water silently, not touching her. "Milady, I promise you, what I send belongs to no whore."

"Then—"

"Certain of my men are married, milady. Though their wives' finery might not be to your standards, still, certain . . ." He paused, his eyes meeting hers with a devilish light. "Certain intimate apparel will be clean and neat and surely acceptable."

Even his silver eyes seemed to touch and stroke her, she thought. She should be far away from him. Far, far away.

She stared across to the shore. "Tell me, Captain, do you intend to let me wear this clean and neat clothing on my own?"

"Milady?"

"Are you—" Her lips were dry, and she was breathless, and they merely stood together and spoke. If only she could forget the past. If only the slightest brush of his arm against hers did not evoke memories of tempest.

"Are you going to leave me in peace, Captain? Your cabin, sir, have you given me that as my own?"

He took a long time answering. When she looked to him at last, he was studying her very seriously. "Until it is time to do otherwise."

"What do you mean?"

"When we've found and taken your father, milady. Then I will return. It will be most difficult for you to keep your promise to me if I am bedded elsewhere."

She did not reply but tore her eyes from his to survey the shore. "With my father on board?" she queried softly.

"You're worried about your father—and not your husband?"

"My husband is not aboard," she murmured miserably.

"Ah . . . so that makes it all right to be an adulteress?"

"Stop it!" she hissed desperately. "Nothing makes it all right!"

"No, it doesn't, does it?" he murmured. He turned her around by the shoulders. She tried to jerk free from his touch, but he would not allow her to go. She stared up at him, her eyes glazing with tears.

"I need your help!" she insisted bitterly. "I had no choice. My father—"

"Aye, your father," he muttered darkly. "And still I tell you, milady, that your husband would have gladly fought and died rather than let you pay this price."

"His blood cannot be payment for my request."

"Aye, milady, for his blood has become your blood, as surely as yours is his. God alone knows how he will feel this time!"

"What do you mean?" she cried, wrenching away from him at last.

"Well, milady, I assume you must have admitted something." The sweep of his eyes told her clearly and boldly that he spoke of her lack of innocence when she entered into her marital bed. "What did you say? That it was fear? Loneliness? Desperation, a bid to save your very life! This time . . . perhaps you need not tell him that you bartered with what was his, that you offered yourself in payment. You can tell him that I am a pirate, a cutthroat, a ravaging rapist, and that I dragged you down before you had a chance to think." He reached out for her again so suddenly that she nearly screamed. His fingers threaded cruelly into the hair at her nape, and he dragged her close. "Maybe he'll be so enraged he'll beat you to within an inch of your life. I wonder what I would do, milady, if you were my wife, under such circumstances. I'd kill the man, that is for certain."

She kicked him savagely, taking him by surprise. He howled with outrage as her foot came in wild contact with his shin, then he jerked harder upon her hair, pulling her flush against him. He gritted his teeth. "Pirates, milady. We are allowed to be savages, remember? But I do wonder just how savage your fine aristocrat of a husband might turn out to be when he hears of this latest maneuver on your part! But then, you told me that you loved him, didn't you?"

"Let me go!" she cried frantically. "He is my concern." Aye, Roc was her concern, just as the Hawk was her concern. And at the moment, he was the man to fill her heart and her thoughts, for she was so completely his prisoner. From head to toe she was flush with the man, achingly aware of the heat of his muscles, the strength of his hands and arms, the fire in his groin. It occurred to her fleetingly then that she knew him more thoroughly still than she did Petroc Cameron, for this one she had seen boldly in the nude, while her husband had seduced her and been seduced in return while never quite shedding his clothing.

Warmth blazed through her as she struggled to be free.

"Captain!"

"Aye!" He released her instantly, striding the deck to come back upon the platform by the helm. It was Jacko calling to him from atop the crow's nest.

"I see ships ahead, far right into the inlet."

"Pirates?"

"Aye, sir! I see Teach's flag atop the one. They're drawing it in, I believe."

"Safe harbor on the islands!" Robert Arrowsmith seemed to growl.

Skye hurried after the Hawk to the platform. "Where are we?" she demanded.

"My glass!" the Hawk demanded. He leaped for the mast and began to shimmy up the length of it. Skye watched his dexterity with perplexity and annoyance, then turned to Robert. "Robert! Where are we? What is going on, here?"

"A party, milady."

"A party!"

"A pirate fete upon a North Carolina island. A number of men have gathered here. Teach just took some incredible prize and enhanced his reputation a thousand times over. We believe he has a certain immunity here, in this area of North Carolina. So do some of the others."

Skye gasped. "So Eden of Carolina has been bribed by the pirates!"

"So goes the rumor."

"But why have we come . . . ?" she began, but even at the last, her voice trailed away. "Logan! The Hawk thinks that Logan has come here with my father!"

"Precisely, Lady Cameron."

Skye fell silent and hurried back to the railing, looking starboard side. She realized that the Hawk was calling down orders to Robert Arrowsmith, and that Robert was then calling out commands to the crew. The sails were drawn in tighter and the ship began to shift. Skye thought that the Hawk meant to sail straight into the land, and she nearly turned to scream that they were insane. But just when she would have done so, she saw the narrow channel leading inland. It was a fair space ahead of the other pirate ships.

They were going to hide, she thought. Hide, until the Hawk could get a fair layout on the land—and its inhabitants.

She was right in her assumptions.

Turning about again, she saw that the order had been given to bring down the longboats.

Then a moment later, in the midst of all the activity, the Hawk was striding back toward her. He was fully armed now, she saw, with his cutlass in his scabbard, a knife in a sheath at his boot, and a brace of pistols shoved into his waistband.

"Go back to the cabin," he told her curtly. "Stay out of sight."

He started to turn away. "Wait!" she cried to him, catching hold of his arm. "Please, don't leave me here—"

"Damn you, stay out of sight!" he told her, his eyes narrowing. "You little witch! Don't you remember the last time, girl? If you hadn't been so determined to escape, Logan might well never have known that you existed!"

And he might not have kidnapped her father. The words went unsaid. Skye stepped back as if she had been stung, but she did not cease her argument, for it was the same as his.

"Please, don't leave me here! It is because—" she hesitated, then continued, "it is because of my very foolish determination at that time that I beg you to bring me along."

He hesitated, and she knew that he recalled how Logan had come to the ship when it had been weak and unguarded.

"Damn it!" he swore. "Damn it! Aye, come along, then! But you heed my words and warnings at all times, and so help me, if you prove to be trouble, I will lash you to a tree! Robert! Get the lady's cloak."

"Robert! And my sword, please!" Skye added.

The Hawk stared at her. He did not refuse her request. "Come, lady," he said at last, as Robert brought her things. "We'll take the first boat."

His touch was far from gentle as he handed her down the ladder to the longboat from the deck. He was not leaving the ship as unguarded as he had in New Providence, but at least twenty-five of his men were accompanying them.

He did not row, but balanced forward, looking ahead. Jacko and Robert and two others were in their boat, rowing steadily. Skye sat tense and silent, watching as they came to land.

When they did, the Hawk asked no by-your-leave, but plucked her up in his arms and thrashed through the water with her in his arms. She smiled suddenly as he carried her, taut and distant, over the sand to the secrecy and shadows of the brush. He glanced down, startled by her gaze.

"Once," she whispered, "you said that I wasn't even worth

a fair price in gold. But you are risking your life for one night in my arms. Should I be flattered, Captain Hawk?"

"Perhaps I value my life less than gold. Perhaps that is a pirate's way."

"I, sir, do not value your life as less!"

She thought that he would be pleased. He stiffened like cold steel and fell to his knees to dump her angrily upon the sand. His men milled behind them but he spoke in a heated whisper anyway.

"What of your life, lady—and all that is of value to your husband?"

She straightened herself, longing to slap him. He knew her intent, for he quickly caught her wrist, and together they rolled across the sand. Breathlessly she shoved against him.

He paused at last. They had come beneath the shadow of spidery trees, on a bed of pines. He rose over her. He cupped her chin in his hands and bent down to kiss her. She tried to twist away. Her resistance was to no avail. His lips found hers. His tongue ravaged them, demanding that they part to him. He was merciless, savage, demanding. She could scarce breathe. She twisted and kicked.

But she could not move, nor could she deny the wild abandon that snaked traitorously into her veins. He brought her alive with fire, with liquid heat. She could fight no more. She tasted his lips and tongue and the deep recesses of his mouth, tears coming to her eyes. She felt his hands upon her, sweeping along her thigh, cupping her breast.

Then at last he broke away. He started to swear at her furiously, incoherently, but then his words broke away. He gently smoothed the tear from her cheek with his forefinger, then he drew her to her feet.

"You will wait here with Robert, do you understand me? I am looking today, nothing more. I may, perhaps, leave you ashore tonight, and enter into the festivities with you safely out of sight and far, far from harm's way. Stay with Robert and my men, and take care. Do you understand me?"

She nodded. He turned and, shouting orders, left her. She waited until he was long gone, then she came over and joined Robert, who sat idly by the shore. Others of the men had stayed behind, too. Five of them. To protect her, Skye thought.

By Robert's side, she suddenly burst into tears. He set his arm around her like a brother, drawing her close. Miserably, awkwardly, he tried to comfort her. "I've tried to tell him. Ah, Skye, I've tried, I'm so sorry. . . ."

"What?" she managed to gasp out. "Tell him what?"

"To leave you be," he whispered. "You don't understand. You can't possibly understand. He . . . never mind. It will be all right. Trust me, milady, trust me, please."

She fell silent and stayed by his side.

Later he rose, looking upward with agitation. "What is it?" Skye demanded.

"Clouds. Storm clouds. I don't like them."

Skye looked up herself. Even as she did so, it seemed that the day darkened. The breeze picked up.

"We should get back," Robert said.

"We can't leave him! We can't leave the Hawk!" Skye protested.

"We won't be leaving him. I'll take you back, and he can come with the others in one of the longboats."

A sudden, brilliant flash of lightning rent the sky. Thunder followed it like a clash of heavenly swords. "Come on!"

Robert dragged her to her feet. Skye whirled around as the other men rose, hurrying toward them.

The rain began to fall.

"We head to the ship in one boat!" Robert cried. He reached for Skye's hand. A second bolt of lightning came, and thunder followed, and the very heavens seemed to open up upon them. "Come, Skye!" Robert grabbed her hand, and they started racing down the beach. Then suddenly she stopped, and she slammed hard against him. "Hawk!"

Skye pushed sodden tendrils of hair from her face to stare ahead of herself. He was indeed coming back. Running along before the main group of his men, he reached them. He spoke quickly to Robert. "They're here all right, a full party of them. Logan, Teach, a fine baker's dozen of others. We'll move in tomorrow. For now, let's hie from here. This storm promises to be fierce!"

He reached behind Robert, finding Skye's hand and pulling her along. He lifted her and shoved her into one of the longboats. Robert and two men crawled in behind them and shoved them away from the shore.

The Hawk ignored Skye, rowing hard with the others. Lightning flashed, thunder cracked, and she flinched. At the shoreline she could see the waves swelling and the trees and bracken bending low to the strength of the wind. She shivered. In a matter of moments, it seemed, a true tempest had swirled upon them.

"Damn!" Robert swore. "I cannot hold her steady!"

"Pull together!" ordered the Hawk.

Skye turned around. She could see the ship, and it still seemed far ahead of them. The ferocity of the waves seemed to push them ever closer toward the shore.

"Take care of the rocks!" the Hawk cried, but he had barely voiced the words when a terrible rending sound was heard. Skye didn't know what had happened at first. The sound seemed part of the horror of the storm, like the crack of thunder, like the high scream of the wind. "Signal the others!" the Hawk cried. Skye stared at him and saw the power he set to the oars, trying to hold the small boat steady. She looked to her feet. Water rushed in upon them. They had struck a rock. They were sinking, she realized.

"Fulton has seen us!" Robert cried. "He's circling back."

"Dive in, we'll take less water, and I'll stay with Skye to the last!" the Hawk shouted. "She cannot make it far in these skirts!"

"I can't leave you—"

"You'll drown us if you stay! It will come right, Robert, if we don't take any more water! Tyler, Havensworth, dive now, and reach Fulton, and bring him around for us!"

Seeing the wisdom of his words, his men quickly obeyed his orders. Skye gasped, her hand coming quickly to her mouth, for it instantly seemed that the wild sea swallowed them over. Grayness prevailed.

Then she saw Robert's head as he broke out of the waves. Then she saw the two other men, and that they could survive; they were swimming hard toward another boat.

She glanced down to her feet again. The water was rising high. She looked to the Hawk. He was staring at her.

"Ready?" he asked.

She lifted her chin with a smile of bravado. "I am afraid of the dark, not the water!" she told him. A slow smile curved into his features. He reached out to her.

"Come then, my love!"

She took his hand. The rescue boat was almost next to them, but Skye realized that they had to jump and swim—else risk the damaged boat crashing with the one that would save them. With her fingers entwined with the Hawk's, she dove over the side.

She was instantly dragged down. The water was cold, heavy, and dark. Her lungs hurt and she tried to kick her way back to the surface. She was so very heavy.

There was a jerk upon her hand. The Hawk was dragging her up. Her face broke the surface. Still, she could scarce breathe. The rain beat against her savagely, the wind screamed and tore at her, stealing away what breath she could gasp in.

"Swim!" the Hawk commanded.

A giant wave crashed down upon her. Their hands were torn apart. Skye felt as if she were lifted by a giant icy hand and tossed about. She was heavy, so heavy! Wildly, desperately, she broke the pull of the sea.

Salt water stung her eyes and filled her mouth as she gasped for air. She strained to see, and horror engulfed her. The longboat seemed to be miles away. Miles and miles away.

And the Hawk was next to it, clinging to it. He could crawl right over to safety, while she . . .

Water rose and crashed over her head again. She started going down. Her lungs were going to burst. Searing pain swept through them. She realized that she was about to die, to drown, to sink down to the sea bed in a swirl of bone and petticoats and skirts, and lie there to be food for sharks and other fishes. Life, sweet tempest that it was, would be over. Death could not be so hard. Not so painful as the agony that came to her lungs. Not so terrifying as the sea green darkness and the cold that was enveloping her. They said that a drowning man saw his life flash before his eyes. What of a drowning woman?

A drowning woman saw her lover's face, she thought, but her air was all but gone, and she did not know if she saw her husband or the Hawk before her. . . .

Pain awoke her just before she opened her mouth to breathe in gallons of the water. Fingers entwined in her hair, dragging her up and up. She broke the surface and through the darkness and gray and pelting of the rain, she saw the Hawk.

"Swim!" he commanded her furiously.

"I cannot! My petticoats—"

"Shut up!"

He was holding her against him, treading the water with a fury and coming at her with a knife. If she had had breath, she would have screamed. He meant to slay her so that she would not drown, she thought incredulously.

But he did not slay her. His knife did not cut into her flesh, but severed away her clothing. Her skirts and petticoats fell, and her legs were free, and she could tread water herself. "Get rid of your shoes!" he shouted.

She reached down and gulped in some water. He spun her around, digging into her hair again, but holding her face above water. She managed to shed her shoes. She realized that he was already swimming, his fingers dragging her along by the hair.

"I can manage!" she cried. Twisting, she began to go with the water. He wasn't fighting the current or the waves. He was allowing the rush of the storm to cast them toward the shore.

Hope surged within her, but then it died. She was tiring so quickly! And it took them so long. The shoreline seemed so close, and then a gray wave would crash over her, and it would seem miles away again. She started to flag. He caught her by the hair again.

"Stop!" she cried. The cold was numbing. It made her want to die. "Stop, you're hurting me. I can't make it. Go on!"

"I'll hurt you like you can't imagine if you don't stop fighting me!" he swore. His fingers were grasping her, biting cruelly into her. They laced through her hair, and he was swimming hard again. She ceased trying to fight him. The rain was all around her, as gray as the sky, as dark as the sea. There was no difference between them. Sky and rain and sea were one, and they were imprisoned by them all.

"There. Hold on!" the Hawk demanded.

She didn't know if she held on or not. The darkness encompassed her. She went limp. She sank beneath the waves. The shore was just ahead of them. She saw that. Then the world was dark.

She came to moments later because she was flat in the sand, and he was straddled over her, his mouth on hers, forcing air into her lungs. She gasped, and breathed on her own. Her eyes flew open.

"We're alive!" she cried.

"We're alive," he said simply. He crashed down beside her. She realized that she could no longer feel the rain. He had brought them into the shelter of a small cove with overhanging rock and ledge.

She could think no more that night. She closed her eyes, and slept.

The sun, hot and beautiful upon her damp body, awoke her. Skye rolled, dazed, to her side. She looked about, and she saw the Hawk. He was still out, sprawled not ten feet away from her. Desperately pleased to see him with her and alive, she crawled the distance to him. If he slept, she could dare to wake him with a tender kiss. This morning, she could not feel guilt or shame.

Yet before she could touch him, she paused. A frown furrowed her brow as she stared down at his face.

Half of his beard had been sheared away. His mustache, too. Bits and pieces of hair clung to his flesh in a very odd manner.

She reached out and touched the hair. It came away in her grasp. It was fake. His beard was fake. He was really clean shaven. And with the beard gone to display the contours and angles of his face, he looked even more like Petroc Cameron. In fact, he looked exactly like Petroc Cameron.

She stared at him, and the truth slowly, slowly dawned upon her. She stood, forgetting their wild fight for life and death, forgetting everything as rage seared into her heart, blinding her to the entire world.

"Bastard!" she shrieked, and she awoke him not with a kiss, but with a wild and savage kick to the midsection.

XVI

"Despicable bastard! Scurvy knave. Worse than a sea slime, worse than the densest pile of—of rat dung! You should be sliced to ribbons, disemboweled! Skinned alive, inch by scurvy inch!"

He was dreaming, Roc thought. The storm and the roiling waves were all about him still and he was dreaming that some Harpy had come flapping around above him to torture him awake.

No . . . he was not dreaming.

It was Skye.

She was railing against him, hollering like a shrew, and tugging upon him, too. His sword . . . she was stealing his sword from his sodden leather scabbard!

Reeling from the pain in his gut, straining to come awake and to terms with the morning, Roc realized slowly that it was indeed Skye, she was standing over him, her left hand upon her hip, her right hand brandishing his sword, and a bit too close to his extremities, at that. Her eyes flashed like sapphires in the sun, she was as tense as steel. She stood disheveled, her hair a wild blaze about her, her skirts torn and shredded, her feet bare. If she weren't so enraged, he would have smiled. She was in a sorry state, except that, even so, she was more captivating than ever. Her legs were bare to her thighs, her breasts strained against the damp material of her bodice, and she might have been some pagan creature from a far barbaric time.

He stared at her blankly. She hissed some other ungodly name his way, and her toe landed hard against his midsection again. His own temper bubbled and soared and skyrocketed with him, exploding like some witch's brew.

He groaned, and she kicked him anew!

He pushed up from the sand in amazement.

"Skye! What the hell is the matter with you?"

"You!" she told him.

Then he touched his face. Half of the beard was there; half of it was gone. He muttered out an expletive and pulled away the remaining false whiskers, wincing as he did so. He was weary. His head was splitting and he ached from head to toe and she was standing there abusing him verbally—and physically—with a vengeance.

"Get up!" she commanded him, bringing the point of his own sword close against his jugular. His eyes narrowed with a flash of anger as he came slowly to his feet, facing her. "I should dice you into tiny pieces, and save the hangman his efforts. My God, the things that you did to me!"

"The things that I did to you!"

"Oh, Captain-Lord-Cameron-Hawk! How could you! How dare you! Hanging will be far too good a fate for you!" She started walking forward in her vehemence, and with that razor-honed blade so close to his throat, he had no choice but to back away from her along the sand. He'd never seen her this angry. He didn't know if she would or wouldn't use it.

"Give me the sword, Skye."

"Give *you* the sword? You must be out of your mind."

"You don't want me to kill me—"

"Kill you!" Her brows shot up eloquently. "Kill you? Oh, my dear captain! I'm longing to kill you, but torture comes first! I should love to see you stew in boiling oil, or perhaps have your fingers and toes and other protrusions chopped off, one by one—"

"Madame—" he began warningly.

"No! Let's see, *who* shall I kill, Lord Cameron? No, my legal husband, a member of the peerage, no . . . 'tis the pirate I should kill. Captain Hawk. The scurvy knave, the rogue, the—"

"Your lover, Lady Cameron?" he inquired with a long, taunting drawl. She hesitated and he continued, daring to put his fingers upon the cold steel and move it away from his throat and bear slowly down upon her in turn. Once more they moved across the sand, with his voice rising in deep angry tones. "Ah, yes! Captain Hawk, the Silver Hawk. That dastardly villain who so crudely and brutally *raped* you upon your first meeting. That was the description of what came between us, wasn't it? Is that what you told your husband, milady, when you threw yourself so completely upon his mercy when trying to disavow your marriage?"

They came against a palm tree. She gasped, startled, as her back hit it. Then her jaw locked and the sword whistled as she smoothly retrieved the blade from his touch. The edge just drew a thin line of blood against his thumb and he made a furious sound like a growl. It did not daunt her in the least. The blade was next to his throat once again.

"You son-of-a-bitch! You *were* cruel and brutal when you seized that ship! You and your announcements that the crew were free to take Tara and Bess . . . but that I was yours! Thrusting me into that dark chamber, seizing my clothing—"

"I thrust you into my cabin because I wanted you safe from the crew. They are good men and loyal, but a captain always needs to take care. And I seized your clothing because they were damp and you might well have gotten pneumonia."

"I might have had some choice in the matter."

"Give me the sword, Skye."

They had come back center on the sand. They circled one another very warily.

"And on that island—" she began.

"What on that island? What? Go ahead, tell me! Was I cruel

on the island, brutal? Ah, yes, that's where I forced you into my arms."

"You did force me—"

"Never, lady, and hence your wrath against me! My God, I had the patience and restraint of a saint—"

"Of a saint!"

"Of a saint. And I warned you time and again, and still you came to me. Vixen, you came to me."

"You knew about—you knew about the marriage!" she charged him.

"Yes, I knew. Of course, I knew. 'Tis my wife I came to rescue."

"And 'twas your wife you seduced?" she snapped.

A slight flush of color touched his cheeks. "I didn't intend to."

"Oh!" She stamped her foot against the sand and prodded the sword further against him. "You slimy, seafaring bastard! You went running from my house to bed another woman, knowing that I would come after you! Don't you ever, ever think to touch me—"

"There was no other woman."

"Liar! We both saw her; her hair was red—"

"I hired her, merely to irritate you." The words were a mistake. Her hand shook. The steel touched him ever more closely. "Skye, give me back my sword!"

"Never! When I give you this steel, Captain Cameron-Hawk, you are going to feel it beyond a doubt."

"There was no woman. But you—you, my love, my dear, darling devoted wife—"

"I never claimed to be a devoted wife!" she spat out. "I was forced to be a wife, just as I was forced to be a pirate's possession!"

"Ah, but the wife didn't mind going off to make a bargain with a pirate. Promises, my love, remember!"

"You are the most despicable man ever!" she hissed.

He ducked down, seeking to retrieve his sword. She sent it slashing dangerously through the air and he quickly danced back a step, circling her. *"Me,* milady! *Me?"*

"You! This double life of yours! Well, I promise you, sir,

they will hang you just as high as the Silver Hawk, even knowing that you are Lord Cameron! You were supposedly my father's friend! And you stole his ship anyway. I should slice you from groin to neck for that alone."

"Oh, so that's it, lady! The hurt is sexual indeed! Slice him to pieces and make sure you damage the man!"

" 'Tis your heart I'd like on a platter!"

"Is it, milady? I seized your father's ship from One-Eyed Jack, lady," he reminded her tensely. "I seized you from him and his band of murdering cutthroats!"

"And you took me to Bone Cay!" Tears were suddenly stinging her eyes, and she didn't want him to see them. She blinked them back furiously and kept moving, watching him very warily at all times. She *should* kill him. She should kill the pirate Silver Hawk right then and there. He would deserve it.

"Give me the sword, Skye!"

"No!"

Suddenly he drew his long knife from the sheath at his calf. He smiled, his eyes glittering silver. "Then slay me," he told her.

"Stop it!" she commanded as he feinted toward her with the short broad blade. Hers was by far the better weapon, and she *did* know how to use it. "Stop it or I shall have to kill you!"

"Come, come, love! Aye, the temptation is great for me!" He dove toward her. She reeled back, slicing at his blow, and their steel clanged together loudly. She swirled around, ready for the next attack. He was coming at her now with a new vengeance. "I should catch you now and beat you silly, madame, redden your aristocratic and sashaying derriere—"

"It's been done before!" she reminded him, her teeth gritted.

"Ah, but the pirate had the pleasure, and not Lord Cameron. Not the injured husband."

"Injured husband!" She was so startled and incensed that she stood still. He lunged, and she was forced to leap back, just barely parrying his blow. "Injured husband indeed!"

"Injured husband. Seduced so sweetly by his angelic and long-suffering wife, just so that she could viciously render him unconscious with a liquor bottle!"

"I had to—"

"You had to! Ah, yes, render Lord Cameron senseless so that you could run off into the arms of another man. To promise to bed him as happily and givingly as a lark for services rendered!"

"Oh, how dare you!" she shouted, and for the moment, she had the advantage again. She moved across the sand in a flurry, and the air cried out with the force of swords and steel as she backed him far across the beach to palm tree again. "How dare you! Fine! You hired a whore just to lie naked with you in a bed to taunt me!"

"Aye!" he cried. "And you were distressed that the Silver Hawk had lain with another woman—not that he asked you to be the *adulteress* to come to him!"

"You bastard, you deserved it! I asked you to leave me be as my good and strong and loyal husband—I warned you about the other man and the fact that I could . . . that I could carry the Hawk's child. But you! You waited until I slept, and then you seduced me, after all that I had said—"

"Exactly, milady! Those words mattered until you meant to leave me for the Hawk—then *you* came and seduced *me!* What of your morals then, eh, Lady Cameron?"

"How dare you—" she began again, but he saw his chance. He had unnerved her, and her grip was slack. He surged forward, catching the tip of his sword with tremendous force. The reverberation of it traveled down the steel and she cried, dropping the blade.

"I dare whatever I please, milady!" he assured her. "You are my wife, remember?"

She stared at him in fury and looked to the sword upon the ground.

They dove for it together.

Skye grappled desperately in the sand to reach the blade. His long bronzed fingers closed over it first, tossing it aside. She tried to reach it. He cast himself against her and they went rolling across the sand. When they came still again, he swiftly straddled her, pinning her beneath him, pinning her to the ground. She writhed and fought against his strength, squirming and kicking, and succeeding only in making the sand fly.

Eventually she was gasping for air, and still his prisoner, exhausted and beaten. She stared at him defiantly. "You *will* hang, sir!"

He cocked his head inquiringly. "And will you come to the spectacle, my love? Will you watch, and perhaps shed a tear or two?"

"I've nothing to say to you. You're a rogue."

"And you're a cunning, manipulative seductress, so which of the two of us is more at fault?"

"You!"

"Milady, I—"

"You! You knew all the while what was going on! You led me on time and time again, and taunted me on purpose. You knew that my soul was in agony and you—"

"Agony! When were you in agony, my love?"

"Oh, never mind! Just get off of me now, and leave me—"

"Get off of you! Well, love, this is typical. There I lay, sleeping deeply after having saved your life, plucking you from the cruel and icy fingers of the sea! Then you come up with your very tender toes and nearly dislocate the whole of my rib cage. You take a sword to my throat, and nearly slice open my veins. Now I am on top again, and so we should quit the fight. Well, no, milady, it does not work that way. I owe you, remember? I owe you for nearly splitting my skull with that bottle, for leaving me to nearly drown in a pool of rum. For trying to sever from my body various protrusions. It is *not* over! You will talk to me, and you will listen—"

"I will not listen!" she snapped. "Ever, ever again! I will be free from you, and so help me, I *will* see you hang! All of those innocents you have fooled! Lieutenant Governor Spotswood believing in you so deeply! How could you! Lord Cameron! You had everything that you could have wanted! But you had to be a pirate anyway. Robbing, stealing, plundering—"

"Raping?" he suggested nonchalantly.

Skye cried out an oath and tried to fight him again. Tears stung her eyes as she writhed and scrambled beneath him. She had so little of her gown left, it was awful. Her shift and shorn petticoats rose about her and she felt his damp thighs clamped hard against her bare hips. She went still, staring at him. He smiled slowly, a devil's taunting, promising, sensual grin. Her heart sank. She could not deny his looks, his appeal. She could not deny the rippling, muscled strength of his arms, or the trembling that seized upon her when he stared at her that way, so very aware of her skirt climbing, and of the distress it caused her.

The silver glitter in his eyes was as wicked as the rogue's curl of his smile. With tension all about him, he leaned toward her. "A pirate's life, ah, yes, milady! The rogue's way. I'm fond of it, yes, I am! Take what a man will, love where he desires, have what he wants! It's a good life, it is! Surely, I will hang for it—and certainly, I will hang, too, for the deceit I played on you!"

She gasped suddenly, staring at him, twisting again with new vigor. "You *are* a—a despicable sea slime! *Oh!* Lord Cameron never doffed his clothes, not even to make love, because you were afraid I would know, that I would find some little mark, that—oh!"

"Yes, it was difficult," he said nonchalantly. "Most difficult. I couldn't have you in the dark—not with your fears, love. That's why the pirate tried so hard not to touch you."

"The pirate touched me again and again!"

He shrugged. "Yes, well, the part of Lord Cameron inside the pirate's clothes didn't want to think that his beloved wife would fall into the arms of another man."

"I didn't know that I was anyone's wife!" she spat out. "Oh, you bastard! You cannot put this on me!"

He leaned low against her, his eyes still wickedly alive, his smile near to a taunting, sensual sneer. "I can do whatever I will, milady. I am a pirate, remember?"

She shook her head furiously. "You will never have me again."

"You are still my wife."

"I disavow you!"

"It isn't that simple."

"So help me, sir, if you ever touch me again, it *will* be rape!"

"Ah, but my lady," he murmured, "you forget so much!

The dread pirate Hawk has already taken you by force, why not again? Your words, milady, not mine. And Lord Cameron surely owes his bride the thrashing of her life. Then there is the main thing, and that is your father. You were willing to sell your . . . er, virture—or what was left of it—to find him first—"

"Oh!" she flared, twisting anew. Her skirt climbed completely and she was bare to the waist and they both knew it. He arched a single brow tauntingly.

"You do make things easy, love. Shall I beat you first, and make love to you—excuse me, that's force you into my arms, I mean—second? Or the other way around? Promises, promises! I am supposed to find your father, you know, for the sweet promise of your willing—and eager—arms."

"Someone should really skewer you through!" Skye announced.

"Should they? Tell me, then, what happened to this tempest inside of you? What of the gentle feelings you bore the Hawk for being tender in the dark? What of the truth that you whispered to Lord Cameron in the forest about your fears? What, lady, of the sweet seduction you played in that room? You told the pirate Hawk that you loved your husband. What of those words?"

She narrowed her eyes carefully, her heart hammering inside her chest with a fierce beat. "Lies, sir. Lies. And that is all!" she said flatly. "Issued about the one man to avoid the other, sir, and that is all."

He shook his head and lowered it against hers. But he wasn't laughing anymore. His features were tense and serious, his eyes were dark, shadowed smoke. "So you care nothing for either man, milady, is that what you're saying?"

"Aye, I care deeply! To see them hang, as one and the same!"

His fingers tensed around hers, his mouth tightened grimly, and for a moment Skye was truly frightened. He had had his fill of her, and he was finished. Perhaps he would play the pirate in truth and slit her throat. Or perhaps his role would be that of the grievously injured husband, and he would strike her where she lay. Thunder touched his features, anger, deep and sure. She did hate him; she despised him for all that he had done.

But she had fallen in love with a man, too. With tenderness, with caring, with flashing silver eyes, and with startling courage against all odds. She had fallen in love with flesh and blood, and she had lain in paradise, be that paradise an island, or a bower within the woods, or a bed upon a soft mattress with white silky sheets. He would hang; and she never be able to bear it.

She closed her eyes, and waited for his blow.

It never came. He released her and came to his feet, and caught her hands and none too gently dragged her up before him. "I am in love with you," he told her softly.

"Love!" she cried. "What can you know of or mean by love, after what has been done!"

"I'd have died to save you any number of times."

"You risk your life each time you sail!" she retorted. "You chose your course in life! You risk your throat every time you step upon the shore of New Providence!"

"What of your father?" he demanded curtly.

"What do you mean?" she asked, faltering.

"You wanted me to find your father."

"Yes, and I still expect you to do so!"

"Under the same conditions."

"What?" Skye cried out.

He didn't reply right away. He asked her another question instead. "What if I could prove myself to you, milady?"

"I don't know what you're talking about."

"What if I could explain my deeds?"

"You shall never explain your deeds to me. And you will hang, eventually, I know it. Lord Cameron or no."

His eyes flashed with renewed anger. "One day, milady, so help me, I will see that you rue those words. For now, however, we will return to the business at hand. The pirate is better suited to finding your father, so the pirate I will remain. You may have my cabin to yourself, milady. But the bargain stays the same. When your father is found and rescued, you had best come to me laughing, your hair draping your shoulders, your clothing at your feet."

"Bastard!"

"Are we agreed?"

"I hate you!"

"Hate me, love me, have it as you will. Until I do hang, madame, you are mine!"

A sudden noise, the cocking of a pistol, sent them both flying around. Skye gasped softly, for they were no longer alone upon the sand.

Logan was there. Captain Logan.

Logan, with two of his henchmen at his side, standing before them.

"I beg to differ with you, Hawk!" Logan announced. "I intend to take her. The lady will be mine."

Roc drew Skye around behind him in an instant, holding her there. He watched Logan very warily, for the man had two pistols aimed straight toward him.

Roc's sword and knife lay in the sand. His pistols were lost to the sea and his powder was sodden anyway. He had nothing, nothing at all with which to fight.

"Move away from the lady, Hawk!"

Behind him, Skye shivered. There was no help; no help anywhere at all. Logan had all the power, and he knew it. He was elegantly dressed in a crimson velvet coat and high black boots, and his hat bore a dashing plume. Skye wondered from where he had pilfered his finery, then she did not care. His lip was curled in an evil grin, and he scratched his chin with the hook he wore for a hand.

He would kill the Hawk, she thought. With the greatest pleasure and relish, he would kill the Hawk, probably ripping him open from groin to gullet with the very hook he wore because of the Hawk's prowess with the sword.

The henchmen with him were not so dandified. They were both young men, in their early twenties perhaps, one blond, one dark. They were both barefoot, in knee breeches with no hose, and in coarse cotton shirts. They were both smiling, too, glad of this confrontation.

Logan's smiled deepened. "Dear, dear, how have we come to find you here? And engaged in this oh, so touching scene!" He laughed to his companions. "Methinks that the lady is no creature of ice! She comes in this fight to the pirate, knowing him so, so well! It seems that the Hawk did teach the lady the finer points of love, which is well enough—I shall enjoy her the more."

"You'll never touch her, Logan!" the Hawk snapped.

"Oh, I think I will," Logan replied pleasantly. "Damn you, Hawk, but you have always been a cocky bastard. The lady is behind you, and you are unarmed, and I have here six pistols and three swords at my disposal. I knew that the girl would have to come if I had her father, and that you would have to come after the girl. I hadn't expected you to fall so easily into my hands, but then the weather was helpful, was it not? And then you two were so engaged with your private affairs that you mightn't have heard the sound of a cannon explosion. Ah, dear lady! But you have done what I never could, you stole the Hawk's guard away. Thank you, my dear. I do appreciate that, and I will be happy to show you just how much!"

"No . . . !" Skye started to cry, but then she was stunned when Roc turned around and slapped her hard across the face. His strength was so great that she went crashing down to the sand, the breath knocked from her, her flesh burning.

"Shut up!" he hissed down to her. Then he turned his attention to Logan. "Take her—you want her so badly. Take her, have done with it!"

"How rude, Hawk! I *shall* take her. Your ruse will not work."

"Over my dead body, only, shall you have her!"

"That will be fine," Logan chortled.

Roc shook his head. Skye's mind continued to swim. She wanted to kill him; she abhorred the thought of Logan.

She could not begin to understand the brutality of Roc's attack.

"She's just a woman, Logan!" Roc called out. "Mine, because I took her. But she's no better or worse than any other. Having her will give you little pleasure!"

"I'll decide on that!" Logan said. "What is this, anyway! I do intend to shoot you and have her. When I tire of her, the others may have her. You will be dead. What will it matter to a corpse?"

"If you kill me, you'll never have the treasure that One-Eyed Jack took off of the Spaniard."

Logan hesitated, his eyes going very narrow against his cadaverous features. "What are you talking about?"

"Don't play games with me, Logan. Jack pirated the Spaniard, *Doña Isabella* out of Cartagena! Everyone knew about it. They talked about it on the islands for months. Why do you think I was so determined to go after the *Silver Messenger?* To take a single merchant sloop? You'd be daft, man! It was Jack I wanted, Jack that I was after. Oh, Logan, you speak of death! Jack died slowly, I tell you! He *had* taken the *Doña Isabella,* and buried all that Spanish gold. Gold that you can't even begin to imagine, Logan."

"The *Doña Isabella?* With the—the Inca gold?"

Roc smiled slowly, folding his hands over his chest. "Aye, Logan, and that's a fact. I'm the only man alive who knows where to find it."

"How do I know that?" Logan demanded.

"I'm telling you that it is so."

Skye stared up at him. She didn't know if it was the truth or not. She didn't know anything at all about him anymore. She was aware only that her choices now lay between two different hells.

Roc wanted Logan to think that she didn't matter so much to him, that she was something to be owned and used, and abused if the mood so struck him. He wanted to save his own life. He was, beyond a doubt, a scurvy bastard.

But, so help her! She could not stand the thought of Logan. What was happening?

Logan cocked his head, staring at Roc. "What is then, a play for time? I keep you alive to take me to this treasure of Jack's—then I slay you anyway. I take the girl, and I find my entertainment, then I ask Spotswood or Lord Cameron for the ransom on them both, the lady and Lord Kinsdale. Any way that one looks at it, Hawk. I win."

Roc shook his head slowly. "You don't take the girl. She's mine."

"What good will she do a corpse?"

"She's mine. She stays with me. We head on to the meeting

here in North Carolina across the island and we go to someone to mediate."

"Mediate!" Logan protested.

"Aye, mediate. Blackbeard."

Logan started to laugh. "You'd give her over to Blackbeard?"

Roc shrugged. "If rumor has it right, he's fourteen young wives. He's women enough."

"They say that he's the fiercest murderer of us all."

"They say—but I know the man. He'd never harm her. And if he swore to me that he'd see her safe back to Virginia, then that is exactly what he would do."

Logan hesitated. "I won't—"

"It's the only way, Logan. It's absolutely the only way that you're going to have the pleasure of killing me and acquiring the treasure, too."

"It's too risky, Captain," the dark-haired man murmured to Logan.

"Risky! What, have you become a coward, Logan? We live at risk, we thrive on risk. Aye, come on, and it is a challenge! I dare you, Logan, take the chance!"

"Send her over to me!" Logan demanded.

Roc came over to Skye, reaching down for her. She lowered her eyes, not about to touch his hand. He had gone insane. She had been there when he had dueled with One-Eyed Jack. The pirate had died cleanly in the fight. There had never been any discussion about gold whatsoever.

Or was there gold? Did he know of it some other way? Had he come after One-Eyed Jack and the *Silver Messenger* because he *had* wanted a bigger prize? Because he needed Jack dead? She didn't know. Her head was still reeling, and she didn't trust him, not in the least.

And still, she was in love with him. Even with her face still stinging, even as she wondered about his double life, certain that he would hang. She did love him. . . .

She started to scramble to her feet on her own, but he wrenched her up and held her close to him. "No. I will not send the girl to you. We do it my way. She's mine."

Logan hesitated a long time. "I *will* kill you when we get

that treasure. If you're telling me the truth, Hawk, I will shoot you clean and simple. If you've lied to me, then I'll have you staked out, and I'll rip your flesh from your body inch by inch with my hook. Savor that, Hawk. And pray that you find that treasure." He pocketed his pistols.

"I haven't lied to you."

Logan shrugged. "Then keep the girl. Enjoy her until your death." He smiled suddenly, watching Roc. "You've lost your beard, sir. Was that to please this lady?"

"It was hot," Roc said. "I do nothing to please anyone, Logan, and you know that."

" 'E looks an awful lot like the other one now," the dark-haired pirate said, eyeing Roc up and down.

"What other one?" Logan demanded.

Roc tensed; Skye felt it as his arms tightened around her.

" 'E looks like the high-and-mighty lord, like his kinsman, Cameron."

"You've seen Cameron?" Logan said sharply.

"At a distance, aboard his ship." The dark-haired fellow grinned. "Eh, Logan! 'E's trying to look like her husband; he's trying to be a gentleman."

Logan cackled, bending over. Roc's fingers tightened on Skye's arm. "Not a word!" he warned her. "Not a word!"

"I should let him skewer you!" she hissed.

"Then think, milady, of what he will do to you!" Roc warned softly. Icy trails sped along her back. He was right. Whatever her anger, he was right.

"And don't he look pretty, minus the whiskers!" Logan said at last. "Didn't work, though, eh, Captain? Not from what I heard. The lady ain't too pleasured to be with you!"

"She's pleasured enough."

"Then come on," Logan said, his eyes riveted on the both of them suspiciously. "We go to Teach, and we sign our agreements. Don't you go against me, not a hair, Hawk. I'll shoot her down where she stands if you betray me, and that will be a fact."

"I won't betray you, not on this."

"Then walk!" Logan commanded.

Roc turned, seeing the direction that Logan indicated. Skye pulled back.

"Where's my father?" she demanded of Logan. "Is he alive? Have you harmed him?"

"He's alive, and his dignity is ruffled, and perhaps he has a bruise or two. That's it, milady. Now, if you will please? There's a feast going on behind those dunes, and we'll be a part of it this night. Move, Hawk."

"I'm not going anywhere," Skye insisted.

"What?" the Hawk demanded.

"Bring me my father. I'm going to sit right here until you prove to me that he's alive."

Logan looked to Roc. "Get her moving, Hawk. Or we'll end it here and now."

"If you kill my father," Skye cried, "then I will not care."

"Move her!" Logan ordered.

Roc dipped low, striking her in the midriff with his shoulder and tossing her over. "Stop it!" she railed, beating against his back. "Stop it, put me down, don't you see that he'll kill you anyway! We have to—"

"We have to shut up!" Roc roared to her. He spun around, searching out Logan. "Lead the way, damn you, will you, please!"

Logan, cackling, stepped forward. He started out walking and Roc followed. Skye continued to protest, rising against him, until he slammed down hard on her rump portion. The action did not hurt her so much, but it reminded her that she was very poorly clad, and that her position was very precarious.

Life had become precarious.

But she didn't trust Logan, and she was certain that Roc had gone mad. He didn't intend to hand her over to Logan, but he did intend to hand her over to Teach, to Blackbeard, while he went off to get killed by Logan himself. It was insanity.

She fell silent as they walked along the dunes. It seemed that they walked forever and ever. The water, though, was always at their side. Pirates needed water, she thought. The land was death; the water was their salvation, their escape.

What was Roc planning . . . ?

"Hear the music?" Logan asked suddenly. He spoke to Roc, who grunted. Skye strained to hear, and the sounds of a fiddle came surely her way. The music grew louder and louder as they walked.

Then she pushed against Roc's shoulder and saw that they had come to a small shanty village. Sparse, crooked buildings made carelessly of thatch and logs lay about a beach where dozens of longboats had been drawn.

Dozens of spits had been set up on the beach. Joints of beef and pork turned and roasted upon the spits, along with numerous fowl and venison. Huge kegs lay about; kegs of ale, Skye thought.

There was a platform in the center of the shantytown. Edward Teach, Blackbeard, with his chinful of illustrious whiskers, sat there as if he sat upon a throne. Before him stood the fiddlers, tapping their toes to the music.

And upon the platform, a woman danced.

She was black-haired, with a lithe slim figure, a startling grace, and a full, firm bosom that rose high against her cotton blouse. She was barefoot and laughing, and she danced like a young doe, like a healthy young animal. The men watched her and cheered.

She was not the only woman there. Others sprawled about with men, leaning against kegs, falling beneath the platform, sitting on the porches of the shanties.

Logan stood behind Roc and smiled at Skye as she lay high against her husband's shoulders.

"The ball, milady, the pirates' grand ball! Welcome. We do not often dare to come so brazenly together on the mainland, but then certain figures of power in North Carolina have been known to turn deaf ears to the sounds of our musicians! Isn't it grand? Not many silks, not many satins, and the petticoats are limited, but we do enjoy ourselves! Welcome!"

There was something about his eyes so hideous that she shivered.

Roc spun around to face Logan. "Remember," Logan warned him. "You play anything other than straight with Blackbeard, and I will shoot and kill this girl who means so little to you!"

"I'll play it fair. Go."

"You go. I'll follow behind with my pistol cocked and aimed for the lady's back. And don't forget. A good number of the men you see about will be off of my ship."

"I'll remember," Roc said. He started to walk. Skye clung to him. Drunken men pointed their way. Some laughed. Some called out. "It's the Hawk! It's the Hawk, and 'e's brought a lady here, can you imagine." Chortles rose up, ringing upon the air. "Damme, but the man would dare anything, anything at all."

"My pistol's aimed at her back, remember!" Logan said.

Roc kept walking. As they neared the platform, Blackbeard's attention was drawn to them, and he leaped to his feet. "What? Ho, there, it's the Hawk, is it not? Aye, and with the lass I was ever so charmed to meet as of late!" His big, bellowing voice rose over the music and over the sounds of the dance. Blackbeard pulled his pipe from his mouth and reached for Roc's hand. "Welcome! We'd thought you'd avoid this place, since you don't much care for the Carolinas, sir! Do you see my Carlotta? My latest 'wife'—she dances for me now. Sit and watch, enjoy. Now there's some warm blood for you, me boy!"

Logan stepped around Roc. "We've come for you to be mediator. The Hawk is my prisoner. He's to take me to a treasure, if you see the girl home. We've agreed it, sworn upon it."

Roc set Skye down upon her feet. Blackbeard gave her a captivating smile. "Lady Kinsdale—no, Cameron, I've heard. Anyway, my lady, you're most welcome here! A flower among us dregs of humanity, and I do mean it!"

"Teach, will you swear to me to see her home?" Roc demanded.

"With my blood. You carry out your bargain, and I'll see her home. I've no wish to hurt a woman, sir, of that you are well aware."

"But *he* comes with me!" Logan cried. "I want it agreed in blood!"

"Raise your arm!" Blackbeard commanded to Roc.

Roc lifted his arm. Blackbeard took his knife and Skye could not help but cry out as the pirate slashed her husband's arm. A trail of blood oozed out. Roc did not protest; he didn't say a word. Blackbeard slashed his own arm and placed it next to Roc's. "Sealed in blood. You owe Logan, and by my honor, I owe you. Now tell me, Hawk, how did you let this scurvy piece of dog meat get the best of you?"

"There's no excuse, Teach. He just did."

Blackbeard swirled around to Skye. "Come, sit with me, we'll drink together.

"I've no wish to drink with you or any of your kind!" Skye spat out.

"A feisty one, yes, I do say!" Blackbeard laughed. He leaned low against her. "Girl, I'm all the hope you've got here, do you understand?" He raised his voice then. "Hawk! You come, too."

"He's my prisoner, bound by blood—" Logan began.

"Yes, but this is my party, my pirate's ball, and I'll not have you leaving with my guests, not tonight. Hawk, you play out your devil's bargain in the morning, and God and Satan be with you both! For now, come with the girl, and watch my beloved dance!"

He pulled the two of them along to join him on his platform. Skye was dragged down beside him on the one side and Roc on the other. The fury of the music increased to a tempestuous tempo. The girl danced ever more swiftly.

A mug was pressed into Skye's hands. She looked into the drunken eyes of a middle-aged, buxom woman with her bodice torn in two. The woman smiled and started to laugh. "Dearie, dearie, a lady! We've a lady among us! Let us take her, Blackbeard, and she'll not be a lady much longer, I'll warrant."

The woman reached for Skye, tearing at her bodice, Skye screamed, trying to draw away. Her chair fell over. Her head cracked against the platform, and she was dazed.

"No!" There was another sound of thunder as a second chair fell back. Roc was on his feet. He came to stand before her, his booted feet planted hard, his hands upon his hips. "She's mine; she's mine this night, and she's Blackbeard's promise of safe conduct when this night is over. No one touches her. No one but me. She's mine, and 'tis my night, and I'll have her in peace from the lot of you scurvies and whores!"

He bent down and lifted her from the floor. "No!" she whispered in desperation.

He barely glanced her way but turned to Blackbeard. "This is your party, Captain Teach! I'm your guest this night, and would request quarters, sir, if I may!"

The pirate Blackbeard laughed and nodded. "Aye, Captain Hawk! If it's a dead man you're to be, you should have this night! Every man gets a last request before the gallows!"

"Wait!" Logan protested. "I did not say—"

"Tomorrow, Logan, you may take the Hawk. Your prisoner, sir! Tonight, he gets his last request!"

Blackbeard indicated a building fifty yards from the platform on the beach. Roc leaped down from the platform with her in his arms and began striding toward the waterfront shanty. Pirates and their doxies applauded and laughed.

"She's a tough one, Captain!"

"Aye, there, lad, feisty but fun!" Roc agreed. Skye hit him, slapping him just as hard as he had slapped her against the cheek. She was just barely aware of the guffaws rising from the pirates sprawled about them with their half-clad drunken whores.

"Take her, Captain!"

Roc, staring at her with fire in his eyes, quickly replied, "I intend to, lad, I intend to!" He lowered her down. Skye screamed, shocked and alarmed as she fell hard upon the sand. He bounded down upon her, seizing her hair in a rough grip, holding her still to his pleasure as he ravaged her lips with his mouth, all the while raking his hands over her breasts.

Laughter arose, whistles and catcalls. He leaped up, jerking her back to her feet, then forcefully into his arms. "I intend to this very minute, lads!" he cried.

"No . . . !" she gasped. Her lips were swollen and bruised and she had never seen such reckless disregard in him before. She gritted her teeth and beat against him in a sudden, desperate fear.

"No!"

"Shut up! Damn you, shut up!"

His eyes lit upon hers, silver and hard. "Open your mouth again and I swear you shall learn something of brute force this very night!"

Skye opened her mouth. She shivered uncontrollably but fell silent to the warning in his eyes.

And Roc dashed up the steps to the shanty and kicked open the door. She was alone again with him, with the pirate, with the lord. With her lover, with her husband.

Alone . . .

With the very devil himself . . .

XVII

Roc kicked the door closed and set Skye down. For a second she remained perfectly still, for shadows fell all around them, and she was frightened of a terrible darkness falling.

Darkness did not come. It was barely afternoon, she thought. She spun around, stared at Roc, and moved away from him, running quickly to the wall, setting her back against it.

He glanced her way with a certain disdain and fell against the door himself, sinking down before it. His eyes closed wearily, then shot open and stared at her with immense displeasure. He pointed a finger at her. "You! You little bitch! You're going to get us both killed!"

Skye stared at him wide-eyed. "Me! You've lost your mind!"

"I am grabbing at straws to keep us going—"

"Straws! There is no treasure!" she hissed.

His lashes fell briefly over his eyes. "That's my problem. I want you out of here. Blackbeard may be many things, but his reputation for cruelty has been deliberately exaggerated. He will keep his word to me. Tomorrow he will see that you are delivered back to Virginia, where you belonged in the first place."

"Then Logan takes you!" she exclaimed.

The anger faded from his eyes and a slow smile touched his lips. "Will you care then, love? You were waiting to attend my hanging, remember? What difference will it make? Alas, you won't get to witness the deed, but the end result will be the same."

"Don't!" Skye murmured.

"Don't what, milady?"

Skye didn't reply. She shook her head and backed against the far wall herself, staring at him. He could not die! And she could not trust herself to speak. She lowered her head, swallowing tightly against the tears that burned hotly behind her eyes. She looked about the room. Sand dusted the floor; there was a plain wooden table with a single candle in a brass holder and two rickety chairs beneath it, and against the far wall was a bed of straw with a gray blanket thrown haphazardly upon it.

"Elegant accommodations," Roc murmured with a certain humor, "but the best that Blackbeard has to offer, I'm afraid. He's a man who falls in love often enough; he's glad to give us the night."

She didn't respond to his words but jumped back up and pushed away from wall and came to kneel down before him. "This is insane! What are you doing? We must escape from here somehow!"

"We?" He arched both brows. She wasn't a foot away from him. Her hair trailed in sunset tendrils over her shoulders and her breasts pushed against the fabric of her bodice and her eyes were earnest and sparkling with emotion. He longed to touch her, but he did not. He allowed his hands to dangle idly over his kneecaps. "We? My love, there is no need for you to escape. Your safety is guaranteed. In certain matters, there is no man you can trust so thoroughly as a rogue such as Blackbeard."

"I can't go back without you!"

"Why ever not? You'll miss a hanging, of course, but you'll live anyway, I'm sure."

"Stop it! Stop being so—nonchalant!"

"What would you have me be?"

"Concerned! Sir, you are to die!"

He sighed deeply. The temptation was too great. He reached out and fingered one of the silky soft curls. Not even the seawater could damage the softness of her hair.

She did not wrench away from him. He went further, and stroked his knuckles over her cheek. "Will you care?" he asked her softly. "This morning you were anxious to see me boiled in oil! Skinned alive. Ah, yes, that is what Logan promised, I think, if I did not lead him to the treasure."

"And there is no treasure!" she said desperately.

"What makes you so sure?"

"I was there the day you killed Jack!"

"Ah, yes, of course. Thank God Logan wasn't about," he muttered.

"Then there is no treasure!"

He shrugged. "Oh, there is a treasure. There really was a *Doña Isabella* that sailed out of Cartagena, and it was supposedly laden with a new cache of Indian gold. And rumor has it that Jack did seize her, steal the cargo, and scuttle the ship. The treasure is supposedly buried somewhere."

"But you haven't the faintest idea of where!" Skye moaned.

He was still smiling at her. Smiling ridiculously. There was sensual silver laughter and tenderness in his eyes; his touch against her was gentle and provocative. His fingertips just moved across her flesh. She wanted to hold him, to cling to him. He had lied to her, he had used her, he had made a fool of her, and he was leading a despicable life, but she loved him. She could fight it; she could deny her heart. But she could not change the emotion deep inside.

"You do care!" he whispered.

"I don't—"

"You do!" he insisted, and then his touch was not so light as he reached out, sweeping her hard and full into his arms. He kissed her again, but this kiss was no hard seizure as it had been outside; this kiss was fierce and demanding but infinitely tender. His lips fell upon her with consuming desire, his tongue teased her mouth, grazed her teeth, sought deep, honeyed recesses. He held her with tenderness, too. His arms were ever ardent, but gentle. His hand cupped her cheek, his fingers trailed her throat as he held her to his kiss. His hands molded her breast, and her waist, and then he broke away, gasping for breath, holding her close. He did love her, too, she thought. He was a rogue, a terror. Demanding, autocratic as the pirate, and as the lord, but his will was fierce and could not be broken, only altered by his own choice, and perhaps, just perhaps, gentled by love.

His eyes probed hers feverishly. "You *do* care!" he repeated.

She moistened her lips, lowering her lashes. She only dared whisper so much upon this occasion. "If I am with child, sir, I'd just as soon he have a living sire."

His smile deepened. "Ah. So that is why you have not betrayed me!"

"Betrayed you?" She lay against his arm, grateful for the curious moment of peace.

"To Logan. He still does not know that Lord Cameron and the Silver Hawk are one and the same."

She swallowed hard, not caring to be reminded of the fact herself. She shrugged. "What difference does it make? He plans to kill the Hawk. He would be only too pleased, I'm sure, to discover that he has killed Lord Cameron, too."

He carefully set her down and stood, pacing the room, his hands upon his hips. "It makes a great deal of difference. If Blackbeard were to know—"

"Your crew is all in on this, I imagine?" Skye interrupted curtly. Robert! Robert Arrowsmith had known all along that her husband and her lover were one and the same. All of them!

And still, there wasn't a single man among his crew she would like to see dangle from a noose!

He paused, casting her a frown, then nodding. "Yes, they all know both of my identities. But these fellows here, they do not. And, thank God, you did not see fit to inform them."

"I'm not a fool."

"You were acting like one out there."

"Because he's going to kill you! Then he'll probably kill my father, too, for good measure!"

Roc shook his head. "Your father is worth too much."

"Oh? Amazing, the pirate Hawk let me go for not so much as a farthing! Perhaps my father is worthless as well."

"The pirate Hawk let you go for not so much as a farthing, my love, to show you not that you were worthless, but rather worth far much more than gold and silver to him."

She stared at him incredulously. Then she saw the tug at the corner of his lip and she came quickly to her feet, hands on her hips, defying him. "You are a liar, sir!"

"All right, so I was deathly afraid of your self-importance becoming exaggerated beyond all measure. I knew that you would return home and discover yourself married and that you would try every trick and wile in the world to escape your husband. And I, milady, was already deeply in love, and not about to let you go."

"You're still a liar!" she accused him.

"And if I'm not?"

"If—you're not?" she whispered.

"What if it's true? What if I really do love you, Skye Cameron? Can you spare just a touch of emotion for an old friend, an old lover?"

She whirled around, not wanting to meet his eyes. "You know that I would be distressed to see you die."

"Ah, for a child. But what about yourself?" He came behind her, setting his hands upon her shoulders. "A child would be nice," he whispered. "An heir to Cameron Hall . . . when I am skinned alive and then shot dead and left for the carrion!"

"Stop it!" she hissed, but she did not turn around.

"Come here!" he told her.

She held still.

"Skye, come here," he repeated, and she did not know what drew her around, but she did turn. And she came to him, too, standing before him, not touching him, but looking up into his eyes. She did not know what emotion was betrayed in her, but he touched her shoulders and bent to touch her lips very lightly. Then he kissed her forehead and drew her against him.

"You do care!" he assured her.

She laid her palms against his chest and pushed him from her and looked at him gravely. "I care, yes, Roc, I care! But I cannot accept you, or what you've done. I've no desire to see you hang, but I wonder at the innocents you've robbed and plundered, and what has created the whole empire you rule at Bone Cay. But for now, I do not think that I can leave you—"

"There is no question that you will leave me," he said harshly. "I will have you safe."

"I don't want you to die! And Logan will kill you, and heinously so, when he discovers there is no treasure!"

He shrugged. "Perhaps I will find treasure. Accidents do happen."

"That would be a miracle!" Skye murmured.

"My men are out there, you know."

Her eyes widened. She had forgotten that, a fact so important that it *was* nearly a miracle. Roc's ship—rather, the Hawk's ship—lay somewhere out on the other side of the island. Unless the storm had torn her to shreds. But Skye was certain that the Hawk and his pirate crew had weathered much worse.

"They'll rescue you—us!" she said happily. "They'll come in here and . . ." Her voice trailed away. He was looking at her sadly.

His crew could not just sail in, she realized. There were many captains here, at Blackbeard's pirates' "ball." More men than the Hawk's crew could possibly meet with any chance of victory.

And it would still leave her father as Logan's prisoner. An enraged Logan, at that.

"There is no miracle to be had!" she whispered brokenly.

"Yes, perhaps there is," he said.

There was a sudden hammering upon the door. "Who is that?" Skye murmured with alarm.

"I don't know. Get over there, on the bed," Roc said swiftly.

"What?" she demanded, frowning.

"Damn you, milady, must you question everything? Get over there!"

She must not have responded quickly enough to suit him, for she found herself flying forcefully across the room and landing hard upon the straw bedding. He was quickly down beside her, gathering her into his arms. Alarmed and furious at his treatment, she struggled against him, kicking out madly. "Damn you, you have lost your mind!" she cried.

His hand landed hard over hers. "Shut up!" he ordered her. "Come in!" he called out.

Outraged, she struggled against him. The door opened and one of the pirates' doxies stood there, dark hair spilling over her enormous breasts, her eyes dark and flashing and her very red lips curled in amusement as she watched Skye struggling.

"Leave her, Hawk!" The girl laughed. "I could provide far more entertainment than this one!"

He shook his head and smiled broadly. "She loves me, Leticia. Honest—she loves me truly. Right, love?" Skye tried to bite his hand. He laughed, a pirate's laugh, and she realized that she was inadvertently playing right along with his ruse.

Leticia shrugged. "Every man to his choice, Captain! But remember if you tire of her . . . you need only call my name." She walked more fully into the room. Roc regretfully pulled himself up from Skye, but dragged her along with him. He held her close, his hand nonchalantly over her breast. She was a possession here, and safe because he had claimed her as his, an *important* possession.

And one he chose to allow to live on beyond him.

"I came to see if you are hungry." She smiled beguilingly and Skye thought that she was really very pretty with her large breasts, trim waist, and dark eyes. Leticia. Roc knew her, he knew her by name. No, the Hawk knew her. Skye wondered just how well the Hawk knew her, and she felt ill. This was insane. She loved him. She despised him. She could not bear his death, and yet she hated this untenable position.

"Hungry . . . for food," Leticia murmured.

"Ravenous," Roc told her.

"I will bring something." She came very close to them both, kneeling by the bedding. She watched Skye with a searing curiosity. Skye raised her chin and the dark-haired woman chuckled huskily. "Ice fires can burn hot, so they say," she murmured, and laughed again. Then her voice lowered and she spoke very softly to Roc alone. "Blackbeard wants to see you. Alone. He thinks that the two of you should talk."

"Does he?" Roc said.

Leticia nodded fervently. "He hates Logan. Always has hated him. You know that."

Roc shrugged. "But Blackbeard is on his honor here. We came to him as a mediator between us."

Leticia tossed back her dark hair. "Blackbeard is his own law, and his own honor. He will do what he chooses, and that will be the honorable thing. If men say that it is cruel and treacherous, he will be glad of it. He savors what they say, as you know well enough. If a man fears the terror of Blackbeard's wrath, he is quick to lay down his arms. You must understand that power, Hawk!"

Roc nodded gravely. "All right. I'll speak with him."

Leticia looked to Skye with amusement. "Not now. I've not come to interrupt anything!" She laughed again. "Later. When darkness has fallen, then I'll come, and I'll bring you to him."

"All right," Roc agreed. Leticia smiled, and whirled around like a young doe to leave them. When the door closed behind her, Skye elbowed Roc with all of her might. She was gratified to feel him release her and grunt painfully.

"Damn you, Skye Cameron!" he swore to her, staggering to his feet.

"Damn me! You tossed me about like so much baggage, and seized hold of me in front of that—that woman! I am not your whore, Captain, and I—"

"Yes, you are," he told her, his tone sharp with warning. He came over to her and she started to back away, but he caught her arm and wrenched her against him. "Here, milady, you are my whore, a cherished whore, and therein lies your safety. So go ahead, scream and fight and lash out, it makes no difference. You will obey me here, or sorely regret it, I promise."

She ground down hard on her teeth, wishing she could think of something horrible enough to say to him. He released her, and as he did, there came a subtle tap on the door again.

Leticia slipped back in. "Food, Captain Hawk. And"—she paused, turning to Skye and curtsying with mock respect—"of course, for you, too, Lady Cameron! The finest, of course. The very finest."

Skye inclined her head toward the woman. "Thank you," she said softly. Her gentle tones seemed to confuse Leticia. She stared at Skye a moment longer, then shrugged and turned back to Roc, setting the tray she carried upon the table. "From Blackbeard's own supply of dark rum, Captain. And for the lady—" She glanced Skye's way quickly again. "For the lady he sends Burgundy off of the French packet *St. Louis.* And there's roast meat and bread, and all the very best cuts, I assure you!"

"Thank you very much, Leticia," the Hawk said. He offered her a wry, grateful smile. Skye felt her stomach twist, for in the midst of all this, he was still a strikingly handsome man, charismatic as the Hawk, charismatic as Lord Cameron.

She lowered her head slightly. Then she lifted her eyes, realizing that the woman was still watching her. "Thank you, Leticia," she repeated. Leticia did not say anything to Skye. She nodded to her, then looked to Roc. "I'll be back when the others are in drunken stupors, when I can bring you to Blackbeard."

She left them. Roc looked to Skye; then, every inch the gentleman, he pulled out her chair for her. He helped her into it before taking the wine from the tray and pouring out a pewter mug of it for her. He sat down himself, lifting a red cloth from the food and then looking to the rum flask provided for him. "Dark Caribbean," he murmured, and drew deeply on it. "It's a fine brew," he told Skye.

"A fine brew!" she exclaimed. "At a time like this—"

"At a time like this," he muttered. "I'm sure that it's an exceptionally fine brew." He drew on it deeply, eyeing her with wary, narrowed eyes.

She didn't look at him but at the tray of food. The meat did smell delicious. Roc set down the rum flask and skewered her a piece of beef with a table knife, setting it upon her plate. "Eat," he told her.

"I can't eat—"

"I'm sure that you can. We haven't had a bite in a day, and I'm famished, if you are not."

He took a rib bone and plowed into it with gusto. Skye watched him and realized that she was starving. It was not so difficult to enjoy the pirate's feast before her. The beef was succulent and delicious and flavored with salt and peppercorns.

The wine, too, was good.

Skye sipped it, watching Roc. "What does this mean?" she asked him. "With—Leticia."

He shrugged. "It means that Blackbeard wants One-Eyed Jack's treasure."

"But there is no treasure."

"There *is* a treasure."

"But not a treasure that you can find!" she wailed.

He set down his food and drank deeply from the rum flask again. "There is a treasure, milady, and that for the moment shall suffice."

"And that for the moment shall suffice!" Impatiently she stood, and her chair fell behind her. "Don't you take that tone with me, Lord Hawk, or whoever you would be today! I am in this, too—"

"And you do not know the rules!" He was up as well, coming around the table to her. She was suddenly drawn into his arms. His fingers raked into her hair and he drew her head back, searching her eyes. "You do not know the rules, my love; you have only your reckless courage, and that will not serve us now! For the love of God, milady, pay heed to me!"

His hold upon her was so very tight. She smiled very slowly, sensually, wistfully. "It is just, sir, that in truth, I would not see you killed."

He stared at her intently, then he drew her to him, burying his head against her throat, emitting some deep-felt sound of passion.

"Skye, Skye," he murmured, "my brave, beautiful love! God! That I could but have you safely away from here this very moment!"

"But I am not away!" she whispered. "And I cannot see you go."

He lifted her up then into his arms. His eyes locked with hers and he strode with her to the crude straw mattress upon the floor with its scanty blanket. He laid her there with tenderness, coming beside her. His mouth covered hers. His kiss ran passionate, and deep, and it ignited her fears and her desires, and she knew that she wanted to cling to him forever. She could not let him go. She wanted him. She wanted to make love to him. She wanted to hold on to the splendor and glory of all that raged between them. She had not forgiven him. . . .

But she had not fallen out of love with him, either, and it seemed that every second now death came closer to their doorway.

He pulled away from her. He saw her eyes, wide and teal and steady upon his. Her lips parted slightly, damp with his kiss. She offered her arms out to him again and he groaned, holding her close.

"I want to make love to you," he whispered. "I want to lie down by crystal waters, with the fragrance of flowers, with the sun overhead burning down upon our flesh, or with the moon offering a gentle glow. I want to give you a soft mattress and silken sheets, or an Eden of sweet earth. I want to love you, and not upon this bare and ugly straw. . . ."

She touched his hair and stroked it from his face. She met his eyes with her smile wistful, her gaze both damp and aflame. "It is Eden, it is paradise," she told him with all of her heart. "Where you are, dear sir, it is paradise, for that is what you create inside of me, within my soul."

He caught her fingers, and kissed them. He met her eyes again. "I do love you, milady. With all of my heart, I love you. As Lord Cameron, as the Silver Hawk, as any man, myself, I love you, and I will do so until my dying day."

She touched his face. His fingers dropped to her bodice and he pulled upon the delicate satin strings until her breasts fell free to his touch. He savored them with his touch, with the sweet intensity of his teeth and tongue and lips. His hands ravaged her thighs, teasing, stroking. He entered into the core of her, and once his touch came so intimately to her, the fires within her soared, and she arched against him, desperate for more of the splendor that churned its fine sweet storm throughout the length of her.

He was the Hawk, he was her husband, and there was no fear any longer that the one might be recognized as the other.

He stood, and shed his clothing, and came back down beside her, stripping away what remained of her gown.

Shadows fell more deeply. Night was falling. Skye did not fear the darkness. He was with her. His hands were upon her. His kiss seared her flesh, and made her warm.

She rose on a wind of fate and glory, desire lapping against her flesh, the fever of it entering her fingers and her lips. She bathed his shoulders with her kiss, she raked his spine with her nails.

She whispered to him of her longing. Of the thing that swirled inside of her. Of the way that she needed him, needed him so desperately to appease the yearning. . . .

And it was paradise. There was no coarse straw, no sandy blanket, no shanty walls around them. The scent of the earth was with them, the music of their heartbeats rose.

Her flesh was silk, and his was splendor. The sun was in his fingertips, spiraling warmth that caressed her naked flesh. Rays that fell against her spine and stroked and rounded her hip, rays that entered intimately, deep, deep within her. . . .

She no longer whispered, she cried out. She strained against him with urgency, her hips undulating to the demanding rhythm of his thrust, her limbs locked around him. She soared and swept ever higher into Eden, then she called out his name, shuddering as the force of his seed racked her again and again. She felt the absolute constriction of his body, the explosion within her, and then she fell softly. Eden was gone, but she drifted on clouds, and those clouds left her sadly satiated and deeply in love upon the raw straw and the sandy blanket. It didn't matter. His arms were still around her. He held her. He stroked her hair.

And that was the paradise of it. Distant and far, as paradise might seem.

"If something does happen—"

"Shush!" she told him, rolling to cover his lips with her fingers.

He drew her hand away and cradled her to his chest, massaging his fingers through the hair at her nape. "Listen to me, Skye, I beg you. I do not believe that it is so simple to conceive an heir, and yet I tell you now that if I have a prayer tonight, it is that you might already carry my child."

"Roc—"

"No, please. I am an eternal optimist, my love—and an eternal rogue, I suppose you might say. I will fight Logan with whatever I might have until the very end. But in case—"

"Roc—"

"No! Listen to me!" Passionately, intently, he rolled her beneath him, demanding that she heed him. "You promise me this, milady, whatever else may come, whatever else may be. If we have created a child, swear to me that you will hold well to his or her heritage."

"Roc—"

"Cameron Hall. The land. The estate."

"Stop it, please!" Skye cried. "You speak of bricks and a handful of earth when—"

"No, lady, no!" he protested gravely. "It is not land, not brick. It is the Tidewater, it is a—dream! It is where my forebears came to live, to find their destinies. It is everything that I am, milady. It is my family. It is the future, and it is the past. There is honor there in the way that we have lived, in the Eden that we have carved from the earth. Promise me that come what may, you will preserve it!"

He was so very tense! Death lay all around them in the shanty, in the night, and he was desperate that she keep his land. She wanted to protest again, but she could not. "I promise."

"A promise you will keep, love."

"I have kept every promise that I have ever given you!" she whispered passionately.

He kissed her lips. "So you have."

"I vow it, Roc. With all of my heart, I vow it," she swore.

He ruffled her hair, falling down beside her, cradling her closer. "It is always beautiful there," he murmured.

She smiled beside him. "Always. The days are not too hot because of the river."

"And winter is never too cold, because of the river."

"The grass is green and blue and rich."

"And the fields are verdant."

He kissed her forehead. "There's an old oak there, down by the river, secluded by other trees and the gardens. The water rushes by almost silently. The leaves are shields against too much sunlight. There are pines there, too, and the earth is moist and soft and giving. It is, I think, Eden, here on earth."

"Is it?" Skye murmured.

"It is. My father used to take my mother there. He told me once. When she died, he told me how she had loved to come there, and how she had laughed. And what great difficulty he'd had convincing her that none could see her if she shed her clothes. And she said then that they were like Adam and Eve in the garden, and he promised her that there were no serpents in his Eden."

"Only wickedly seductive Camerons!" Skye murmured.

His arms tightened about her, then he suddenly bolted up.

"What is it?" Skye demanded.

He didn't answer her, but drew the blanket around her. He reached for his breeches just as a quick knock sounded, and was still stepping into them even as the door opened. Leticia slipped quietly into the room.

Skye held the blanket close to her breast, watching as Leticia drew a finger to her lips, beckoning for Roc to come with her. Skye thought that the woman looked at her curiously where she lay silent upon the straw, but she could not tell. Shadows filled the room.

"I'll be back!" Roc promised her softly. Skye watched him go to the woman and whisper something to her. He glanced Skye's way. "She'll come back to light the candle."

Skye smiled, catching her lower lip between her teeth as she fell back against the straw. She watched them leave, then she closed her eyes, shivering.

It had not been a frightening place when he had been with her.

It had, for a time, been created a paradise.

But he was gone now, and it had become a shanty, chilled by sea breezes, covered in sand, barren and stark.

Skye rolled upon her stomach and rested her head upon her arm, exhausted and yet keenly aware that she couldn't be so, that she needed desperately to think. This was a world of madness. She could be safe from it, but Roc would sail away to certain death, and she could not let him. And Logan still held her father. It was the worst nightmare she might have ever imagined.

Skye was dimly aware that the door opened again. She wasn't worried. Leticia was coming back to light the candle. Skye was so deeply enmeshed in her worries that little could have moved her then, for she knew that she could not leave Roc, not ever; she hadn't known that she had taken vows when she did, but there was but one thing that could part them, and that was death.

Her father! Where did Logan have him? If Blackbeard decided to help them, Logan would still have her father. . . .

She frowned suddenly, aware that no candle was being lit, that Leticia was murmuring no words to her, mocking or other. She started to spin around but halted as something cold and steel touched upon her bare back.

"Be very still, my dear."

Skye froze instantly. It was Logan. He spoke softly in the night, but the evil and menace in his tone was unmistakable.

The cold steel skimmed along her naked back from her nape to the small of her spine. Logan chuckled softly. "Once I had fingers, milady, and now you feel what is there, a hook for a hand, fashioned of metal. There is ice where once there was warmth. And still, it is an interesting caress, is it not? Feel my touch, lady. Brood upon it, if you will."

She bit down on the flesh inside her jaw, trying hard not to scream as she felt the hook skim over her again. He touched her with the curve of the hook until he came to the end of her spine, then he teased her flesh with the rough edge of the hook, a touch that hinted of drawn blood any second.

He did not want her blood, she realized. He wanted the Hawk's blood. He only wanted her because she was the Hawk's.

"Have you enjoyed your evening, my dear? Your last night with Captain Hawk. It's a pity that he cannot be trusted. He did try to buy your freedom, but I'm afraid that I can't let that be. If Blackbeard takes you, then I've nothing left to use against him. Blackbeard is a greedy man. And this time, he cannot have it all. Turn around. Look at me."

"No!"

He caught her arm with his good hand and wrenched her over. She would have fought him in a frenzy, but his hook landed instantly against her throat and she went still, staring at him with hate and venom afire in her eyes.

Then she realized that he was not alone. Two of his men stood silently, just inside the door. How many of them were behind it? Would Roc come back and stumble into a trap? She needed to scream, she needed to warn him, she needed to call help. She didn't know Logan's intentions, but she had to warn Roc that he was here.

Logan chuckled huskily, drawing her attention back to his face. She met his eyes once again, and drew breath to scream.

"Don't! Don't do it!" The point of the hook lay against her jugular. Slowly, her breath escaped her. She could not scream.

He smiled slowly and idly drew the curve of his hook down the length of her throat to her collarbone, then taunting, a curious caress indeed, over the rise of her breast. The hook continued downward, dislodging her blanket, leaving her bare to his assessment. She bit down ever harder upon her lip to keep from panic. A scream rose and bubbled in her throat, but as his eyes returned to hers, she knew that he would not hesitate to slit her open with the weapon he wore upon his severed wrist.

"That's right, love, quiet!" he whispered, and laughed. Something of regret passed over his eyes. "Milady, how I'd like you now, this very minute, alive and attuned to sensation by the most unique and tender stroke of my adoring . . . fingers. I'd like your Hawk to enter into his room and find you touched and filled by his dearest enemy. Alas! What a pity that I cannot do so."

Relief escaped her in a long gasp. His smile, however, was not reassuring.

"Nay, lady, first I must take you to my ship. You are so concerned for your father, eh? Well, now, perhaps we should let the old man watch, too. That's where we shall capture the Hawk for real, milady. And when we see that he is coming, that is when I shall have you, in bold light, upon the deck. You'll feel the true kiss of this steel, my love, and he'll know that I'll use it against you in truth when I am done."

"Perhaps he will not come," Skye said.

"I think that he will."

"But he won't. You've seen him with me. He demands things because that is his way, but I'm nothing to him, not really. He's women everywhere, what is one more, or one less?"

Logan sat back on his haunches, his eyes alight with a leering humor. His hook raked around the fullness of her breast as he answered, "Lady, you are worth your weight in gold. That was long ago decided. You are worth even more to me. He will live to rue the day that he caused me to wear this hook. Now, get up!"

He stood, and reached down with his good hand, wrenching her to her feet. His eyes assessed the length of her in the shadows, and she had never felt more violated. From the doorway, she felt his men, staring at her, too.

She jerked her hand free. "I cannot come like this!" she told him. "Let me dress." She bent down to retrieve the tattered remnants of her dress. Logan's foot fell upon the material. "We haven't time," he said harshly. "Morgan, toss her the cloak."

A woolen garment fell her way. Skye retrieved it quickly, grating her teeth as she quickly slipped the scratchy wool cape around her shoulders. She drew it close about her and stared at Logan again, waiting.

He bowed deeply to her. "My dear?"

She passed him by. The two men at the doorway stepped aside, opening the door for her. They were all behind her.

Skye quickly stepped out the doorway of the little shanty.

Fires still burned upon the sand, warmth against the night and the sea breezes. There was no music, though, no one danced. Men and women still lay sprawled about, but they lay in sleep, some snoring, some dead to the world in drunken stupors.

Logan, she thought, had no more than the two men with him. They were all behind her.

She hurried down the few steps to the sand, screamed as loudly as she could, and started to run.

"Catch her, you fools!" Logan shouted.

She didn't know where to go, nor did it matter. She couldn't possibly have navigated a course in the darkness.

And it was dark. Away from the fires, the night closed in. The sky met the sea, and the wilderness beyond the beach. There were more shanties, more ramshackle and makeshift homes and buildings.

Roc would be within one, she thought. Bargaining with Blackbeard.

But where?

She couldn't pause to determine that fact, she had to run. "Help me! Help me! Someone, for the love of God, help me!" she shrieked.

There were various stirrings about, but few heeded her cries.

The pirates were accustomed to hearing pleas for mercy—and equally accustomed to ignoring them, Skye thought bleakly.

She whirled around. Logan's men were almost upon her.

She was losing time, racing around the shanty buildings on the beach. They could trap her that way. They were trying to do so right then, she thought. "Take her! Take her from the left!" one of them cried, and another waved, running around to encircle the building.

Skye screamed again, and turned to flee toward the beach.

Her legs flying, she raced past the platform where Blackbeard had held his pirates' court that day. She went onward, seeing that a startled Leticia stood upon the steps to the shanty where she had spent the day. "Tell the Hawk!" Skye screamed.

Leticia jumped back and Skye realized that the men were almost upon her. She tore on down the beach, her lungs afire, her heart thundering, her calves cramping mercilessly. She could hear the sound of the waves rushing up on the beach, beckoning to her. Their dark invitation called to her.

The sea! she thought.

The night was frightening, the darkness unimaginable, but it might well be her only hope. If she could strike out and shed the cape, she could swim. She didn't know if her strength would hold out against the currents, but she had no other choice. She had only to pass the shadows of twin palms and plunge into the waves to find freedom.

Suddenly a figure stepped out from the palms. She could not stop running, her momentum was so great.

She collided with Logan. She screamed; his arms came around and they fell hard into the sand together. They rolled and she kicked and fought desperately.

"Logan!"

The thunder of the Hawk's voice interrupted their wild fight. Logan looked up, and Skye tried to dislodge him again. He was wiry and strong. He had his hook, and he carried a sharp and lethal knife. He caught her about the waist with his arm, dragging her to her feet. He stared back toward the fires of the night.

Skye, sobbing for breath, tossed back her hair. He was there, the Hawk was there, feet wide apart, his hands on his hips, defying Logan. A sword dangled now from his scabbard. There was a lineup of men behind him, Blackbeard among them.

"Let her go!" Roc demanded.

Logan laughed. With his good hand he pulled open her cape, placed the blade squarely against her heart, upon her bared flesh.

"I've warned you, Hawk. Back off, or she will die!"

"Let her go!" Roc demanded again. "This fight is between us. It is between men! Don't drag the girl in!"

"Ah, because she's a part of you, eh, Hawk? Like my hand was a part of my body? Severed now! Back off, Hawk, and I mean it! My knife shivers with the beat of her heart. I'll slice it out for you, Hawk, so help me God! You want her back so badly? I'll slice her heart from her body, and hand to you, sir, still beating."

"What the bloody hell is this?" Blackbeard demanded.

"Now, Logan, you were with me, we were all agreed upon the details! I got the girl, and you took the Hawk."

"You're a slimy, scurvy backstabber, Edward Teach, and that's what you are!" Logan called out.

"Now, sir, I take offense at that!" Blackbeard bellowed.

"Take all the offense that you want. I'm leaving in me boat with the girl. If one of you makes a move, it's her heart, and that's a fact. Are we understood?"

No one moved. Least of all Skye. The razor-sharp edge of his blade just scratched her flesh and she felt faint. He meant it. Logan would carve out her heart without a moment's thought.

"You move now!" he ordered her harshly. He jerked her, dragging her toward the water's edge. She heard the sound of oars and knew that Logan's longboats awaited them.

"I'll be on me deck!" Logan called out to the Hawk. "You want her alive, you row out alone. I'll be waiting to see you, Hawk. I'll be waiting right on the deck, and she'll be with me. She'll be right in my arms. You come, and she lives!"

Seawater, cold with the night, rose over Skye's ankles. They backed against Logan's longboat. His men were in it, she saw from the corner of her eye. The two who had come after her, and another two, who had probably remained with the boat, ready and awaiting his command. Logan was no fool; neither did he know the slightest thing about mercy.

"Hawk! Don't come! He'll kill us both!" Skye cried. Then she gasped, for the steel came hard and cold and deadly against her.

Logan spoke against her ear. "Get in! And not another word, and not a move. I'll cut you yet, my pretty!"

Stumbling, Skye stepped into the longboat with Logan still behind her. He dragged her down before him with the blade of the knife still tight against her breast.

"Shove off!" Logan commanded, and the longboat shot into the dark.

For several seconds, Skye could still see the Hawk. He stood on shore, tall and formidable, his legs arrogantly apart, his feet firm upon his sand, his fingers knotted upon his sword.

He could not come for her! They would both die. She was certain of it.

Good-bye, my love, she thought. And you are my love, in every way.

Suddenly she wished that she could go back, just for a few hours. Just long enough to tell him that she did love him, that she didn't care about the past, that the future was what needed forging. No matter what he had been, she would hold her silence unto the grave, and she would live with him and love him in his Tidewater paradise forever, for as long as they both should live. He was everything to her, everything in life.

"There she is, the ship!" Logan cried. His arm tightened around Skye. "No diving, my love, no swimming this night! No tricks, no fun, and I am in no mood for games! Climb aboard now, and know that my knife urges you upward."

Skye grated her teeth and gripped the ladder. Logan's men had crawled up before her, and Logan himself was behind her. She looked longingly back to the sea.

Logan's knife prodded her rump. "No swimming, my love. Remember, we've been this road before!"

Arms reached down for her and his men dragged her aboard. She landed in a heap upon the deck, the cloak drawn around her. Logan crawled over the railing and looked down at her, smiling.

"Here we are, my love, alone at last. Well, not alone." He lifted an arm, indicating the many men of his crew, pirates in all manner of dress, some in the rigging, one climbing to the crow's nest, one at the helm, and gunners as ease, their breeches and shirts blackened by powder.

Logan took a step toward her. "But alone enough. Away from the Hawk." He reached out his good hand to her. "Come. Come on, milady. Take my hand. You see, love, you and I are going to await the good Hawk. We're going to await him together."

XVIII

In the whole of her life, Skye had never been so frightened. No darkness surrounded her now, but rather Logan's ship was ablaze with lanterns against the darkness of the night, and of the sea. Perhaps it seemed that the very creature of her nightmares had stepped forth from the darkness to meet her in the light, and the face of fear was far uglier in light than it could ever be in shadow. Logan threatened all that mattered in life. He threatened her father, he threatened Roc, and he very definitely threatened her person, and did so at that very moment.

She stared at his hand. She knew that she would never take it.

"Get up!" he bellowed. "Come—to me!"

She hesitated. Then she leaped to her feet with speed and agility, racing past Logan across the deck.

"Stop her!" Logan ordered. "She'll jump!"

She would have jumped; it was her whole intent. She would rather face a shark or any monster of the blue depths than face Logan.

But his men were quick and agile, too. She had just reached the railing when her cloak was seized from behind, and she was dragged back, spinning into the arms of a black-toothed hearty. He laughed, enjoying her discomfort. Skye faced him, and carefully smiled in return. She was thrust against him. She inhaled the filth of his body and the reek of rum upon his breath, but she endured the horror for the sake of freedom. He did not know just how far she was willing to go to achieve her freedom, and so he was totally unprepared when she drew his sword from the scabbard at his side.

"Damme!" the man swore.

"Fool!" Logan raged. "Seize her, take her! She cannot best you all! By God, I thought I had men on this ship!"

She could not best them all, Skye knew that. But she spun away from the pirate who had stopped her plunge into the sea and backed herself to the railing again. The pirates surged toward her, but they were forced to take care. She parried their steel swiftly and desperately, aided by Logan's next bellowed order.

"I need her alive! Idiots! What good will she be against the Hawk if she lies dead!"

Two of her attackers backed away. Skye eyed them warily, and they watched her like sharks, waiting for her to blink, to drop her guard for a single second.

"Ahoy, Captain Logan!" someone cried. "A ship approaches!"

Logan's attention was temporarily distracted. "The Hawk!" he called, savoring the words.

"Nay, sir, I think not. Or perhaps it is! 'Tis Blackbeard, sir, I can see him standing toward the bow!"

"Then the Hawk is with him!" Logan said. "I need the girl! Now!"

Skye was already crawling up atop the railing. She screamed when she was caught by the hair and thrown down hard to the deck. She looked up, gasping for breath. It was Logan himself. She still held her sword. She lifted it in a definite threat.

"You want to fight, little girl?" he demanded. "All right, then, we will fight! Toss me my sword, gents! Someone toss me my sword."

A blade swirled through the air and landed at his feet. Skye feinted toward him as he reached for the weapon, but he was quick, and he was good. He lunged toward her, and it was all that she could do to evade the heavy thrust.

"Milady, have to!" Logan cried. He attacked and she parried, and he attacked again, and she parried once again. His men backed away now as they fought, and she thought that she knew why. Logan didn't believe that she could really kill him. She was good, very good. But she didn't have his strength or stamina, and if he kept a fair distance, he would eventually wear her down.

She could not let him do so.

He smiled at her as they fought. "Milady! Your cleavage is showing!"

She smiled in turn, aware that the cloak gaped open, then it spun and flew as she fought. She could not seek modesty now. Logan hoped to unnerve her with that ruse.

"Does it, sir?" she inquired, undaunted. Their swords clashed hard and the momentum brought them together, face-to-face. He reached out as if to touch her with his hook and she cried out, flinging herself away. She leaped toward the mainmast, and kept it to her back. When Logan charged, she quickly sliced the air.

She caught him in the cheek. A thin stream of blood appeared against his flesh. He paused, wiping it away with the back of his sleeve, then staring at the blood that stained his sleeve. His eyes shot back to Skye's with undimmed hatred.

"Little girl, you play rough. But I will play however you want, and lady, you will wish that you were dead!" He thrust toward her hard and she screamed, ducking. His sword sliced into the masthead, dropping rigging, and Skye screamed again, rushing over to the side of the boat. Blackbeard was coming. He would be there any second.

She could not believe that she was waiting for the infamous Blackbeard to save her, but she was. If he would just arrive while she still held her own, the pirates could all engage in battle, and she would be free.

But her father would not. Where was he? Somewhere

aboard the ship? She prayed that she could help him, but she could hardly help herself.

"Hold her, seize her, take her!" Logan ordered, and suddenly they were all coming after her again.

She held her own. She fought valiantly, and she fought well, and she was certain that no lad could have lasted longer. But the sailors were already upon her. While she parried the one, the next was striking. She was forced further and further along the deck to the stern, and then she parried and turned to leap but found that her way was blocked. Logan was there, and his sword was ready this time. He cast the point hard against her throat.

"Drop the sword," he ordered her.

"I'd—I'd rather die!" she managed to cry, even though she shivered and quaked with the fear of it. She wanted so desperately to live!

"Fine. Drop the sword, or I will slice you from head to toe. And when I am done, I will drag the old man up here on deck, and while you bleed slowly to death, I will hack him into little pieces before you."

"And you will never have the Hawk."

"One day I will have him. It is inevitable."

"You will never have the treasure."

"Is there a treasure, my dear?"

"Of course!"

"I think not."

"There is—"

"Drop the sword."

"Logan! Captain Logan!"

The call came from the longboats, far below the railing. It was Blackbeard's voice. The pirate had arrived at last. Too late.

"Drop it!"

Skye did not respond, and Logan surged forward with a fury. He caught her blade with his, and it fell flat to the deck. He wrenched her to him by her hands, hurrying over the fallen rigging to reach the portside of his ship and the new arrivals. "Blackbeard, you common traitor! Get away!" Logan roared.

"Now, Captain Logan, that's not atall nice, sir, not atall nice! Now I've come in good faith—"

"You've come for more treasure, you greedy viper, and that's that. You'd kill me, you'd kill the Hawk, you'd kill your own mother's every living son or daughter for more treasure!"

"Yer hurtin' me, Logan, yer hurtin' me deep!" Blackbeard called out sarcastically.

Slammed against the railing with Logan behind her, Skye could see that longboats were arriving with men by the dozen. Her heart caught in her throat, then suddenly soared. Against the lantern glare and the darkness, she could see Robert Arrowsmith. The Hawk's own men had arrived. There would be a mighty battle here, indeed.

"Where's the Hawk?" Logan raged.

"Not with me!" Blackbeard called.

"He'd best be. It's the Hawk I want. If I don't get him, I kill the girl, and that's that. Stay out of it, Blackbeard. This is no business of yours."

"Now Logan—"

"Shut up!"

In a fury, Logan turned around, thrusting Skye toward one of his burliest men. The man caught her hard, sweeping his arm around her and dragging her across the deck again. He held her against the railing while Logan looked down to Blackbeard. "I want the Hawk. I don't know what he's playing but I want him now. Don't think to storm the ship. Hans has Lady Cameron, and he has a blade at her heart now, and he'll kill her quicker than you can blink. Get the Hawk before me, and get him now."

"Now, Logan!"

"I'm done!" Logan thundered. "Man, I am done, and she is nearly dead!"

Nearly dead . . .

And that she was, Skye thought, for the man with his arms about her was huge, well over six feet, and each of his arms was greater in circumference than her own waist. His arm was clamped around her, holding her tight against him. And as Logan spoke, he drew out his dagger and smiled as he moved the cold steel between the valley of her breasts. His hold was so tight she could scarcely breathe. He would smother her before he could stab her, she thought. And yet she was afraid. Deathly afraid.

"He'll come!" someone called out. "Don't fear, lady, the Hawk will come!"

And then silence reigned. There was nothing, nothing but the night, nothing but the darkness and the eerie glow of the lanterns, and the sound of the water lapping against the ship at night.

"He'll come!" Logan laughed, casting back his head. "She'll die!"

His laughter faded, and the silence continued. Logan strode over to her furiously. He plucked up a piece of her golden-russet hair and fingered it slowly. "Pray, lady! Pray now, pray deep, for if I do not soon see his face before me, you will swiftly die!"

He dropped the lock of her hair. He stroked the length of her cheek and he jerked open her cloak, drawing the palm of his hand slowly down to cup her breast. Skye moved to fight him but Hans jerked her back, his hold as secure as rock.

"Blackbeard!" Logan called. "Can you hear me?"

"Aye, Logan!"

"Tell him—tell the Hawk that her hair is satin and her flesh is velvet. Tell him that her breasts are lush and firm and ripe. Tell him that I'm touching her."

Skye spat at him. He started, and wiped his cheek. He stared at her and smiled and she cried out, for he viciously caught and twisted her breast. "Next time, milady, it will be the hook!" he warned her.

He smiled, and his touch lingered, and she barely dared breathe, nor could she move. Logan tired of staring at her. He strode back across the deck. Silence held the night once more. Silence . . .

She heard something. It was nothing, she told herself. It was just water lapping against the hull of Logan's ship. It was nothing, nothing at all.

But then she managed to cast her gaze behind Hans, and

she was glad then that she was so nearly smothered, for she could not gasp out in startled surprise.

He was coming . . . he *had* come. To save her. The Hawk.

He had crawled up along the hull of the ship, barefoot and bare-chested, his knife between his teeth. He silently leaped over the edge of the starboard hull, landing with the softest thud upon the wooden deck. Hans started to turn, his knife still taut against her breast.

But Hans turned too late. He dropped his hold on Skye to defend himself against the Hawk. Roc attacked quickly, catching the bulky Hans right in the rib cage. Hans didn't get to say a word. The breath left him with a soft *whooshing* sound, and he crumpled to the deck.

That was when Logan turned.

"Hawk!"

"Aye, 'tis me, Logan! Here, where you have her!" Roc cried. He grabbed Skye, throwing her behind him to the rigging. "Climb!" he ordered her. "Climb high!"

She obeyed him, clinging to the rigging for dear life. She paused, and looked back.

Roc had found the sword Logan had forced her to discard. He held to the rigging, balancing as he fought with speed and fury, knees bent, the whole of him as agile as a dancer. "Come, fellows! You'd fight a mere girl and threaten her life as one, come, take me on, too."

Steel clashed. He parried forward, he allowed himself to be thrust back, only to surge forward with a whole new force again. Men fell before him. One sailor leaped over the side; Roc caught his midriff with the sword and the fellow screamed as he crashed into the water.

"Come, Logan!" Roc cried out. "It's you and me, isn't it? Isn't that what this melee is about? Come, sir, let us have at it again."

"Sir!" Logan stormed. "As you wish it! And understand that there will be no mercy for you!"

The sounds of a score of cries, battle cries, suddenly burst through the night as Blackbeard and his men and the Hawk's crew climbed aboard Logan's ship, all of them entering into the fray. Skye, climbing high atop the rigging, looked down and saw the fight. She saw Robert Arrowsmith and Fulton, fighting finely, their swords flashing, bringing about victory. Then she gasped softly, for she saw young Davie, too, and she was stunned.

Roc had taken the innocent lad aboard a pirate ship! she thought, but then her thoughts gave way, and her attention was riveted back to the pirates fighting below her.

Logan and the Hawk.

This was, she knew, a duel, and a duel to the death. Neither man would leave this fray until one of them lay bleeding life away upon the decks.

Pray God that it would be Logan dead, Skye thought!

"You bastard, hold still!" Logan shouted. "Then I may skewer you through!"

"Skewer me? Why, sir, it seems that you cannot touch me!"

Logan bellowed at Roc's words, leaping forward. Roc caught hold of the rigging and swung clear of the man's lunge, turning swiftly to renew his own attack.

"She was sweet and wonderful!" Logan taunted, backing away.

"What?" Roc demanded quickly.

"I touched her, I had her, all of her. I held her taut and I let her scream, but I had her, deep and sweet and sure—"

"Lying bastard!" Roc roared, surging forward. It was the advantage Logan wanted. He lifted his sword to crack it down upon Roc's shoulder with all of his might. Just at the last second, Roc dropped down and back, spinning about, reappearing on the other side of the mainmast.

"I'll have your ears!" Logan called. "I'll slice your ears and your toes and your privates, and I'll stuff them down your own throat, and you'll choke to death on your own flesh, knave!"

"You'll have to best me to do it, rogue!" Roc retorted.

Logan looked up suddenly. He smiled, seeing Skye perched high upon the rigging. He suddenly lifted his sword and brought it hacking down hard upon the ropes.

"No!" Roc bellowed.

Skye screamed as the rope sagged and the wood beams could be heard to crack and shiver. She held tight, afraid to climb upward, afraid to climb down.

Someone knocked over a lamp. A fire caught in the forward section.

"So help me, by God, by the very devil! This night will be the end of you, Hawk!" Logan screamed.

"Abandon the bloody ship!" a voice raged out.

Skye's heart sank. Her father!

"Roc!" she screamed. He paused, his gaze still warily upon Logan as he listened to her. "My father, Roc! He's aboard! He'll burn to death aboard this bloody death trap."

He looked up at her, and smiled slowly. He looked out to the sea, then over to Logan. Logan started to laugh. "Ah, the Hawk is in trouble at last, is he? Save the girl, save the man—or slay me, and save his own hide!"

"Do you mind a bit of a swim, love?" Roc murmured.

She shook her head, frowning, having no idea of what he meant to do. Suddenly he lifted his own sword and hacked with a swift clean blow against the rigging. She couldn't help but scream and hold tight as the mast seemed to sway and tottered with her and the rigging, then started plunging toward the sea.

She fell . . . fell and fell and fell, and felt the cold embrace of the water. She plunged downward, downward into darkness at first. There was nothing, nothing but the cold, nothing but the darkness. Her lungs were near bursting. She closed her eyes against the darkness, kicked with all her strength, and went shooting back up to the surface of the water again.

It seemed that all of the ship was ablaze. Men were screaming; men were leaping into the water. The night was alive with light, with activity, with shouts, and still, with the clang of steel.

Skye grabbed on to a floating log. The cloak had been dragging her down but she clung to it once she had the log; it seemed to offer her a certain warmth, sodden as it was. Or maybe the fire was warming up the water, she didn't know.

Perhaps her heart and soul had gone so cold that she could not feel any ice external to herself. Her father and her husband remained aboard the ship, and it burned with an ever-wilder frenzy.

"Scurry, men! If you would. By God, see! There's enemy sails afloat!" someone called out.

More cries broke out in the night. Longboats broke away in the night, but Skye didn't try to reach any of the pirates. She would wait. She would hold tight to her log and . . . pray.

"Lady Cameron! Lady Cameron!" someone shouted to her.

She turned about, and a gasp formed and froze upon her lips.

Lieutenant Governor Alexander Spotswood was sitting forward in a longboat, reaching out a hand to her.

"I—I can't—" she began.

"Child, look who I have with me!" Spotswood demanded.

She looked past him. Lord Theodore Kinsdale peeked around the lieutenant governor's shoulder, his eyes rheumy with tears, his mouth breaking into a hearty smile.

"Father!" she cried.

"Help the lass, help her!" Spotswood demanded.

Spotswood's sailors reached into the sea for her. Skye flushed, and the men politely turned aside as she tried to adjust the sodden cloak and find a seat within the longboat. Theo's ferocious hug nearly upset all of the boat, and she found herself held warmly in her father's arms. She shivered and chattered insanely. Someone pressed a bottle to her lips. The brew threatened to burn her mouth.

"Drink it!" she was ordered.

She swallowed. Then she swallowed more deeply. The shivering at long last seemed to subside. "More!"

She swallowed more. The world was hazy around her. Maybe some of the rough edges of pain were eased.

"Bless God and the saints above us!" Theo muttered.

Skye pulled back. Her father—her dear, fastidious father—was torn and disheveled, from his unpowdered hair to his filthy mustard breeches and snagged stockings. He smelled like an animal hold and he was every bit as sodden as she, but she cried out and hugged him again, because he was alive and well. "Father! Oh, Father! Why did you come for me! I was safe; you could have been safe! And now . . ." Her voice trailed away. In her relief to see her father, she had momentarily forgotten the Hawk.

"I had to come, you're my life, my only child. You are everything to me!" Theo reminded her.

"Oh, Father! I do love you. But now—"

"The Hawk!" Theo said.

"My God!" she breathed.

"My God, indeed!" Spotswood murmured, and he turned to her. "There, milady. I see him there, still aboard the ship!"

She strained to see past the fire and the smoke and she saw that the lieutenant governor spoke the truth. The figures of two dueling men could be seen, outlined clearly like black silhouettes against the fiery furnace of the blaze. They feinted forward, and they feinted back.

Theo placed his hand upon her shoulder. " 'Tis the Hawk," he murmured. "He tossed me overboard to the boats below with that vile Logan a-breathing right down his shoulder."

"He'll best Logan. He has to win, Skye. You understand that?"

She didn't understand anything. She screamed suddenly, leaping up, for the pirate ship exploded, bursting in the night. But just as it happened, the silhouettes were still stark and visible. And one of them drew back his sword with a fierce and mighty swing, and sent it flying like a headsman across the other's throat. And even as the explosion rent the air, sending both silhouettes flying into the dark and waiting water of the night, she could see a severed head go flying from a torso.

She screamed and screamed, clutching her throat. The explosion had killed the other man, surely! It was an inferno, and they were scarcely far enough away themselves not to feel the horrid heat of the blaze.

"Skye!" Spotswood called to her. "Dammit, child, sit, will you? Skye!"

Their boat tipped, and capsized.

And for the life of her, she could not care. She wanted to sink at that moment into the darkness. Life, she thought, had been darkness until he had lifted her from it. She wanted no part of the light, if she could not share it with him.

"Daughter!"

"Skye Cameron, come over here!"

Whether she wanted life or no, she was going to be forced

to live. The sailors righted the boat; her father grabbed her. When the boat was righted, they dragged her up. They all sat shivering.

Another explosion rent the pirate ship. The fire crackled high in the night, and then it began to fade. It would burn for hours, Skye thought, but never so brightly as now. By morning, the fire would be gone.

Spotswood inhaled and exhaled. "All right, men. I see no other of ours in the waves. Head toward the *Bonne Belle.*"

"No! We can't leave!" Skye protested.

"My dear, there are other boats about."

"No man could have survived that explosion!" one of the sailors said. He whispered, but Skye heard him.

"Now, now. The Hawk is known to be a survivor. Perhaps he has gone on with his pirate friends, and maybe that is best," Spotswood said.

No, Skye thought. The sailor had been right. No man could have survived the explosion. Not unless he had leaped clear when the ship went to splinters.

Oars lapped the water. Theo pulled her close to him again and Skye rested her head on her father's shoulders.

"Damn child, if I'm not quite a mess!" Spotswood murmured, very unhappily wringing out his wig. "I'm not even supposed to be here—this is North Carolina territory, you know. Not supposed to be here—I'm *not* here! If any man ever says it, I will deny it! Blimey, but you have given us a good soaking girl."

She couldn't respond. Theo took her face tenderly between his hands. "Did he hurt you, Skye? Are you well, are you fine? I was so terrified for you; all I could think of all the time was how very afraid you must be of the darkness."

"I'm not afraid of the dark, Father," she whispered, and she squeezed his hand. He loved her, and that was why he had come for her. She had to understand that. She had been willing to sell her own soul for Theo's sake, and she was grateful beyond measure that he was alive. "I'm not afraid of the dark, not anymore."

"There she is, right ahead, the *Bonne Belle.* And not too far from our own waters at that!"

The longboat came alongside the ship the *Bonne Belle.* "Captain, lower the ladder if you will!" Spotswood called out. "I've Lady Cameron and Lord Kinsdale safe and sound and with me!"

A cheer went up. Skye was helped up the ladder and over the edge, and she tried to smile to the young man who helped her so intently. She fell against the railing, though, and as her father and Spotswood crawled up behind her, she turned about to stare out to the sea, out to the night.

"Peter! Bring your mistress a dry blanket, and quickly!" Spotswood called out.

Peter! Skye whirled around and, indeed, Peter was there, rushing to her with a dry, warm blanket. He set it about her shoulders. "My lady, are we grateful to see you!"

"Peter!" She forgot protocol and hugged him fiercely, then looked to Spotswood. Spotswood shrugged.

"I already told you, dear—I am not here this evening. The *Bonne Belle* is another of your husband's ships."

"Oh!" she cried, then she turned back to the water again, and she started to shake and cry in earnest, tears cascading down her cheeks. She couldn't bear it. She just couldn't. She loved him too deeply, for all his sins, because of all his sins. He had always been there for her. He had risked his life time and again to save hers. He had come to her in darkness, and in light, and all that mattered now was that he was gone, and that life held no meaning.

"Skye!"

She heard her name as a rasping whisper, calling out to her from the fog of anguish that covered her heart. It was not real, she thought, but she turned slowly, and then her heart started to leap. *He was there.* Standing before her, drenched and dripping over the deck, barefoot and bare-chested still. He held no weapons, but faced her with his palms out, his heart within his silver eyes. He was alive.

"Roc!" she screamed his name in gladness, hurtling toward him, throwing herself against him. She cried his name again and again, holding close to him. She clutched his face between her hands and she showered him with kisses, his forehead, his lips, his cheeks, his sea-wet bare chest and shoulders. His arms folded around her. He pulled her close, holding her wet and sleek to his heart. His fingers combed through her sodden hair.

"Skye . . . beloved . . ."

His mouth covered hers, and the warmth of a summer day exploded within her. He was alive! He was warm, he was real, he was with her, beside her upon the deck of the *Bonne Belle.*

"Really!" Theo Kinsdale groaned. "They're barely clad, between the two of them."

"Theo!" Spotswood reprimanded him. "Have a heart, sir! They are duly wed, and I might remind you, it was all your doing. Give them a moment's peace, then I shall part them myself."

A moment's peace . . .

Skye didn't hear the words. She was in her own world.

In paradise . . .

Touching him, feeling him, convincing herself with all of her senses that he was truly alive. Then he broke away from her, and she saw his face, stripped of his beard. His hair unpowdered, wet and trailing down his back. His shoulders sleek and bronze and rippling with muscle.

And Spotswood was here. The lieutenant governor! He would know—just as she knew!—that the Hawk and Lord Cameron were one and the same. And there would be no escape now. No escape at all. Roc had survived Logan and the fire just to hang!

"No!" she gasped in horror, staring at him.

"Skye—" he murmured.

"All right, my dear young friends," Spotswood said, coming toward them. "I'm afraid I must interrupt you now—"

"No! No!" Skye cried. She held her husband tightly. "You don't understand! You mustn't take him—"

"But, my dear, I must—"

"No!" she cried.

"Skye . . ." Roc murmured.

But it was suddenly too much for her. She fought for reason; she fought for light. Darkness was overwhelming her. She clung to her husband, and his arms came around her. But it was not enough. She fell into his arms, and the world closed in darkness around her.

"My God, what's happened to her!" Theo demanded, pushing forward.

"Nothing, Theo, nothing. And it seems that the lad has her well in hand. She's fainted, Theo, and that's all. And for the night that the poor thing has endured, it seems little enough!"

"I will take her to bed," Roc said softly.

"But—" Theo sputtered.

"They're married, Theo!"

Theo tried with dignity to adjust his ragged clothing. "Quite right, Alexander, quite right. It's just that . . ."

"Quite right, and that's that!" Alexander said. "Lord Cameron! I need a word with you as soon as she's settled."

When she woke up, it was light. The sun streamed in upon her and she rose up, amazed to discover that she was home.

Home. Cameron Hall.

She was dressed in a soft blue nightgown with lace at the collar and the cuffs and hem. Her hair was dried and soft and she was comfortable. She had been out a very long time.

She lay upon her husband's bed, and the very sight of it brought her up, amazed. "Roc!" she cried out his name, but he was not with her, and she had known that he would not be. Spotswood would have arrested him for piracy by now. They would take him to the jail in Williamsburg, and as soon as the court met, they would try him.

And hang him.

"Oh, no!" She leaped out of the bed, and she was amazed that she could have been out so long, and so completely. It was the liquor they had made her drink, she thought. Her head was still pounding. She pushed up from the bed, and she stared about the room. How ironic! Now, at long last, she slept in her husband's handsome bed. But he was not with her. The sun streamed into this place that he loved so much, and she was alone with it. She let her hand fall to her abdomen, and she thought of all the time that had passed since she had first encountered the Hawk, and she trembled. He had wanted an heir. Perhaps that was what she had left. Perhaps she could live to give him that which he had so desired, the son to carry on his name in this all-important land. "Please God, let it be that it is so!" she whispered.

Then she spun around, determined. She would not let the father hang so quickly, she could not! Her father would help her. Theo would testify that the Hawk had saved his life during the fire. There would be enough men to stand for the Hawk, oh surely.

She had to find her father, or the governor, or Peter, or someone. Ignoring her state of undress, she tore out of the bedroom and along the hallway with the portraits of the Cameron lords and ladies. She paused, and her heart beat fiercely. "I shall not let you down, I swear it! I will save him, I promise. I did not want to come here, that is true, but it's my blood, too, now, you see. I think I'm to have his child, and besides, you see . . . I love him. With all my heart. He is my life, and this land is his passion, and therefore, it is mine."

She was talking to portraits, she realized. But the Camerons looked down upon her, and she thought that they smiled their encouragement. The men with their silver eyes, the women with their knowing warmth and soft beauty.

She turned away from the portraits and ran down the elegant stairway. From the grand hallway she burst into the office.

Spotswood and her father were there. They were seated quite comfortably, lighting pipes, sipping coffee—out of fine Cameron cups.

Skye strode to the desk, facing Spotswood. "Where is he? I demand to know." She spun around. "Father, you make him tell me where my husband is! I want to see him now. You may arrest him, but you'll not hang him. I'll fight you. I'll fight you both tooth and nail until we are all nothing but blood. Father! He saved your life!"

"I know that, daughter—"

"And Alexander! You were all willing and eager for the Hawk to do your dirty work. The government of Virginia cannot interfere with the government of North Carolina, and so you didn't mind seeing him attack other pirates in Carolina waters. Now I'm telling you, I demand to know where he is."

Theo looked at Alexander, and Alexander looked at Theo.

The lieutenant governor shrugged. "By the river, I believe. He mentioned a certain spot. It's quite lovely and private. Down past the docks, beyond the graveyard. You'll not see him if you don't run down the slope by the old oaks."

"What?" Skye murmured. "But—"

"Find him. Speak with him."

Skye backed away from the desk. They had both gone mad, but Roc was out there somewhere. She could see him and touch him. She could cling tightly to him and tell him that there would be an heir to Cameron Hall. She could love him, before they could take him.

She stared at her father and the lieutenant governor, then she whirled around and raced out of the house.

"Milady!" Peter called to her, startled that she should be running out in her night attire. She ignored him. She burst from the house and into the day and down the slope. She saw the docks before her, and the family graveyard to the right, and she kept running upon the soft green grass. Her feet were bare, and she stumbled, but she didn't care. She had to reach him.

"Roc!" she screamed. She raced far past the graveyard, and by the mound of oaks.

She saw him then. He was clean and bathed and handsomely dressed in fawn breeches and buckled shoes and a deep red frockcoat. His dark hair was unpowdered, but neatly queued. He rested a hand against a pine tree, and he looked out to sea.

Until he heard her call. He turned about, and his eyes came alight with a silver blaze, and his lazy, slow, sensual smile curved his lips. Perhaps he would have reached out to her. She didn't know. She tripped and went stumbling down the slope of grass there, and fell at last into his arms.

"Skye!"

Her force nearly knocked them both over. He swept her into his arms, and down then upon the ground, in a bed of pine needles. He cradled her gently and searched her eyes while her fingers fell tenderly upon his clean-shaven cheeks. She gasped for breath, then kissed him. He arched his brow and brought his palm against her thundering heart. "My love—" he murmured.

"Aye, Roc, and I do love you!" she gasped. "I'll not let them have you!"

"Them?" he inquired.

She could smell the sweet pine needles beneath her and the cleanliness of the river air. She felt both the sun and the shade of the trees, the birch and the oaks and the pines. She felt the searing warmth and sweet fire of the man, the silver blaze within his eyes. She held tightly to him. This was indeed his Eden. It was where his parents had come. It was a garden where a man could love a woman, and a woman love a man, far from the cares of the world.

"Oh, Roc!" she whispered. "We are, I think, I'm almost sure—"

"What?" he demanded, his arms tightening around her.

"We're—we're going to have a child." His arms came like steel, warm and loving, and she spoke on quickly. "I don't know whether Lord Cameron or the Hawk has fathered the babe, but Roc, I will raise him, I swear it, come what may! Yet I swear, my love, too, that I haven't given up on his sire as yet—"

"I should hope not!" Roc said indignantly. "Oh, my love, a babe, really?" The tenderness in his voice tore into her heart. It brought tears to her eyes.

"Really, I believe. Now, Roc—"

His kiss cut off her words. It was deep and sweeping and sensual, and it enveloped and enwrapped her in splendor and warmth. It filled her with sweet longing and desire, and left her trembling in his arms. When he rose above her, the tenderness was still with him. "My dear lady, bless you. With all of my heart, madame, I do love you. You believe that now, don't you?"

"Yes, I believe you!" she whispered. He smiled, and reached to her gown, tugging upon the laces at the bodice. The material fell away and he lowered his head against her, taking her nipple deeply into his mouth and laving it with his teeth and tongue.

"Roc!" she cried out, tugging upon his hair. "Stop, please, we must talk. . . ."

He spoke huskily against her flesh. "We've a lifetime to talk!"

"No!" She tugged fiercely upon him, drawing him back up to face her. He was a handsome devil, she thought. Handsome, strong, seductive. She could not bear life without him now! "No, Roc, now listen to me. We must think. We must find you legal representation, the very best. And witnesses, the proper witnesses."

He was nuzzling her breast once again. Sensations blazed into her, but she fought them all fiercely. "Roc, this is serious!"

He groaned.

"Roc, they'll hang you!"

His eyes fell upon her, wicked and silver, and hungry like a gray wolf's.

"If I am a condemned man, then love me, wife!"

"Roc! You mustn't—you must listen to me. Roc—"

"Have you ever seen such a glorious place?" he murmured, and again he spoke against her flesh. He edged her gown from her shoulders, and his words and kisses fell against them, then he moved lower as he stripped her completely in the bower of pines. "It is Eden. Feel the breeze, love, upon your flesh. Like my touch, I swear it. Gentle always, soft sometimes, with heady passion at others. Feel where the air touches you where my lips have just lingered, the coolness against the heat. Hear the birds, my love? Sweet and never strident. Smell the earth, the verdancy, the flowers. Never so good as the sweet scent of you, never so provocative, yet always enticing. . . ."

"Stop!" she pleaded, catching his dark hair as he teased her belly with the hot tip of his tongue. Swallowing, seeking breath, she dragged him to her. She pressed her lips passionately to his, then drew away. Tears glazed her eyes. "I cannot! I will not let them hang you!"

His lashes fell, dark over his eyes. "They are not going to hang me, love."

"What?" she cried. "Oh, Roc! You must not be overconfident because you are Lord Cameron!"

He paused then, and cradled her in his arms. He ran his palms over her naked breasts tenderly, and he thought that he had never seen her more beautiful, more gentle, than at this moment. The trees rocked their branches above. Her nightgown hovered in a soft blue swirl about her hips while the beauty of her throat and breasts and torso were bared to his eyes. Her hair cascaded all about her, sunlight, sunset. Her eyes were all teal, liquid with her love for him.

He had never felt more humble, and he trembled. He had never known what love could be. Now, it was his. It was more precious that life, limb, earth, or country. She was life. His life. Their child grew within her. Their future stretched before them. He had loved the land before; now it was everything. Now it would be shared.

"My God!" he whispered, and his fingers shook as he smoothed away her hair. "Skye, I love you. I cannot say it deeply enough. I love you."

"I love you!" she whispered, and the tears still stung her eyes.

He smiled, holding her tight, cherishing and savoring the soft feel of her naked chest as he held her against his body. "I'm not going to hang, my love, because the lieutenant governor has been in on it all the time."

"What!" Stunned, she broke away from him. He was reminded of the daring temptress who had fought him so fiercely on the deck of the *Silver Messenger,* the very first day he had seen her.

He nodded slowly, watching her flashing eyes. "I was asked to be a pirate, milady. I stole nothing. I tried to learn the plans of the real rogues at their hideaways, and I captured ships, but only my own ships, or imaginary ships, or ships that I captured from other pirates to send on home."

"But—but—"

He lifted his hands. "Spotswood would deny it, of course. He is a servant of the Crown. But several years ago I had a ship taken and my crew was butchered, and I could not help but want to seek revenge. Alexander and I spent a night drinking and . . . the Silver Hawk was born."

"But the place on Bone Cay—"

"I own it. The Camerons have owned it for at least fifty years."

"Oh!"

"Love, I'm sorry! I could not tell you. You already despised the man you were to marry, and I had sworn to Alexander that I would never divulge the truth to anyone."

"But Robert—"

"Robert Arrowsmith has always been one of my best friends. I have given him a plot of land connecting ours. He is going to become a gentleman planter now."

"What of Mr. Soames and Señor Rivas and—"

He shrugged. "They like the Caribbean. And I have no intention of giving up my island. It holds wonderful memories for me, and can be fine to visit in the winter. The pardon you spoke of before has come through. Men in authority have gone to take control of New Providence. The Silver Hawk will seek a pardon, turn his property over to his deserving cousin—Lord Cameron—and then disappear into the pages of history."

"Then you won't—you won't set sail again?" she whispered.

"Alas, no, my love. My pirating days are over. Jack is gone, and Logan is gone. One day Spotswood will have Blackbeard, but I haven't the heart for that fight, and the lieutenant governor has decided that my usefulness to the Crown is over. I am a changed man, love! I swear it!"

"Oh!" she gasped.

He stroked her cheek, and laid her down upon the pines. "I love this place," he whispered. "I want our son to grow here. I want it to be the finest estate in all Tidewater Virginia."

"Ummm," she murmured.

"Say something!" he implored her. "Will you mind so very much that the Hawk is not to hang?"

She shook her head. She stretched her arms around him and drew him close, loving the masculine hardness of his body as it pressed against hers on their bed of pines. "I'm glad he's not to hang," she whispered. "And since he is not . . ."

"Since he is not?"

"Then I demand that he love me here, in this Eden. Perhaps

he is of no more use to the Crown, but his lady shall always demand his time, and his energy."

"Ah, but the Hawk will be gone! 'Tis Lord Cameron who will give you his life and his love and his passion."

She laughed with sweet delight and raked her fingers through his dark hair, drawing him close. "Perhaps. But perhaps my legal lord will always be the valiant pirate Hawk in my heart. And perhaps I will always lie with him now, forever, in this Eden."

"Perhaps . . ."

"And then, perhaps, it matters not at all, for I love the man, you see. Whether he is the Hawk or the lord, the rogue or the noble gentleman, I love him. And would have him love me now."

He smiled to her, and caught her lips, and rose above her, his eyes—silver eyes, dancing eyes, rogue's eyes—alight with his passion.

"Gladly, milady, gladly," he assured, and set forth with fire and passion and tenderness to prove to her the bold beguiling truth of his ardent assurance.

Epilogue ❧

March 20, 1719

Lying beneath the oaks, Skye was half-asleep when Roc came upon her. He smiled down at his wife, for she looked beautiful and pure and childlike, with her hair all tousled about, and at the same time mature, for she was huge with their child—the babe was due any day.

"My love!" he murmured, sitting down beside her.

She jerked up and he laughed, smoothing back her hair. " 'Tis just me," he assured her, and drew her close. He kissed her forehead. "No one is allowed in Eden with Eve except for Adam, you know."

She smiled, and stretched lazily and then leaned against him, as content as a kitten. "How are things in Williamsburg? How is Father?" she asked. "What of the pirates?"

"Your father is fine and feisty as always," he said. "The

pirates . . ." He sighed. Spotswood had managed to get his hands on Blackbeard at last. There had been a battle at Ocracoke Island last fall, and Blackbeard had fallen.

His head, it was rumored, had been severed and hoisted up on the bow of Lieutenant Maynard's ship for all to see. "Woe to all pirates!" was the message.

Well, Blackbeard had been a rogue and caught at it, and perhaps he had rightfully deserved to die, Roc thought. But in his own dealings with him, he had seen Blackbeard maintain a curious honor, and so he was sorry for the end of it in a way.

Skye squeezed his hand. "At least he was not captured and taken prisoner with the others!"

Men *had* been taken. They had been sent to the Williamsburg jail, and they had been tried on March 12. All but one gentleman—who had been able to prove himself a guest and no more on Blackbeard's ship, the *Adventurer*—had been sentenced to hang.

"Aye. Well, it's over now."

"Is it?" Skye asked him.

He nodded, looking out to the James that swept by them, the very life of their land, their property, their estate, their future.

Their children's future. Their destiny.

"Yes," he said, drawing his wife close. "I think that it is over. I told you once that the Crown created pirates—Sir Francis Drake was a fine example. We warred with Spain, so the kings and queens cried, 'Rob them blind!' Then men began to forget that they should pirate only foreigners, the enemy. The islands gave the rogues bases. Now Woodes is cleaning up New Providence, and Ocracoke will never welcome pirates again. An age is coming to an end. The age of piracy. Maybe that was our age, my love. When the settlers arrived here last century, they had to survive against the Indians. They had to hold fast to the land. For us, it was the menace of the pirates. We had to endure, and survive. Who knows now what the future, what our children shall face? It's all to God, isn't it? Fate. And we can only pray that each generation will endure."

Skye touched his cheek. She started to smile, started to speak. "Oh!" she cried instead.

"What is it?"

She sighed, and flushed, and smiled again. "It's quite all right. I mean, I think that it's some time yet."

"What?"

"Well, you remember, I met *you* when the age of pirates was flourishing! And you were an absolutely irresistible and ravishing pirate. And—"

"Skye!"

"Well, I believe it's time for a certain ravishment or seduction—whichever it was!—to bear fruit."

"The babe!"

"Yes!"

"Oh!"

He leaped to his feet and drew into his arms. He groaned slightly. "Well, you're not as light as air at the moment!" he apologized.

"And I can walk perfectly well!"

"Not on your life, my love."

He carried her to the house, and up the stairs, and to the bed they shared. Mattie was there, and Tara and Bess, and Peter hovered by the door with Davey and some of the others ready to run and fetch whatever might be required. Davey was sent for the doctor, then Mattie expelled Roc, too. "It's a long, long time!" she assured him.

He paced the portrait gallery, and then he went out walking again, and he came down to the cemetery, and looked out over the tombstones. He walked over to those belonging to Jamie and Jassy, and he touched the cold stone, and he smiled. "I *am* mad!" He laughed aloud. "But it all came out so very well." He paused. "Life is good. It is Eden. I—I thank you for this place."

He decided that he *was* mad, smiled again, and turned around. He came back to the house, and he paused by the beautiful portrait of his great-great-grandmother, then he walked on again and went to his office down the stairs.

Robert Arrowsmith arrived, and drank with him.

He had several snifters of brandy, and smoked several pipes.

Then he heard one cry, and then another, and he glanced

toward Robert, and he tore up the stairs, two at the time. He burst into the room, where Mattie was just swaddling the babe. Roc looked at her expectantly. Mattie smiled and handed him the squirming bundle.

"A . . . ?" he inquired.

"What else, Lord Cameron? A boy."

"A boy! Wonderful. But don't you what-else-me, Mattie! A girl would have been just as welcome!"

"Well, sir . . ."

"What?"

"I'm glad to hear that, for the second is a little girl, wee and fine and golden-haired."

"Two!"

"Twins, Roc!" Skye called from the bed. He hurried over to her. She was pale, but she smiled beautifully, and the happiness that radiated from her was glorious. He knelt down beside her and he kissed her hand. Mattie brought their son over, while Bess carried over their scarcely bathed daughter.

They inspected their infants, hesitant, curious, laughing. Adoring the infants, more deeply in love than ever with one another. Mattie and the girls left them alone. The babies fussed, and Skye, laughing and awkward, tried to nurse them both. Roc helped, trading infants while she traded breasts, and together they laughed again, until he saw that her eyes were closing, and that she was exhausted.

"I'll call for Mattie and Tara," he assured her, kissing her forehead.

She nodded sleepily, and he called to the servants, and then it was Mattie's turn to cluck proudly over the newborns. Roc came back beside his wife and sat down, cradling her hand. She was nearly asleep. Clean and bathed and beautiful after the ordeal, she was again sweetly innocent and pure to him. It was hard to recall her as the passionate vixen who had come to his arms to create their marvelous new additions, but he knew that he would meet the vixen again. He kissed her forehead. Her eyes fluttered open, teal, beautiful.

"I'll let you sleep. I'll send a message to your father. I'm sure he can be here by tonight."

She nodded, and squeezed his hand. He kissed her again

and stood. Her eyes opened again, devilish slits. "Make sure you tell *them* we have twins," she whispered.

"Them."

She winked. "Jamie and Jassy. I think that they'd like to know."

He laughed, and said indignantly, "My love, one day our children's children will live here. In the world we work to build year by year."

"And one of our great-great-great-grandchildren, a handsome lad, a rogue with dancing silver eyes, will come by us, and whisper of what has come!" she said.

"Vixen!" he teased her, and kissed her again.

"It takes one to love a rogue," she assured him demurely.

And he laughed, and it turned out that he didn't leave so quickly after all, for she was not so tired that she could resist being taken into his arms and giving him a kiss of infinite tenderness and passion and promise.

A kiss . . . to the future.

About the Author

New York Times and *USA Today* bestselling author Heather Graham has written over one hundred novels and novellas, including category, romantic suspense, historical romance, and paranormal. Married since high school graduation and the mother of five, her greatest love in life remains her family, but she also believes her career has been an incredible gift. Romance Writers of America presented Heather with a Lifetime Achievement Award in 2003.